MW00860712

LUNARIA

Book One of The Unraveled Fate Series

LUNARIA

KARA DOUGLAS

KARA DOUGLAS, FANTASY AUTHOR

THE VALON EMPIRE

THE HUMAN REALM

KINGDOM OF PENYTH

KING'S BORDER

PRINCE'S END

THE ANDRONICUS SEA

SALTAIN

LYLAND

KINGDOM OF CREA

KILSPIRE

GRANTFORD

MARKET PORT

RUNNSWICK MARKET

WISEBECH

WALKING PATH

ROYAL TRAINING CAMP

STABLES

NORTHERN SPARRING RING

SOUTHERN SPARRING RING

Second Edition 2024
All designs, art, and formatting 2023 by Rena Violet
Editing by Sophie Ramsey

ISBN: 979-8-9885772-0-1

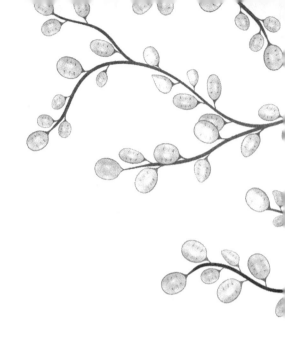

Lost inside the forest, but it feels fine.
-Dermot Kennedy, Innocence and Sadness

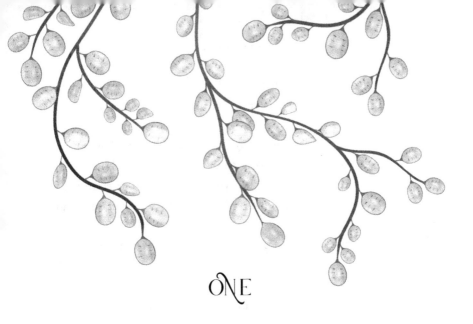

ONE

Xerographica Tillandsia

I step out onto the busy market road, so close to the outside world I can taste it. Jealousy fills my veins as I watch the marketgoers move about so freely. I glance back at my guard, readying myself for yet another day of tracking down the things I was demanded to retrieve. I take in the aromas of spices, baking bread, and dozens of other scents that always seem to envelop this place. I'm still exhausted from yesterday, but somehow these comforting, familiar scents draw me forward.

The textured tapestries that hang over each stand sway gently with the early morning breeze. The dull colors are dried out from basking in the sun all day, but they still manage to look as beautiful as the day they were made. Oh, the stories these cloths could tell.

As I traverse the thick, mud-coated pathway I step carefully on the uneven stones. I glance down at the list again and clench my jaw while trying to set my mind to the task before me.

The moment I left the desolate training camp for the market I tried to make myself relax, but it feels like more work than ease. Even so, it's always brighter in the market, bustling with townspeople and the tradesmen that have traveled here from across Crea by ship or horse.

I can always tell who's from Runnswick and who has traveled outside the town's reach. Many people flood in from the port side of town as they exit their ships with goods to sell or empty bags to fill. Even with the sun just beginning to rise, people are already swarming the square.

The noisy chatter of townspeople bargaining with the tradesman—often to no avail—accompanies the market daily. The unwavering on both sides makes the corners of my mouth want to turn up into a smile, but they don't. Or maybe they don't remember how to anymore.

At least the present excursion gets me away from Father for the morning. I loathe going into the market to fetch items he needs as if I'm a servant, and yet I guess I'm merely that to him.

I alternate between flexing my fingers and squeezing my fist as I make my way past the cramped stands. Glancing back down at the list, I search it for the tenth time, not wanting to forget something from it again.

From the corner of my eye, I see a market seller wave his hand, flagging my attention. "These earrings would look *lovely* with your hair, miss," he says, emphasizing *lovely* in a way clearly intended to flatter me. The merchants all try the same tactics. It never works.

I shake my head and quickly step past him without speaking.

Not eager to go back to the camp, I slow my steps. Nothing good waits at the camp—only Father with his demanding lists and disapproving glances. I may have spent my entire life growing up near the castle, but that doesn't mean I have a place there.

My father's goal has always been for me to be as invisible as possible, especially when he has his meetings with the king. When

I'm one out of two females in the entire training camp it makes remaining unseen a lot more work.

I straighten my spine and push back my shoulders to assert a measure of calm, decided confidence, even if I don't feel it. The stress of the camp finally starts to slowly melt away as I drift through the market.

I carry on with my usual routine, bargaining with a few of the sellers I know will take a coin or two off, pocketing everything left over, and feeling treasonous but powerful. I'm not allowed to have my own money, but that doesn't stop me from trying.

Father always wants the fruit of the season from a specific stand, which means seizing the opportunity to visit my favorite tradesman, who's nestled into a corner shop by the port. Even well into his older years, his arms are toned from a lifetime of working on his farm. His hair is mostly gray, and his skin is creased from spending too much time in the heat while harvesting and selling fruit.

Some days, it's the only kindness I get. He offers me the same smile he has every day for years now, his eyes wrinkling at the corners when his mouth turns up.

"Another list of things to get today?" His voice is worn and soft as he shifts his eyes to the list clenched in my hand. His smile slips for a moment, and I clear my throat, hoping he'll let it go today.

My cheeks redden as I say, "The usual please, Linnick."

Thankfully, he doesn't say what I can see written on his face.

He shoves the fruit into the sack I brought with me before saying, "I'll give you these three for five coins less today and throw in a lemon for you. I like taking your father's money, but I like to see you spend it on something for yourself even more." He holds the sack out, his eyes narrowing with uncharacteristic ire. "Anything I can do to feel like I'm ripping that bastard off."

My eyes sweep through the crowd, searching for my ever-present guard. James looks more bored than anything these last few seasons, his rough features hardly focused on what I'm doing. But when his gaze sweeps in my direction, a moment of fear courses through my body. I freeze, not wanting this trip to be over yet. His eyes don't focus on me, and his gaze skips past me to his favorite establishment. The fear is quickly washed away in a wave of relief at seeing James distracted by the madam's house.

By now, James is surely disinterested. His lack of concern is both relieving and infuriating, and I almost run away to spite him. But where would I go? The ports are thick with Father's allies. I watch him a moment longer and relax further when he dips into the brothel. I realize that I won't have long, but it's more than enough time to sneak over to my favorite stand.

I turn back to Linnick and give a barely audible "Thank you" and he nods in return, his smile not reaching his eyes this time. Most of my regular tradesmen will bargain with me for the same reason, but none look out for me as Linnick has all these years.

"I'll be back the same time next week," I say, though I'm aware Linnick will be expecting me. He always expects me. "Father seems to be taking more meetings with the king these past months." Which means more errands for me to run so I'm out of his way. It's hard to keep the bite from my words as I speak about him. I squeeze my fists at my sides before I say something I shouldn't, knowing there are always listening ears.

Linnick can always hear what I don't say, but he never pushes me to talk about it. Instead, he just forces another smile and nods when he says, "See you next time, Amira."

After double-checking I've crossed each item from the list, I zip through the paths that connect the market and spot the row I'm most eager to see.

I quicken my feet to match the exhilaration coursing through my veins, dodging all the comments thrown my way: "Try this new scented oil!" and "This bread will be the best you've ever tasted!" and always "Buy this talisman! It protects from the cruelty of Penyth!" I give a polite nod but don't give the sellers a second to stop me.

My fingers fumble around in my pockets, fishing the coins out. It takes me longer than necessary with my gaze distracted by the flowers filling the stand, containers filled with the most gorgeous solid white blossoms I've ever seen. They are round and flat with a golden sheen, resembling the loose coins sitting heavy in my palm.

Flowers are so rare in this part of the kingdom that I can't stop myself from going to the stand, the magnetic pull of the earth drawing me closer to them. They must've been brought on a ship just this morning.

The scent of lavender surrounds me from where they are squished beside the large coin-like buds, small yellow bumblebees buzzing around the purple stalks. The flowers tilt and stretch toward the sun, their petals poised as if to grasp the warm, vast columns of light draped across the market square.

My fingertips caress the stems and skip the ones the bees have nestled themselves against. I envy the bees for that. I would love to make a safe home surrounded by vibrant color and this intoxicating aroma, gravitating as if by pure instinct toward the comfort of the sun. I gaze up at the sky, longing to sprout wings and take flight.

I gather up a few bushels and hand my coin over, sighing as I place one of the lavender flowers behind my ear like a talisman. Someone bumps into my shoulder as they pass by, pushing me into another person on my other side. The day is now well underway as the market begins to fill.

I spot James coming toward me as he adjusts his belt and sword at his hips. His roughly scarred face is half covered by the patchy hair on his cheeks and chin. He doesn't acknowledge me, but I know by now it means it's time to return to the camp. Heads turn my way as the local marketgoers notice James accompanying me, but quickly avert their eyes when they realize who I am…whose daughter I am.

I lift my chin and fight against the urge to let the avoidance affect me. They split apart in a wide berth as I pass, creating a gaping hole in the shoulder-to-shoulder square. I don't take it personally. I wouldn't want to interact with the royal merchant's daughter, either.

It's not like the townspeople or tradesmen wear anything close to my usual attire. Not only does my clothing always stand out, but so does my hair. The long, plain brown is braided down my back and tied at the end with whatever frayed ribbon I can find for the day, a dead giveaway that I don't belong.

Even the less wealthy townspeople have their hair freely flowing or in some elaborate knot on the top of their head. I wince at the thought of having my head poked and stabbed with pins to hold everything in place. Beauty isn't the top priority in the training camp.

I pinch the bridge of my nose and squeeze my eyes shut for a moment, breathing in slowly to calm my now-racing pulse. Any pretense of confidence crumbles beneath the pressure of returning, and the temporary comfort from the flower stand is already fading. I notice how far into the sky the sun has settled and realize I've been here longer than I should have been. My shadow and I pass through the market, dread coiling in my stomach.

Another soldier nods to us. "How's the camp these days?"

James grunts in response, the guard nodding as if that suffices as an answer. I hear a brief acknowledgment between James and the castle sentry, his position seemingly more boring than James's.

I dull out their conversation, eyes wandering. As we pass by, my eyes land on the enormity of the walled castle before me. It overshadows the market. Even a small maid from one of the cramped, tiny stone cottages beyond the market can easily spot the castle gates. I wonder if the people inside feel trapped like I do.

James nudges me ahead with a sharp poke. Wincing at the direction I need to start heading in, I sigh and sling my sack behind me. My palms begin to sweat, and my heart matches the quick cadence of my feet. If only I didn't have to return. There's an entire world of things I'll never be able to experience, but I'm not foolish enough to believe I can escape Father's tight grasp.

Turning my back on the castle, I weave through the stands toward the end of the market. The one and only path connecting the royal training camp to this part of Runnswick is one I wish to never take again.

My footprints trail behind me as each plop in the mud coats my shoes with heaviness. James trails lazily behind me, clearly not in a rush to return to his training. His large build is ever-present even when I try to ignore it.

Suddenly I spot a flash of familiar blonde, the figure's hair swishing as she trudges through a side path coming from the woods and feeding into the path back to camp.

"Opal!" I shout her name and jog to catch up to her, the only person in the world who comes close to understanding my pain. Our childhood friendship quickly turned into a lifelong bond. Her father being the commander of the army and mine being the royal merchant, we latched onto each other as a means of survival.

She smiles and spins around. "Well *Lu*, how nice of you to join me on the trek back to our *glorious* camp."

I sputter a laugh at the nickname from years ago, her ease never failing to distract my mind from what lies ahead. Still chuckling, I say, "Well I don't think our fathers would appreciate us getting distracted from their tasks, so we better hurry back *home*."

She laughs with me, and we loop our arms together while letting the path guide us to a place neither of us will ever truly call home. Her wavy blonde hair is a stark contrast to my messy brown braid. Standing a forehead taller than me, she's outspoken and always plastering on a smile. Her ivory complexion is complimented by the subtle rosiness that always tints her cheeks, whereas my skin is rough and scarred.

I've spent countless years schooling my expression into neutrality, but she can sense what my words don't say. She turns her head and narrows her gaze at James behind us.

"Do you know how creepy you look? Following a girl around and lurking in the shadows?"

James rolls his eyes at her and ignores our giggling.

Opal turns back to me and shakes her head at the flowers in my hand. "Again, Lu?"

I sigh and turn away from her penetrating glare. Even if it's a risk to buy these flowers, it's one worth taking. If it keeps my incessant need to explore at bay, then that's a small price to pay over the alternative. Like trying to run away and getting caught.

I train my eyes on the narrow path that is now quiet with the sounds of the market fading in the distance behind us. For a moment, the only thing I can hear is the sound of our boots squishing in the dirt.

"He didn't notice the flowers," I say when James falls far enough behind. "He's too absorbed with going to the madam's house. Besides, if I'm back at camp before dusk, his job is complete."

She's already shaking her head bitterly before I can finish my sentence. She lowers her voice and speaks in a quiet fury. "You should be more careful; you know your father wouldn't approve of spending his money on something he didn't put on that list." She plucks a stalk of lavender from me, bringing it to her nose before promptly tossing it in the mud. "The faster we play their game, the faster we can get out of here."

I move to speak, but she doesn't stop there.

"You know as well as I do, the best thing for us is to find a husband and get away from the men that raised us. It doesn't even have to be for love, just someone less of an ass than they are." Opal squeezes my arm looped in hers and huffs several times when she finishes talking.

I take a deep breath and tilt my head back toward the sky without answering her right away. A bird swoops by the trees surrounding us and dives toward one of the tallest branches for a perch. He lets out a gentle caw at us walking past, then takes off back into the air. Never did I think I'd find myself jealous of an animal, but the creature possesses an easy access to freedom I'll never know.

I want to experience what it would be like to move about without a guard to escort me back to the training camp. Or to leave the camp for a season to see what one of the mountainous towns is like in the spring. How could I know what I like if I've never been far outside of Runnswick?

That's twice today I've found myself envious of something other than humans.

I shake my head and wrap my arms around myself. "It doesn't matter how much my father complains about me spending his precious money. He'll wait until it benefits him the most to give me over to a husband and use me as his servant in the meantime. Your father has more sons than he can count, but lucky me for my father to only have a daughter. I also must have an offer to begin with."

Opal rolls her eyes again. "'Servant'? You mean his favorite slave? At least servants get paid something in return."

I know she's right. But as much as I despise my father, it's still difficult to think of him as caring so little for me. Being viewed as someone only to be tolerated didn't make for a pleasant childhood.

We walk in silence for a few moments as we draw nearer to the camp. Her brows knit together in what I can only interpret as fear with our proximity to what lies behind the gates.

She certainly won't have a problem finding a husband. What man wouldn't want someone like Opal with her striking features and her charming smile?

"When are you going to accept one of their proposals?" I ask in what I hope is a light tone.

She glances at me with narrowed eyes and says, "Someone will ask you in time, just be patient. And maybe try to smile more. I don't think glaring at every man is going to make him want to make you his wife. You could have any man you want, but we both know you don't want a husband."

The words strike me hard, like a cold blast of wind sprinting through the trees.

My shoulders tense, defensive. "I'm just not meant to be someone's wife. We've both spent our whole lives serving our fathers. I don't want to do the same for a husband. I want to be free. I just refuse to escape one master, only to run headfirst into the clutches of another."

She shakes her head but says nothing as the camp comes into view. We unloop our arms and I let my hand rest on the dagger at my hip. Any lingering happiness fades from my face as I toss my bouquet into the forest beside me. I reach up and grab the stalk behind my ear, wiggling it in front of Opal's face so she sees that I removed it.

The ugliness before me is no place for flowers.

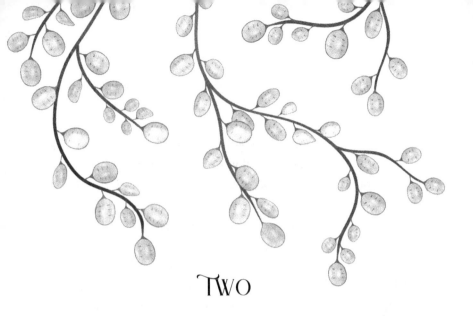

Two

Clematis

We reach the outskirts of the camp, the guards at the massive gate glancing our way. The mouth of the camp gapes open like a hungry fish, eating whole everyone who steps through. We step carefully past the threshold, not feeling safe no matter how many times we cross through. The guards silently let us pass, and we split off on our own paths back home.

My shadow returns to my father's area of the camp, not bothering to give a goodbye. I pass through the only opening to the wall that surrounds the enormous training area and out to the start of camp.

I wipe my hands against my leathers, dread trickling into my core and twisting my insides. Two tall watchtowers rest at the start of camp, a man in each turret with a wooden bow ready in his hands. Six other watchtowers are scattered about the camp, placed strategically apart to be able to see this side of the wall and the woods beyond it.

Keeping our enemies out, but also keeping me in.

I hold my chin high as I pass through the first training area with a few soldiers training together. None look my way, most of them used to my presence by now. I keep walking with my sack fastened over my shoulder, not bothering to pause at the central square. The heart of the camp lacks any real warmth or comradery.

Worn tents litter just beyond the square, right before the next training area. Soldiers preparing to join the King's Army are packed tightly together, like the fish crammed into overflowing baskets in the market.

The men enter the camp as farmers, tradesmen, and everything in between. A lot of them need the very small coin that comes along with joining the King's Army and send what little they make back to their families. They come in waves, inexperienced and unknowing about the particulars of being a soldier, and leave as trained combatants to be stationed around Crea.

I look over at an unclaimed area and watch as new recruits put their tents up, a clear line being drawn between the new, laughing soldiers and the grim-faced veterans who have been here longer. Their shoulders sag with the conditions of the camp bearing down on them for months on end.

At least I don't live in a cramped space like that. My bed is soft and plush, nothing like the jagged terrain the soldiers' tents rest on that touch the cold ground. This is the way Father says it must be: that there are winners and losers. But I can't help but feel sorry for them. Maybe that's why they stay so tightly packed together in the tent, huddling together for warmth on a chilly night.

I grind my teeth together as I clear the tents and pass the stables holding the highest-ranking soldiers' steeds. The smell of them lingers around the majority of the camp, but I don't mind it. Most of those horses have more sense than the men riding them. The sound of howling hounds fills the air, causing the horses to kick uneasily at their wooden stalls.

My eyes catch on a soldier who stands just outside the dog's pen, yelling commands at them. When he holds up a slab of meat, they all sit on cue. He tosses the meat to the first dog to sit while the others watch hungrily. When he gives another command, the dogs all bark in unison, causing him to smile and toss another slab of meat. The dogs clamor for it, their teeth gnashing and nipping. But the biggest beats the others out, its tail wagging victoriously. The rest fall silent, waiting for his next command.

I swear the animals train faster than some of the men that end up here.

The deeper I get into the belly of the fish, the more I can feel beads of sweat collect at the nape of my neck. With the tents behind me, I get a small moment of reprieve before I reach the training rings. Knowing it's filled with soldiers going through their combat lessons—ones that I won't be invited to join—fills me with jealousy.

I walk in silence, tapping my fingers against my thigh as the sounds of commanders yelling grow louder. Even with the number of soldiers filling the circular training camp, the massiveness of it still makes it easy to find small spaces of silence.

I stick to the rut in the ground, the makeshift path that's been created from boots stomping through the cluster of main training tents. The tented structure is the most prominent thing in the camp. Two tall wooden posts are staked into the ground on each side of the opening to the tent. Atop the posts is Crea's emblem stitched into a bloodred cloth, the ends tattered from the wind and rain. Two officers stand stationed outside of it, keeping track of the trainees inside who sometimes take the fighting too far. The opening flap is pulled wide open, giving a clear view of the lesson they're running through.

Another area has just been roped off, leaving a group to train out in the open. The ropes line the edge of the path I'm walking, leaving me far too close to the glares tossed my way. Opal's father is running more experienced soldiers through sword work already. Heavy wooden training swords smack into each other, sending splinters flying off toward me. Now that I've made it to the northern sparring rings, I'm surrounded by hundreds of soldiers. Different groups are broken up to run through their respective training sessions, commands being shouted out from all directions.

The soldiers are lumped together by their skill level, more areas than I can count bustling with men. The distant sound of bells and the slowly sinking sun signal that the evening meal is ready. The bustle suddenly shifts as the men put their weapons down and head out for dinner.

The training rings sit just before Father's cabin. He says he likes to see how his money is paying off. But it makes for a hell of a trudge. Someone could get lost in here—in fact, people do. I notice what must be a squadron of new recruits still sparring, unaware of the dinner bell. A new batch of overly self-confident boys with no ability to fight. As the thought crosses my mind, I can feel a smile coming into form before I shove it back down.

I narrow my eyes at one of them looking my way, his eyes trailing slowly from my head to my toes.

"Hey, come over here, watch me fight!" The boy speaking is gangly, his limbs long and lacking control like a newborn deer. I honestly don't know how his body can hold up the largeness of his head. His stance is terrible, and he doesn't look a day over sixteen.

He won't last a week.

"How about I join instead?" I offer expectantly.

The other new recruits roar with laughter and turn their backs to me, effectively blocking me out.

I take a defiant step toward them but freeze when I hear a voice speak through the cluster of soldiers, scraping against my insides like claws dragging down tree bark.

"Welcome home." Father stands with his arms crossed in the distance. A seemingly innocent phrase, but somehow chilling my heart to a standstill.

The recruits all glance my way again; I can see the realization settling on their faces. The gangly boy grows pale when he makes the connection that I'm the royal merchant's daughter, the blood draining from his face. In many ways, my father is more feared than the royal commander of the King's Army. Not from the fear of a violent presence like the commander, but fear of his influence that reaches out in strangling tendrils throughout the kingdom.

Father's face is a quiet mask of calm as he approaches from across the ring, the world around us slowing to a stop. Much like the breath stuck in my throat.

His height sticks above the crowd, and the dark brown hair atop his head sits in perfect condition. The edges are all stiff and brushed back, giving it an almost wet look though it's entirely dry. His slim nose matches my own, a piece of me I've always hated. Soldiers part for him to pass through, his features aimed straight at me like one of the army's archers readying his arrows, with me as the bullseye.

"Did you find everything today?" His face is neutral, but I can see the almost imperceptible narrowing of his eyes as his gaze flicks to the sack fastened over my shoulder. The soldiers around us resume their routine, leaving me alone with him.

I shoulder the sack and hand it over to him. He smiles stiffly, lacking any warmth in his cold eyes. It's less about the items and more about following his command.

Every piece of him is sharp and calculated, and he can't stand the possibility of being outmaneuvered by anyone. That's why, in a calculated ploy, he befriended the royal commander, moving us here to be trained under the most skilled soldier in the kingdom.

Being the royal merchant, Father is wealthy and trained expertly as much in the moving of money as in combat. He knows how to mask weakness better than anyone I have ever known. But his most frightening quality is his ability to find the weakness in others. In his early days, the only weakness in my father's arsenal was his inability to fight. And if you want to live and sit on the king's council, you must be able to defend yourself and your seat in the inner circle.

So, he moved us and his enormous wealth to the king's camp to sharpen his skills as a combatant. I think my father felt this would complete him. That this was the final piece missing from his life, rounding him out into the formidable figure he so desperately sought to become: the embodiment of wealth, power, and fear. But he's as miserable as everyone else here.

"Amira?"

I realize I'm still holding the sack between us, and I drop it into his outstretched palm with a sudden jerk.

My father shakes his head as he examines the contents. "And the change?"

"In the bag," I answer shortly.

His eyes narrow. "I know where it is. I'm asking you to account how much."

I furrow my brows. I should know this—he asks every time. My mind blank, I open my mouth just as he interrupts.

"You seem distracted, Amira. You should know better than to let your mind wander. And you should know that I will spot a single copper piece that isn't in its rightful spot."

My breath staggers even though I'm certain I counted right.

His mouth curdles into an insincere smile. "Hurry home, now."

I stare longingly at the new recruits.

"Now," Father reiterates, his voice darkening.

I head back, empty-handed.

I lie in bed staring up at the wooden ceiling, viewing the arch of the wood sloping down to meet the floorboards unevenly, causing small cracks to litter the corners of my room as the cool night air slips through them. I roll over in bed with frustration as sleep evades me yet again. Memories of my mother try to claw their way to the surface, but I force them back down, not wanting to torture myself with distant memories of her. I can't help but wonder how different my life would be if I had ended up with her instead.

The old, gold-framed mirror leaning against the wall across from me reveals a girl I now hardly recognize. The eyes of the girl in the mirror don't reflect the longing to escape that fills me. While I despise the nose and shape of my body that resembles too much of my father, my eyes belong entirely to my mother. The only memory of her face the hazel eyes staring back at me in the mirror.

I toss the blankets aside and sit on the edge of my bed. To get out of here, I must be strong enough to leave. I already know fighting my way out through hundreds of soldiers won't work, but can I even make it out there alone? Maybe I can convince Opal to leave behind her fantasy of marriage and join me. There's strength in numbers, right?

Taking off my thick nightgown, I slip into my training leathers. I welcome the familiarity of the material like an old friend as I lace up my pants. I separate my plain brown hair into two braids, placing one over each shoulder and tying them with a thin ribbon at the end.

I take one last look into the old mirror at a girl now properly ready for her day. A girl thin from the small rations allotted by the cooks. A face slim and speckled with freckles down the bridge of her nose and across her cheeks. A girl that trades sleeping for training—a girl yearning for her escape.

I am Amira Ramsey, and I am not going to spend the rest of my life like this.

I just have to find a way out.

I force a grin at the girl staring back at me from the mirror, and she grins too. Squaring my shoulders and lifting my chin, I swing open my bedroom door and silently make my way through the cabin.

It's still before dawn, the sky outside my window black and cold. I tiptoe light-footed in my boots, careful not to wake the sleeping beast that lies behind the room facing mine. I snatch old fruit off the table and quickly mix my daily tonic with a glass of water. It burns as I gulp it down, but the alternative to not taking it would be much worse.

I step onto the porch to find the camp dog waiting for me. He's supposed to be in his pen with the other hounds, but he spends most of his time following me around instead. He lifts his head as soon as I close the front door and starts to sweep his tail back and forth excitedly.

"You know you're not supposed to keep sneaking out of your pen. They might throw you out if you don't train well, Dog." I smile down at him, and his ears perk up when he hears his name. Or lack thereof.

No one saw the point in giving him a name, so everyone just kept calling him Dog. All the other hounds were given names to intimidate Penyth's men. With their army using strange tactics that frequently end in victory, our king finally decided to use animals to our advantage too. Most of the training mutts have names like Striker, Beast, Hurricane, and Fang, but Dog was found a few years into his age and didn't seem to take to listening to anyone unless he wanted to.

I tried calling him a few different names for a while, but he never responds to anything but Dog. I squat down on the porch to scratch his head and his fuzzy white ears. As soon as I stand up, he starts to follow me. We make our way to the outer perimeter of the camp for our early run while I scarf down my small breakfast. He's so tall that his head brushes my hip while he sticks close to me.

"Up for a little run?"

He swishes his tail back and forth and tilts his head at the question. After a quick stretch, we begin at a steady pace through the camp. We pass a blur of tents, drunken trainees, guards, and cooks gathering their ingredients for the morning breakfast mush.

Most of the soldiers begin their day the same way: breakfast, body strengthening, hand-to-hand combat training, running the wall perimeter, strategy lessons, sword mastery, and dinner. With the number of new recruits coming in each month, the rations have been cut even smaller. The soldiers have already started lining up at different cooks' stations, even though morning training won't start for some time. They shove each other and push the smaller men to the back of the line.

As soon as we get to the less populated area of the camp, I start to relax, leaning into the burn working its way through my limbs. The stars are still shining above me, but the soft glow from the sun is just beginning to lighten the eastern sky. We make our way through the outskirts of the camp all the way to the giant wall closing us in. While the number of tents lessens to almost none and trees fill the area, I let my mind drift with the breeze of night ending.

I sprint harder than I have the past few weeks, letting frustration push me swiftly through the woods. I dodge fallen tree branches and roots scattered across the forest floor. Dog howls in excitement and speeds ahead of me in chase of a squirrel. I shake my head with a small laugh, happy to see him about so freely and not caged in his pen. Most of the soldiers seem to be too scared of him to mention he should be locked up with the other hounds.

The damp and sloshy mud squishes beneath my boots, causing my feet to occasionally slip. Dog's paws sink into the ground, his fur changing from a crisp white to a deep and muddy brown. His tongue lolls to the side of his wide-open mouth as he runs in circles after the creature in front of me. Much stealthier on his feet than I am, he can navigate in the muck just as well as he does on dry land.

When we pass the thin stream that travels along the back half of the camp, I ache to pause and enjoy the silence that accompanies the area. This is the most alone I can ever be right here. But I know there's no time for that.

Dog finally gives up on chasing the squirrel and returns to my side as we continue through the thickening forest. We race along the wall encircling the camp that's too tall to think about jumping, and the watchtowers that loom high off the ground, making it almost impossible to do so anyway.

I finally break through the woods a final time after a few runs around the camp and stop to brace my hands on my knees to catch my ragged breath. Dog darts toward the cooks to no doubt beg for food that they will eventually cave in and toss his way. More of the camp is awake now with trainees pushing out of their tents to get their breakfast, the newer ones likely unaware of the need to get in line early.

The smell of the food is even less appetizing than the sight of it. The slop smacks from the cook's ladle and into the bowls of starving soldiers.

I watch as a soldier accepts his food eagerly, only for his mouth to deepen into a frown as the sludge splatters out of the bowl and onto his face. The next in line gags slightly as his portion is slapped into his bowl. The men are so different from one another, ranging from boys with their voices still changing to middle-aged men. Though their disappointed grumbles are always the same each mealtime.

I walk past the cooks' stations without stopping, not eager to approach the men still shoving each other to get their slim helpings. Even if the food smells worse than the stables, a hungry man will weather the worst of it. One of the larger ones in line snatches a boy's bowl out of his hands and pours it into his own, doubling his portions and leaving the boy with nothing.

The other soldiers in line continue about, unaffected. No one stands up for them, the smaller and younger boys all wasting away with the passing days and food stolen from their fingertips.

Ever since I was a little girl, Father has always told me weakness isn't tolerated in the king's camp. The kingdom needed to plant soldiers like seeds around the kingdom, but only seeds that would sprout and flourish—not die and wither away with a gust of wind. A part of me wonders if they serve the food they do on purpose, to try and weed out the ones who can't handle the hunger.

It always made me wonder if my mother was weak; if she really died like Father said, or if he casted her off because he perceived her to be frail and purposeless. Or maybe she was smart enough to leave this dreadful place behind, and for that, I wouldn't blame her.

Once again, I'm left with a growling stomach and a hint of a memory of the woman I assumed was my mother. Her face was one I could pass and never recognize, but the scent of lilies and lavender would always cause me to look around, hoping to catch a glimpse of her.

"Amira!" Opal waves and smiles brightly at me as she hurries over, pulling me out of my thoughts. Her golden hair is twisted into a tight bun on top of her head and soft curls frame her face, her bright blue eyes somehow brimming with hope in this desolate camp. Opal may be a pretty face, but looks can certainly be deceiving. She's like a clever little fox always assessing and adapting, the look in her eye showing me she's up to something.

"Want to train together today?" I ask. "We probably could trade our morning portions for a lesson or two from one of the hungrier recruits."

The camp, now almost fully awake, begins to take notice of us. Those who have been in training longer often see Opal and me together, but curiosity toward us lingers all the same.

"Deal." Opal dips her chin down once in confirmation and lets a smile that's almost predatory slip. We both love a challenge, and tricking the new soldiers is always a fun warm-up for the day.

THREE

HELIOTROPE

THE DAYS BLEED TOGETHER IN a haze of routine as I wake up earlier than the rest of the soldiers to train. After today's circuit, Opal and I lounge by the stream that lines the camp. The muddied water is stained the color of dirt from the amount of rain that falls in Crea. Sprawled out on a rock jutting out over the stream, I skim my bare toes along the cold water. Small fish dodge my feet as they race toward the sea into which the stream will eventually feed.

The water is so murky it's almost impossible to see the little animals swimming about. They swim in a perfect circle around my toes. I tilt my head to the side, curious as I watch them continue around my feet in the strange pattern, the fish each no bigger than a pebble but following each other in flawless unison. Opal splashes her feet into the water and the fish scatter, the hunger gnawing at my stomach making me wonder if I imagined them.

Small gnats flood the surface above the stream, and I swat them away with no progress in removing them. I sigh and lie back in the grass to look at the night sky that's holding on above me. Dawn will be breaking through soon, but the moon shows no signs of lowering.

"Can't we just rest for a moment, Lu?"

Something flutters in my chest when I hear the nickname that I chose for myself so long ago—a simpler time of running around the camp with Opal, not yet with the mounting responsibilities we now have. We would run around the camp calling each other by our pretend names, ignoring the glares of all the soldiers.

"Tired already, Ava?" I emphasize the name Opal chose for herself and she laughs.

"I hate that I chose that name. Yours is so much better."

I smile to myself, a piece of me agreeing with her, as it's partly the reason I still let her call me Lu so often. Somehow, calling her Ava never really stuck past our childhood. I still my swinging feet just as I hear Opal's soft snores beside me. The world around us quiets with our stillness, and with hours left before daybreak, the camp hasn't yet awoken.

Opal—the only friend to have shared almost the same childhood as me. Her father nearly as terrifying as my own.

Above me, the thick coverage of trees tries to conceal the outside world, but the slivers of sky peeking through are enough to let me play pretend I'm somewhere else.

"Let's play a game, Lu. It's called pretend." A soothing woman's voice drifts from beside me while she strokes my hair.

"What's pretend?" I ask, fighting sleep. I rub my tiny fists across my eyes, trying to clear the sleep away.

The woman smiles and says in a low whisper, "It's imagining something the way you wish it to be. You dream of something wonderful, and you act like you're in it. Like this: we play pretend that we are in a field filled with white lilies. Their round, white, bell-shaped tops are visible as far as your precious little eyes can see. Butterflies are flying around, and one lands on you. When it lands on you it turns you into a butterfly too. You sprout beautiful, big, yellow wings and fly into the sky to gaze at the lilies in the valley below."

I feel my eyes widen with the thought. "And then what do I do?"

She smiles again and says, "And then you fly far from here and the beautiful lilies of our quiet valley."

I frown in confusion because the story is sad. I don't want to leave the pretty flowers.

The woman laughs quietly and says, "But this is the fun part of pretend. If you don't want to leave you don't have to. You can come back."

I scoot closer to her, and my eyelids start to weigh down with sleep, calling me into a night of dreaming about flying through the lily field with the pretty woman. The woman joins me in my dream and grabs my hand while we fly together from petal to petal and laugh our way down the field of flowers.

I startle awake to Opal raising her voice. I scramble to my feet and find the source of her frustration.

"This is truly how you believe spending your time will benefit you the most?" Father's disapproving frown tilts across his angular face.

A blush splashes across my cheeks, and I grind my teeth to stop myself from speaking.

He cuts his eyes to Opal and narrows his gaze at her.

I clear my throat, trying to turn his attention back to me. "Attending business so far from the camp this morning?" I ask with the most neutral tone I can muster, squashing any signs that I'm afraid.

He takes a step closer, and Opal does the same.

"Letting another fight your battles for you, daughter?" He stares at the two of us for a moment, and we both know it's better if we remain silent. But I still can't stop the words from spilling out.

"You've taught me better than that, haven't you?"

With the way his face hardens, he takes offense to it as I thought he would. "You forgot your tonic powder. Do you think it truly wise to break out in hives from your allergy? Or is it that you enjoy your throat and lungs closing entirely?"

On reflex, I reach for its resting place in my pocket. I usually don't leave the cabin without it. The blood drains from my face when I find it empty.

"Have you forgotten the last time you forgot to take it?"

No, but he has no problem reminding me.

"The moment you touched a blade of grass your throat closed up, and you writhed around on the ground unable to breathe."

I shudder, the memory of writhing in the lily field returning. No amount of play pretend could change the fear that memory left in me. It's almost as if nature is entirely against me with how severe my reaction is to any green, living thing.

"You almost died several times." He sneers. He holds out my leather pouch containing my medicine, a knowing look on his face. Now that he's gotten the last word, he turns on his heel, walking back in the direction of the camp.

I pinch out the amount I need and drop it into my mouth dry. Without anything to mix it with, he knew I would have to take it this way. I swallow thickly until the bitter substance is fully dissolved and sliding slowly down my throat.

The sun has mostly pushed itself into the sky, and we make our way back to camp while keeping a safe distance away from Father. We walk slowly through the woods and slightly off the small worn path, avoiding the dodder plants that litter most of our land.

I wouldn't want any of those nasty little seeds coming back to camp with me. They weave their way around the little speckles of clovers trying to sprout up, wound so tightly that I doubt the clover will last the day. I wonder if Penyth has to deal with the irritating plant in their kingdom. Although, they likely have much more dangerous things growing.

Morning brings a small amount of warmth and starts to chase away the chill of the night. Twigs snap under my leather boots as I walk alongside Opal, neither of us mentioning the run-in with my father. The wariness of the tasks for the day makes me feel like crawling back into bed.

"So, what are you going to do when I get married? You know it'll happen eventually." Her voice is a gentle nudge. Her bright blue eyes sear into me. "I can't leave you here alone with him."

I consider her words and chew on the inside of my cheek. As much as I hate to admit it, the idea of being here without Opal isn't an easy thought to bear.

She sighs and gives my hands a squeeze. Her eyes are sympathetic, knowing the world we want isn't the world we live in. "Sounds like a good morning to spend time in the southern training ring. Let a little of our frustrations out, maybe? It probably isn't crowded yet if we skip breakfast. Not that you can call *that* stuff food."

We make it through the thickly wooded forest and start off toward the southern sparring ring. Only a few other soldiers mill about, cycling through their own lessons, but none I recognize.

Soldiers come and go so frequently that it's hard to keep up with who remains. Most of them are only here for a short amount of time to learn how to be a soldier, and then are shipped off to different villages as guards of the kingdom. All in the name of keeping Crea safe, the villagers in line, and protecting the kingdom from Penyth. The men that are here the longest are usually the ones being trained for more specialized positions, like stations at the castle or becoming trainers in the camp.

Even though I typically become familiar with those who remain, I never allow them close enough to stab me in the back—because they always will.

"You only gain power by taking it for yourself, daughter, and once you have it there will always be someone trying to take it back."

I blink away the memory of Father's words as Opal tugs me into one of the sparring rings.

Her tightly wound bun bobs on top of her head as she speaks while bouncing on her toes. "Ready to run through the first set?"

I grab a practice sword from the rack and flip it over in my hand twice as I circle her. Any hint of a smile between the two of us dissipates into concentration. Being best friends doesn't mean we go easier on each other. We've spent years training together, learning each other's weaknesses, and finding ways to strengthen them.

She lunges first like I expected she would, and I let her weight collide with mine. Using her surprise that I let her hit me, I throw her off balance and sweep her feet from beneath her. She throws her hands under herself to brace her fall and rolls to the side—just in time for my knees to heavily hit the ground before I can land on top of her. She laughs and jumps to her feet, still bouncing back and forth on her toes. My eyes must give away the anger bubbling inside of me because her laughter quickly quiets.

"What? You said to get our frustration out," I say with a shrug.

She nods, her eyes narrowing as she spits a strand of hair out of her mouth. I wonder if I look as ferocious as she does, two tigers circling in on each other.

"You're always so serious, Lu. You need to lighten up a bit."

I answer her by swinging my blade at her left side. Her weaker side. She blocks my swing a moment too late, and my blade meets her leather top. She jerks her head up at me in a mixture of surprise and irritation. While not swinging hard enough to severely injure her, I still manage to leave a small cut.

We may not go easy on each other, but we typically don't draw blood. I pause a moment, frustrated with myself for letting my anger reach the surface. She takes advantage of my pause and elbows me in the chest, causing me to release my blade to catch my breath.

The second my blade lands in the muddied ring, I grab a small dagger from each thigh. I work better with them anyway. The closer the combat, the more skill that's involved, and while Opal is a decent fighter, she isn't nearly as skilled as I am.

A fight isn't about who can get more hits in; it's about who can finish it.

In a short burst of movements, I disarm her of her blade. She reaches to her thigh to grab her own dagger, then looks over to the edge of the ring. The extra dagger and various weapons she typically hides on herself are lying on the ground. She looks back at me and shakes her head, prepared for her loss. As resourceful as she is, she can't outmatch me while I hold a dagger in each hand.

By the end of it, we are both breathing heavily and beginning to bruise. When one of the recruits whistles at our display, Opal flashes him her middle finger.

We look at each other. An apology sits on the tip of my tongue, but we both know I won't say it. I let the apology shine through my eyes, and she nods in understanding. She knows me well enough by now to know what lies behind what's left unsaid.

We break into a series of circuits with my frustration now mostly deflated. We speak in hushed voices during our lesson, so the others won't hear. Heads turn our way every so often, and ears are clearly straining to get a slice of information from the royal merchant's daughter and the royal commander's daughter. Everyone wants an advantage, but we never give lessons to the new recruits. Much like we aren't allowed to join in getting them.

We practice our own version of hand-to-hand combat drills until the ring is full of recruits about to begin their own lessons.

"The trainer will be over here soon; we should get to our chores." Opal nods at the trainees starting to trickle in.

I reluctantly follow behind her, taking one last glimpse back at the roped-off area. One soldier picks up a sword, slashing through the air once or twice to try out its size, before replacing it on the rack and choosing a larger one. Another is crouched down on the ground, re-lacing his boots.

Every scrap of information we've gathered on fighting has been something we've had to trick someone into giving us or eavesdrop on while completing our chores from our fathers.

I usually use the new recruits to practice new techniques against, not with. Even if the technique is a failure, I can still usually beat them. A more skilled fighter will use each failure to their advantage against their opponent, but most of the new ones don't have a fighting background.

I use every spar with a newcomer to learn something. In most cases, I can easily disarm them in a few moves—but I always take my time and remain calm. Except today. I rarely allow my emotions to cloud my judgment while fighting, but today's different.

It feels as if the walls of the camp are closing in around me, throwing my footing off. Both in my head and in the ring. A mistake like that with Opal is fine, but if it were a real fight I would've been left wounded—or worse.

I won't be caught unprepared again.

Later that night, Opal and I sit around the fire eating our dinner, the briskness of the evening chased away by the warmth of the fire heating my skin.

I watch as Opal pinches her nose and shovels the soupy grains into her mouth. Her antics to avoid tasting the food have always amused me. Sometimes she swears squeezing both eyes shut and picturing a warm pie makes it taste better. Once she tried to smell a clover as she was chewing. I still don't know if any of those things worked.

I massage away the soreness in my legs without much ease in the pain. The lukewarm oats feel like ash in my mouth tonight. I push them around my bowl without making much of an effort to continue eating. At least the smoky smell of the fire covers the unappetizing whiffs coming from my bowl.

"Tomorrow's market day, right?" Opal is staring at her food like it's going to jump out at her.

I sigh and look up at the sky. "Want me to sneak you anything? I can bring you back one of those small apple pies you like from Mrs. Sutherland's stand."

The fire crackles loudly and specks of embers float into the night sky away from the camp. I stare after them as they each make their escape. Some of them slowly turn into ashes and fall back down to the earth beneath my boots, but some make it out. All it takes is choosing the right path to float away—or end up back on the camp's muddy soil.

"No thanks. Last thing you need is your father catching you with something you're not supposed to have. All his disapproving looks wouldn't be worth it. I don't know how you stand the guy."

The same could be said for her father. But at least she doesn't have a guard following her around when she goes out.

I remain quiet and instead watch the small bugs that light up with bright hues of yellows, their illumination pulsing in waves growing from bright to dark and back again. They circle above our heads, trying to light up the darkness of the camp. It would take a thousand of them to brighten it here.

"Would you rather be a bird or a bear?" Opal wiggles her eyebrows up and down like it's the most important question she's ever asked.

I let out a small breath of laughter and say, "A butterfly. I would be a butterfly, but if I had to choose between those two, I guess a bird since they at least have wings. Butterflies are prettier though."

"That's not really how the game works when I said *bird* or *bear*, but honestly, I'm not that surprised that you—" Her voice is abruptly cut off by another.

"Two women in a camp filled with soldiers. Remind me why we waste our food on you two when you should be cooking a nice dinner for a husband?"

A soldier I recognize as one that's been here at least a few years juts his chin out at Opal. She narrows her eyes at him and sticks another spoonful into her mouth. Much to her credit, she doesn't gag this time.

"I'm not sure what manners your fathers are teaching you girls, but give me that food, or I'm going to take it from you. You're so skinny you don't need much to fill you anyways. Some of us spend all day training around here," he taunts.

Before Opal can speak, I thread my fingers behind my head and lean back against the bench behind me. Opal's likely to talk herself into a fight she can't win, not against him anyway. I've seen him; he's ruthless, and revels in crossing the line when training.

"Glover. That's your name, right? Or is it Grover?"

Even with the fire splashing small amounts of light across his face, I can still see it turning bright red. "It's Rover and you know it, Amira." He spits at the fire and causes more embers to escape into the night sky.

The corners of my mouth turn into a smile that is anything but friendly. "Ah yes, Rover. So many of you look and fight the same it's hard to keep up." From my place on the ground, I slowly unlace my fingers from behind my head and stretch my arms out by my side. I unsheathe one of my daggers and push it beneath my sleeve as I stand up. Always be prepared.

I may be a few inches shorter than whatever-his-name-is, but he takes a step back the moment I'm upright. His face is still twisted in a burning rage that is likely to reach the surface soon…with a little prodding at least. Unease taps on my shoulder and tries to stop me, but I shove it back down.

"I honestly thought you didn't make it. Haven't seen you in a while. I'm pleased you've lasted this long, but I send my regards in advance for when you finally decide to quit. Or die." I shrug, and with that, the rage in him reaches its boiling point.

"Bitch." He spits the word at my smiling face, and Opal jumps to her feet as a few soldiers near us begin to take notice.

I turn my head to the side, my grin wide, and say, "Sounds like you're up for a challenge to me."

"Amira, I'm fine. He can have my portion, let's just go."

I ignore Opal and take a step closer to the soldier. The fire is blazing hotly beside us, so close a small step to the side could burn me. The flames lick dangerously close to my leathers.

Letting him take Opal's portion would only show she's someone the other soldiers can push around, her easy smile setting an even easier target on her back to be picked apart by the vultures.

But not if I'm here.

His eyes widen in realization of what I'm doing. Several soldiers eating around us stand up in excitement. There's nothing better than a little fight to get soldiers interested—it's not as if they have much entertainment around here.

The soldier notices the watching eyes and speaks through gritted teeth. "A challenge you want? A challenge you'll get." He knows he's too stuck to say no with the audience we've gained.

"To the southern sparring ring!" someone shouts, and everyone begins to move. The older soldiers look at us with disinterest and continue eating, but most can't resist.

"I know you're a great fighter. One of the best, but he's been here awhile as I'm sure you know." Opal continues to ramble, offering reasons why I should sit this challenge out. None are enough to convince me.

We walk deeper into the belly of the fish, away from the cooks' stations and toward the southern training area. Torches light up around the main ring, and several people lift their sticks of fire into the air with shouts of excitement. Others clap their hands together, applause filling the space as I shake away the regret biting at my heels.

Too late to turn back now.

There's no formal start to a challenge; the moment we step in, we both know it will begin.

I cut Opal off as she continues to try and talk me out of it. "Opal, I will be fine. I always am. We can't let them think of us as easy pickings."

Before she can reply, I step into the ring. The moment I do, I can feel the gathering crowd slowly quiet themselves.

I stand just inside the curved line and casually examine my nails without looking at my competitor, hoping to give off an air of arrogance I don't quite feel. The dagger I still have in my sleeve sits heavily against my wrist, so I slide it back to its resting place at my thigh.

"You realize to fight you have to actually look at me?" he spits out.

I slowly look up and roll my eyes at him. "You realize to win you need to actually know how to fight?"

His face seems to be stuck in anger, and it grows redder than I thought possible—so red it almost looks purple. Like a grape about to pop.

He takes a step toward me, but I make no move toward him. He grunts in frustration and tosses his sword outside of the ring.

"No weapons. Hand-to-hand only. Tap out quickly, and I'll try to not hurt you too badly, girl."

I smile and nod my head once in agreement.

He swings his giant fist at me, and I duck easily at the slowness of his attack. Before he notices I've moved, I jab my elbow into his stomach. He twists to the side and attempts to swing his arm at me again. This time, his fist slams into my temple and I stumble back to avoid the second strike.

I laugh and roll my shoulders. He takes two steps forward and swings his fist toward me again. I lean back far enough to avoid his hit and kick his knee as hard as I can. His knee bends back further than it should, and he yells in anger. Dropping to his hands, he cries out, this time in pain as the full effect of something tearing hits him. I take a step forward to finish the fight.

"Stop! I yield!" he shouts before I can step closer.

"You see, the angrier you allow yourself to be, the less focused you are. You really should relax a little." I flick my braid off my shoulder and walk out of the ring.

Some men cheer, but most are staring at the south side of the ring, where my father is standing with his arms crossed.

I don't know why I expected him to show any sort of pride, but he simply narrows his eyes and walks away. The crowd quickly parts for him. Disappointment washes over me.

Rover still gets to go to training tomorrow, and Opal seems more mad than grateful.

All I'm left with is a throbbing temple.

FOUR

ACOCOTLI

I ROLL OVER AND DECIDE to skip my morning exercise as a reward for my win yesterday. I slowly sit up on the edge of my bed and stretch every cramped muscle, closing my eyes as I focus my breathing to a steady in-and-out pace. The feel of the warm bed beckons me to lie back down and avoid facing the day, but the market awaits.

I hear a shuffle of steps, and something slides against the wooden floorboards. A piece of paper shoots from beneath the door and lands close to my feet. A headache already forms at the list scrawled out in Father's handwriting.

Still sore from my match yesterday, I stiffly get dressed and pull my hair into a single braid, then snatch the list off the floor to examine it.

Two apples
Loaf of bread
Leather waistband for a sword
Bag of grain

Bottle of ale
Jar of honey
Bundle of cheese
Sack of wool
Handful of fish
A fresh supply of tonic is on the counter

The list continues onto the back page, but I shove it into the pocket of my cotton pants without bothering to read the rest of it. To the market it is.

I breathe in the rich spices of the fragrant stands. The cramped market square is crowded more than usual today, like rats packed into an alley all forcing their way in different directions. James follows behind me with a disinterested, blank stare on his face.

"Welcome to the market town of Runnswick! So close to the castle you can watch the king's address today." The seller is clearly new to town if he thinks the king will have anything worthwhile to say. His speeches have grown more and more incoherent by the year.

Before I can respond, he's already turning and repeating the same line to a few wide-eyed women. A flurry of noise fills my ears, bursts of laughter from friends walking together and shouts of anger from sellers yelling at children to scatter.

One small child plucks an apple off a stand while the tradesman is busy yelling at the other children. He turns his big green eyes and notices me watching him. His eyes widen in panic, and he freezes with his hand still grasping the apple. But instead of waving the constable over, I wink. He grins a toothless grin at me, immediately jerking his hand—and the apple—away from the stand.

The tradesman turns back toward his fruit stand just as the child darts away with his prize. I shake my head and watch, amused, as the child continues along to claim more treats.

While the kingdom isn't poor, it isn't exactly wealthy either. Father makes sure there's a clearly defined line between the wealthy and the poor. After all, Royal Merchant isn't a title freely given. Even now, Father makes sure I know my place from his by casting me out to do the servants' work. Yet James's presence—and the camp's crimson crest emblazoned across my back—informs others I'm well enough off to be treated better. He keeps me just enough afloat to avoid drowning, but not enough to surface.

I nod my head in the direction of my guard as we approach Linnick's stand, and he immediately bombards him with offers to taste-test his delicate fruits. When James turns his back and Linnick gives me a wink, I dart off.

I run to a barmaid heckling men to come inside the main tavern, one of James's favorites. "Lucy, could you distract him a little longer today?" I ask, handing her two coins.

Her eyes narrow at James across the way, a smile forming on her lips. "Anything for my favorite cash cow." She pockets the coin and fluffs her hair. "You got until midday."

I push through the crowd, getting elbowed in the side and back at least twice. I find Linnick's stand as he and James finish with their tastings.

"Good morning Linnick, two apples today."

Just as Linnick begins to bag up the apples, Lucy ambles over to us.

"You don't want to miss today's show, Captain. It's going to be a good one."

James leaves with Lucy, and the crowd swallows him from sight.

"Be careful, Lu—he's going to catch on one of these days. Or he'll get sent somewhere else, and the next guard won't be so easy to trick."

I sit down behind Linnick's stand on his small wooden stool, smiling to myself at my nickname. He's the only person to whom I'd reveal that embarrassing story, the years Opal and I spent playing pretend and calling each other different names as our imagination took us to a better place.

The tattered tapestry above us has been stitched together with several different patterned cloths. The air has a cold bite to it with the warmth of the sun obscured. The covering does little to block the loudness of the market around us.

"Most men are the same, all distracted by a woman." I shrug and watch as Linnick sells a few lemons to a couple who look like they just departed from the dock this morning. Their belongings rest at their sides as they hand over their coin.

Once Linnick is back beside me, he brings his hand to his chin and makes a humming noise as he stares at the stand across from us.

"Are you up for a game of pretend?" he asks.

I laugh and nod, joy filling my heart. Linnick's the only other person I've let in on my little game, other than Opal. "Looks to me you've already started playing."

He smiles, keeping a watchful eye on the tradesman across from us. "The guy over there selling cattle pelts, you see him?" He points to the stand.

I look over to the stand that has more than twenty cattle pelts strung up or laid out over the front of the wooden station. I nod and try to keep myself from laughing. Linnick sometimes gets more into the game than me, even if it should be a game for a child.

"Well, he's not selling any ordinary cattle pelts..." His voice trails off and he lifts an eyebrow at me, waiting for me to finish the sentence.

"They're magical." I fill in the blank. "If you buy one, then you'll have luck brought upon your house. Coins will be left at your doorstep each night if you hang the pelt on the inside of your door."

Linnick nods his head and stares harder at the seller. "Right, and if you leave it over your table in the early hours of morning, then a full spread of jellies, breakfast pies, meats, and bread will fill your table." His voice holds poorly concealed laughter, causing the seller to turn and look at us with narrowed eyes.

"But unfortunately, you learn that everything you're given must be given back tenfold. So, you spend your days being the maid for a smelly little troll. The same one that used to bring you your prize."

Our laughter rises, and we try to hold it back.

"And the troll turns out to be that tradesman!" Linnick's outburst causes us both to howl with laughter, earning a scowl from the seller.

I sigh, wiping a tear from my eye as the last of the laughter leaves my body. The sky above us fills with deeply colored clouds, the scent of rain filling the air. Linnick looks up at the sky, noticing the storm rolling in.

"Rain is always a good day on the farm. It means we can take the day off and relax a little. It means that the grass is going to grow and the fruit is going to flourish." He starts to pack his fruit into the crates he brought them in, knowing the rain will leave the market empty in no time. The laughter in his voice nowhere to be found.

"That sounds nice," I say, watching the trollish tradesman gathering his pelts into his arms. "The rain at the camp means I get the training area mostly to myself. Opal doesn't usually venture off in this weather. She says it messes with her hair."

He laughs and looks back up at the sky. "My wife used to be the same way."

His wife? The way he said it—"used to be"—makes me not want to ask about her. I've always wondered, but in all the years I've been visiting his stand, she's never once come up. A lump forms in my throat at the tears welling in his wrinkled eyes and the misery written across his face. Too scared to make him talk about the pain behind his tears, I leave it alone.

The flashes of lightning bring James back sooner than I would've wished, his crimson tunic flashing toward us from the scattered crowd.

I nod a goodbye to my friend. "See you next week, Linnick. Be safe getting back with the weather like this."

James returns like my shadow as I make my way through the market, knocking into travelers and townspeople through the busy street. I quickly make my way through the rest of my list as the rolls of thunder begin to sound through the sky. Now seems like a good time to return to camp. Once the rain begins to fall, it likely won't stop for days.

Sellers finish frantically packing up their stands as townspeople race back to their homes. Ships quickly dock at the port due to the impending weather that will stop them from sailing for the rest of the day. Travelers look around at the frenzy in confusion, clearly not prepared for the immense downpour soon to start, and certainly not quick to end.

I hasten my feet as the first drops of rain splash onto the ground. In my urgency, I slam into the shoulder of someone speeding in the opposite direction, causing my feet to slide on the dampening ground and lose control. I fall, landing on my belly and launching the bag of goods.

I'm face to face with worn leather boots.

"Shoot," says the stranger, voice rife with concern. "I'm so sorry, let me—"

He bends down, collecting my spilled sack. I flush with anger. Father will be livid the items got ruined.

I stand up on my own. "You have eyes," I say, snagging the sack, "so use them."

Before he can speak, I'm off.

It's going to be a long trek back. I fasten my sack behind me and start to run at my typical pace with James jogging beside me this time. The rain deepens along with the claps of thunder. The forest around me blurs with the speed I need to make it back home before the items on the list today are totally ruined.

The bread is certainly a soggy mess by now. Father isn't going to be pleased. Flashes of lightning are followed by thunder so loud it sends animals scattering about. Rain means that most of the soldiers are hiding out in their tents, and the training areas will likely be vacant. The sky empties what seems to be every ounce of rain it had stored up.

I make it back to the camp without an inch of me left dry. As soon as we make it through the gates, I'm left sprinting alone through the camp. I keep a swift pace as the loud downpour quiets the sounds of the dogs in their pens and the horses kicking their stalls.

When I reach Father's cabin, I sling the sack off of me and toss it onto the porch, hearing the wet slap against the wood.

Most of it's ruined now anyway. I bend down and try to shake the water from the items, without much success. My hair is drenched and sticking to my face. I run my fingers through and retie my braid over my shoulder.

The sky above me clangs loudly, making me jump. Fear spikes through my chest at the ferocity of the storm. Flashes of lightning brighten the dark sky, the cabin porch lighting up. Lightning storms near here don't usually end well, their streaking blows hitting trees and homes.

Runnswick may be a place to live for many, but do they truly feel they belong? People do what they can simply to survive in this town, like Lucy. It makes me wonder if the smaller towns are the same way, or if it's just how many people are clustered together near the market.

The conditions here can't be much different from the rest of Crea. This isn't the first time the weather has ruined an entire day's worth of goods.

I look out at the empty sparring rings and jog toward them to begin my isolated training.

FIVE

ACONITE

I TOSS IN MY BED, feeling hot and suffocated, blankets in a cocoon around my body causing me to feel a swell of panic that I'm trapped. The exhaustion from training the day before tries to lull me into a deep sleep that I fight against. I cannot be vulnerable in a house where vulnerability is not tolerated. Not even in sleep.

I stare at myself in the old mirror leaning in the corner of my dark room, the cracks in the walls allowing moonlight to stream in from outside. Staring at my father's nose that sits on my face, I'm dragged into a dream or a memory, unable to stop it from filling my thoughts.

"You only gain power by taking it for yourself, daughter. And once you have it there will always be someone trying to take it back."

The memory causes my jaw to clench in anger as I'm yanked into a day I often try not to think about.

His nineteen-year-old face splits into a wide grin as he catches me looking at him. He notices my staring like he always does. Though four years older than me, he still manages to make me feel like I'm not a child. Because I'm not.

I grew up in this terrible camp with a calculated father and grew up faster than any fifteen-year-old should have to. He stands up and walks over to join me on my porch. Few soldiers would dare to step this close to the royal merchant's cabin, let alone his very off-limits daughter. But Evans does.

Most girls my age are already promised to another, but Father always says, "Not good enough," or my favorite, "It isn't the most opportune time."

"Hey, Lu."

My nickname tumbles from his mouth. I feel my cheeks redden at him so casually calling me something so intimate. He doesn't even know why we use it. In all the years we've been sneaking off to train, he's never teased me with the made-up name, but I kind of like it.

"Hi." My voice is quiet but not timid. I quickly learned how to turn off feelings like being shy after growing up here. But I feel as if I don't have to hide those emotions around Evans. He's never treated me the way the other soldiers do. Which is probably why my pulse races with nerves every time he looks at me the way he is now.

"Want to go spar? We had new lessons this week in hand-to-hand."

Delight warms my heart at his offer. The other officers and soldiers never let me join them or learn during their practice. I feel so special that he always makes time for me, but not convinced this time of day is best.

"Come on, Lu, your father never technically said you couldn't train."

I chew on the inside of my cheek, unsure if it's a good idea to train in front of Father's cabin. He may not have said I wasn't allowed to train, but I doubt all the officers thought to exclude me from learning on their own.

"We usually do it when he's away meeting with the king or going on tax runs through Crea."

Evans bumps my shoulder with his and wiggles his eyebrows up and down as if to say, "So?"

I laugh despite the unease filling me.

"I've been training you for years now; I'm sure he's caught on. You said it yourself that there isn't much that goes on at the camp that your father doesn't find out about. There are too many soldiers here for one of them to not mention it. Besides, does he think you magically started to win fights against Opal's older brothers when they pick on you two?"

I give in. "Fine, let's go before weaponry lessons begin."

He rewards me with a smile, and a thousand butterflies take flight in my stomach, flittering throughout my chest. Then when he grabs my hand to lead me to the sparring ring, the butterflies morph into falcons that carry me to the clouds.

"I like your hair braided to the side like that." He's smiling his easy smile and reaches out to tug on the end of my braid.

I smile and look around to see if any of the soldiers are watching us. They are. Some of them are laughing.

"Hey, don't worry about them, Amira. They're just jealous you only talk to me. Who wouldn't want the most beautiful girl in the camp with them?"

We step into one of the training rings and I raise my eyebrow at him. "I'm almost the only girl in camp."

He laughs and releases my hand, a cold wake left at the break of contact.

"Then you're the most beautiful girl in all of Crea. I don't think I've ever seen a girl with eyes like yours, the perfect mixture of green and brown. You have no idea how many of the soldiers watch you when you aren't looking."

My cheeks redden, instantly embarrassed at his flattery.

"Do you want to meet up tonight after the camp is asleep? We can take a walk on the back half if you'd like. Whatever you want, name it and I'll make it happen."

"A walk sounds nice," I admit softly.

He grabs my hands and positions them in front of my face in a fighting stance.

Evans grins even bigger than I thought possible as he says, "Ready to learn some new punches?"

My eyes snap open and my heart is beating so wildly that it feels as if it's trying to escape the cage in which it's been trapped. I blink several times and attempt to steady my rapid breaths. They're coming in quick succession, a cadence so fast that I can't catch up with the breath that's running away from me. I close my eyes and squeeze my blanket tighter to my chest. Why won't his face leave my memories?

The air is too thick, and my room is too small. The walls close in around me as night begins to greet the glimpses of morning. I shove the blankets off my shaking body and swing my legs over to the side of the bed. My hair is slick with sweat as I gather it into a bun that sits off-kilter on top of my head. My heartbeat begins to calm, but my body is still shaking in rage and fear.

I count each of my toes and then each of my fingers. Starting with my left hand, then my right. Then counting all over again until the fear recedes. All are accounted for and present. I sigh and stand up. The creaking floorboards protest, and I freeze in alarm of waking the monster who sleeps a room down.

Carefully, I make my way to my clothing chest and change into my training leathers. I quickly swallow down my mixture of tonic and water before quietly slipping outside. I have a feeling today's run will be a long one. I want to erase these memories in the morning fog.

Dog is waiting for me on the porch with a wagging tail and a line of slobber stretching from his mouth to the porch floor.

"Better be ready for a long one this morning."

His eyes perk to attention on top of his head.

We run for what feels like hours. We make several laps around the circular camp, following along the edge and staying close to the walls that barricade us in. I pass the archer towers and watch as the guards stiffen when they see my figure running through the veil of darkness. The weapons are brought to the ready, but still once I come into their line of sight.

Just as the day eats away the darkness of night, I break in front of the cook's station, collapsing against the ground and breathing heavily. Dog licks my face in one big, slobbery swipe before trotting off, presumably to find water and sneak back into his pen before the trainers awake.

I peel myself off the ground and stagger back to my room before Father sees me. I hastily wash the sweat away with a cold bucket of water and put on my square-necked leather tunic, breathable trousers, and sturdy boots. Just as I finish lacing up, Father bangs on the door and slips his list beneath it. I freeze as I watch his feet disappear from under the door.

I wait long enough to hear his steps make their way to the front and for the door to swing shut behind him. I swallow a deep breath and quickly finish lacing my shoes, excited to leave the camp for the day and eager to explore the market. I pick up his list and shove it into my pocket.

Today I'm in unusually high spirits. I swing my empty sack and hum to myself as I watch a bird chasing a dragonfly. The sky seems to be matching my good mood as the sun shines down on the world below, so I let myself play pretend and ignore James trailing behind me. If just for a moment.

"Let's play our game, Lu." The soothing voice I try to hold onto whispers into my memories.

Today I pretend I'm one of the travelers in the market. I've spent my whole life mobile, moving from one town to another. The market town of Runnswick is one I've never been to before. The sun is shining, but there still seems to be mud everywhere, and on everything.

The busy market street is buzzing with traders and buyers. I have money left to me by my late husband, and not near enough things to spend it on. I walk past the flowers stuffed into an old rickety stand and pause. The stand itself is nothing special; I've seen far more luxurious markets in the many places I've traveled to. The flowers within the stand, though, draw my attention almost immediately.

I smile broadly at the seller and tell him I'll take a large bouquet of whatever he thinks goes well together. He smiles at me enthusiastically while he wraps a beautiful large bundle in a thick brown wrapping sheet.

I grab the lilies and inhale their sweet scent deeply. These will go well sitting in my carriage as I make my way to another new town hours away.

The bird squeals at the dragonfly and snaps me out of my little game of pretend. I clear my throat at the tightness in my chest and realize that we've made it to the market. I rush to the Linnick's stand first, not having enough time to wander today. Animals of all shapes and sizes abound in the square. Livestock day. Strong odors slam into my nostrils as flies buzz in hordes around the stalls. The sheep, cattle, and goats move about restlessly at the commotion of the marketgoers filling the square.

"You could be a little more polite when you almost barrel someone over." A light and playful voice directs itself to me.

"Excuse me?" I turn around to the owner of the voice, irritated at this interruption in my day. I have to distract my guard soon, so I have more time to see Linnick and maybe even buy a flower or two.

"You ran into me. The day of the last storm?" The owner of the voice is not what I was expecting. He's a handful of inches taller than me with a slender but muscular frame. His blond hair is kept short, but slightly unkempt under the hood he's wearing.

His tattered clothes speak the untold story of the harshness that has likely been his life.

"Sorry, you must have me mistaken." His charm may have caused me to momentarily pause, but it doesn't deter me from my plans for the day. I turn to walk away, but he stops me with a hand on my elbow.

I look down at where his hand is connected to my body. As opposed to his tattered clothes, his hands are surprisingly clean and uncalloused.

The unwelcoming feel of his touch must show on my face because he removes his hand the moment my eyes connect with his. I have to tilt my head up slightly to meet his gaze.

"I don't mistake anything." His sideways smile looks like he's used to getting his way.

I narrow my eyes at him and cross my arms over my chest without responding. I should probably walk away before James takes too much notice of our exchange.

"I'm Adrian. Are you traveling from outside of Runnswick?" He extends his hand in front of him, expecting me to take it in greeting.

I ignore it.

"No." I turn to leave again and pause when he plows forward, surprising me with his persistence.

"Wait! You didn't tell me your name." The boyish grin on his face makes it impossible to ignore him.

I pause, half-turned, and say, "Amira." This time when I walk away, the stranger lets me.

He shouts, "I'll be here on this day next week too. See you then."

I keep walking as the crowded path swallows him from view behind me. He doesn't ask it as a question, but rather says it as a statement.

I'm frustrated by his arrogance. Charm has little value to me—especially after what Evans did—but there was something in his eyes that seemed sweet. Different than the men from camp.

As I clutch my list, I think of what Father would do to him if he found out I was wasting time talking to someone without status or a title. What he might do to me.

But I don't want to be hurt again. My focus shouldn't drift to the first boy to stop and speak with me; that doesn't bring me any closer to the freedom I crave.

Maybe that's why I was lying to myself when I insisted I didn't have butterflies.

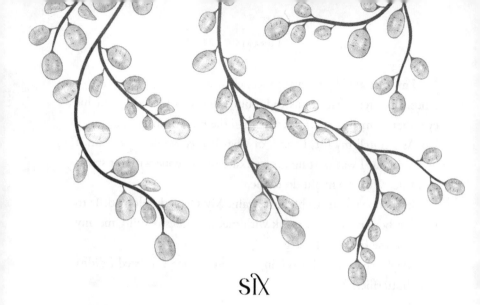

SIX

COLTSFOOT

I POSITION MYSELF BETWEEN TWO tall trees, hoping I have enough coverage from the watchtowers to where they can't see us running through our training. If you can call what Opal's doing "training," that is.

"You know your hair is just going to get messed up, right?"

Opal runs her fingers through her hair for the hundredth time, adjusting a small piece that always sticks up further than the rest. She lets out a frustrated grunt.

"*Please* let me do your hair after we train today. I can practice for when you go to the market next to see the mystery boy," she pleads dramatically with her hands clasped in front of her and winks.

I roll my eyes and begin my circuit of swings. I knew I shouldn't have mentioned him to her; she'll never let it go.

"Seeing as what happened the last time I talked with a boy, I'd rather not."

From where she's seated on a fallen log, still messing with her flyaway strands, she grimaces.

"That was different, and a long time ago." She speaks softly, the joking gone from her voice and her attention fully on me.

The pity in her eyes causes me to fidget and turn away from her. The mention of Evans turns my thoughts inside out, bringing me back to that night long ago.

"Amira! I'm glad you came. I was afraid you weren't going to show." His smile that's always so easy and carefree lights up his face.

I smile immediately in return. The night sky is clear and twinkling brightly above our heads. This far from the fires of the camp, we only have the moonlight cascading light onto us, creating a dance of shadows with every move we make.

"Well, you asked me to come, didn't you?"

His laughter fills my ears and echoes through the woods. I didn't mean to be funny. I've never thought of myself as funny. He steps forward and pulls my braid over my shoulder. His fingers trail down the length of my hair, making me self-conscious that I didn't do something more with it.

Most girls are probably spending time perfecting their hair and wearing something other than their muddied training leathers, like Opal. I should've asked her to do mine like she does hers.

And yet he still says, "I love your hair like this."

He's so close I forget how to breathe. I've never been this close to anyone before, let alone a boy. Our proximity during training is different: we have a job to do. I'm focused on learning as much as I possibly can, eating up every morsel of teaching he has to offer on how to become a better fighter.

He gently reaches down to cup my cheeks, which are most definitely covered in splotches of pink. I nervously wipe my palms against my thighs as he stares at me.

I suddenly feel jittery with nerves. He glances down at my thighs where I'm still trying to get the sweat off my palms.

"Nervous?"

Instead of making me feel more at ease, his smile increases my uncertainty. I smile, though, unsure what to say. He must take that as a cue to accelerate things faster than I was planning for, because he leans in and closes his mouth over mine.

Our lips touch, unmoving, for a solid minute. I squirm beneath his grasp and pull away from him. Still, he doesn't notice my apprehension. This must be how everyone feels about their first kiss. He clearly knows what to do, and that must be why he's so confident.

"Think we could convince your father to let us get married?"

His question startles me. He's always hinted at us running away together or sneaking off to get married, but never so bluntly. I almost thought I imagined every accidental brush of his hand against my waist, or the look in his eyes that lingered on me as I walked past him.

I stutter, attempting to form a cohesive sentence. "I, um, don't... maybe..." I cough to cover up the flurry of nerves eating away at me like worms on a leaf.

"You've got to know I like you, Amira. When we were younger, I was certain you were just using me to learn how to fight."

I was. He was cute, but learning to protect Opal and myself was more important than anything else. It still is.

"I can't just leave Opal. We made a pact to get married at the same time and her father told her she could choose who she marries. Sometimes I think she's holding out until I'm ready. Besides, she hasn't met someone in a high enough position to pay her dowry..." My voice trails off and I'm acutely aware of his hand now lightly touching my lower back. This time there's no mistaking it as accidental.

Evans moves closer to me, wrapping his arms around my waist. I instantly relax into him, safe in his arms.

"I love you, Amira. And one day I'm going to marry you."

I smile, and I'm rewarded with my second kiss. It's much better than the first.

It leaves me feeling breathless and giddy. I smile against his mouth as warmth spreads across my chest. If I had known it could be like this I would've done it sooner. He lets out a breathy laugh, intertwining his fingers in my hair. He pulls me closer to him, and I greedily accept.

"Hello, earth to Lu? Are you playing pretend without me?" Opal snaps her fingers in front of my face.

I shake my head and try to smile at her, annoyed that I let myself think about him. "I wouldn't dare."

She gives me an odd look, likely reading into the lie thick in my words. "Come on, we need to start our chores."

I reluctantly follow her back to the heart of the camp. We glare at the watchtowers as we pass, hating their presence; they were made to protect us from Penyth, but I can feel their eyes tracking my daily movements.

We go to the stables and shovel muck until our hands are blistered and we're covered in sweat. After we've finished, the soldiers leave a mountain of clothes out behind the stalls.

The washing station is dangerously close to the dogs' muddied pen and their incessant barking. Opal looks at me and I shake my head, knowing our fathers would be glad to see us working on our "wifely" duties.

"No time for lunch today, it seems."

We gather the laundry and spend the rest of the day washing smelly clothes, gagging and trying to pinch our noses while cleaning them.

"It's like the soldiers drag their garments through the dogs' pen before they drop them off for us."

I look down at the filth-covered clothing and nod my head in agreement. By the time the dinner bells ring, we're hanging up shirts, pants, and under-trousers to dry on the clothing line.

We work through the start of dinner and watch the training ring as the newest soldiers run through their weaponry training.

"I heard from one of my brothers the new men arrived just last night from another training camp that was attacked by Penyth. *Everything* in the camp was burned to the ground. Strange Penyth was able to pull that off with the last few days of rain we've had; everything should've been too damp for a match to even be lit. Those twenty or so men were the only ones to survive."

As Opal talks, I watch the new arrivals, their worn expressions solemn and closed off. I feel a surprising twinge of pity as I watch them listen to the officer instructing them. Many of them have their eyes trained on the ground, their movements slow.

We're too far away to hear the officer's lesson, but we both watch silently, absorbing their movements. I mentally take notes to practice the swinging motion they're learning with daggers.

I take a deep breath and close my eyes, leaning forward just as he breaks the spell he's cast on me.

"So what does your father think of me?" Evans's voice is strange and different from his usual confidence.

I snap my eyes open and pull away, the warning bells sounding loudly throughout my mind. "What?" My voice comes out breathier than I meant for it to.

He scratches the back of his head and laughs again. "Yeah, I mean if he's let me train you this long, he must think highly of me, right? Obviously, Commander Lyle isn't around much with him being away on missions, but everyone knows the great Royal Merchant Reichardt is more in charge than he is. He does fund us, after all. You're lucky to have Reichardt Ramsey as a father."

Something feels wrong. In all the years we've spent sneaking off to train, he usually doesn't bring up Father.

"Of course, if we get married that would raise my position. Wouldn't that be great? I could take care of you. Put in a good word for me and then maybe he won't be so mad when we get married without his consent." He smiles at me, but it's off this time. The curve of his lips

doesn't match the hardness in his eyes. The eyes that usually crinkle at the corners and gleam with delight when he sees me. The eyes that wink at me from across the sparring ring when Opal and I wash the soldiers' dirty clothes.

I take another step back. This is about my father. I reach down for the dagger attached to my thigh and slowly unsheathe it, trying to quietly bring it out. His once-soft eyes dart down, my movements not going unnoticed, and for the first time I feel afraid of being alone with Evans. My forehead dampens with sweat, and I try to quiet my breathing as it becomes laced with panic.

"What? Come on, Amira, you're all I think about. It wouldn't be so bad if you mentioned how well I do in training to your father, though. You know, for us." His voice grates against my ears, the hair on the back of my neck standing up.

We're so far out that we're almost to the wall, too far from the sleeping soldiers to be heard if I scream. The camp is entirely too large; in this area covered by woods, nobody would hear me other than the creatures of the night.

"Take a step back, Evans."

His eyes darken and flick between my blade and my unwavering glare. "You aren't the only daughter of someone in power at this camp, Amira." His voice is different, rougher.

"Don't touch her." I force my words to sound icy this time. Detached. But panic swells at the thought of him trying to use Opal in the same way.

He laughs again; he won't stop laughing. I clench the dagger in my hand and pray I can bring myself to use it, the sting of betrayal causing my hand to shake.

He was just using me. This whole time he was using me to get closer to my father.

"Then I need you to tell your father how you've noticed my skill, how vital I could be if he placed me at his side."

He never wanted me.

"You want me to tell my father about you? I'll gladly mention to him your poor attempt to weasel your way into his attention. Best of luck, Evans."

He catches me by the arm and yanks me closer to him. His breath twists together with mine as he inches closer to my face. I look down at the mouth that only moments ago made me feel something entirely different.

"If you think for a second—"

A voice I never thought I'd be relieved to hear cuts through the night. "Remove your hand, soldier."

Even in the darkness I can see Evans's cheeks redden. He drops my arm like it's made of molten metal, my head spinning with the way the night has changed directions so quickly.

Evans is frozen with fear, seemingly unable to make his lips move. The silence stretches thickly between the three of us.

"Royal Merchant Reichardt, sir. We were just talking; your daughter asked me to meet her here, and I didn't want to tell her no."

Father is many things, but he is not easily deceived. He takes a few strides toward us with his hands folded behind his back. My anger is replaced with a newfound fear of what he'll do.

"Leave us. Leave this camp. There is no space here for weak-minded boys who use deceitful tactics to win the attention of someone in power. Only having true skill would capture my attention, and you clearly do not possess it."

Evans begins to stammer in an attempt to smooth over the situation.

Father takes another step forward and, in this moment, he is every bit the Predatory Merchant the townspeople whisper about. With a quiet voice that I know is not to be questioned, he says, "Leave."

Evans glances a final disgusted look in my direction and stalks away.

The moon is barely visible through the trees. I feel the darkness spread over my heart. Father turns to me. Weak, I lean into his chest.

He puts his hands on my shoulders, pushing me away. His eyes are hard. "You only gain power by taking it for yourself, daughter, and once you have it there will always be someone trying to take it back."

For a moment I'm stunned into silence that he protected me, but then his words hit me deeper than Evans's betrayal.

"You have failed miserably yet again. You should've anticipated his lies. No one here is interested in claiming your childish heart. You hardly look like a girl by wearing pants, and you certainly are not a woman. Likely never will be."

I will myself to not let the tears fall, but I can't stop them from spilling over, my pride broken into just as many pieces as my heart.

He doesn't miss the wetness streaking my face. He shakes his head in disappointment and sighs. "Truly, daughter, I will not be so easy on you the next time you fail. I will find you a suitable husband when the time is right, and when the advantage benefits me."

My entire body begins to shake as he turns and leaves me in the woods. The moment he's far enough away I release the rest of my tears. Of course Evans only wanted a chance to be noticed by my father. His friends must have known; I cringe as I remember their laughter.

The walk back to camp is cold, my arms wrapped tightly around myself and doing little to bring me warmth. Father's words play on a continuous loop in my mind, my only companion beneath the glowing moon. "You only gain power by taking it for yourself, daughter."

I don't want power. I want freedom. And one day I will find it.

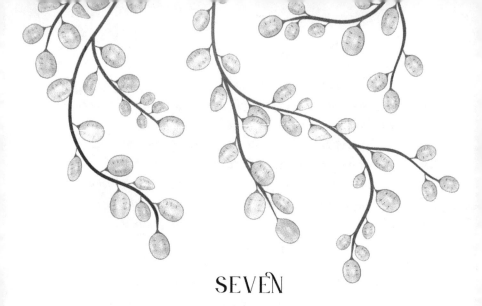

SEVEN

LAVANDULA

I AWAKE TO SCREAMS FILLING my ears. I startle from my dreamless sleep and quickly put on my leathers. My two daggers slide easily into the sheaths on each side of my hips. I sling on my sword belt but keep the blade in my hand. The frenzy of shouts crying out from around the walls of the cabin bombard my ears.

Flashes of fire blaze through the small cracks of wood, but not enough for me to make out what's happening. A loud thud slams into one of the walls and causes me to jump back. The small tip of a sword is sticking through the panel with blood now pooling from behind it, where it seems a person has just been killed.

I wrap the ribbon from yesterday tightly around my hair to secure it at the nape of my neck. At the last second, I run to my small dresser and open the top drawer, rummaging around until I find what I'm looking for. I find the small cloth and unravel it, clasping the golden chain around my neck for good luck. The pendant rests lightly against my chest, giving me the courage to step out.

I bolt out of my room and find Father rushing out of his at the same time. He looks at me with his own sword drawn. "If you die here today, then I'll know for certain I have failed to raise someone I can claim as my daughter." With that, he leaves out the front door, not bothering to close it.

I shake my head and step out into the blackness of night.

The camp has been set ablaze. In the distance, fire engulfs at least half of the tents, and soldiers are scrambling around trying to put them out. With the tents so close together, the flame is faster than the small buckets of water can hold it off. The horses have all been let out of their stalls and are racing around in a panic with chaos fueling their speed. A few of the soldiers who were trained to ride try to wrangle the horses enough to mount them. I spin around and raise my sword while assessing the carnage in front of me.

Many soldiers are lying on the ground either dead or not far from it. I clench my jaw and search for an unknown target. I see soldiers I know still in their nightclothes, unprepared and clearly awoken from sleep.

Where is Opal? Looking wildly around, I try to catch a glimpse of her, but the mayhem of the attack offers little time to find her. My sword hand begins to shake as the panic seeps in.

I hear shouting from every angle; some men fighting are ones that I recognize as being on my side. The others stand out in stark contrast to the men they're battling. The soldiers attacking us are *twice* the size of our soldiers. They fight in a strange sort of rhythm, almost as if they're all connected and making the same methodic movements. Their armor is light, and their swords have a golden glint to them. A strange symbol is stitched into the backs of their tunics. There aren't more than thirty of them, but they're holding off our *entire* training camp.

How are just a handful of soldiers against hundreds able to cause this much chaos?

I spot the hound handler letting the dogs out of their pen and watch in amazement as he puts their training to the test. In the fray of the fighting, the dogs must've been given a command, because all at once they form a line in front of their handler.

The blazing fire around me heats my skin as it trails dangerously close to the cabin.

"Penyth!" a soldier screams, reaching out to grab my ankle from where he lays in the dirt. I let out a small scream and kick him off me before I realize he's one of ours. It's the soldier I challenged a few weeks ago. Rover.

I bend down to see if I can help, but the red sticky substance covering his stomach tells me there isn't much I can do for him now. Guided by the light of the moon and fire, I try to press down on his wound. He yells out in agony, reaching up to grip my arm.

"I'll get help, just wait here." I look around wildly and then back at the soldier. His eyes are frozen on me, now unmoving and empty, his chest no longer rising and falling with his breath. I blink a few times, trying to pull myself together to make sense of what's happening. The fighting blurs, the world slowing down around me.

Penyth attacked *here?* They would never be so bold as to attack the royal training camp. They might attack the other camps, but with us being so close to the castle, what would bring them here?

Before I have any time to contemplate why they would risk waging war against our kingdom, the squishing of mud fills my ears from behind. I spin around with my sword up just in time for it to be met by a clash of metal. The sounds of screaming soldiers are almost completely silenced by the ringing in my ears as steel clangs against steel.

The Penyth attacker meets each of my swings blow for blow. He's much taller and stronger than I am, but I've fought his size before. He looks worn from travel, yet his lips are firmly pressed with determination not many of our soldiers possess. I must admit,

Penyth trains their soldiers well. The rumored ruthlessness of their queen is certain to be behind it.

He looks surprised at my ability to keep up with him, but the sound of a soldier screaming captures his attention. The look of agony on his face makes it clear that it was one of his.

I find my opening, taking advantage of his distraction, and feel my sword thrust through his chest. His head swivels to meet me, his features twisting in anger. He brings his sword toward me, and I struggle to keep my blade lodged within him while trying to stop his from bringing me to the same fate he's soon to meet.

An unreadable look crosses over his face as he stares into my eyes. His once-determined look is now frantic, and his blade releases from his hand, falling to the ground without a sound.

"Forgive me."

My eyebrows twitch in confusion, but before I think to ask him why, he reaches his hand to mine and digs the sword deeper into his own chest. The chaos around us flurries, but the moment freezes to a halt.

The breath in my throat catches as I watch him fall to the ground. My chest heaves rapidly, stunned.

Before I can think more, I spot two Penyth soldiers closing in on one of ours. I charge forward, a scream tearing from my throat as the soldiers turn in surprise toward me.

I distract them enough for several soldiers near us to surround them from the other side. As one, we close in tighter until the two soldiers are overwhelmed. The soldiers beside me give brief nods in appreciation, the only acknowledgment I'm likely to get for the aid I've given. I wipe my hand across my forehead and make my way to Opal's cabin. She's learned to fight, but never took much interest in practicing like I did when we were growing up.

"Opal!" I shout as loudly as I can, panic twisting my insides at my friend's safety. The narrow path past the stables toward her cabin is barricaded in flames. I see the dark silhouette of a Penyth soldier further along the path, terror filling my veins at the thought of his blade at Opal's neck. The smell of burning tents fills my nose, and the screams of dying soldiers overwhelm my senses.

I cup my hands around my mouth and scream again. *"Opal!"*

The fire blazing across the camp brightens every inch. The watchtowers are all burning and crumbling to the ground. Just as I feel tears begin to prick behind my eyes, I hear her voice behind me.

"Amira!"

I spin around to see her emerge from behind the main training tent, sword drawn. Her eyes look red from the fire's reflection, her blonde hair for once unruly and unkempt. I rush to hug her, looking her over for any cuts or wounds. We nod once at each other as we enter formation: back to back, a unit of two ready to fight.

Somehow, the few Penyth soldiers are still holding on—dwindling slowly, but still managing to kill more than twice the amount they have with them.

A tall, slender soldier rushes toward us, his golden sword rising. I can feel Opal tense behind me, but she holds her ground. Together, we fight the soldier. Well, I fight. Opal distracts. She has an uncanny ability to catch the attacker's eye, drawing him to her. The moment his attention is off of me, I press forward. With my weight centered, I strike.

He's fast enough to stop me just before my blade reaches him, the edge hovering a hair away from his nose. He lets out a feral snarl and forces me to back up a step. The noise shoots a spike of fear through my body, but the adrenaline keeps it at bay.

He circles us, each of our swords drawn. For a moment, it's just us and him. My vision is tunneled to his movements, to the flexing of his fingers against the hilt of his sword. A clear sign he's about to make a move.

Opal raises her blade higher, causing his eyes to snap to her. I jump in front of her at the same time he swings. Until now, my life has been filled with daydreaming. What if this is it? It can't be.

A scream tears through me as I raise my sword to meet his. The piercing cry brings a flash of movement from the corner of my eye. Someone drags the soldier away from me before the metal can touch. I flinch at the slender arm that wraps around my waist, but relax when I realize it's Opal.

"Ember and Mica can handle it."

Even as she says it, I doubt her two brothers alone can. I take a step toward them, prepared to help, but her oldest brother, Beryl, rushes past us, shoving the youngest of the five into our arms.

"Emeril, there you are." She squeezes her little brother, his sandy hair nearly the same color as hers.

When the Penyth soldier falls, I step back and notice most of the fires have now been put out. The fighting around us has reached a standstill. My breathing is heavy as I sheathe my sword.

The first soldier I encountered sticks in my mind. His words clutter my thoughts: *Forgive me. Forgive me. Forgive me.*

I shake my head as Opal and I exchange a look of relief. Beryl stalks over to us and snatches her sword from her hand. His clenched jaw doesn't leave her room to protest. His face is caked with mud, but the resemblance is still there. His eyes are just as blue, the Lyle siblings' trademark.

Ember and Mica share a look but make no comment about his harshness. They never do. Opal slides her hand across Emeril's shoulders. He gives me a tentative wave, small around the towering height of his brothers. She tosses me an apologetic look over her shoulder and I watch as they disappear through the carnage. Smoke settles thickly over the camp in place of the blazing fires. A few horses stand out of place where they've yet to be rounded up.

Exhaustion weighs me down, but the adrenaline still coursing through me carries me forward while I walk back to my cabin. I need answers, and my father is likely to have them. I spot him walking across what used to be the northern training rings with a terrifying look in his eyes. His shoulders are tense, and his sword is bloodied. His face, usually calm and collected, is smeared with dirt and twisted in anger. Blood drenches his right knee as he walks with a slight limp.

Father pushes into the cabin with Commander Lyle, trailed by a few high-ranking guards. Though I hate to admit it, the two of them together are a force to be reckoned with. Just as I take a step closer to follow, they slam the door behind them.

With the other soldiers distracted doing cleanup, no one sees me slip beneath our cabin's porch. I crawl on my stomach through the mud until I can see the dust falling from the floorboards where they stand above me, their voices coming out in poorly concealed, hushed words.

"What the hell happened, Lyle?"

Father's voice comes out steady, holding its composure. Only the slightest hint of panic seeps through, barely noticeable in contrast to the rest of the frantic soldiers.

"How am I to know, Ramsey? You're the one with all the money and spies. You should've known before any of us." Opal's father is nearly shouting at mine; the floorboards groan in protest as he shifts angrily on his feet.

"Seeing as you're the Commander, Remburt, this one is on you. Where were the guards at the gate, and why didn't they alert the camp?" Father's condescending tone is the one I'm most familiar with, but I must admit that I don't mind it being used on Opal's father.

At this, Commander Lyle falls silent and another one of the guards speaks up. "They seem to be missing, sir."

Someone slams something onto the dining table, which I imagine is a very unhappy fist connected to an equally unhappy father of mine.

"Missing? Lyle, you better hope and pray they are dead or deserted instead of spilling our secrets to our enemies." Father walks out of the cabin and slams the door so hard that I wonder when the hinges won't be able to take it anymore.

The mud is beginning to soak through my leathers. As I back out, the muffled words begin again.

"Penyth is getting out of control, sir. This is the third attack this week on one of our camps. They're looking for something. Taking small groups of highly trained soldiers and pillaging each camp. With the size of our camp, we should've been able to take them down quickly." The soldier speaking is the only one brave enough to speak, and I pause to listen.

"Daughter!" Father bellows from the other side of the cabin, and I scramble out before he walks back around to the porch. I don't have time to stand, so I work the laces of my boots until I hear him clear his throat. I stand up a little too quickly. For a moment I think I can see relief in his eyes, but just quickly as it appears, it vanishes. He clenches his jaw and sets his eyes to the task beyond me.

"Good. If you find any survivors, have them brought to me." His eyes flick to my pocket. "And take your tonic." He walks away without another word and begins rolling over bodies, looking for anyone alive to give him information on the attack.

After mixing my medicine, I join the rest of the camp. The night is spent searching for someone to hold responsible for the attack, no soldier spared from interrogation. But most end up reporting the same thing: somehow, Penyth snuck past our defenses unseen. When they became outnumbered, they all ended their own lives, saying, "For Penyth."

I don't mention that the soldier I fought said "*Forgive me*" as he looked directly into my eyes. My mind races with the possibilities of his words. The men around me whisper about what the attack means, but my mind is stuck on the memory of this exchange.

Is it because he was fighting a woman? Most soldiers aren't used to fighting women. The surprise of a woman being in Crea's army is enough to throw our own soldiers off, let alone one of the enemy soldiers. Or was it my ability to fight him so well that took him by surprise? My question is only met with more questions, the sole person able to answer it now entirely devoid of life.

We all spend the early morning hours cleaning up the rest of the camp. The fires that ravaged most of the tents are now gone and are nothing more than smoldering piles of smoke. The bodies of the Penyth soldiers are searched for any useful documents. It's obvious nothing of use is found given everyone's general air of defeat and the foul mood that radiates off my father.

Penyth is careful and meticulous when it comes to revealing their hand. The Valon Empire was split down the middle for a reason. With the Kingdom of Penyth ruling in the northernmost and the Kingdom of Crea ruling the southernmost, both kingdoms have always been evenly matched and unable to overthrow the other. Even if that's always been each kingdom's goal.

As the sun begins to bleed into the horizon, many of the soldiers find a place to rest for what short hours they can. I stiffly walk into the cabin to change out of my dirtied clothes.

A bucket of water is already waiting outside my room, no doubt left by some unknown soldier under my father's command. I pick up the heavy bucket, water sloshing over the sides as I haul it into my room. The water is ice-cold, but I methodically and quickly wash away what remains from the attack.

My mind is wandering, my limbs slow with the ache of fatigue. The quietness of the cabin echoes too loudly. Father is surely in meetings with the other commanders. My ears ring with the stunning silence, almost as if I can still hear the clanging of sword against sword.

After cleaning up as much as possible, I skip the soft linen sleepwear and slip into a fresh pair of leathers, falling heavily onto my bed. While a follow-up attack is unlikely, it isn't entirely inconceivable. Too restless yet to sleep, I twist my necklace against its chain, studying the old round pendant set in plated gold. Vines etched into the outer ring twist and tangle around it, encasing the coin in a delicate hold. This necklace likely couldn't even buy me a grain of rice at the market, its worth meaning more to me than anyone who could ever come across it.

I run my thumb over the grooves in the back, and I feel my eyelids falling closed, heavy with sleep. For a moment I imagine the etched scribbles as if they make sense to me. A word rises to the surface just as I sink deeper into sleep. But before I can arrange my thoughts, I drift into the darkness.

The forest floor stretches out beyond me in a vast expanse of glowing golden leaves. The trees are now mostly bare and empty. The leaves crunch under my feet as I walk toward my home. The ground is covered in so much gold that the grass below is completely covered by the changing of the seasons.

Winter will be coming soon, and yet the earth around me still flourishes; beyond the forests, bright green fields of grass still grow. I feel a dizzying sense of joy and warmth as the sun settles into a soft glow across the woods. Without the trees' thick canopy above me, I can feel more of the sky's embrace. The sun casts warm, golden hues through the air, bouncing and reflecting off the puffy white clouds.

I tilt my face upwards while I walk my usual path, closing my eyes for a moment. Muscle memory takes over as I blindly spread my arms out for balance, anticipating each twist and turn on the path I've taken countless times. A bird flits from branch to branch alongside me, and I peel my eyes open to leisurely admire the flowers poking through the leaves. Lilies and clovers sprout up randomly in the empty spaces they can squeeze through.

"How lucky I am to have such a beautiful home. Most of the other kids aren't allowed anywhere without an adult, but I get this forest garden all to myself," I tell the little blue bird. It chirps at me in what seems to be agreement. I smile to myself, a wide, toothless grin where my two front teeth have yet to come in. Mother says it'll be any day now.

My hair catches on straying branches, but I don't care. How can I care when the world around me is so happy? My dress swishes noisily alongside the dried leaves as it picks them up and drags them about from their resting place on the forest ground, leaving a small trail in my wake.

The blue bird flies away suddenly just as I hear the crunching of boots. I swivel around so fast my short pigtails whip wildly around my head. At least a dozen men stare back at me. I don't recognize them; their faces obscured by a thick cloth covering. They don't wear our colors, and their faces are angry, which makes me scared. I suck in a quick breath to scream just as someone from behind covers my mouth and nose with a damp cloth.

A tall, slender man steps into view just as the golden forest around me blurs into blackness.

I awake with a gasping breath and jolt upright. My leathers are sticky with sweat and my hair is matted to my neck. My chest is rising and falling in short bursts of panic as the dream subsides. It was so vivid that it's difficult to shake the little girl's terror.

Even the gentlest start to a dream somehow always turns into a nightmare.

The strange men that stared at me are all a blur, but the brilliant shine of the golden leaves is freshly stamped in my mind. Colors I've never seen here in Crea. Colors so painfully bright and only reachable in dreams, because my world could never be so beautifully painted.

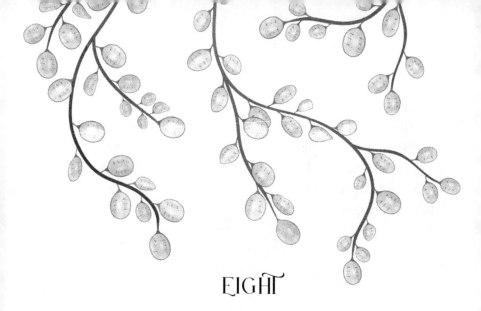

EIGHT

ANGREC

DICE ROLL ACROSS MY PATH as gamblers yell at me for stepping into their game. Bits of bone have been wielded into small game pieces used by anyone willing to bet their coin. The usual group of men huddles together, drunk and losing more money than they have to spare.

I tighten my furs around my shoulders as the winter chill breezes through the market. The muddy days seem endless in Crea, but the winters hold out even longer. More market dwellers turn to ale to substitute for the lack of warmth, and in return, there are such vile brawls that even I shy away from them. There's nothing to gain from getting in a fight with someone who is starving and drunk.

Today's list is short, and even though it's my normal market day I'm surprised Father still sent me off after the attack.

Heap of cloth for wounded soldiers

Jar of ale

Log of goat's cheese

Two cattle pelts

I look back at James, wishing I could leave him behind and set sail on one of the many ships docked at the port. I catch sight of the small child with quick fingers and big green eyes. I laugh as he yet again zips undetected from stand to stand. He notices me and winks. I laugh, louder than last time.

Fascinated with how he gets away with this so often, I can't tear my eyes away. No more than six or seven, he is awfully sneaky for his age. He snags himself a fur overcoat, which he promptly puts on, an apple—again—which he immediately bites into and keeps in his mouth, and a handful of cheese, which he stuffs into his pockets.

He vanishes from my sight, and I raise myself onto the tips of my toes to see where he's scurried off to. By this time, the market is far too busy to see over the sea of people. Travelers are arriving from the port and on horseback from the multiple paths that feed into the market.

It must be driving Father mad that his spies hadn't caught wind of the plotting. The thought pleases me more than it probably should. I take my time and stop to speak with the occasional seller to get a feel for how prices might change in the cold months to come. Items of need always seem to increase during this unbearable season. Many of the businesses around the market are filled with people trying to get out of the cold, seeking warm broth to fill their bellies.

Horns sound loudly and bounce around the market and everyone looks toward the source of the playing. That noise can only mean one thing when it's coming from the direction of the castle. Even with the loudness of the market, the clamor still pierces through the chatter.

The horns keep sounding until every marketgoer is silent and looking toward the whitewashed platform that juts out from the castle and looms above the square.

"Silence for His Majesty, King Avalon Stewart!"

The already silent square remains eerily restless as the king steps forward. His crown sits off-kilter on his head. The furs he's wearing are fluffy and ordained in golden chains and jewels. The cup he's holding sloshes liquid over the edge, the substance a deep maroon color. He drains the liquid from the cup and tosses it, the guard beside him fumbling to catch it. King Avalon wipes the back of his hand across his mouth and stares out into the crowd.

"People of Crea, as I'm sure you could either hear or see, the events of the attack last night—"

The king abruptly burps, and a few people nervously laugh. The guards shout for order and silence.

"Last night my royal training camp was attacked by Penyth."

There's a collective gasp; several of the women near me wipe fresh tears from their cheeks.

"Their evil knows no end! Use this as a reminder of what they're capable of."

People around me shift uncomfortably. Whispers sound throughout the crowd, rumors of wicked men and forbidden sorcery tossed around like seeds cast in the wind. Their words fall and take root, sprouting into the crowd as they grow louder and more panicked.

"Do not fear, we won last night's battle and we will win every battle after!" The king sways slightly on his feet and the crowd murmurs with uncertainty.

I refrain from rolling my eyes, knowing that if the king was there last night to see how poorly we handled only thirty men, he wouldn't be counting us as victorious yet. If they would've had a hundred men, the outcome would've been much different.

The king pats his protruding belly and walks back into the castle. Not much comfort being offered, if you ask me. The marketgoers disperse, somewhat uncertain at the abrupt end to the king's address. If you could call it that.

"You came back." A boy's gentle voice carries over the rumble of the crowd.

Without looking, I slip into a busy side street to escape my follower. I don't have time for him today, or any other day.

The crowd swallows the space between us, and I quickly set to ticking off the rest of the items on my list. His hood sticks above the crowd, weaving through the cramped square and coming closer. I spin around and see James walking to the madam's house. After the events of last night, he doesn't seem to need much nudging to head in that direction.

I duck behind a stand and mutter an apology to the seller as he eyes me suspiciously. I crouch and wait for the boy to pass. When he does, a pang of guilt washes over me: his clothes are still the same tattered cloths poorly stitched together. He can't possibly be staying warm during the day—let alone in the frigidness of night—with those scraps he's passing off as clothing.

I glance down at my own fur surcoat and thick leathers beneath. I may not have an interest in the boy's games, but that doesn't mean I want him to freeze to death. I release a breath in frustration as I stand up and step in front of him before I can think better of it.

"Here." I strip off my furs and hand them over.

He stops, shocked, as his eyes fly from the furs back to my face. He shakes his head, leaving the offering unclaimed in my outstretched hand.

I let out a huff and toss the surcoat over his shoulder. "I don't want your money. Take it. I have more."

He's still staring at me, unmoving. "I don't need it, thank you," he says as he blinks rapidly a few times and starts to hand it back to me.

"You must not be from here if you don't know that a winter night without the proper clothing can bring you to an early death." It may sound dramatic, but it's the truth. "Judging from the current state of your clothes, you don't have a warm place to sleep tonight."

He studies me for a moment longer and then slings it over his head. Even with the furs nowhere near his size, it still covers the majority of his torso and arms.

"My name is Adrian, in case you've forgotten." A slow smile spreads across his face, and I notice the warmth of the fur already bringing a slight pinkness back to his flushed cheeks.

I give him a tight smile before spinning around and disappearing through the crowd again. His smile stays in my mind even after I've turned around. The curve of his lips brings heat creeping across my cheeks. I shake the image away, annoyed at myself for noticing it in the first place.

Love is a trap covered in leaves. You don't notice until it has you in its clutches and you've fallen into a hole too deep to get out of. It takes your mind and empties it of its contents until you're unable to make sense of the world.

Women in this town are so blinded in seeking love that they'll give up every part of themselves in hopes of finding it. They trade their own freedom for the protection and safety of a man.

I gather one or two items from my list and pause when I get to Linnick, his back to me as he stacks cases of fruit on top of each other. When he turns around, he drops his crate and rushes toward me, wrapping me in a tight hug.

"I thought about coming to find you when I heard about the attack. I'm glad you're safe, kid. You shouldn't have to go through something like that." His usually wrinkled face looks more tired and worn today.

"I'm okay, Linnick, I promise." His worry over my safety tugs at the edges of my heart, and I have to blink away the tears forming behind my eyes.

"And your friend Opal?"

I smile at him, thankful to have such a constant and steady person in my life. "She's okay too."

He releases a long breath and walks back to his stand, which I notice is unusually bare.

"Already sold most of your fruit today?"

He looks up at me, his small frame looking fragile and frail. His shoulders curve inward as he avoids my gaze. "I won't have much more fruit to sell after today."

My mouth falls open. "Are you leaving?" My voice is hoarse, and my eyebrows pull together tighter than the pain stabbing at my chest.

"No, Amira. My farm has been reaching the end of its harvest for a while now. The dodders infested my farm about a month back. We tried burning them off, but…all I could spare was a single citrus tree. My favorite one. I don't have enough money to start from scratch. It took my whole life for me to build up what I had before."

I gasp, my fear of him leaving turning into sadness at his loss. "But you still have your home—is there other work for you to find?"

He shakes his head and looks down at his small number of crates. "The tax on the land is too much to keep up with."

I have to look away from him, knowing he doesn't blame me but nonetheless feeling the shame of the high taxes my father and the king have placed on everyone in the kingdom.

"What are you going to do?" I watch him as he looks down at the dwindling crates. He doesn't speak for a long time, and we both stand there in silence.

"I have a small bit saved up, but it won't last me forever. It'll give me some time to figure out what to do next." I nod, not sure what to say. "Or the two of us could call it quits on this town and get out of here. You don't belong at that camp any more than I know what to do next."

My heart sinks at his offer. I'd love nothing more than to get out of Runnswick and find somewhere else in Crea to explore. I search the crowd for my guard, dread coiling in the pit of my stomach at the thought that he might be listening.

"Relax, kid, I've been watching the door. He hasn't left yet." Linnick waves me off.

My shoulders release some of their tension, but I keep my gaze bouncing around us.

"You're one of the best fighters in that camp and everyone knows it. I say you fight your way out in the dead of night, and I'll be waiting on the other side. The town's been talking about how much of the camp got destroyed. You can easily make it past the guards now that the watchtowers are burned down."

My hand reaches to my stomach on reflex, tracing the jagged scar that runs from my hip and across my abdomen. "I tried once a few years ago. It didn't end well for me."

"What do you mean—" His voice is cut off by one I'm now beginning to recognize.

"Amira! There you are." The beggar boy appears beside us, out of breath. His overly eager smile slips as he sees the defeated look that Linnick and I both have on our faces. He practically skips over to us, his blond hair still wild beneath his hood. I didn't notice before how neatly defined his jaw is, a perfect shape to surround the deep dimples in his cheeks.

"Oh, did I interrupt something?" He looks between us, and Linnick looks to me, raising his eyebrow.

"Yes," I say curtly, "you did."

Linnick makes a *tsk*ing noise against his teeth, chastising me for my rudeness. "My name is Linnick. Don't mind her, she doesn't know how to make friends. She'll come around."

I stare with my mouth open as the two shake hands.

"So, how do you know her, boy?" This time Linnick crosses his arms over his chest and stares at Adrian with narrowed eyes.

Well, now I'm embarrassed.

"I don't, not yet at least." Adrian looks at me and winks. "She gave me her cloak and I just wanted to thank her."

Linnick studies him for a moment before nodding his head. "Well, you two better get going then, so you can thank her." He turns his back to us.

I try with everything in me not to stick my tongue out at Linnick's turned head. Traitor.

"Promise I don't bite. Adrian, remember?"

I nod my head slowly, still skeptical and internally cursing Linnick for betraying me.

"My father is very…cautious. I come to the market with a guard. He's…busy right now, but I'm sure he'll be done soon." I look to the madam's house and Adrian's gaze follows mine. His golden-brown eyes study the house like he just realized it sits there. He nods his head in understanding and points to the docks sitting across from it.

"I know a spot we can sit where he won't see us."

Suspicion must show on my face because he says, "It's close enough to people that if you decide you don't want to sit with me anymore you can easily leave."

I look back to Linnick, who nods encouragingly at me.

"Okay," I concede, "but we won't have long."

Adrian smiles, making him look more boyish and less like someone who goes to bed without food. His smile doesn't match the life he seems to lead.

I follow him through the crowded market as we squeeze our way to the port. He occasionally looks over his shoulder to make sure we didn't get separated, or that I didn't decide to sneak off. The water is calmer today than I feel; the seas of the Andronicus are smooth and steady. He leads us past a few of the docking planks until a small separation splits open between the last two docks.

Slabs of stone have been formed into a staircase, leading down to the clam-infested wall that lines the sea beside the port. He plops down on the edge of it, swinging his feet and humming to himself. I look behind me. Sure enough, even though the people trading in the market would have a difficult time seeing us, I can still see them.

I sigh and walk forward to take a seat beside him. Leaving a wide enough space between us, I determine I could probably kick him into the sea if it came to it.

"So, why do you have to have a guard with you when you come to the market? Do you always come on this day?"

I kick my feet against the edge of the wall, wondering how he found this little hidden spot. Also wondering how I let myself get here and how much to share with this stranger. The clams crack beneath my shoes tapping against them, and I watch as they fall in pieces to the sea. The waves swallow them up as they disappear into the deep.

"Just something my father decided to start doing. And yes, I typically come on this day."

He nods his head, seemingly unbothered by my short answer. "He must care a lot about your safety to send a guard here with you every time you come."

I can't stop the fit of laughter that bursts out of me. He startles, his gaze confused and questioning at my response.

"Sorry, it's just that no one has *ever* mistaken my father as someone who cares that greatly for me. His motives have nothing

to do with my safety and mostly to do with seeing I don't run off."
I'm surprised with my honesty and clamp my mouth shut.

"Oh, I see. My father can be…difficult sometimes too."

We sit in comfortable silence as we watch the sea crash into
the docked ships. The water occasionally rushes in and sprays up,
hitting our feet before receding back into itself. The port is busy
today, people loading and unloading various items to sell at the
market. The ship closest to us is boarding to set sail. The temptation
to jump on and never return tugs at my mind, but I stay rooted to
my spot on the wall. Stuck like a rock in the mud.

I hear a familiar whistle and whip my head around to see
Linnick waving his hand in the air.

"That's my cue to leave. It was…nice. To meet you." I hope
that my voice doesn't sound as awkward as it feels. The amusement
in Adrian's eyes tells me it's definitely clear how uncomfortable I
sounded saying it.

"See you next week?"

I hesitate, and then nod, turning to push my way through the
crowd and put myself within James's eyesight so he can find me. I
turn around one last time to see Adrian watching me with a smile
on his face. He brings his hand up and waves at me.

I surprise myself when I wave back.

Back at the camp, I nod to the guards, who have since been
doubled after last night's attack. They hardly look in my direction
before turning back to the trees, daring someone to come through
them again.

The camp looks worse during the day. How such a small group
of soldiers could do so much damage to the king's royal training
camp is beyond me. Many of the training soldiers' faces are grim
with the loss that weighs on them. Most had joined the army with

brothers, friends, and cousins. Joining the king's army as their sole means for a meal each day and a place to sleep against the elements of the winter months was the only option for many of them. Loss is inevitable in the army, but to have it within the largest training camp in all of Crea is a shock.

The fires are all now completely put out and no longer smoldering, but the flames seemed to have reached the majority of the camp. A pile has been made of what was unsalvageable, and another of what could possibly be patched back together.

"You're on patchwork duty! Get to it after you put my items inside." Father's voice carries from a hundred paces away, causing several of the soldiers to stop and stare at our exchange.

I nod curtly at him, careful to keep my face neutral in his presence, like I've practiced for so many years. Not wanting to be picked apart for what he deems a flaw.

I grab a few needles and join the soldiers threading together bits of fabric that have already been ripped apart from the burnt pieces. They lay the finished fabrics over the fence to the dogs' pen, and the irreparable sections in a heap beneath.

The soldiers closest to me take two steps away from me before going back to their work, flashes of fear evident in their eyes before resuming their conversations. How I wish it was because they were afraid of me and not my father. I hold back a sharp remark from escaping my lips for the sole reason that they likely have experienced my father's wrath today. His foul mood is palpable throughout the entire camp.

It's not that he's mourning the loss of life. His precious pride is wounded after being caught unaware.

The end of the needle catches my finger. "Ouch." A trickle of blood immediately rises to the top.

The soldiers beside me pause their work and stare at me. The fear is replaced with visible anger.

"Hurt yourself with a little prick, Amira? Why don't you ask Rover if that would bother him?" One snickers with laughter.

I can't, since his wound led to his death.

Another lifts his tunic and points to a particularly deep gash still oozing blood. "This one was made with something a bit bigger than a little needle."

No longer able to ignore their taunting, I turn around and put my back to them. They won't attack me here. Probably.

One of them mumbles under his breath and the others laugh. I spin around to face them.

"Say that again, soldier," I snap. Their laughter dies down, but none of them speak. "Well?"

They share a look between each other. The largest of the bunch is the first to talk.

"We wanted to know how it felt in that comfortable bed of yours tucked away from the attack while the rest of us lost good men." A few of them shift uncomfortably on their feet while the one speaking loses confidence with each word.

"I didn't stay in there. I came out and fought alongside each of you," I say firmly.

They burst into laughter again, completely abandoning their tasks. Their amusement spurs on as they talk over one another— "That's the only funny thing I've heard all day!" and "As if she was out there more than a few moments!" and finally "How did the merchant raise such a coward?"

I swallow the anger building in my chest as their laughter stokes the annoyance I'm fighting to shove down. "The point is I didn't shy away from the fight. If you idiots would shut up long enough for me to speak, I could tell you that."

I turn back around to my stitching and make quick work of it. I hope one of those soldiers will get this one; he'll be caught with a tent full of rain from the holes in it. Their snickers quiet down, but their whispers carry easily to my ears.

Amira, the spoiled royal merchant's daughter. Amira, the silly girl playing pretend that she's a real soldier. Amira, the girl incapable of getting a marriage proposal like she's supposed to.

I don't hide from the poorly concealed insults flung at me. I stand until the sun sets and most of the camp is putting down their work for the night. I remain in the same spot doing an imperfect job and catching my fingers on the needle several times. Still, I don't leave until my cut-up hands are staining the tents red, and all of them have been done.

This, I can handle. Their words mean nothing to me. If I were that little girl in the golden forest, I'd be afraid of what I could lose, but here it's all the same.

At least I've avoided my nightmares for this evening.

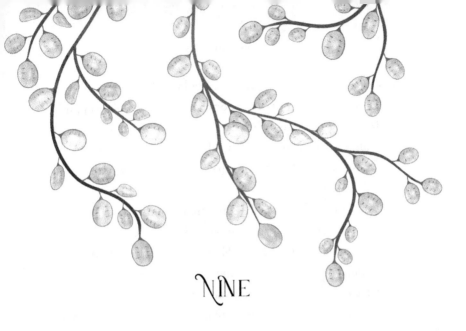

NINE

ZINNIA

"PACK YOUR BAGS. YOU'RE GOING with a group setting off in a few hours and we need to speak before you leave. They're going to gather new recruits and bring them to the camp. We lost too many."

I roll over in my bed and shove my pillow over my face. I wait until Father's steps disappear down the hallway before making a move to get up. The small hours of sleep I managed to get aren't enough to offer me the energy for a day's journey. I slowly get out of bed and grab whatever clothes are lying around to stuff into a bag.

My eyes are so heavy with sleep that I'll likely forget a few things, but I'm more excited about a day out rather than looking for everything I need. I find Father standing on the porch, overlooking the waking camp.

"You know your task today?" He asks the question each time.

"Report to you what happens and anything of note that someone says."

He nods his head, not looking at me. "James will accompany you if you need anything. A new supply of tonic came in." He drops a new sack and I fumble to catch it. I hold back a grumble as I slip my half-empty pouch out of my pocket and pour the new supply in.

He folds his hands behind him and walks off of the porch, dismissing me to spy on his own soldiers for the day. I scurry out of the cabin and head straight to the stables, which were thankfully spared during the attack.

I skip past the first three stalls in search of one horse in particular. A petite white mare with gray spots waits for me. She pokes her head over the side to peer at me. She's not mine to claim, but being the first one here gives me a few moments with her.

Her back is bare of a saddle and her mane has been braided tightly to her neck. She is calmer than the other war horses. She is small, but faster than any of the others. I pick up her solid-treed saddle and rest it on the edge of the stall. She sniffs deeply at the cracked leather covering the wood. I open the stall and walk in to greet her, but her nose finds its way to my pocket for her treat before we can say hello.

"Now, Veyron, that's not a polite way to greet someone coming to see you."

She brings her head up to mine, her height barely rising above my own.

I reach into my pocket and offer her the apple, which she greedily accepts. She chews noisily on her treat while I dress her in riding gear. By the time I finish up, the other riders are just arriving at the stables.

"Ramsey ordered his daughter to join us on the journey." The voice, which I don't recognize, seems to be unaware of my presence.

Veyron shifts on the hay-filled ground, and I give her a pat to keep her quiet.

"Of course he did. The king and the prince are coming to visit the camp. They want to see firsthand what came out of the attack.

He can hardly keep the girl in line as it is. Don't need her making a fool of us with the king around. She doesn't ride with us. The merchant's orders."

I open the stall and lead Veyron behind me.

The men stop talking, their eyes widening.

"See you on the trail." I throw a smile at them and watch, amused, as their expressions turn into concern. They stammer apologies. I continue without a backward glance.

Once out of the stables, I find the only person worth telling of my departure. Opal's eating her small breakfast alone. She smiles and waves us over, reaching up to glide her hand along Veyron's long neck. Veyron nudges her hand when she tries to stop petting her.

"The king must be coming to see the damage on the camp since you're being sent off. Is your father letting you ride today?"

I shake my head and pat Veyron's back. "Just getting her ready for whoever it'll be. A few of us will be on foot so I won't be the only one this time." I stare longingly at the soldiers mounting their horses, aching to join them on their ride.

"Be careful out there, Lu. Make sure to stay out of their way."

I grimace, still burning with jealousy. But I swallow it down and force a smile. "Of course."

I trail the group alone with James lingering by my side, not close enough to count as company. The other twelve soldiers walk in rows of two and talk among themselves, the rest of the company riding ahead of us on horseback. I spot Veyron's gray tail swishing at the end of the pack, my only true companion on this trip. She throws her head around, making the soldier atop burst with anger.

The wind bites at my cheeks as the chill of the air fights to seep through my leathers. A thick fog has begun to settle low on the earth, and the horses grow restless. Their hooves send the fog into a swirling mess, the haze twirling in a circular motion in their wake.

The trees twist up into odd angles, creating a crooked canopy above us. The branches are curved and rounded, like an arch of wood lining the path.

The soldier at the front of the line calls back to the rest of us. "We'll hit the first town before the sun reaches its highest. We're to offer the coin to the family of the men who choose to join us, and bring them back to camp."

A few groans sound throughout the group as they speak in hushed tones to one another. A couple of the soldiers pull out skins of ale to warm up, and pass the drink around.

"Here you are." A soldier sticks out the container and I reach for it—just as his arm extends past me to the soldier on my other side. I should know better than to expect that by now, but the anger still stirs within me.

The path is mostly encased with the coverage of fog, but I can hear the horses squishing the mud into the earth. The grueling travel is only halfway done, but at the same time, I feel relieved. It's nice being this far from camp.

I notice Veyron growing uneasy ahead of me. She stops walking, her ears flicking from side to side. "Move!" the soldier riding her yells. The group in front of me continues their chattering, not noticing their stop. The soldier pushes her forward with a kick of his heels in her side, and her ears pin down flat on top of her head. My hand comes to rest on my sword, annoyed that the soldiers can't pick up her cues. I look over to James and see that he's trying to squeeze the last drop of ale into his mouth.

The group continues along with the ale flowing and the cold increasing. I keep one hand on my blade and listen closely. The woods around us are too silent. The birds have ceased their singing, and the bugs aren't flying. And yet, no threat appears.

The first town we come to is small and only made up of a few worn clay and mud houses. A few of the roofs have holes in them, and the people are thinner than the soldiers at the camp. A small, circular stone makes up the center of the little town. Children play in the middle of it with dolls sewn together by burlap and hay. Their faces are dirty, and their feet bare.

I see a boy around my age watching us warily, so I try my luck with recruiting him. "Hello, as you can see—"

I'm cut off before I can finish.

"We're with the king's royal training camp," a soldier declares. "Your kingdom needs you to fight against the evils of Penyth so that your family will be safe and prosper. We have wages you can send to them." The soldier glares at me, continuing the message they were told to recite to each man they could find.

I roll my shoulders, frustrated.

There's a middle-aged man warily watching us from the center of the town. I try a small smile with him as I approach.

"We're with the king's—"

"I know who you're with." He spits angrily at the ground and lifts his arm, untucking it from his side. "The fire is hot, but surprisingly cold."

I bite back the bile rising in my throat at the sight of the jagged end of his wrist, where his hand is missing.

He begins muttering incessantly. To me, to himself—it's near impossible to tell.

"The half-breed will bring us to ruin."

I scrunch my face at his jumbled words. "I'm sorry?"

His harrowingly slim body quakes with a passing tremor. He begins rocking forward and back, a twitch flickering his right eyelid.

An older woman with fine lines and gray hair walks over to us, a stack of papers in her hand. Her clothes have several patches stitched over holes from what looks like years of wear.

"Don't mind Lance. He hasn't been right in his mind since the merchant came for him for not paying his tax." I can feel my heart stop. She pats him on the back, soothing his muttering. "Care for a trade?"

I offer a weak smile and look over the pamphlets. The top one reads: *A rhyme and a song to grow a day's worth of grain. Sell your secret to the wind, and never toil again.*

I gasp and shove the papers back into her hands. The ends of her nails are black. From the looks of it they're beginning to rot.

"Dabble in the old ways, miss? I'll trade you this rhyme for your lowest wage." The woman smiles a toothless grin.

"Unless you want to be arrested, I suggest you lower your voice." I turn my back to her, hoping no one took notice of us. She doesn't know the number of eyes paid to watch over me, placing her in far more danger than she realizes.

I sit back down close to Veyron with my arms crossed. The woman must be desperate to try such a thing with the king's army present. The soldiers work to gather the able-bodied men of the village, adding them to our charge.

I don't try to help any more after that. Why help build an army if they're all just going to treat each other so poorly? As if this kingdom needs more men like my father. Instead, Crea needs more people like Linnick and Opal.

By the time the moon reaches the sky, we have added almost fifty more to our company. Most of them take cues from the soldiers and keep their distance from me. I arrange a place to lie down next to Veyron, her ever-watchful eye scanning the trees around us. The furs I lie down on aren't near enough to create a barrier between me and the damp ground. Won't be getting much sleep tonight, it seems.

The majority of the men are drunk and passed out beside a small fire. The others are huddled in the tents they managed to set up. James is settled beneath a tree close by, stretching his legs out and closing his eyes. I study the soldiers closest to me, knowing they likely wouldn't say anything of note while I'm nearby.

I stare into the crackling fire, my legs itching to carry me away without a glance back. The forest is quiet tonight, making each pop of the burning logs envelop me. Several of the soldiers are snoring, but my mind drowns the noise out the longer I look into the flames.

Sometimes I wonder if Father sends me on these trips to test me—to place me so close to freedom, knowing I won't run. Not after last time. I bring my hand to cover the now-healed wound over my stomach. Occasionally, I can still feel the edge of the blade biting into my skin, the soldier that yanked me by the arm and down to the ground to stop me. *"Your father said bring you back whatever means necessary."* I shiver at the memory of the coldness in his voice.

I don't remember much from that night. Just that I wasn't fast enough.

Suddenly, Veyron pulls tightly against where she's tied to a tree, straining to get away. I sit up and pull my sword into my hand. This time the other horses become restless alongside her. None of the men awake from their sleep. I silently stand to calm Veyron and ready myself to wake everyone else up.

A figure darts just out of my line of sight the moment I turn my back to the woods. I whirl around and feel the pace of my breathing increase. *Stay calm,* I tell myself. A shape that resembles a wolf bounces through the trees, coming closer. I lift my sword as Veyron snorts loudly, her hooves stomping fiercely against the ground. Just as I open my mouth to scream, the animal pounces on top of me and we both roll to the ground. My sword is knocked out of my hand with the heaviness of the blow.

As I begin to think of all the things I haven't seen or done, I feel a tongue scrape across my face. I open my eyes as my brows knit in confusion. Dog is staring at me with his tongue lolled to the side and his breath coming out in quick pants. Veyron still pulls, and I stand back up to quiet her.

"What are you *doing* here, Dog?"

His blue eyes look at me without answering my question. I sit down beside him and hold my hand over my still-pounding chest. He nuzzles his massive head against my side and lies down against me. Well, now I suppose I have two companions for the rest of this journey.

I sigh and settle back onto my furs. I only manage to get a little sleep before my eyes inevitably snap open, my heartbeat dancing wildly against my chest. Even with the new company, my dreams are riddled with nightmares.

The unsettling voice in my dream recedes to the back of my mind. But I remember that it was calling to me.

"Come closer, child…"

Day is just beginning to break when we make it back to camp. Soldiers show the new men to their tents and are issued a pair of training leathers, armor, and a sword. I drag myself across camp, so hungry I'm actually eager to eat this morning's breakfast.

I dig into my pocket for my leather pouch with one hand and try to wipe the sleep out of my eyes with the other. I drop a pinch of the powder into my waterskin, watching with a frown as it clumps at the surface. I try not to think too hard about the taste, and toss it back.

I look to the spot where Opal and I usually sit to eat but find it empty of her presence, the place taken by a group of soldiers. They're doubled over in laughter. I walk over to them, annoyed they might've taken advantage while I was away.

"Has anyone seen Opal at her chores already?"

One of the men turns to me, his features still lit up from the story he was telling.

"You didn't hear?" a gravelly voice calls out from behind us. We turn around to see a soldier stretching as he awakes from a nap. I narrow my eyes at him, not wanting to take the bait.

"You would think being her only friend you would know such a thing. She didn't bother to tell you?"

I give him a gesture that tells him exactly how I feel about him and turn back around.

"Poor little Amira. Stuck here being the only girl now that her friend has run off to get married." He laughs and walks away, joining his friends as they roar with laughter and playfully shove each other.

I feel the color drain from my face. She wouldn't leave without saying goodbye. She wouldn't leave. We both knew one day she would marry, but not this soon, and certainly not disappearing without a word.

"Sorry, Amira. Her father got the offer he's been waiting on while you were gone. You just missed her; they collected her last night. She sure did put up a fight at first—might want to remember that when it's your turn so you don't embarrass your family." The soldier turns to the others surrounding him and they resume their laughter.

Heat prickles in my chest at the way he used the word *collected*, like she was a gift to be given away at her father's choosing.

My breath stays caged in my chest as I struggle to process Opal being gone. I rest my hands on the base of my throat as I will myself to slowly sip on air.

I will not cry. I will not cry. I will not cry.

I spin around and choke out, "Who?"

He laughs harder and says, "Does it matter?"

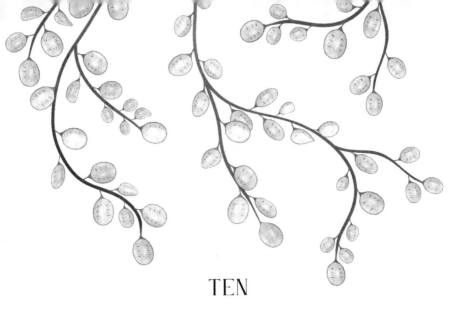

TEN

ASTRAGALUS

I MOPE AROUND THE CAMP like a forgotten flower wilting away and drifting in the wind. I methodically run through my usual routine, minus Opal. I complete my morning run, stare at breakfast without eating it, and try to finish my daily tasks.

I've never felt so alone. Opal's smiling face was a welcome reprieve from the war always raging in my mind. Before Linnick came along, she was the only friend I'd ever had. She was there when Evans betrayed my trust, and each time my father tore me down bit by bit. She was the deeply rooted tree that kept me grounded, and without her, I feel more isolated than ever before.

While washing the soldiers' clothes in the buckets in front of me, I don't bother with trying to watch today's training lessons. Several soldiers walk past and toss their dirty garments at me, causing the bucket at my knees to spill and soak the ground I'm kneeling on.

Tears well in my eyes as I realize I didn't tell Opal what her friendship meant to me. She was just always there, and I never thought to thank her for being my only friend for so many years. I bite the inside of my cheek and look to the sky, willing the tears to not fall. But a few slip out.

Someone has to know something that can help me find her. I hear a burst of laughter from the stables, two sandy blond heads that are identical in height and build ambling into it. The twins: the easiest to crack.

I bolt upright, knocking my bucket of water over in the process. It would be pointless to try and get information out of Beryl, but if he knows anything, then he surely shared it with Ember and Mica. The twins hardly leave Beryl's side these days.

I wipe away the trail of tear stains from my cheeks and rush toward the stables. After casting a look around the area and finding it empty, I slip in behind them.

Ember is pulling a bucket of grain from the shelf, while Mica is walking into the stall with one of the horses. I've never been particularly close to any of them, but Mica has always been the nicest to me.

"We need to talk."

He jerks his head. His hand is frozen on the mare's mane, brush in hand. "Amira, it isn't worth asking."

"Where is she, Mica?"

He shakes his head and resumes brushing the mare's mane.

"Do you even care about her? She's your only sister."

"Of course I care, but we don't know anything." His jaw is hard but his voice softens. "I'm sorry." The wooden door creaks open behind me and his Lyle-blue eyes snap over to the entrance.

"Go home, Amira." Ember's voice edges on annoyed. He talks to me like he would Opal, as if he's my brother. I've known them for so long, I may as well be related to them too.

I twist around to Ember. His features are identical to Mica's but I could always tell the two apart. Mica is soft, whereas Ember is all sharp edges like Beryl. It's always made me wonder if he does it to seem more like the eldest brother.

"Tell me where she is. Just one hint that I can use to piece it together." I jab a finger in Ember's direction. "If you two care about her, then you can at least help me with that. I just want to check on her to make sure she's okay."

"We all tried to ask our father, but he refused to say anything. He said we should focus on our training and move on." Ember's jaw is tightly flexed.

The unspoken rule that none of us question our fathers hangs in the air.

"There's no use in trying to convince us to tell you anything—even Beryl doesn't know." Something in Mica's voice tells me he isn't lying. Coming from him, I believe it.

"You must've heard something useful," I insist.

Mica shakes his head, his mouth pressed into a line. "Sorry, Amira."

My fingers curl into fists. If none of the Lyle siblings know anything, then that leaves me at a dead end.

"Amira! Come over here."

I jerk at the sound of Father's voice coming from outside of the stables, not fooled by the calmness of it. *Act calm,* I command myself. *He will see straight through you.*

The twins share a look, a silent conversation passing between them. Both of them shoot me an apologetic glance, but that's the most I'll get from them. Their eyes are so like Opal's, it hurts.

I walk out of the stables toward the cabin. I focus on keeping my eyes downcast like I've trained myself to do. Father is standing on the porch, looking out at the camp with a steaming cup of tea in his hand. I relax my face into neutrality and stare blankly at him. Breathe. In. Out. In. Out. *Relax your fingers; he'll notice your hands curled into fists.*

Still gazing out at the soldiers training, he speaks quietly. "I need you to go to the market today. I suppose you're capable of handling that?"

My eyes remain fixed on my feet, and I can feel the scrutiny in his voice. I give him a small, rehearsed nod and say, "Of course, Father."

He smiles, resembling a serpent preparing to strike. "Wonderful. Don't forget your medicine."

It's been years since I've had any allergic reactions. What if it went away? It would mean I've been putting this disgusting mixture into my body for no reason. Maybe I can cut it down to every other day. Then every several days, until I know for certain.

What's the worst that could happen? I've never had so much as a sniffle or bump since I was a child. I reach into my pocket and squeeze the leather pouch. It doesn't leave my pocket with my hand. For the first time in years, I don't take it.

My ordinarily bored guard eyes me and my unusually sulking mood but says nothing. When we get to the market, I clench my jaw as I look at the castle. The tall stone building looms over the market—so close to the starving and begging people beyond its gates, but completely removed by a single stone wall that separates the two.

The king and my father continue to make coin off the backs of the international market town of Runnswick. People from around the entire northernmost part of the kingdom make their way here to sell, buy, and beg for money at the castle gates. Little do they know that no one other than the select few in power is allowed to enter beyond the castle walls, and even those select few have been mostly cast out during one of the king's drunken stupors.

Father and Commander Lyle are among the few who go in for meetings when called upon by the king. Usually, Father can't be bothered to go to the castle. More times than not, the king himself will come to the training camp to see the great royal merchant.

The castle is mostly gray but speckled with white stones throughout. From this point, it's hard to see past the height of the surrounding wall, which is more than triple the height of the seller's carts. Archers line the top of the wall, guarding the castle from a very unlikely attack.

Someone taps my shoulder, and I instinctively bring my hand to the hilt of my dagger.

"Whoa, I come in peace and with no intentions of bringing you harm." Adrian stands there with his palms lifted in the air and a smirk on his lips.

The furs I gave him are still resting on his shoulders. His sandy hair sticks out of his hood in a mussed mess on the edges, and his smile stretches freely across his face, showing off the deep dimples on each side of his mouth. I look around quickly in search of James, hoping Adrian didn't think I was staring at his mouth.

"Embarrassed to be seen with me now?" His words are light, but his smile doesn't meet his eyes.

"It's not that." James is nowhere to be seen, and he couldn't have made it to the madam's house from here so quickly.

"Three weeks in a row seems like a pattern to me. Are you trying to see me, Amira? You even came a few days early just to talk to me," he taunts me, but I'm hardly listening as anxiety squeezes my racing heart.

"Your guard is going to be busy for *quite* a while."

I jump when Adrian whispers into my ear, his closeness causing me to take a step back. I tilt my head up and study him, wondering how serious he is.

"What do you mean?"

He rubs his hands together and sighs heavily, a smile playing at the corners of his mouth. "Ye of little faith, Amira."

I narrow my eyes at him, not buying into whatever act he's playing at. I try to muster the most annoyed look I can, but I just don't have it in me today. His smile falters when he sees the sadness I'm poorly concealing.

"I had a friend distract him for a bit. He's very…convincing." He offers a shrug, and I can tell he's holding something back.

"Are you sure your friend is capable of that?"

Adrian slaps his hand across his heart in feigned shock. "He is perfectly capable, actually."

I grab Adrian by the elbow, dragging him to our small spot on the port. My eyes still search for any signs of my guard. I don't speak until we're safely tucked away and alone. Once we reach the small, crooked staircase leading down to the sea wall, I feel safe enough to talk to him.

"What makes you so confident in his ability?"

Adrian shrugs and seems to think this is a sufficient answer.

I look up at the docks and see a blonde girl boarding a ship, her laughter carrying to us. I sit up straight, my spine snapping to attention as I strain my neck to look at her. The girl turns in our direction and my shoulders sag when it isn't the person I wasn't hoping to see. I feel a rogue tear slip down my cheek and don't bother to wipe it away.

"What happened?" Adrian asks.

I sniffle in response, not caring he's sitting beside me. I study him as he looks longingly out at the sea where ships are coming and going. I'm surprised to find my own sadness mirrored in his face as he looks at the restless ocean. The Andronicus Sea has claimed many lives. The unforgivable pull of the sea calls like a siren for all brave enough to enter it.

We both sit in silence. We get lost in our own thoughts of escaping our current lives. His hood is still fashioned on top of his head like it always is, and not for the first time, it makes me wonder why he always chooses to wear it.

"My friend left. Her father married her off and I don't know where she went. Where I live, I don't have any allies. I don't have many people I trust enough in my life to call a friend. I have three, and that's it. One is married off—someone I'll likely never see again—one is an old man, and the other is a dog with no name." I hold his stare to show him I don't pity myself. Having three people you trust completely is better than having none.

He studies me a moment without looking away from my gaze. His bright brown eyes lock with mine. "Well, now you have one more." He gives me a small smile and looks back out at the sea.

I mumble under my breath, "We'll see." But it's difficult to stop the smile from tugging at the corners of my mouth.

The waves lap below our feet as we watch more ships unload their goods.

"So, it's agreed upon? Friends?" He sticks his hand out for me to shake.

I hesitate. Something in his eyes causes me to extend my hand toward his, a well of sincerity shining through their depths. "Agreed." And with that conclusion, we clasp hands, and I add one more friend to my short list of companions.

"So, what's with the old man?"

I wipe my sleeve under my running nose and laugh, seeing Linnick's disapproving look in my head. "You know the man you met who told me to give you a chance? We've become friends through years of trading. I've bought fruit from his stand for a long time."

He looks out for me in a way my father never has. I thank the heavens that I have Linnick in my life.

"That sounds really nice. I suppose I could make a few runs to his stand to buy from him too."

Adrian's comment makes my stomach drop.

"Did something happen to him?" he asks knowingly.

I shift where I'm seated, uncomfortable with how well he can read me. "The dodder plant has taken over so many of the farmers' harvests these past few years. His farm was hit just as the season started changing; he tried to salvage some of it, but once it starts it can't be stopped. All the fruit gone just like that." I swallow the lump that's formed in my throat. I don't think I can take talking about this anymore.

Something in Adrian's eyes hardens at the comment. "How long has this been going on?" His voice is quiet and unsure.

"Have you not heard the farmers around you mention it? It's all most of them talk about these days. The vines are making their way through all of Crea. A lot of farmers have lost their income because of it. And of course, it means there's less food to go around. People are restless that there isn't something more that can be done to stop them."

Adrian hesitates, studying me for a moment before speaking. "Can't he just appeal to the king for additional wages or food until he can replant more fruit? For a small debt to repay, there has to be something he can do."

I tilt my head, almost feeling sorry for him that he doesn't understand. "There's nothing left to give. The king hasn't answered a request for extra portions in the past few seasons. Besides, once the dodders roll in, the soil becomes unusable. He'd have to buy an entire new lot with undisturbed soil."

Adrian's brows draw together as he lets out a long breath. He pulls off his hood, running his hand through his sandy hair. His arms aren't muscular like the men in the camp, but they're defined enough that his forearms flex with the motion. I quickly turn my gaze back toward the sea.

"Friends tell each other things. Since you told me what's on your mind, I guess I could tell you something in return. Remember when I said my father was difficult too?" He must sense the shift in my mood with the change of subject.

I nod my head and wait for him to continue, silently thanking him.

"Well, I'm taking over the family farm soon. My mother died when I was born, and I don't think my father sees anything but her when he looks at me. I've heard from a lot of people he hasn't been the same since we lost her."

I nod again, his honesty hitting a little too close to home.

"I don't have any brothers or sisters. I have an uncle but he stays fairly busy. Just my father and me. The pressure of doing a good job for the family name just gets to me sometimes."

I grind my teeth together, trying to stop my tears from flowing. I almost feel like I'm being tricked with how his words seem to expose my very life.

"It's mostly just me," I say. "My mother died when I was young, and I have few memories of her. Now that my friend is gone, I don't have anyone left at camp."

He looks at me, eyebrows raised. "The royal training camp?"

I panic, my breath stalling in my throat. Fear seizes me that he's about to figure out whose daughter I am, but he just looks back out at the sea and clenches the side of the wall.

"I do. It's…home. Of sorts." Unnerved, I try to find a way to talk myself out of that truth.

"You were there when Penyth attacked?" he asks quietly. "And you're unharmed?"

His concern surprises me, and warmth tries to penetrate my cold chest. My sword piercing the Penyth soldier flashes into my mind. Guilt gnaws at my insides, even if that's the last thing I should feel for a Penyth soldier.

Looking at Adrian, I wonder why he hasn't joined the king's army. A man his age and build would be recruited quickly.

"Have you never thought about joining the army?"

He laughs, surprising me as he shakes his head. "No. That's not for me. You know you aren't the best at reading people? You also thought I didn't have a place to sleep at night."

I eye him, still not convinced he does.

"And how are you not married yet? A girl like you, I'd figure…" His voice trails off and his cheeks redden again. As poor as he thinks I am at reading people, he sure seems to leave his emotions on display.

"I don't want to be tied to a husband. Besides, it'll be my father's choice eventually. I try to delay it as long as I can." I watch a young couple boarding a ship, their laughter bounding off of them and their happiness stronger than the waves below us. As they climb onto the boarding plank, I imagine they're setting sail somewhere far away, and much, much brighter than here.

I almost forget Adrian is sitting beside me until he speaks in a low voice, as if to not frighten me. "You must have to work pretty hard to stop someone from offering you their hand."

I stiffen at the words, but don't snap back in response. "I just want to see the world. I wanted to see the world with Opal." I bring my knees to my chest and rest my chin on top of them, the sting of her departure tearing my heart in half.

"Well, I really only have one friend. He isn't what most people would consider friendly, but neither are you." He playfully nudges my shoulder with his and I find myself laughing. He manages to pull me out of the rain cloud I stuck myself beneath.

"That's because almost everyone I've placed my trust in has either left me or betrayed me. When someone lies to me I just—" I take a deep breath and try to collect the thoughts running through my mind. They fall like leaves and scatter around the ground in an unorganized mess. "It's hard for me to trust people. I don't make friends easily because I'm afraid they'll lie to me to try and get closer to my father." I bury my face in my knees that are still curled to my chest, too embarrassed by my honesty to look at Adrian.

"I won't lie to you."

I bite the inside of my cheek; nobody's promised me this before.

"We should get going. I don't want you to get caught. I'll see you next week then, Amira."

His words echo in my mind, somehow collapsing the wall I built between the two of us.

"Lu," I say suddenly.

He looks at me quizzically, his mouth opening to respond, but I hold my hand up. He waits patiently as I get the words out.

"My friends call me Lu."

I don't give him the same courtesy of responding, leaving before I can see his smile grow any further.

"'Til next time, Lu!" I hear from behind me.

My steps are light on the way back to camp. Much lighter than they've been in a long time. I barely notice James, I make quick work of my final chores, and I even manage to avoid a run-in with my father.

I take a deep, full breath, my lungs clear and strong. After finishing all of my tasks, I slip into my bed and, for once, drift into a peaceful sleep.

My eyelids flutter open. My arms itch. A lot. I look down at them, squinting through the darkness of my room. Large welts cover my skin. A searing pain blisters from every rising splotch of red.

I scramble out of my bed, scratching furiously at the marks. My tonic. I need my medicine. My heart beats wildly in my chest, causing my breath to come out in quick pants. I bolt out of bed, stumbling to the ground with a loud thud, twisted in my blankets.

"Amira?" My throat tightens further at the sound of Father's voice. He'll know I didn't take it.

I take in a jagged breath. Why is it so hard to breathe?

I crawl over to my trunk and throw the lid open. My hands tear through the contents until I find my leather pouch. The door creaks open, revealing Father on the other side.

His jaw flexes, and without a word, he shoves a glass of water toward me. I don't question it, needing it to go down quickly. I quickly scoop a bit of powder out and stir the mixture with my finger.

The welts are beginning to burn and spread. Without hesitation, I raise the glass to my mouth and drain the cup of every last drop within it. Almost immediately, I can feel my airway ease open and the welts begin to melt away.

"This is what happens," he says, stabbing his finger into an open welt, "when you don't listen to me."

I cry out, snatching my arm away from him.

"I'm—sorry." It's still hard to breathe.

"I suppose I'll be getting myself a new glass of water now." He turns on his heel and leaves me heaving on the floor.

Even though I'm inside now, it must have been enough to just be outside all day.

It's shocking how quickly the powder eases the pain from the welts and brings air back into my lungs. I thought this would be the final link—that by cutting this tie between us, I might finally break away. But it didn't work, and I still don't know where he gets the supply.

It's just one more thing keeping me bound to him and this life I'm stuck in.

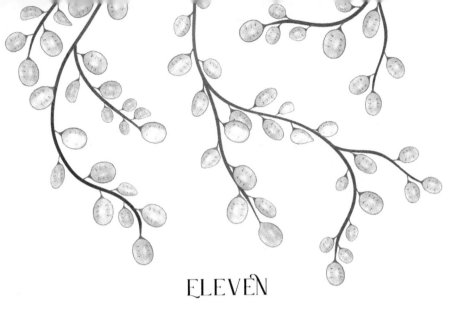

ELEVEN

BEGONIA

"WHAT'S LIFE LIKE ON A farm?"

Adrian hesitates, lost in thought. I scold myself for bringing up something he's been tentative to talk about.

"Sometimes it's beautiful. The days can be filled with lounging around inside or endless amounts of work to get done without making any real progress by the end of the day. It isn't always as easy as it sounds. From the outside it looks like we wouldn't have anything to complain about, but lately it feels like we're crumbling each day on the inside."

I nod my head, knowing that what lies inside your home isn't what others think it may be

"My father loves me, but he loves other things more. He'd sooner pick up a bottle than save our farm, even if it were burning to the ground." His voice is quiet and hoarse; I have to angle my body away from him to avoid letting his emotions penetrate my heart too deeply.

"What kind of farm do you have?" I ask to break his thoughts away from his father.

"A sheep farm. We're in charge of a large herd. With my father's mind shrouded in a haze, it's my responsibility to keep the sheep safe most of the time. You'd love it there, there's so much life and light."

While Linnick's farm sits ridden in dodder vines.

"That seems like a lot for you to be in charge of."

He laughs, though I'm not sure why. He shakes his head and runs his hand through his hair. "It can be. Sometimes I just want to be…" His voice trails off and he looks out at the sea, the restlessness of the waves matching his troubled gaze.

"Free," I finish for him.

He turns to face me, a small and fleeting smile forming on his lips. "Where did the name Lu come from?"

His abrupt question catches me off guard, my thoughts momentarily distracted from my stolen friend. The past week without Opal passed faster than I thought possible. Looking forward to spending time with Adrian kept my head above water, too close to drowning without someone to hold me afloat.

"Opal and I decided to change our names when we were younger. I chose Lu for myself, and she chose Ava." It was our escape from the camp and our fathers. We played pretend and dreamt of being someone else. "She claims I chose the better name, so she still calls me Lu. Or did." Not knowing how far away Opal was taken is frustrating. I kick the heel of my foot against the wall we're sitting on, watching as rubble loosens from the rock and tumbles into the sea beneath.

The waves slam into ships docked at the port, signaling the imminent weather. Large wooden masts sway side to side, the crew rushing around in a frenzy to tie thick ropes to the dock to secure them for the night.

"Any luck on finding her?"

LUNARIA

I sigh, having known this question was coming. I place my hands on the ground behind me and lean back, reticent to admit I've found nothing. "Everyone I've asked has remained silent. Even her brothers don't know. Their father said to mind their own." A chill runs down my spine; it's like she's disappeared. "Her father's probably just glad I can't get close to her anymore. He's always said I was a bad influence."

Deep down I feel there's a way to find her. "I just want to make sure she's safe, wherever she is." And that she's happy.

"Are you safe?"

His question makes me hesitate. I've never thought about my position in the camp as *unsafe,* but being the only female in the camp has brought an uneasiness to the back of my mind. He must take my uncertainty as an answer, his jaw clenching. His eyes are colder than I've seen since meeting him.

"I can help you, but you have to trust me."

I meet his gaze, though not fully following. "I hardly know you." Even if my words are true, the curiosity sneaks through my attempt to sound skeptical.

"I'll explain as soon as I know it's happening for certain." The softness of his smile smooths over the anxiety building inside of me.

"Sure." My voice lacks any confidence, but I appreciate that he thinks he can help.

His brown eyes soften, sensing my wariness. "Just trust me, okay? You can't be content stuck in that camp, surrounded by savagery and ruthlessness."

He doesn't know how growing up in that world made me numb to things that are considered savage to others. A boy that spends his days farming and harvesting doesn't understand what it's like to live in the camp.

"I can give you a place better than where you are now. You deserve so much more, Lu.

He looks like he has more to say by the way he keeps opening his mouth and closing it, but instead just runs his hands roughly through his hair without making a sound. Before he can get out what he's struggling to say, horns reverberate through the market. I whip around, but it's hard to see what's happening from where.

Adrian jumps to his feet, his eyes wide. "I need to go, but I'll find you soon. I promise.

Confused, I watch as he ascends the stairs out of our safe spot tucked away from the people of Runnswick. The horns sound again, and I follow behind him. Marketgoers surge toward the castle walls as people shove and push those around them to get a closer look.

Someone steps on my foot and I turn around to glare at them; when I pivot back to Adrian, the crowd has already swallowed him from view. "Bye to you too," I mumble to myself.

The crowd is growing quickly in size, though the platform remains empty. We all stand there in wait, though the addresses typically hardly inform us of much.

The wait is long, leaving my thoughts to center on Adrian's offer to help. The refuge of staying on his farm is tempting, and it's a more generous offer than I've ever been given. I can see myself working alongside him until I make enough money to leave. I'd eventually have to tell him who my father is, but that can wait.

I imagine his farm matches the sense of warmth that radiates from him. The way he's described the fields of golden hay and sheep scattered about sounds safe. His days of tending to his flock and keeping watch over them is something I'd gladly accept doing. My life could consist of being surrounded by farm animals instead of the soldiers at the camp. I smile to myself, hopeful I can make the daydream real.

The horns sound a final time, snapping me out of my thoughts as King Avalon steps out onto his platform above the market.

"People of Crea. It's been brought to my attention that our land is in need of alliances to be made within the kingdom. Several highborn women will be brought to the castle to be matched with a suitor. Marrying houses together will strengthen our bonds and produce strong heirs for each family."

I feel bad for whoever has to be subjected to that task. Whispers spread like wildfire through the market at which women will be chosen and brought in.

An older woman mutters to someone beside her, "The castle has been empty for so long, the king will likely send everyone away again after a night of wine like last time."

Several people near us murmur their agreements. I roll my eyes, the stories of the past flying from lips and being retold a slightly different way each time.

"I heard people couldn't stand to be around him losing the contents of his stomach at all hours of the day from the amount of ale and boar he consumed."

Several others add their own versions as to why the castle hasn't had a visitor in years.

A stout man waves his hand, dismissive. "The way I see it, the whole Stewart line is doomed. The prince is hardly a leader. He should've secured himself an alliance by now, and yet he parades about the castle to do as he pleases." The man snickers. "Maybe he'll be forced to participate in the match. The sooner our kingdom gets an heir, the better."

The king sways on his feet and rests his hand against the banister in front of him. "My advisor will be reading the nobles that are chosen to participate." The crowd waits for more, but the king just smiles and teeters unsteadily back into the castle.

A man walks onto the platform with a large leatherbound book in his hands. He gives the king a pat on the back briefly when they pass each other.

"Kingdom of Crea. The following have been selected to participate in the royally sanctioned matching. The matching will consist of various events, planned meetings, and free time to get to know the others in attendance. Everyone who attends will not leave until they have found their match. Invitations are being sent out to ensure all families are notified." The man clears his throat and holds the book up to read from.

My pulse quickens with the energy of the buzzing crowd.

"Sir Edmond Briar, Lady Gwendolyn Stone, Lady Edith Frarison…"

My attention wavers to the people around me as the names continue one after another.

"Lady Edith is sure to catch the eye of the prince," a woman whispers to another. "Lord Frarison has been trying to make that happen for years," is the answer she receives in turn.

"Sir Christopher Lander." The announcer's voice rings out through the now-chattering crowd.

"Lord Lander? Those poor women."

I bite down on a smile as I try to focus on the names. Dozens have been called out already. The names all blend together, and my attention drifts again.

"Sir Nolan Tanner." The announcer turns the page, a smile on his mouth. "Lady Amira Ramsey."

I freeze. Several people around me turn in my direction, making me feel closed in.

I must've heard them wrong. Me? At the castle? There's no way. This isn't how I wanted to get away from the camp. This is *so* much worse. Right?

"Lady Amira."

I flinch at the sound of James's voice from beside me. I turn to look at him and he nods in the direction of the path back to camp. His face is pinched in a tense expression, and he throws a glare at the now-empty platform before turning to leave. I follow after him, studying the stiffness in his posture. Seeing the opposite of his routine disinterest he usually wears causes my eyes to track his abnormal behavior. It's the only thing I can focus on with the thoughts racing through my mind.

I can't go to the castle to be matched. Finding a husband is the last thing I want to do right now. I'll be surrounded by people who have spent their lives learning how to act a certain way, which is very different from how I've spent my life. I swallow down the lump rising in my throat.

"The royal merchant requests you to see him." James's posture remains rigid as he stalks off in the opposite direction. My eyes follow his heavy footsteps slamming into the muddied ground as he heads straight for the southern sparring rings.

My palms become slick with sweat, and I shake my hands out at my sides, trying to keep my rage at bay. I find Father sitting on the porch in a wooden rocking chair.

He rocks forward and backward, the chair eerily creaking as I approach, the rhythm precise as a steady drip of water. Markings indent the wooden slats on the porch from where he's rocked ruts into them. He watches me approach and continues his motion in the chair without stopping. His gaze neutral and jaw set. Not a good sign.

I come to a stop at the edge of the porch, not wanting to climb the steps to where he's seated. He slows his rocking to a complete stop, still saying nothing. The boards beneath his feet creak as he shifts his weight forward in the chair.

"Don't feel bad for not bringing anything from the list back today."

My heart clenches, knowing he's not being kind from the goodness within him. I remain quiet and nod my head, not knowing what the right thing to say is, hoping it's safe to remain silent.

"And how was the king's address? Brief as it was." He chuckles to himself as he leans back in the chair and resumes rocking.

"It was different today." My tone is clipped.

His face doesn't reveal surprise; instead he nods his head and gestures with his hand for me to continue. Of course he already knows about the address. He has ears everywhere.

"He's summoning a few highborns to the castle to be matched with a husband."

At this, Father's passive face spreads into a grin. This is a look that I've seen on rare occasions, and it typically means he's up to something. A plan he has spun into action is playing out how he wants it to. It's a smile of him getting his way.

"It seems I'm one of them," I say tightly.

"Wonderful. I'm pleased I secured you an invitation."

I swallow thickly, fighting to remain calm in his presence. My voice is trapped within my throat, a rabbit stuck in a hidden snare.

"The king informed me of this only last night in our meeting."

He knew the king would give the announcement today, and chose to keep it to himself until the opportunity to tell me was most beneficial to him.

"I've allowed you to remain unmarried for too long. I have a strong feeling you'll meet an appropriate match while there."

I struggle to keep my face impartial to his words. "Father—"

He doesn't need his voice to silence me. The scathing look he's giving me is enough to make me hesitate for a moment. His beady black eyes zero in on my every move, waiting for me to say something against his request. It's clear there's no getting out of this, but maybe I can help someone else in the process.

"I'll go," I say at last.

His eyes narrow as he senses there's more coming. His rocking ceases as he stands from his chair. From my position still on the ground he towers high above me, perched on his stoop and watching me closely.

I take a deep, steadying breath. "If I can bring someone with me."

"And how does this benefit me?"

I pause. Asking him for a favor doesn't usually end well.

"I have a friend that's about to lose his farm to the dodders. He could accompany me as my servant. It's better than being a beggar in the market. What lady travels without a servant? It'll seem strange enough when I arrive without a lady's maid."

His sharp cheekbones are so tense they could slice through my attempt at asking him for this favor. But I press on.

"Without the income of selling his fruit he needs somewhere to go, but would need someone higher up to recommend him for the castle. If your answer is yes to this, then so is mine to your request."

He studies me for a moment. I lift my chin slightly, knowing if I back down now he won't agree.

"Again, how does this benefit me?" he inquires.

I force myself to breathe, knowing he already has the answer to this question but is choosing to make me say it.

"You know servants have all the secrets. That's why you make sure James is always with me. Not to protect me, but to protect everything I know about you." I know I'm close to crossing a line, but I need this. "Nobody will suspect him of being a spy; he's too old, and too kind. But he'll report everything he learns to James. And you."

I hold my breath, waiting for the biting words to tell me how wrong I am.

"Pack light, the castle will have what you need."

It's hard to keep the surprise from my face. He hands me a new supply of tonic, this one larger than my typical stock. How long does he think I'll be there?

I wait until his back is to me before I deflate. I wrap my arms slowly around myself and ball my hands into tight fists. My fingernails bite into the flesh of my palms. I can do this for Linnick, but if Father thinks I'll bind myself into marriage with someone, he's mistaken. My mind briefly betrays me, bringing an image of Adrian's face to the forefront of my thoughts.

A pinch of regret pierces my chest, but I doubt he could've helped me. The dream of life on his farm was nice while it lasted. But my dreams always turn to nightmares. I'd be a fool to be surprised anymore. And if I have to stay trapped in this life, at least I can save Linnick.

TWELVE

PROTEA

"ABSOLUTELY NOT, LU. I'M NOT stepping a foot in that crumbling castle and neither should you."

I sigh heavily as Linnick packs up his stand for the last time. The once-overflowing crates are now empty and bare.

"And where are you to go? How are you to survive?"

He grunts irritably instead of answering. Several people pass by and a few pat Linnick on the back, offering their condolences on the loss of his farm. With each pitying look he's given, the further his shoulders slump forward, looking more his true age than I've seen before.

"You wouldn't be allowed to join the army," I continue, "and you know as well as I do that the castle will give you a place to sleep and warm food to eat."

He sits down heavily on his empty stack of crates, bringing his hand to his chin and resting his head atop it. "I won't be a slave to your father. He'd never just let me go once you're finished, and I'd certainly be in his debt after. This task could turn into the rest of your life if you aren't careful."

He has a point. He looks over my shoulder; I turn to follow his gaze to where James stands nearby. My small case of personal items rests at his feet.

I slip my hand into my pocket for the tenth time, just to make sure my medicine is still resting inside. My shoulders lose some of their tension when my fingers wrap around the familiar leather seams that hold the tonic pouch together.

"Eventually we'll find a way to leave the castle, and Runnswick, for good." I give him a pleading look. "Trust me." Maybe someone at the castle can help me figure out where Opal is. With all the wealth and high positions there, someone is sure to know.

"It won't be easy." I can see the answer on his face; he can't tell me no. "Still, I can't just leave you to deal with this alone. Just know I'd sooner starve than do your father's bidding, but for you, I'll do it." A kernel of guilt taps against my chest, causing my heart to constrict and thud painfully. "Someone's got to look out for you, kid." And someone has to look out for him too.

He stands from his resting place and pats me on the shoulder before walking to James. I'm left alone at his barren stand. Memories of playing pretend with him and playing tricks on James now feel like a fading echo.

I straighten myself and join the two waiting for me. James is wearing a tight expression once again. Linnick's brows are knit in apprehension at what lies beyond the castle walls. I take a deep breath, and the three of us make the short walk to the castle gates.

"Remind me why I'm the only one from the camp having to do this?" I ask. None of Opal's siblings had to be subjected to this invitation, yet the Lyle family was highly titled.

"They have their duties, you have yours. They turned down the invitation." James's aloof response wasn't much of an answer.

They had the option to decline?

The muscles in my shoulders tense as we near the entrance. My eyes dart to the heavily guarded wall that encompasses the castle on all sides. Castle sentries are crowded together near the opening of the gate, their faces mostly covered with heavy steel helmets.

I squeeze my hands tightly at my sides, trying to prepare myself for this new cage. Linnick clears his throat beside me, giving me a pointed look to relax. I release a quick breath as a group of men arrive on several horses near us. My heart thuds faster in my chest at the guests already arriving, but they trot past, hardly stealing a second glance at us as they shout and laugh among themselves. Their joy is a glaring contrast to our heavy mood as we approach the castle walls.

I catch sight of one of men in the back, his red curly head facing my direction. His eyes travel over my clothing, the look of disgust on his face revealing his opinion.

"I didn't think servants were allowed out front!" he yells at me as he ambles past.

Several people turn and stare at me. I twist around and ignore his jab, refusing to show a hint of embarrassment.

There are already several people waiting in line to enter the castle. Each woman joining the line brings along a new flurry of chatter and brightly colored dresses. The newest to come up waves to the group around me.

"Edith, you made it!"

The girls jump out of line to stand with her. It seems like everyone arriving already knows someone here. The longer we stand in line, the more anxious I become. Lords and ladies are arriving from all directions, making me feel suffocated already.

More than half of the people here so far all came from the port, brought in by ships. The rest walk their horses to the stables to demount and hand them off to the stablehands. We're the only ones who've arrived on foot. My palms sweat at the idea of being stuck inside with so many people I don't know who live so differently than me. I wipe furiously at my leathers to try and dry my hands.

Soldiers walk the length of the line, stopping every few people. "Documents?"

We aren't even to the front yet. Father never lets me keep my own papers. I'm too likely to lose them, or so he says. I look to James, waiting for him to hand them over.

"What? I don't have them. Your father didn't hand them to you before you left?"

My eyes widen, certain they couldn't have forgotten such an important thing.

"Lady Amira Ramsey, daughter of Royal Merchant Reichardt Ramsey." The words feel like sand in my mouth, but I have to try. The title *lady* doesn't match the training leathers I'm wearing, and the messy side braid my hair is tossed into won't help either.

The guard pales at my father's name but doesn't step aside. "Documents, or you don't enter."

Several other guards begin to take notice of us, drawing closer with their hands positioned on their swords.

"I can vouch for them. I was sent to be their guide today." A man not much younger than my father turns the corner nearest to us. He wears an elaborate tunic of fine, dark golden material, his hair a deep brown with streaks of gray peppered throughout. His features are familiar, but I don't recognize him no matter how long I look.

"Welcome to the castle," he says with a smile as he addresses us. The guards immediately step back at the man's presence. They move on to the rest of the line, but their eyes remain narrowed on us.

"A pleasure to meet you, Lady Amira. Your father has spoken well of you."

Of course he has.

The man's gaze sweeps my unusual clothing, doing well to mask the surprise. "I was pleased to read your name at the address."

It clicks.

"Lord Wyman, Duke of Runnswick," the castle guard introduces him; the name matches the fine clothing.

He leans forward in a slight bow. "Your guard can bring your items in before he returns back to camp." His face slips into an easy smile before he abruptly turns and guides us into the castle. The duke is stranger than Father ever described him.

He and the guard lead us through a dark passageway, our footsteps echoing on the stone. The guard holds a small torch that lights our way as we near a large wooden gate.

The guard calls out into the darkness. "Lady Amira Ramsey, daughter of Royal Merchant Reichardt Ramsey, and Lord Wyman, Duke of Runnswick." The wooden gate creaks and slowly opens high enough for us to step past. Just after pass under to the other side, it's released back down, closing us in.

The tunnel is dark and cold, smelling faintly of wet vermin. We walk in silence through the damp passageway. Each step fills me with dread. We reach the end and are left standing in front of a tall metal door occupied by two more castle guards.

Though I don't recognize them, I feel their eyes on me. They all have the same blank expression, but surely at least one of them recognizes me from their days of training at the camp. I'd bet my nonexistent savings that at least a handful of the guards are still being instructed to track me by Father. They all are swept into the royal training camp and pushed out to the castle on the same undercurrent. A lot of the castle guards are hand-selected by my father and the commander for being the "brightest" of the trainees. More like the ones who are loyal spies.

Their bloodred tunics are covered by chainmail. They stand at attention, a large shield painted with Crea's insignia resting in the right arm while a tall spear twice their height is clenched in their left. I stare at the shield while we wait for them to grant us passage into the castle.

A gold lion with a crown atop its head stands on its hind legs, a large bird clenched within its jaws, depicting the lion for the Stewart family line, which has ruled the kingdom since the split of the empire. The bird, a phoenix, represents the Kingdom of Penyth, though both kingdoms have remained at a standstill for hundreds of years, neither gaining power over the other.

Linnick is escorted away from us before we step into the castle. He looks over his shoulder and winks before he disappears altogether. I close my eyes and try to steady my racing pulse, hoping desperately I didn't get us both in over our heads.

The corridor the duke leads me into is barren, though the dark room is dimly lit by the occasional window and sconces bolted to the stone every few steps. With the height of the wall separating the castle from the market, the sun struggles to light the area.

The corridor is wide enough that it could fit ten men walking shoulder to shoulder without knocking into the other. The ceiling above us is so high that the light from the sconces doesn't come close to illuminating it, leaving it dark enough to look like there's no ceiling at all.

"Your father wanted you here early before the other highborns—looks like they were eager to arrive, though. He wanted you to prepare for this evening." Duke Wyman's voice causes me to jump in the quietness of the corridor.

"Prepare for what?"

My question goes without an answer as we turn around a corner, passing room after room. I try to keep count of the ways we turn so I know how to make my way to the entrance, but after the twelfth turn, I lose count.

Several of the doors we pass are open, a flurry of maids rushing around inside to organize the chambers. They dust the floors and fluff the linens on the beds. The corridor remains empty other than the occasional servant passing, their hands full of large baskets or cleaning items.

"This way, Lady Amira." Duke Wyman takes a sharp turn into a small, almost invisible walkway. The slim entry connects to an even narrower winding staircase with a poorly lit path. I follow behind, thankful I'm not wearing a dress while ascending the slick stone steps. Though I have a feeling that's about to change.

For a moment we're plunged into darkness, one of the sconces on the wall devoid of a fire. With my sight gone, the only thing to focus on is the scuffing of our feet on the steps and my short breaths.

Before I have the time to feel any fear, the pathway opens to the next floor of the castle. This hallway looks much the same, a wide berth with more empty chambers being prepared for guests.

"What's on this floor?"

The guard with us doesn't turn around or slow his steps but instead lets out a sigh. "More bed chambers, two celebration halls, the throne room, and the great hall. Your chamber is the next level up, along with the prince's chambers, the king's, and the chapel. It's of great honor to stay on the same level as His Majesty."

I nearly laugh. My father no doubt had a hand in that.

"Lord Wyman, a moment?" An older man shuffles over to us and leads Duke Wyman far enough away I can't fully hear them. The two look back at me before resuming in hushed tones. I strain my ears to listen, but their whispers weave jumbled words, indiscernible.

The longer they speak with their heads hunched together, the more bored I become. I wander over to the nearest window, hoping to catch a glimpse outside. From this level I can see the market stretch out below, and beyond that the choppy waves of the

Andronicus. The space between the wall and the castle is narrow, just a slim walkway.

A blur of motion catches my eye against the rocky shore. A tall, dark-haired figure stands over a servant curled into a ball with his arms covering his face. With the distance separating us, it's hard to make out the two, but the man on the ground is unmistakably older than the one standing over him. The waves rush up the shore and lap against the man on the ground, whose clothing is the same drab, rough wool that all the servants wear. He does nothing other than try to block the brutal blows of the man's fists raining down on him.

As the attacker pulls his arm back to strike again, a golden ring on his middle finger glints in the sun. The fabric of his black tunic stretches easily with the movement, conformed to his body in a way that suggests he can afford finer clothing to be tailored to him.

My eyes widen and I twist around to find someone to help. "We need to go down and help that servant!"

The guard ambles over, lacking any sort of haste. He peers out the window, his movements slow and unhurried. "Are you feeling well?"

I make a face at him, jabbing my finger in the direction of the attacker. "There. A servant is being—" When I turn to look at them, my hand falls to my side. The rocky shore is now entirely empty.

"I apologize for the delay. Are you ready to continue?"

I study the depths of the walkway once more before finally tearing my gaze away. Duke Wyman studies me curiously.

"Is everything all right, Lady Amira?"

I cast one last fleeting look over my shoulder, a chill running down my spine. "My servant? Where will he be?"

Calling Linnick my servant burns my throat. I bite the inside of my cheek, already anxious I've made a mistake. If servants get treated like that often here, then it's no different than the camp.

"In the lower level below the main floor in the servants' quarters. He'll spend most of his time in the kitchens and pantries. You've had a lady's maid assigned to you."

I resist the urge to cringe. "What are the higher levels for?"

At this the guard turns his head to me, narrowing his gaze in my direction.

"Curious, is she not?" says Duke Wyman with a smile that fills me with unease. "This must be your first time in the castle. Now how could your father keep such a flower hidden?"

I burn with embarrassment. "I—"

James clears his throat to stop me. I can practically hear my father's voice insisting I be more discreet. Being at the castle is already exhausting.

Thankfully, we've reached the end of the narrow stairs and stop in front of a wooden door, oddly shaped and rounded at the top.

"Your lady's maid will be here shortly to help you get ready for the evening festivities." The castle guard turns to James before I can ask him more. "I'll escort you back out after you set her belongings down."

James kicks open the entrance, earning a small glare from Duke Wyman as he steps through with my trunk in his arms.

"A pleasure to finally be introduced." Duke Wyman bows, leaving me with a poor taste in my mouth.

James leaves without a single glance in my direction.

Once everyone is gone, I take a small step inside. My shoulders lose some of their tension. I'm finally alone.

Tall windows line at least half the room, allowing ribbons of streaming sunlight to flood in. A sheer white linen canopy hangs above the massive, cushioned bed. Each corner is gathered where it hangs from the tall wooden posts that run up the bedframe to the high ceiling. The fabric looks so soft I have to restrain myself from walking over to touch it. It sways slightly with the breeze flowing in from one of the open windows, the bed poorly concealed behind it.

The walls are covered in heavy green tapestries from top to bottom. Swirls of gold have been sewn into patterns of military might: Crea's soldiers make a pattern around the king at the center on his throne. The cold stone floor has been layered with giant rugs woven in more colors than I've seen in one place: deep maroon, green, and endless shades of gold. There's a small area carved out of the wall beside my bed, separated by a door; I assume it's the washroom.

I breathe in a shaky breath. Father outdid himself with this one.

I walk over to a small, plush lounging seat and sink down onto it, unsure of what to do with myself in this massive room.

As I study the carvings that border the rounded threshold, it creaks open. A woman who looks to be slightly older than me walks in with her shoulders back and her head lifted high. Her smooth, pale skin is radiant, her features soft with big, round eyes and smiling lips. If she weren't wearing a maid's smock, I would likely mistake her for a princess.

She steps closer to me, coming to a stop just a few paces away and giving a quick dip with her head bowed. "I was instructed to get you ready for tonight. There are several things we need to do." Her eyes remain trained on my feet, causing me to shift my weight uncomfortably.

Even if I'm considered a lady with my father's position on the royal council, I've never been treated as such.

"What's your name?"

At this her gaze shoots up to mine, a questioning gleam in her eyes. "Avery, miss."

I nod my head, taking note to not forget her name. The small smile forming on her face causes me to immediately take to her. She nods and motions for me to turn around, where I find a large trunk resting at the foot of the bed.

"A few dresses are in there for you. We'll need to get you washed and cleaned before you pick out which you'd like to wear tonight." The trunk is almost as long as the bed and is as tall as it is high. It's sizeable enough it could house ten dresses, maybe more.

"What's tonight?"

Avery's hand comes to her mouth, stifling her laugh. "There's a celebration tonight. The commander of Penyth's army was captured, the very one who initiated the attack on your camp. It seems like a wonderful time to introduce everyone who was invited for the matching. You could meet yours tonight!" The dreamy look in her eyes reminds me so much of Opal that I feel a painful twist in my gut. It sounds just like something she would say if she were here with me right now.

Avery helps me undress, chattering away about things to keep in mind.

"Remember, when you meet the prince—" Her words fall away, eyes transfixed to the mark on my stomach.

On instinct, I use my hand to shield it from her the best I can, though the jagged scar reaches far past the width of my two hands. The deep, puckered surface runs all the way from my hip and up past my belly button. It's impossible to miss.

She recovers quickly, but the slight hesitation lingers between us. "You'll need to give him a small curtsy and introduce yourself."

I'm thankful she doesn't ask about the scar, but her curiosity is almost tangible. I can already tell she's someone I can trust, which is likely going to be hard to say the more people I meet in the castle. But I don't talk about it with anyone, not even Opal. It's a memory I keep locked away for good reason.

"After you bathe, we'll need to have a few lessons on the nature of the court. Since we haven't had guests in ages, it's easily forgotten.

King Avalon has instructed the guests to learn what's expected and how to behave."

Her voice is gentle, but her words paint a picture of an atmosphere very unlike the one in which I grew up. I've been trained to swing a sword, throw a punch, and take a hit. Not how to behave like the women I was surrounded by when entering the castle.

Was it always Father's plan to have me marry at this age? It couldn't be, otherwise he would've never allowed me to fight. And now, I feel entirely out of my element. The camp is all that I've known, and this isn't exactly how I expected to escape it.

Still, I'm not under the same roof as my father. I can pretend to be here for the same reason as everyone else, even if it's only to have time away from the camp.

"Tell me what I need to learn." It makes me wonder if *all* the guests are getting this lesson, or just the one that has spent her entire life surrounded by soldiers.

But I can still play the part if that's what it takes.

THIRTEEN

MULBERRY

AFTER BATHING MY SKIN RAW, Avery takes a comb and begins to untangle the mass of hair that sits stick-straight against my head from the cold water. She puts a gooey substance in my hair with a stiff wooden brush.

The washroom is a small, round room that juts out the side of the castle, hardly enough space for the two of us to be in here with the large copper tub resting in the center.

"The water is usually heated by the fire, but we don't have time to wait for that this morning."

I just nod my head, thankful for a tub at all. My normal bathing at the camp consisted of a small pail and quickly scrubbing my skin until there was no visible dirt. This bath has small stalks of lavender floating in it, letting off a bursting floral aroma.

"What's that you're putting in my hair?" The light brown thistles of the brush are turned completely black by the thick muck coating it.

"It deepens the color of your hair and gives it a beautiful shine. All the highborns use it."

I twist in the tub, baffled.

"It'll also make your hair soft and add some waviness," Avery adds.

I turn back in the tub so she can continue, strange as it seems to me.

She washes my hair once more and brushes it out again, finding more tangles that have worked their way back in—and people wonder why I always keep my hair braided. She hands me a fluffy, soft towel to dry off. Its velvety feel makes me want to wrap myself in it and take a nap, but she quickly hastens on to dressing me.

Avery paints a faint pink color onto my lips and lines my eyes thinly with charcoal. After getting dressed and letting my hair completely dry, I feel poked and prodded enough for a year. My waist is cinched tighter than ever before, and I try my hardest to take a full breath against the stiff material.

"Here are your shoes, miss. They'll make you look elegant."

I step into heels that are far too high to be considered safe. This certainly will not do. I take a few steps forward and stumble, catching myself on the stone wall.

"We can spend the next moments…longer maybe…practicing. We can add this to the lessons as well. The sun hasn't begun to set yet."

Avery is the only kind person I've met so far; I feel a little better knowing she's going to take the time to teach me.

She spends well into midday teaching me the art of walking in uncomfortable footwear, simultaneously running through important facts to know about the majority of the other highborns. Lord Tristan's liable to step on my toes, so avoid his hand during the waltz. Sir Christopher, whom she promises I can't miss due to his persistence, will almost certainly try to ply me with drinks.

"And the prince?" I ask.

Avery holds my hand as I learn to hold myself upright; she squeezes especially hard as I trip.

"He's a charmer, that one. Judging by the boys he's friends with he may not be ready to settle down. His closest friend is notorious with women." She pauses. "Well, you'll see," she says ambiguously as I right myself.

"Is there even anyone to befriend?" At least one ally would be nice.

"There is a younger boy, Emilio. He comes from a respectable family that doesn't seem to involve themselves with court politics. He'll likely be the youngest one in attendance, so he should be easy to spot."

I nod. At least that's one.

"With your seclusion in the camp for so long you'll be at a slight disadvantage to the rest of the guests. Many of them studied together growing up or have connections through their parents."

Not a problem seeing as I don't intend to find a husband while I'm here.

"Will the king be present tonight?" I ask.

Avery pauses and I do the same, unsure if I can walk yet without her steadying hand.

"Likely not. The prince is usually at events in his stead, as well as the majority of the royal council and the prince's advisor."

I've heard about him before; there likely isn't a soul in the kingdom that hasn't heard of the Prince's Snake, Graylen Garriden. He does all of the crown's dirty work, which means he might be the only person in the kingdom less popular than the royal merchant.

Avery continues working her way from the most important in attendance to the lesser highborns: Edith Frarison, said to be the most eligible woman in attendance due to her family's holdings and land; Penelope Larksong, a cousin of the crown, whose insistence on singing at parties is particularly offensive; Sarah Frederick, youngest daughter of the Lord of Grantford…

I lose track of the rest, my interest waning with the sinking sun.

The top part of my hair has been braided into a coronet, reaching from one ear to another, like a small crown has been laid upon my head. The rest of my hair flows freely down my back in waves. The substance Avery put in it has already turned it from a dull brown to a deep onyx.

A forest green dress is cut in a square at my chest, clinging tight around my waist and fanning out slightly at my hips. The sleeves are snug and run all the way to my wrists. The only thing that remains the same are the small nicks and scars on my hands.

"I'll be waiting outside when you're ready." Avery gives me a wink and another quick dip before breezing out of the chambers entirely.

I rifle through the pocket of my leathers and slide my tonic pouch into a small pocket in my dress.

I pace in front of the door, occasionally holding my arms out for balance. I'm tempted to leave the room without shoes at all, but I'm certain that would be frowned upon. Not that anyone could possibly see my feet with the amount of fabric I'm drowning in.

I take a deep breath and step out into the corridor. Avery beams at me, though the steps I'm taking can hardly pass as graceful. One foot in front of the other. Falling in front of everyone is not the first impression I'd like to make.

We walk in silence for a long while, making our way to the second floor where the celebration is being held. With the sun nearly set for the evening, the hallway is even more dimly lit. Fire dances against the stone walls, bouncing around and leaving bits of unlit areas in between the sconces.

We pass several guests leaving their rooms, all of them escorted by either a castle guard or a lady's maid. The highborn girls wear large and colorful dresses, adorned in sparkling jewels and elaborate hairpins. On reflex, I reach to my pendant, nervously playing with it.

Finally, I hear the chatter of a full room and string instruments getting closer. The room is larger than any room I've ever seen, like a long hall stretched out with a length much larger than its width. Chandeliers adorn the ceiling in a row of three, going from one end of the room to the other, casting a twinkling and dancing light over the attendees.

The large golden mirrors lining the walls give the illusion that the chandeliers are endless on either side. Tall golden sculptures sit in between each mirror, topped with a basket of fresh flowers. The ceiling is intricately painted in swirls and whirls of gold and white.

Tables scattered around the room bear trays of fruit, meat, cheese, and wine. The over extravagance is in sharp contrast to the state of things just outside these walls.

"This is as far as I go, miss," Avery murmurs. "Enjoy your evening."

I feel the absence of her comforting presence as she leaves me surrounded by strangers and feeling utterly alone.

My eyes drink in the crowded room, hoping to find someone familiar among the sea of nameless faces. Occasionally, people turn my way to see who's passing, but most continue about without a second glance. Even with Avery's hard work to make me look like someone of importance, my seclusion in the camp has left me unrecognizable to the highborns.

With the amount of gawking I've been doing, I almost miss the man walking toward me. My mouth falls open.

He's devastating. The hair falling around his face is so dark that I can't tell if it's a deep brown or black. It's almost the same color as mine now. His jaw is defined and lined with a few days' worth of stubble. Either he was too busy to remove it or simply didn't care.

Ink flows up both of his arms, disappearing underneath the hem of his sleeve. The flexing of his corded muscles disturbs the strange pattern etched into his skin, rendering it indiscernible. Even in all my time among soldiers, I've never seen markings on someone like that.

His frame towers above the crowd as people part for him. He's almost a foot taller than everyone around him. The intensity in his gaze is nearly impossible to escape, his eyes so green that it sends a memory skittering across my mind of plush green fields lined with lilies. Yet his expression reveals none of his thoughts. I feel a discomforting thrill when I realize he's also watching me.

"Who is that?" I ask a woman beside me as he makes his way over.

"Sir Graylen Garriden, advisor to the prince." She says it more as a warning than an introduction.

My eyes find their way back to Graylen, who seems to understand that we're speaking about him even at a distance.

"You likely won't be the first or the last to try and speak with him tonight," the woman says. "You should try your luck elsewhere."

I bristle at her assumption, though I can't deny the curiosity I feel deep in my bones.

Graylen stops in front of me, devastating, and for a moment I forget the reputation that comes with his name.

"Interesting." His eyes follow the length of my dress from my shoulders to the floor. Something about him is familiar. He reaches across me to grab a pint of ale from a servant's tray. He leans in so closely that his chest brushes against mine, and I take a step back. Before I can say anything, his ring draws my attention.

The golden ring rests on his middle finger, nothing out of the ordinary if it weren't for his knuckles covered in fresh cuts. Like the man beating the servant.

My veins ice over, the blood within my body chilling to a freeze. He brushes past me and continues around the room, several girls stepping into his path like gnats swarming a piece of meat. He draws a lovely girl with strawberry-colored hair onto the dance floor, her cheeks tinted the same pink. Just past them, I spot Father's familiar sneer from across the room. He nods his head.

"You look lovely, Lady Amira," a voice interjects. "So glad your father could join us for once—he stays so busy with the camp these days."

I turn to find Duke Wyman in a new tunic, this one more ornate than the last. Being brother to the king has more benefits than just the title of duke, I suppose.

"My wife is around here somewhere; I'd love for you two to meet." His smile doesn't match the glare in his eyes, a look I've come to recognize quickly in my father's smile.

I nod and move throughout the room, feeling the need to be further away from him.

"Lady Amira, right?" a light voice says, interrupting my escape. "Lady Adley of Saltain." The girl smiles widely, her clear blue eyes as wild as the ocean. Her hair makes it difficult not to stare, so long and straight it touches her waist. But that isn't what catches my attention. The color is almost as white as fresh snow, contrasting brightly against her rich, dark skin.

"You can call me Addie," she says with a wink, flipping her striking white hair behind her. She's soon whisked away by two different men courting her. It's going to be a long night.

I observe the young crowd as highborn women are introduced to boys and men in high standings, several names that I recognize as wealthy families with both land and titles, and a few more from Avery's lessons.

"Hello, I don't believe I've seen you before, Lady…" A young man who looks to be close to my age stands patiently beside me, his tunic perfectly suited and expensively made.

"Lady Amira Ramsey." I smile as I watch the color drain from his face the moment the name leaves my lips.

He coughs awkwardly and gives me a tight smile before nodding his head and walking away. As wealthy as my father is, most aren't quick to have his attention turned on them. Any secrets they possess will be quickly brought to light and exploited if needed by my father.

I can at least thank him that most men bristle at the name Ramsey. Surely, that will put a hold on Father's sudden push to find me a husband.

"A delight to see you as well."

A voice from behind freezes me to my spot. I close my eyes for a moment and release a short, painful breath. I must be imagining it, yet the laughter carrying over to me is impossible to misplace. It's one I've heard far too many times to not recognize.

I slowly spin around, my vision sharp as my eyes land on the last person I expected to see here. The moment I see him, our eyes meet.

"*Adrian*," I breathe to myself.

His face splits into a wide grin as he finishes his conversation with the person beside him. He shakes the man's hand and pats him on the back before returning his gaze to mine. The world moves in slow motion as my brain works to catch up with what's happening. My heart drifts deeply into my stomach, deeper than a pebble sinking into the depths of the Andronicus Sea.

Someone bumps into me, causing my feet to tangle and my arms to flail out to right myself. How could Adrian be *here?* What could he possibly have done to get himself into the castle for the matching event?

My mind buzzes with the possible reasons for why he's here. My heart feels torn: one half relieved to have an ally among the pack of wolves, the other wary and uncertain of what this could mean. Something doesn't feel right. His clothing is far finer than the son of a farmer could ever afford. Even if he sold his land and sheep, he wouldn't be able to buy such fine clothes.

Warning bells sound within the recesses of my mind, telling me to turn around and leave before the world comes crashing down around me. I spin around, having lost sight of him in the crowd. People turn to look at me, casting concerned looks in my direction. Like a wild animal caught in a bright light.

Everything around me blurs, overwhelmed by the laughing mouths, the endless eyes glued to me.

I have to find him and figure out what's going on. I shove my way through the swarm of guests, sweeping the room for the one person who can answer my questions. My mouth drops open as the crowd separates, revealing his path to me. I didn't imagine it. It's Adrian.

My farmer boy, my only friend outside the camp. Who'd never lie to me.

Fourteen

ARTEMISIA ABSINTHIUM

His brown eyes are just as I remember, but gone is the boy in tattered clothes from the market. In his place is a man distinctly polished, with clothing formed perfectly to his body. He politely smiles as he dodges the many people in the crowd trying to stop and speak with him.

The royal crest sits embroidered over his heart, laced elegantly into his jacket. Rings made of gold and precious stones adorn his fingers. The only thing remaining from the boy in the market is the same unkempt blond hair and golden-brown eyes. My stomach drops, leaving my palms sweating and my heart pounding in confusion.

"It's not what you think, please just let me explain."

My mind hasn't fully connected with his presence here, and my words stay stuck within my throat.

"Prince Adrian! You're looking well tonight." A short, stout man claps Adrian on the back.

Prince Adrian? My mouth plops open, my heart flopping around in my chest like a dry fish on land trying to make its way back to sea.

Adrian gives the man a friendly nod and turns back to me, effectively cutting him off. I want to scream at him or walk away and gather my thoughts, but I do neither. Instead, I stand there, unmoving and unspeaking. I need the missing pieces to the story to make sense of what's happening.

"Hi, Lu." His smile is soft and shy, awaiting my reaction.

I press my lips into a thin line, not wanting to speak but having so much to say.

He plows ahead, rushing to try and explain. "I know this is confusing, but I wasn't lying when I said my name was Adrian. Or about all the things I opened up to you about. I've never been that honest with anyone before."

The words barely make it into my ears. A large number of people name their boys Adrian in honor of the prince. When I saw a boy in farmer's clothes, it didn't cross my mind that instead of being *named* after the prince, he *was* the prince.

"And technically, I do lead many sheep. Those sheep just happen to be people, and the entire kingdom."

People are starting to take notice of our lengthy conversation. Adrian's voice is low, and his proximity makes it clear this isn't our first time meeting. My surprise shifts to anger, the heat rising to the surface.

"Look," Adrian says, "I know this is a lot to process. The moment you said you lived in the camp it was an easy connection to figure out who your father is. I had to help you, and I can explain everything. We'll talk soon, I promise."

I realize I still haven't spoken a word. He tries to smile reassuringly as he reaches forward and squeezes my elbow gently. His promises seem to change like the waves of the sea.

A cloud forms over my head and follows me around the room, the guests no longer looking my way for introductions once my last name has made its rounds. Like the people at the market, they turn their backs to me and step out of my path.

I look to where I last saw my father and see the disapproving narrowing of his eyes. My head swims and my vision sways. I need air.

The crowd around me gapes open as another figure steps through; Graylen's tall form rises above the guests, moving toward me. People avoid him much in the way they do me, the Prince's Snake less liked than even the Ramsey name. If he truly is Adrian's minion, then maybe they've spoken about me. His green eyes search mine, his face revealing nothing.

"Fresh air?" His voice is deep but soft.

My eyes flick down to his hand holding his cup, the same hand that rained punches down on someone weaker. I need a moment, but not with someone who beats servants on the shore.

"No, thank you." Does he not realize who he's speaking with? Even the Prince's Snake is no match for my father's spies. Although Graylen's the first person I've met who might be able to go toe to toe with my father.

"There's a terrace that overlooks the Runnswick Gardens at the end of this celebration hall."

The Runnswick Gardens? I'd only ever heard of them from Opal, like a fairy tale. The twins once accompanied their father there during a meeting. Mica spent the entire next day talking about the tall, spiraling trees and the ripe apples in the orchard. Opal and I have always dreamed of seeing it.

Graylen must notice my interest because he turns and walks away. He truly thinks I'll blindly follow out to the terrace. Probably used to women doing just that. I contemplate letting him go and turning the other direction, but something about his arrogance distracts me. A part of me wants him to admit what he's done. How could no one have noticed?

"Lady Amira, daughter of Royal Merchant Reichardt Ramsey." The words rush out, anticipating a reaction. But there is none. He continues walking, hardly glancing down at me. "And?"

I gape at his question. Unable to speak for a second time tonight, my mind is more confused than it's ever been. People part widely for the two of us, whispers sounding from all angles. If he notices, he doesn't let on. His gaze is fixed ahead, bored and uncaring of the events around him.

The subtle fear in people's eyes when he approaches them is evident. He likely knows secrets that could ruin every person in this castle. If the rumors are true—and the incident with the servant makes it feel like more than gossip—he also has the ability to dispose of them discreetly. The kingdom respects the king and the prince, but almost everyone fears the Prince's Snake. I'm beginning to understand why.

I turn to look at Graylen and find him studying me. He doesn't turn away or flush in embarrassment; instead the corners of his mouth slope upward into a brief smile.

The closer we get to the terrace, the easier it is to make out the guests gathered there. I see a familiar, perfectly coiffed head of black hair. Father's back is to us, but it's an outline I can't mistake.

"I'm going to find something to eat." I hurry away, my interest in the gardens gone. I spin on my heel, annoyed to find Graylen trailing behind me.

As the party drags on around us, I notice something that doesn't fit the celebratory spirit, easier to see the closer we get to the end of the hall. In the middle of the drinking and dancing is a man in a small metal cage—not tall enough for him to stand or rise above the heads of the partygoers. He's been stripped of most of his clothing, but a deep green commander's sash is unmistakably draped over his bare chest. Muddied and streaked with old, dried blood that has matted most of his hair in odd directions, fresh bruises mix with old ones as they splotch in various sizes across his exposed body. His face is shaded as it hangs, unreadable.

I gasp at the state of this man. Finely dressed women and men splash drinks on him through the bars. A pale woman in a tight-corseted gown flings a grape at him. "Catch!" she jeers, her red, over-lined lips curling into a smile. The grape bounces, rolling all the way to the hem of my dress.

The man's head stays bowed as if in prayer, not flinching at any of the insults or objects thrown at him. I head straight to the cage, needing a closer look. Surprisingly, Graylen doesn't try to stop me, but walks closely behind me until I'm nearly face-to-face with the man, wrapping my hands around the metal bars.

"Penyth scum," the man next to me spits at him while others murmur in agreement. Graylen says nothing, curiosity marring his features as he watches me.

My father's words haunt me as I look at the power stripped from this man.

"You only gain power by taking it for yourself, daughter—and once you have it there will always be someone trying to take it back."

Regardless of where he's from, he shouldn't be made a spectacle in this way. A shudder runs through me as I watch people get drunk from wine and fill their bellies with delicate food. Nausea eats away at me, causing any appetite I may have had to disappear. From the corner of my eye, I see Graylen bend down and lean toward my ear.

"Shouldn't show pity for the commander of the rival kingdom, Lady Amira. At least remove the emotion from your face." His voice is so quiet I can hardly hear it, and his breath tickles my skin as it dances across. I shoot him a look and quickly relax my expression.

Before I can respond to Graylen, the stringed instruments halt and horns pierce through the crowd. Every head in the room lowers as they bow in unison. Graylen tugs on my hand to get me to do the same. The contact of his hand in mine sends a sickening twist through my stomach. I jerk out of his grasp and follow along with the rest of the crowd.

The king is escorted in by six guards, three on either side of him. The guards' bloodred tunics stick out among the crowd, and their chain-link armor clinks noisily.

A chair has been placed on a small, elevated surface just behind the prisoner. The crowd separates down the middle as the king walks through. Adrian peels out from the crowd, his face poorly concealing his shock at seeing his father here. I feel as if I'm in a daydream, my body wading through mud as I try to sort through who Adrian is. He stops on one side of the king's chair, while Duke Wyman is positioned on the other. He's so unlike himself, rigid and unable to look in the direction of the cage.

Everyone stays in a lowered bow as the king strolls leisurely by, his gait wavering and somewhat sloppy. He pauses a moment to admire the humiliation of the prisoner, looking slightly confused as his brows draw together. The moment he sits on his makeshift throne, everyone stands and watches him for what is to come next. Most of the guests' faces look stunned at seeing him here, but Adrian's most of all.

"Who put that poor man in that little cage?" His words slur together drunkenly as he gazes out at the commander.

The duke hands him another drink and he takes a deep sip.

"So, we are all here tonight to…" His voice trails off as he sways to the side, his arm coming to rest heavily on the arm of the chair to hold himself up. He scratches his thick beard as he searches for the words. The duke leans over and whispers something into his ear, and his eyes light up in recognition.

"Ah, yes! We're here to welcome the honored guests who begin their quests to find a royally sanctioned match." He pauses to allow the crowd to cheer as if he were a puppeteer, telling them when and how to react. The duke leans over and speaks into his ear again.

"Thank you, brother. As your king, I want to be the first to welcome you to the castle."

The king stands from his chair and clasps Adrian on the shoulder while smiling down at him. At a wave of Duke Wyman's hand, the music begins again; people immediately take to the dance floor in celebration, the wine-drinking fully underway and laughter growing louder with each passing song.

"If we aren't going to speak then perhaps we should at least dance," Graylen says.

Dancing is very low on my list of things to do tonight. The camp doesn't teach many dancing lessons, and the few I learned from Avery haven't prepared me for this.

"I don't dance. Besides, I can point out at least four hopeful women waiting for you to ask them." I continue to search the crowd and relax a fraction when I don't recognize my father anywhere. I see a flash of blonde hair and rise onto the tips of my toes to see the girl attached to the hair so like Opal's. I plop back down onto my heels when I lose sight of the girl, disappointed.

Graylen pulls me forward suddenly, not giving me a chance to say no. He laughs as I roll my eyes, but it doesn't look convincing with the smile tugging at my lips. I avoid eye contact with him, but play along while I look for Adrian. I spot him at the far side of the room, opposite where I had entered. He's easy to find, most of the guests fighting to gain his attention. The future king is almost more popular than the current king, who's now nowhere to be seen.

Even with his height and broad chest, Graylen moves surprisingly lightly. I stumble more than once, but he says nothing. My balance has less to do with my dancing ability, and more to do with the man dancing with me.

"How'd you hurt your hand?" I ask him, fishing for an answer, not wanting him to know I saw him, but curious at what he'll say about it.

"Hurt it while training with a guard." His answer is short, but his eyes narrow.

I look away from him, a spike of fear running through me.

Adrian's still there, free from the crowd of guests. His brown eyes watching us dance. His brows are drawn together as his gaze bounces between me and Graylen. I'm twirled around, and have to look back to my dance partner so I don't lose balance. His eyes are fixed wholly on me. He seems to be drinking in every inch of my face, memorizing the curve of my cheek and the slope of my nose. The intensity of his gaze causes my cheeks to flush, which his eyes immediately catch onto. He tilts his head, curious. He doesn't even *try* to conceal his stare. The song comes to an end, and everyone bows to each other. I quickly take a step away from him, wanting to put space between us.

"Mind if I steal her for a dance?" Adrian's light voice causes me to suck in a quick breath. Frustration heats my cheeks that he feels the need to ask Graylen instead of me.

"We were just about to get some wine."

Adrian winces at the harshness behind my words, but nods as I pull Graylen with me to the nearest tray. The moment we're there, I quickly drain the contents of the glass and set it back down. I feel stuck between an immovable rock and the sea, not wanting to hear what Adrian has to say yet and not wanting to be around someone who hurts people for sport.

"You care for him." Graylen says it as a statement instead of a question.

The last thing I want to do is admit to Adrian's only friend I care for him. Known for being as slimy as a snake and revealing any and all secrets to the prince does not make for a good gossiping partner.

"I don't even know him." I try to keep my answer short, without revealing my emotions.

"Goodnight," I say, eager to leave this overly eventful evening, and I slip away before he has the chance to stop me. I steal a glance over my shoulder and find a new girl already in my place dancing with him. Adrian's nowhere to be found. My feet throb where the footwear bites into every piece of flesh it touches, the thought of taking them off propelling me forward until I find the path back to my chambers.

FIFTEEN

ANEMONES

"THE BOY FROM THE MARKET was the *prince?*" Linnick's voice echoes through my chambers loudly.

"He lied to me, Linnick. He promised me he would never lie, and he did."

Linnick paces in front of where I'm seated on the small lounging chair. It's strange to see him in servant's clothing, his hands red from the night he's already spent in the kitchens.

"I know. The boy shouldn't have lied to you about his farm. Would you have believed him if he said he was the prince, though?"

I throw my hands into the air with frustration. "You're taking his side?" I say in a half-whisper, half-shout. I let out a deep breath, trying to calm myself.

"I'm always on your side, kid. But it seems to me this whole thing is happening because that boy wanted to help get you away from the camp." He pauses and takes a seat beside me

"Yes, but only to find a husband here. He knows I have about as much interest in finding a husband as he does being locked in a castle."

Linnick nods, leaning onto his knees as he thinks through my words. "He's given you time to figure out what to do without being stuck at that horrible camp. As much as I don't like his lies, I can't say I'm upset to see you away from that place."

I huff, still not sure why Linnick isn't as angry as I am.

But a part of me understands why Adrian did it—understands the lies. He knew who I was, and he still wanted to be my friend. I can understand feeling so stuck in your life that you try to pretend you're someone else. He felt safe enough to escape with me, even if it was just for a few moments at the market. For some unfathomable reason, I felt safe enough to do the same with him.

"Then I'll give him a chance to explain. Maybe he has a plan." I nervously reach for my necklace, twisting the pendant against its chain. I'm still not convinced he understands me at all if this is what he thinks I would want for my life.

"There's something else. I need you to be careful, Linnick. Just watch out for the prince's advisor, the one covered in ink markings?"

Linnick eyes me, curiosity lingering in his gaze, but nods his head. He knows me well enough to believe me without a second thought.

"I saw him—"

A knock at the door startles us.

Linnick picks up the breakfast tray and nods to me before saying loudly, "I'm glad you enjoyed the breakfast, Lady Amira." He winks at me before opening the door, revealing who lies behind it.

"Your Highness." Linnick bows deeply to Adrian as I remain upright. Adrian nods to him and smiles widely, unaware of the rising anger within me. As Linnick steps out of the room, he turns back to me and mouths, *Be nice.* I smile a tight, close-lipped smile at him, and he laughs before disappearing around the corner.

Adrian closes the door, immediately turning to me. "Amira—" He stops himself, letting out a deep breath and looking out the window that reveals the market below. "Do you like your chambers? I wanted to ensure you had the nicest ones. You're the only guest on this floor; I was hoping you would feel better if you weren't around all the others. I told you I would make things right for you."

My mouth falls open. It was Adrian who arranged my chambers, not my father.

"Of course, if you aren't comfortable, I can have you moved immediately—"

"No! They're perfect, I just…" My voice trails off. I have to look away from the openness of his eyes to stop myself from falling into their depths. It's far too easy to fall prey to the emotions so plainly written across his face, to his adoring smile. "Did you suggest I become one of the highborns brought here?" I need to know for certain it wasn't all my father's plan.

"Well, I had to get you out of the camp somehow, Lu. Convincing my father to agree to this event was the quickest way."

I stiffen slightly at the use of my nickname and his smile slips. He orchestrated this *entire* thing?

"I'm sorry, I know it isn't how you thought you'd be getting out. I couldn't leave you unprotected in a camp of angry men and a father that likely doesn't deserve the title." His smile has fully vanished.

I watch the market dwellers below us through the window, and my eyes travel to the area where we once hid out beside the sea. Seems like a lifetime ago.

"You'll get used to the castle. This isn't quite a farm, but I couldn't very well tell you who I was just yet. I know you don't want a husband, but if you just give the idea a chance so you can leave your father—"

My head swivels to meet his gaze. My eyes widen as round as the full moon. "You *lied* to me, Adrian." My voice is just above a whisper as tears begin to prick behind my eyes. I blink rapidly and look back out at the market, jabbing a finger toward our secret hideout.

"We sat right there, and you let me believe you were just a farm boy. I had no idea…" I clear my throat and struggle to keep my voice even.

"Would it have made a difference? Given who your father is I don't see how me being the prince would've made you trust me. Everything I said is still true. I yearn to be free, as do you. But our reality isn't that we get what we want; people like us don't get the luxury of that."

He isn't wrong.

"I understand if you're angry with me, but I hope in time you'll forgive me. Besides Graylen, you're the only friend I have. I don't want to lose you."

His words hit me in the center of my chest. I knew Graylen was Adrian's advisor, but how is he friends with him? Is he blind to the things Graylen does in his spare time?

"About Graylen…how well do you know him? The things he's capable of… He isn't someone I would consider a trustworthy friend." My voice is small. I look down, unsure of how he'll react.

"Graylen has his reasons for the things he does," Adrian replies. "I know the rumors, most of them being true."

But does he truly know? Adrian hasn't seen how cruel the world can be. He likely hasn't felt the sting of betrayal from someone he thought was on his side. As frustrated as I am with him, I can't help but want to wrap him in a tight hug, to help shield him from the people trying to hurt or use him.

"I'm often busy with meetings, but I'll see you when I can." He shifts his weight, bringing my attention back to him. Half of me is torn by his good intentions even if he did lie to me.

"I need a small favor."

He looks to me, his eyes bright and ready to help with anything I may ask.

"Can it be arranged that I eat my breakfast in my chambers each morning?"

I don't explain why, and he doesn't ask. His eyes dim at the simplicity of the task, but he nods in agreement. The truth is, I know I'll need to find quiet where I can. My privacy is about to shrink tenfold.

"Consider it done." His sincerity edges away my anger bit by bit. He smiles as he bows deeply. I can't think when he's smiling at me like that.

"I believe the women are being gathered for an afternoon activity in the great hall." He winks at me, the dimples in his cheeks deepening as my lips curve into a frown.

"What activity?" I call after him as he slips out of the room, but he laughs instead of giving me an answer. Great—I'm screwed.

Avery comes bustling in behind him, not questioning me, but following his exit with a lingering gaze.

"An invitation came for you." She hands me a folded piece of parchment. I carefully unfold it and take a deep breath.

Lady Amira,

Your presence is required in the great ball for a women's-only activity to better acquaint you with preparing yourself for a husband. Please await your servant's arrival to lead you to the great ball.

An activity to better prepare me to find a husband? I crumple the thin parchment into a ball and throw it against my window, letting out a small, frustrated scream.

"Ready, miss?" Avery's face is warm and calm, but the small pinch in her eyebrows gives away the pity she feels for me. "It won't last long, promise." She smiles easily, her voice confident enough that I believe her.

I nod my head and follow alongside her down the corridor.

"How has your sleep been since you've arrived?"

Now that she mentions it, I realize I haven't had a single nightmare since being here. "Much better than at camp."

Avery smiles, pleased with the answer.

Several other girls are being led out of their rooms as we make our way to the great hall, their cheery and wide eyes fixed in a permanent state of excitement.

"I can think of ten different things I'd rather be doing," one girl whispers loudly to another in front of me. She glances over her shoulder, a blush spreading across her face when she realizes I heard her. I shrug, feeling the same way but surprised I'm not the only one.

"Just nod your head and smile occasionally," Avery whispers sympathetically. I nod again as I plaster on the fakest smile I can muster. She laughs, covering her mouth with her hand before shaking her head and turning away from me.

The great hall is tall and wide, larger than the celebration room, but somehow we're crowded shoulder to shoulder, squeezing tighter as the women continue to pour in. Tables are shoved against the perimeter of the room, preventing us from spreading out.

"Do you think the prince will be here?" a small, dark-haired girl beside me asks, poking my shoulder. When I don't answer her, she makes a face.

"He's far too busy for us, Edith!" a girl in front of us whirls around to say. This sparks a wonderfully delightful conversation about the prince's social calendar.

I sigh, looking longingly out the window. I'd much rather be running through a sword circuit with Opal.

"I'm sure if he was here, he wouldn't waste his time speaking with any of you. Not when my father and mother are so close to the king. They're practically family." The girl, Edith, makes several others around us roll their eyes.

"Keep telling yourself that," the other girl replies.

I smile to myself, thankful she said what we were all thinking.

"Ladies! Ladies!" A woman at the front of the room claps her hands together until silence ensues. "Welcome to the castle! What an honor to be invited here."

The women around me clap their hands together. I begrudgingly join.

"Today, we learn how to appropriately approach the men who were also invited here to be royally matched."

I fight against rolling my eyes and zoning out entirely. A girl beside me watches carefully as the instructor demonstrates a dance. She bites her nails as she repeats the steps to herself. She's wearing a simple yet elegant plum-colored dress. The other girls went a bit over the top, but this girl stands out with her graceful style.

"I love your dress."

Her head jerks to look at me, her shoulders losing some of their tension. "Thanks." She smiles, pausing her nail-biting. "My mother sewed it for me. They couldn't afford the amount of dresses the other girls brought with them. I'm saving some good ones for the next event, though."

I nod. The girls around us have expensively woven dresses and flashy jewelry.

"I have some that are a little small for me; I can have them brought to your room if you'd like?" I try to keep my tone casual, not wanting to embarrass her. I know what it's like to feel out of place in a room that everyone else seems to melt into seamlessly.

"Oh, I couldn't accept that." Her eyes dart down to her feet.

"Please, they're just sitting unused in my trunk. You would be doing me a favor."

"If you're sure?" Her smile grows, excited now. "My name is Sarah, by the way."

"I'm Amira." Her excitement slips a fraction. "Ramsey," I add belatedly, but she's already recovered her smile.

"Thanks, Amira." She turns back to the instructor, looking a little less panicked.

"Just as we practiced moments ago, ladies!"

In unison, the girls around me hold their hands to their chests and smile softly, beginning a series of steps for a dance I have no clue how to mimic.

"Wonderful! Next!"

At this command, they all curtsy deeply and hold it low, leaving me awkwardly standing above the crowd. The woman at the front of the room shakes her head and *tsks* softly. I spot familiar, strikingly white hair that does not dip either. She notices me and winks, trying to keep a laugh in.

"Up!"

They all rise together and smile as the instructor claps, pleased at the performance.

"Lovely work! Please wait outside until the dining tables are prepared for everyone to eat."

Now *that* I can be excited about, though I'd much rather be eating in my chambers instead. As we file out of the room and wait for the room to be transformed, the men trickle slowly into the corridor.

The doors are opened once more by a servant, who motions for us to enter. Everyone rushes in for a seat, quickly finding their friends or potential partners. I look around at the filling tables, unable to find a face I recognize.

"Amira, over here!"

I relax when I see Addie waving me over to an empty seat beside her, right at the end of the table where we wouldn't really be facing anyone else. I walk over to her quickly, ready to eat and go back to my room.

"The pottage isn't too bad, just check both sides of the bread before you eat it," Addie advises me.

I don't ask how she knows this but once the food is served, I'm glad she does. The meat, vegetable, and bran-filled bowl look well enough. But the moment I turn the bread over, I notice little ants crawling on it.

I take a bite of the pottage, my eyes closing from the flavor of it. It's better than not too bad. This is far tastier than the slop at camp. I scoop the food up eagerly. On the next bite, I'm reminded of why I'm here. *Who* brought me here.

Adrian didn't have to take care of me, yet he did. The castle isn't my first choice but it's better than the alternative. I'm away from Father, the camp, and the terrible food, all because Adrian made it happen.

I smile, thankful. No one has gone to such lengths to keep me safe.

"Unbelievable everyone was sent here just to be married," Addie says. "Might as well stick with arranged marriages to make it quicker. It's just as painful either way."

Soup jumps around my throat, my laughter mixed with coughing. "It certainly is different."

Addie seems like someone I could truly be friends with, but it's difficult to know how far my father's reach extends. And how many spies he has within the walls.

I'm relieved that she doesn't press me for information as we finish our meals in silence. The rest of the guests settle down too, the sound of silverware clinking against bowls loud in the quiet room. While I finally feel as if I've made a friend among the other guests here, I'm not sure how long I can last with these ridiculous lessons.

Addie has only shown me kindness, but she still fits in seamlessly with the rest of the group. I glance down at my dress, feeling like an outsider in my own skin.

"Amira, you're using the wrong spoon." Edith's voice cuts through the clinking and Addie freezes with her spoon mid-air.

Well, the silence was nice while it lasted.

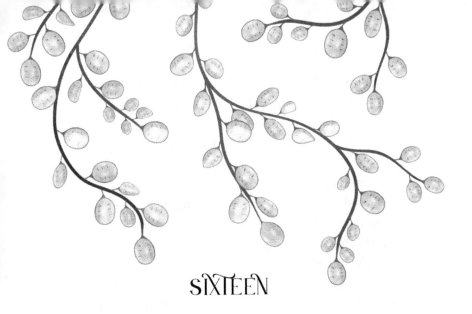

SIXTEEN

BORAGE

"Any ideas on what to pass to your father that'll appease him for a while?"

I chew on the inside of my lip, clueless. "I'm sure he has enough eyes in here to know I haven't made any obvious connections with the men yet. I'll think of something."

Linnick's eyes crinkle at the edges as he smiles, the circles beneath them more prominent with the endless time in the kitchen. "Other than the prince?"

My eyes cut to Linnick and the room is filled with his laughter.

"We haven't been able to see each other much."

But that doesn't mean he doesn't drift into my thoughts occasionally.

"He cares about you," Linnick declares.

"I know. I think I care for him too," I say, quietly.

Linnick pats me on the back. "You'll figure it out, kid. Time to get back to work, can't let them think I'm taking it easy. I have a reputation to uphold down there." He smiles at me, lessening the sting of the reminder of him having to cook all day.

He turns as he leaves, a knowing gleam in his eyes. "You should see the library today; I've heard there's no other like it in the entire kingdom."

My eyes widen. "A library?"

He winks and leaves without divulging any more information.

I spring to my feet, eager to explore the castle now. I nearly run out of my chambers, trying to remind myself to slow down.

"Lady Amira!"

I'm stopped before I can make it a few paces away from my door. A short boy pauses in front of me. I likely met him at the celebration, but neither his face nor his name are coming to mind.

"Sir Lucas Tucker?" He says it like a question, like he doesn't know his own name.

I peer around him, trying to find an excuse to continue my search for the library. I could ask him where it is, but he might take that as an invitation to come with me. No, that won't work. The silence stretches thickly between us as I struggle to find something to say, like a flightless bird that keeps falling back down to the ground.

"I…" I chew on the inside of my cheek, failing to think of something polite I can say to get out of this.

"There you are. I thought we were meeting at the garden entrance?" A voice I'm loath to hear joins us.

Lucas's eyes bulge out of his head as he takes in our new company. "Sir Graylen, I apologize. I stopped her a moment to say hello." The poor boy visibly shakes as Graylen continues to stare at me and not acknowledge his presence.

"Ready?" Graylen offers his arm, but I don't accept it.

I don't want to entertain either of the boys' possible advances, I just want to go see the library. But he at least offered to show me the gardens, which is almost equally as enticing.

"A pleasure to see you, Sir Lucas." I give him what I hope looks like a sincere smile and he grins in return. His eyes dart from me to Graylen, clearly trying to gauge the two of us together. I don't intend to have a *together* with anyone while I'm here.

When Lucas is out of earshot, I expect Graylen to say something. Some kind of offhand compliment or uninteresting fact about his wealth. Instead, he remains silent. So silent I can't stand it.

"Is that how you win every woman? Lies and a deep frown?"

I wait for a laugh, or a charming response. Instead, his face remains passive.

"Or is it your delightfully cheerful personality?" I try again, doubting why he stepped in to help me in the first place.

"You looked less than pleased to be speaking with him. In fact, you seemed to be begging someone to get you out of there." His voice sounds uninterested, like he could be watching a painting dry. "And no, I have no interest in matching long-term."

"But everyone is here to be matched?"

The corner of his mouth twitches, as if wanting to smile. "Not everyone."

I nod, begrudgingly agreeing with him. I want to know why he hurt the servant, and what happened to him. But I can't outright ask him. Is the man even still alive?

We walk down the corridor in more silence. I follow him down each level until we're back on the ground floor, passing two guards at every hallway entry and exit. Sunup to sundown they hold their shields, emblazoned with Crea's insignia.

"You clearly aren't interested in matching with anyone either," Graylen remarks.

I fight to keep my face as neutral as his, not wanting to give anything away. "What makes you believe that?"

Graylen peers down at me, towering high above me and the people we pass. "At the celebration you ignored most of everyone in attendance, while the other women nearly fought one another to speak with the men."

I narrow my eyes at him, uneasy that he was watching me that closely.

"Your secret is safe with me."

I jump at the nearness of his voice, his face far too close for my liking. My secrets are likely safer in the hands of the town gossip than they are with Graylen Garriden. Everyone in the castle must think I'm here to find a match like the rest of the girls, especially him.

"I just haven't been introduced to the right person yet."

Again, the faintest whisper of a smile graces his mouth. "I have a feeling he's closer than you think, Ramsey."

I frown at the name. "My name is Amira."

"And my name is Graylen, nice to meet you." He slides his hands into his pockets, looking more relaxed than ever. "We're here."

He gestures to two large glass doors. Curling iron bars frame panes of glass, formed into weaving lines. "Enjoy the gardens, Ramsey."

He's clearly choosing to not say my title just to bother me. Just because he can, and no one will correct him.

I could care less about the title. Still, I can't stop myself from being annoyed.

"*Lady* Amira."

This time both corners of his mouth turn upward into a small grin. I'm about to say more when I notice a set of guards standing at their post, large swords sheathed in their belts. I press my lips together. Their gazes remain fixed forward, although I can barely tell with their faces fully covered by their helmets.

Graylen tilts his head, studying me. But surprisingly, he walks away and leaves me alone

"The gardens close at sunset. Do not veer from the path. We lock the doors when the sun is fully set," one of the guards recites as if reading from a script. He opens the door for me, and my hand coming to cover my eyes with the brightness of the sun glaring in.

The gardens are so large, they surround the entire eastern back of the castle. Tall trees are somehow trimmed into a spiral formation, reaching as high as the second level. They grace both sides of a small path that begins at the entrance of the glass doors.

Large, round shrubs are squished so close together that there's no way to veer off. I feel myself begin to relax for the first time since arriving at the castle, taking a deep and steadying breath in the fresh air.

Several other people had the same idea. Small groups of women stroll through a narrow orchard to my left. They laugh and talk to each other as if they've known each other forever—and maybe they have.

"Edith! Wait for me!"

I spot the overly self-focused girl from last night and dodge behind one of the spiraling trees closest to me. I peer around the side, waiting for them to pass.

"Uh, what are you doing?"

I spin around, smiling with too many teeth. Addie laughs and joins me to peer around the side.

"I see. Edith is certainly someone I would jump behind a tree to avoid too." She smiles, her shockingly white-as-snow hair twisted into a low knot at the nape of her neck. "Don't be a stranger." She winks at me and peers one last time around the tree before turning to me with a thumbs up and humming as she continues her own walk.

The sun above me is warm against the small chill in the air. There's a gentle breeze that lifts strands of my hair, which wrap around my face. Smiling, I close my eyes. I almost forgot how much the outside air calms my racing nerves. My freedom is never so close as it is when surrounded by the beautiful, natural world around me. Even if I'm always within eyesight of a guard out here.

I wish Adrian was here to walk with me, to show me around. He's grown up in these gardens, and likely knows every hidden nook.

The path ahead of me forks in two different directions, and I choose to go left, curious to map out every inch of this place. Shrubs continue to line the many different turns, most of which become dead ends where I have to turn around a time or two. Their height is slightly taller than me, blocking me from seeing how to get out. Realizing this side of the garden is a maze, I hop into the air to try and find the exit.

I eventually find my way back to the fork and go in the opposite direction instead. This path takes me to where I can see the water. Far enough down the garden, there's a steep cliff edge that leads to the Andronicus Sea below.

There has to be a way to the port from these cliffs. A plan begins to bud with this newfound access to the water. Linnick and I can't stay at the castle forever, and Father won't allow me to return to the camp unless I marry. Being bound as his permanent fixture in the castle is not the life I intend on living.

With the amount of people and guards in the castle, we couldn't walk directly to a ship in the port. That leaves too much space to be followed and found out. I tuck away the idea for later and spare as much time as I can to stare out at the sea, drinking in the seclusion of the gardens.

I retrace my steps back to the castle, not wanting to ask any of the guards for help. They stare straight ahead without glancing at me as I pass. By the time I make it back to the entrance of the gardens, I've collected a healthy amount of sweat on my brow.

I spend the rest of the day avoiding any of the men that try to stop and speak with me and attempting to find the library. I finally break down and ask one of the guards how to get there. A few guards later, I'm able to piece together how to somewhat navigate the large castle. One wrong turn and I would end up back where I started.

"Lady Amira!"

I internally groan at another nasally male voice aiming itself at me. He's not short, but he isn't much taller than me. His long red hair is curled so tightly to his head it doesn't move as he bounds closer.

I try to nod and continue walking, not eager to entertain anyone else for the day.

"You certainly are difficult to find. Most of the women are in the celebration hall or walking about the corridors from sunup to sundown. Your father wanted me to introduce myself. Sir Christopher Lander." He bows deeply at the waist, baring the top of his red hair to me.

If my father wanted me to meet him, then I certainly don't want to. Then I recognize the curly head of red hair, pausing as I remember the boy atop his horse yelling, telling me I shouldn't be in front of the castle because he thought I was a servant.

I wasn't offended he mistook me for a servant, but the disgust in his features told me how lowly he thought of them. Rage simmers in my gut once again.

"Lovely to see you again," I say smoothly.

He tilts his head, oblivious to our first meeting on arrival day. I simply smile and choose to not elaborate.

"I'll be honest with you. When your father approached me, I was hoping it was going to be about you. I've heard tales of the royal merchant's alluring and enchanting daughter. I must admit, you lived up to the tale."

The way he pauses to watch my reaction turns my insides cold.

His wide and overly confident smile slowly melts away with the stretching silence between us. The men here are like vultures preparing to swoop down and devour the timid blushing brides.

"Lady Amira, I've spoken at length with your father. He's given me some very…enticing offers in exchange for such an appealing trade-off. I would be honored to have your hand and take you as my wife."

Take me as his *wife*? I've never disliked that word as much as I do right now. Given that my father threw me at his feet, he assumed I would gladly accept. I've only just met this boy and he's already proposing.

"I'll need to consider it, you understand?" I'd love nothing more than to tell him he can *take* a walk off the cliffs and into the Andronicus, but Father wouldn't be pleased with that. If Father hears of my *unacceptable* behavior, then he'll likely bring me back to the camp, stealing what slim chance I have to escape Runnswick for good.

Sir Christopher stiffens at the response but nods his head. "I'll be patiently waiting."

I force a smile onto my face, the movement like knives twisting inside of me. I'll play the game long enough that I can devise a plan to leave for good.

By the time I figure out the library is located on the fourth floor, I'm close to giving up. I pass a large room filled with a small congregation of highborn guests. I pause at the door, listening.

"I heard that the king drinks himself to sleep midday, *every day.*"

A girl that I can now easily identify as Edith is speaking far too loud about the king's habits. A few people turn to glare at her, not wanting to be in trouble for speaking ill of the king.

I reach the large oak doors that sit open, revealing the library inside. The setting sun causes me to squint into the mostly empty room, save for a single person reading at a small, square table. I avoid the figure reading on the opposite end as I step further in.

The room is shaped like an oval and reaches three stories high. In the middle of the tall room, a place for a window has been carved out of the ceiling, filled with colored glass in a mosaic pattern. When the sun is out, I can imagine the floor below would shimmer with different shapes when the light hits it the right way.

Ladders to reach the higher shelves are stationed all around, and there's a narrow spiraling staircase to take me to each floor. I can see myself spending most of my days here, amid the quietness of dusty books, stuck between stiff pages. Not surprisingly, people in the castle do just about everything other than spend time in the library, which makes it a perfect place for me to be.

There have to be hundreds of books on maps of each territory in the kingdom and who owns the land. Beyond that, there are likely even books about the Kingdom of Penyth and its territories as well. Doesn't hurt to add to the items to learn on my list. Libraries are a rarity; most houses would be lucky to have even one book in them. Some of the nobles hardly have more than a handful.

I need something to help me familiarize myself with my own kingdom. Spending my entire life in the same camp and only ever venturing to the market or the few closest towns didn't give me much room to learn what lies beyond.

I walk toward the nearest shelf, running my fingers along their spines and admiring how well-made they are. Even with the darkness of evening, I can see how the wealth of the castle has benefited this specific room.

"Following me now, Ramsey?"

I jump, never hearing him near me. I spin around, annoyed at how often he shows up without me realizing it.

"No," I snap. "I don't creep around in the shadows trying to follow people. But you seem to have that fully handled."

Graylen raises a single brow at me, intrigued. "Then what exactly is it you're doing in the darkness of the library?"

"Exploring."

His lips curl into a cruel smile. Mischief swirls behind his eyes, which are wholly fixed on me. "No one explores the library unless they plan to meet another on the abandoned third floor. I can guarantee you that reading is not what they intend to do."

Even with the room devoid of light, I can see his eyes darken.

"And I'm sure you know each and every one of those places around the castle."

"Would you like for me to show you?"

My breathing hitches. He reaches forward and grazes his knuckle against my hand. The image of him grabbing my hand and leading me up the winding staircases to the third level crosses my mind. I let out a laugh, causing him to smirk. I'm taking too long to respond, and the look in his gaze suggests he's well aware of where my mind has drifted.

"Actually no, I prefer to be alone. But please, don't let me stop you from whatever deplorable acts you were about to commit." Heat dances across my cheeks.

He takes a step toward me, and I find myself gravitating toward him.

"Deplorable? You're giving me a complex." He's mocking me.

"You did that all on your own."

"I'm starting to think you just don't get me."

"And I'm wondering if you know yourself well at all."

His smile loosens, and I immediately wish it would return.

He turns to the bookcase to pluck a book off its shelf. He taps the cover hard, like it's evidence. "They say don't judge a book by its cover, you know. Tattoos and black clothes don't make me a villain, just like your gowns don't turn a soldier into a princess. You would change your mind if you got to know me."

He thinks I'm judging him because of his tattoos. Is he serious?

I can't stop myself from laughing. He looks surprised by my reaction, like he can't imagine what he's said that's funny, but he waits for me to explain.

"I think you're full of yourself." My voice comes out breathy with laughter.

His voice lowers, causing my insides to twist. "I might be arrogant, but the same could be said when you assume so much about someone you barely know."

"I've seen plenty."

He tilts his head to the side, studying me. It's as if he can't help but get under my skin. "No, you haven't."

He steps toward me again and I spin around, my back to the bookshelf. He leans forward, crowding my space with his size. His gaze lowers to my mouth.

"Amira?"

A pair of shoes claps against the stone floor. We both turn; Adrian's standing at the entrance of the library. A guard comes from behind him and begins lighting sconces on the walls, the room instantly brightening with the glow.

I shake my head. I'm already losing my mind in this castle.

Graylen reaches above me to slide the book back into place. He takes a step away from me, the moment now gone and replaced with something else. Not that there *was* a moment, because this is Graylen. Judging by the smirk on his face, he was trying to get a reaction from me. Spinning his charm to see where it could get him.

Adrian walks closer and looks between the two of us. Together. In the dark. Tension crackles in the air. I open my mouth, but Graylen beats me to it.

"Good evening. Tired of being a prince for the day already?"

The two smile at each other as Adrian shoves Graylen playfully. Their friendship is more apparent without so many people around, the tension easing.

"Slinking in the darkness as usual, brother?"

The use of the word causes Graylen to roll his eyes, but the small smirk on his face is the closest thing I've seen to a genuine smile from him yet.

"Amira, good evening," Adrian says. "Please excuse this rude and less-than-pleasant person to be around."

The two boys laugh, and I watch them, fascinated. Adrian's light words don't match his posture. He looks stiff and formal.

"Now, I know you don't want to hear this right now. I met two earls who wouldn't drive you completely insane. You should speak with them."

He knows there's no chance of me being interested in anyone here. Even as the thought crosses my mind, I find myself looking down at my feet, not wanting to look at Adrian as he goes on.

"I know their families fairly well; they would make for decent husbands, I think."

I glance at Graylen, whose face is neutral. Adrian likely already told Graylen about our visits in the market. I wonder what else he's told him.

"You should give it a try, Amira. You'll have to get engaged at some point." As Adrian says the last part, he grimaces slightly, like it pained him to say it.

Maybe Adrian doesn't think of me as more than a friend. Helping me leave the camp is something a friend would do, setting me up to be matched with another man is something *only* a friend would do. I swallow my feelings; I can't be angry at him for the suggestion. That's what everyone was invited here for, after all.

"Amira?"

I try to hide the emotions broiling inside. He's the prince—how could I ever expect anything more? His offer to introduce me to a possible suitor is all that I need to finally begin making plans to leave, anyway. I just have to find a way to buy some time while everyone around me is getting engaged.

"I'll consider it," I say suddenly, forcing a smile.

I was fooling myself with Adrian. I needed to focus on what mattered. Freedom.

SEVENTEEN

IBERIS

"Ladies! When I chime the bell it's time for you to move to your next suitor. Remember to tell them anything you feel is important, as you'll only have a few moments to do so before moving on to the next person."

The women's faces around me convey a wide range of emotions.

"We'll get to talk to so many of them," someone next to me whispers, an eager smile lighting up her face.

"Maybe I can talk to Sir Nicholas finally," another from my left says.

More light laughter sounds from the women until the person leading this little game spins around, a cold look aimed at us to silence ourselves.

"Think they'll have food for us later? I'm starving." I laugh, my stomach threatening to grumble noisily at the thought of food.

"You may begin."

Everyone hurriedly finds a place to sit in front of each suitor. All the men are lined up and seated at small stations, set far enough apart that we can speak comfortably without hearing the person next to us. The instructor walks over to me, giving me a small nudge to join the rest of the group as they make their introductions.

I see Sir Christopher's station and quickly turn in the opposite direction, hoping I can position myself to avoid him during this game. I reluctantly walk over to the only other empty station, where a boy with a thick head of dark hair smiles widely at me, pleased to have someone in front of him. What looks to be a leaf of cabbage is currently clinging desperately to his front tooth, and I try to not grimace.

"Hello, my name is Sir Frederick. Son of Lord Richard Hughes." He stares at me expectantly, waiting for my response as he fights a losing battle of keeping his eyes on my face instead of my chest.

"Amira Ramsey."

His smile falls, obscuring my view of the cabbage still attached to his tooth. A bead of sweat slowly trickles down his forehead and rounded cheek. He absentmindedly begins rubbing at his wrist, running his hands over a thick scar that encircles it.

"Do I know you from somewhere?" I ask. He looks familiar the longer I sit in front of him, but he quickly shakes his head.

"N-no," he stammers as he pushes his chair back, preparing to rise, his face now leeched of its color.

"I'm almost certain I've seen you before."

He shakes his head again and looks from side to side, trying to escape the conversation. Great, my first one of the day and he already wants to run away screaming. I've been more productive than I thought.

He touches his wrist again, and a memory flashes through my mind of a few years past. A boy strikingly similar to the one in front of me snuck into the camp one evening. He was dressed in fine enough clothes that I knew he wasn't a beggar. I watched curiously from my laundry washing as he crept to the dog pen, snickering with another boy. He ran up to the gate and opened it, running away as the dogs spilled out, and made a beeline to the cook's station to find something to eat. Two soldiers caught him on the way out as my father approached them, but his friend got away. I never figured out what happened to them.

A piercing chime sounds to indicate it's time to move to the next person. The boy visibly relaxes, his shoulders losing tension as they slump down. I throw an apologetic look at him as I stand to move to the next station.

The next boy is one I've seen around the castle but have never interacted with. I sit there as he drones on about his father Lord So-and-So, and his great friend Lord Something-or-Other.

"Where did you say you were from?"

I didn't say, because he never asked. Just like he had yet to ask my name.

"Prince's End." I smile at the lie. Maybe I could have fun with this speedy game of meeting suitors.

"Really? Who do you know from there? I know quite a few lords and ladies there."

Of course he does.

I search for a lie, knowing I have no answer. "I keep to myself mostly."

He nods, accepting this answer as the bell chimes.

The next boy looks hardly old enough to be anyone's husband, his thin arms rubbing at his big, bored eyes. At least I wasn't fully alone in that regard today.

"Can we just pretend we talked and stuff?"

I laugh at his question, finally not minding the person sitting across from me. He'd be the perfect younger brother.

"I'd rather be cooking in the kitchens than doing this right now."

He returns my laughter and looks relieved. "They've made us do so many strange things to meet others here."

I nod and make a mental note to stop and speak with him if I see him around again. "Only offer your hand if it's what you want. You'll find someone."

He smiles at this, relief washing over his young face.

"What's your name?"

"Emilio. You can call me Milo." I remember Avery telling me about him. "You're Amira?" He doesn't shy away from speaking with me. I like that about him.

"Nice to meet you, Milo. If you ever need to escape someone trying to wed you, the library is usually empty."

His grin widens, making him look even younger.

The bell chimes once again, and we say our goodbyes. We're not even halfway through yet.

"Sarah!" I wave her over, her smile timid but relieved to see someone she knows. True to her word, she's wearing a new dress, this one fashionably decorated and fitting her small frame perfectly.

"You should sit with Milo next; he seems really nice."

She glances sidelong at him, bringing her nails to her mouth. They have to be fairly close in age. She takes a deep breath and walks over to his seat, forcing her hands at her side and gripping her dress. He says something to make her laugh, and I smile.

There are far too many suitors left. I'm so lost in trying to count how many are left, I miss the person sitting right in front of me.

"Isn't this my favorite kind of surprise."

I jerk my head toward the voice, taking in Graylen's relaxed posture against the chair. Both of his hands rest in his pockets as he leans casually back.

I should've picked any other station. "Torture any commoners today?" I ask, falsely upbeat with a sickly-sweet smile on my face.

"I love it when you speak to me like that."

My smile dissolves. I narrow my eyes at him, seeing through his fake charm. "Does that line ever actually work?"

His laugh comes out breathy and quiet. "I've gotten no complaints."

Or so he says.

"Keep telling yourself that. Could it be they're wanting to use you to get closer to the prince?"

My question is met with silence as he leans forward in the chair, bringing his ink-covered arms to rest on the table separating us. His dark hair falls into his eyes with the movement, though he seems unbothered and makes no move to fix it.

"Tell me, Amira. What is your favorite color?"

Is he *serious?* That's his important question?

"Why are you even here, Graylen? Didn't you say you aren't looking to be matched?" He shrugs, not openly admitting anything. "Or do you just like to annoy people because you have nothing better to do?"

"Specialty round!" comes a call from the front of the room. "Enjoy a few extended moments with your current partner!"

I fight against the urge to throw the closest object at the announcer. Graylen's eyes remain fixed on me, studying my every movement.

"Care to join me in the gardens later?" He leans forward more, and I lean back.

"No, thanks." I cross my arms.

Instead of looking offended, he laughs.

We spend the rest of the round in a silent competition, neither of us willing to speak first. I'm not entirely sure how this particular feud began, but I wasn't going to lose, sitting upright with my spine locked straight and jaw set. Graylen remains lounging against his chair as if there's no place he'd rather be.

The bell finally chimes, and I bolt out of my chair, eager to be away from him. All the girls stand and shuffle to the next station, slightly less energetic than they were when we started. A tall, slender girl I recognize breezes past. Her smooth, dark skin glows against her unforgettably bright hair.

"This is the worst, isn't it?" Addie winks, her whispered annoyance catching me so off guard that I stop between stations. Knowing that there's another woman here who might not enjoy this as much as everyone else gives me a brief moment of ease.

The man waiting clears his throat, bringing my attention back to the game. I smile, feeling like I can fake it just a while longer to make it to the end of this event.

"I understand that your father is a highly respected member of the king's council, though I apologize it isn't the match my family would have in mind..." His excuses about why he wouldn't want to match with me drone on, but my mind drifts away from them.

I watch Addie giving an unimpressed tilt of her head at her partner a few stations down. Her pair is animatedly telling a story, paying no mind to her response. Beside her, Sarah sits with Milo still; the two both have splotches of red splashing across their cheeks.

At least someone in this castle likes me.

EIGHTEEN

CORIANDER

"LULU, SWEETIE, YOUR SISTER IS sorry." She brushes away the tears that are streaming down my little face. I wanted to look like her. Everyone loves her.

"No, she's not. I just wanted to borrow her clothes, so I would look like her. Why did she get so mad?" I cry harder and look down at my muddy clothes.

"You can't take someone's things without asking them, sweetie. You should've asked her permission. She shouldn't have pushed you down, but you can't steal her things." She pats my bed and I lie down as she pulls the warm covers over me.

"But I was going to give them back!"

She shushes me and scolds me for raising my voice at her.

"Taking someone's things without asking—even if you were planning on returning—is still stealing. How would you like it if she took your flower from the window without talking to you first?"

She doesn't understand. That's different. That's special to me. My sister has hundreds of clothes that she only wears once and never touches again.

Instead, I just nod my head and close my eyes while she smooths my hair over my face. She hums a soft song about a girl going on a great adventure.

As soon as I feel myself drifting into sleep, the door creaks open. I freeze, my hand slowly reaching for the knife hidden beneath my pillow. My eyes remain closed as I hear boots scuff on the floor. This person is skilled, but not silent enough to avoid my notice. I feel my stomach clench as the boots near my head, keeping myself still until I can catch the intruder unaware.

The figure creeps closer to my bed, and I jolt upright with my knife aimed in the direction of the noise. But I'm met with an empty room. I whip my head to the side, slowly searching the chambers for anything out of place. I find nothing. My heart pounds against my chest. I rub my hand over it to steady its painful rhythm.

I must've been half asleep, dreaming someone was in my room. I lower the knife but hold it in my hand as I scoot back to rest against the bedframe. Now I'll never go back to sleep.

With my knife clutched in my fist and my back against the wooden frame, I stay this way until the room glows with the rising sun.

Only when a soft knock sounds on the door and Linnick steps in do I find myself relaxing. He's carrying a tray of steaming tea and biscuits, the cup chattering on the tray with his unsteady hands. He looks over to me, stopping when his eyes zero in on the knife in my grip.

"Lu?" He takes a tentative step forward, concern creasing his forehead as he sets the breakfast tray on my lounging seat.

"I'm going crazy here, Linnick. I need to get out," I whisper through clenched teeth, knowing how deranged I must look with my hair sticking out in all directions and a blade in my hand.

He takes a seat on the lounging chair, silently assessing me. "What makes you feel like that?"

Linnick's calm presence relaxes me almost instantly.

"For starters, I feel as if marriage is being shoved down my throat here. Even with my father not being around, his influence is still evident in the introductions he's orchestrated." A shiver rolls down my spine. Not to mention the people he's paid to be his eyes here. I look out the window, toward the market now filling with travelers and sellers.

"And on top of that, the men are insufferable! *Especially* Graylen. He's rude, arrogant, and only cares about himself," I huff out.

"I see. Then should we find an opening to leave?"

I nod, knowing there's no clear answer as to how to make that happen.

"We'll figure it out," Linnick murmurs. "Just hang in there."

I breathe in unsteadily through my nose and release it through my mouth.

Another knock at the door makes Linnick jump to his feet and grab the breakfast tray.

Avery slips in, looking well-rested and relaxed. "Good morning, miss."

I tilt my head at her, her good mood infectious. "You look well today, Avery."

She smiles. "I was able to stay with some of my friends in town last night. It was a very pleasant visit."

At least one of us got some sleep.

"Your father passed a message through one of the other servants and will be here tomorrow. He would like to speak with you at the introduction banquet."

I nearly lay back down on the bed and cover myself with blankets. At the *what?*

"He said he'll have Sir Christopher with him when he arrives. He's eager for the two of you to make things official from the sound of it."

I wince. Suddenly Avery's smile is nowhere to be found.

"Sounds like we don't have long to come up with something. I'll try to come back tonight," Linnick whispers, giving me a sympathetic look.

"What's an introduction banquet?" I dare to ask.

Linnick's smile is nothing short of a slice of courage for what he's about to tell me. "A banquet is being thrown tomorrow night in the gardens. I believe it's to give the guests a chance to mingle and meet one another."

I groan loudly, like a child stomping their feet and crossing their arms.

"Lovely," I mumble softly to myself.

Linnick pats my back, the most reassurance I'll get from him as he leaves.

Avery helps me dress, her brows furrowed. Her silence is out of place for her. I don't pry, knowing how much sharing my own thoughts makes me uncomfortable.

"Do you need a nap before you begin your day?" she asks.

I must look more tired than I thought. I shake my head, even though I'd like to say yes. I pull my leather pouch out of my pocket and pinch some powder into my morning tea. The floral flavor of the steaming tea thankfully chases away the bitter medicine.

I spend the rest of the day hiding out in the library, reading book after book, looking for some clue on how to escape my situation. I'm close to tossing my current one across the room when the doors open in front of me. I watch as Adrian comes in, muttering to himself and completely unaware of my presence.

I study him a moment as he walks in and paces in front of a bookshelf. He's turned from the books, clearly here for some time alone to clear his thoughts, rather than to read. His blond hair is messy like he ran his hands through it a time or two. His brown eyes squint and widen as his lips move unintelligibly, still talking even though no one's there.

Unable to take my eyes away from him, I lean back in my chair. I recline further and feel the legs wobble as my world tilts, a small yelp leaving my throat as the chair falls backward. I hear a curse and look up.

Adrian is hovering above me.

"Lu? Are you okay?"

Embarrassment prickles at my neck as he helps me off the ground. I rub the back of my head and feel my cheeks redden at his concerned gaze.

"Um, yes." I wince at the pain.

Adrian steps closer to inspect the back of my head. "Do you mind?"

I shake my head, the motion causing me to grimace. His frown deepens with concern, his face scrunching as he closely examines me. His fingers are gentle as they comb my hair aside, careful to not cause me more pain.

"No blood, that's a good sign. I'll call for a healer to be sent in." Adrian begins moving away from me, but I quickly grab his arm.

"I'm fine, I promise."

His brown eyes seem torn between doing as I ask and going to find a real healer to look at my head. Something in my face must be convincing enough because he nods and doesn't move away.

"What are you doing in here?" he asks.

I look down at the piles of books scattered across the table. I chew on the inside of my cheek, not sure if I should be honest with him or not.

"Hey, we're friends, remember? And friends tell each other things. Whatever you're thinking, it's safe with me."

I look back at him, a confident smile spread wide across his face.

"It's complicated."

He nods, knowing that with me, most things are. He sits down slowly, his hand resting in mine as he guides me to sit beside him.

"My father will be at the introduction banquet tomorrow,"

At these words, Adrian stiffens. Clearly he doesn't like the idea of my father being near any more than I do.

"Why?" He asks tightly.

I shrug, unsure. I don't know myself.

"You can hang around with me tomorrow night. I doubt he'd say anything in my presence."

I smile weakly, hoping he's right. I turn to face him, his dimples momentarily gone as he studies my face for any signs of distress.

"Thank you."

At this, his dimples return. We face each other in our chairs, our knees bumping into each other at the slightest movement.

He reaches forward and gently touches the back of my head, tentatively checking it again for any bleeding. I watch the concentration in his eyes, the light hitting them golden and bright. His gaze trails from my hair to my ear, down my jaw, and lands on my mouth.

I can feel my lips part in surprise as he leans closer toward me. He shakes his head slightly and returns his gaze to meet mine, his breath shallow. His mouth opens to speak, but I cut him off, too afraid of what he might say.

"Do you ever dream about your mother?" I don't know why that's the only thing I could think to say.

His face shifts into a look of surprise, his eyebrows raising. "Sometimes, but not often. I have a hard time remembering what she looks like." He looks down, his voice quiet.

"Me too," I say and, not wanting to explore it further, I stand from my chair. "Save a dance for me tomorrow night?"

The moment I'm on my feet, he follows suit. He nods and smiles softly, no dimples in sight. "Of course, Lu."

Hearing that name come from him causes my heart to speed rapidly inside my chest, so loud I'm afraid he can hear its beat.

He walks me back to my chambers without another word. We both remain silent on the short trek, his hands clasped loosely behind his back.

Nineteen

Gladiolus

I sit on my bed, my leg bouncing furiously while I wait on Avery to help me dress for the day. I already washed, gulped down my tonic, and picked out a pale green dress to wear to tonight's banquet. At least it was being set up in the gardens. Hopefully I could escape into them and get lost in the maze while everyone else paraded around inside. I haven't had the chance to see them at night since they get locked at sundown.

My father will be here soon, and Sir Christopher's proposal hangs over my head like an axe preparing to swing. I stand up and walk over to the window, doing anything to keep occupied for the moment.

My door swings open, and I feel my body stiffen at the sound.

"Lady Amira." Avery shuffles in holding a large box in her hands. She walks over and lays it gently down on my lounging seat, carefully unwrapping it for me. "A present from the prince." She flicks her gaze to me, a knowing smile playing across her face.

"What is it?" I can't help the excitement that is laced within the question.

Her bright eyes wink at me as she waves me over. "I think you'll like this one."

I peer over her shoulder at the present lying inside of the wrapping. A shimmery violet dress sits perfectly folded inside. I pick it up to inspect it. It's delicate and soft, composed of a rich, silky material. The light from the window dances off the sparkles that encase the dress.

"*Everyone* will look at me in this dress, Avery." My excitement fades into dread as I realize what wearing something like this would mean. It's far more elegant than anything I've ever owned before. The material is so light in my fingertips, if I closed my eyes, I could almost convince myself I was holding nothing.

"I think that's the point, miss."

I drop the dress, suddenly feeling like my lungs are collapsing and the room is far smaller than it was just a moment ago. I sit heavily down, and Avery comes to my side, rubbing my back in soothing circular motions.

"It's just one night, miss. Many people will pair up after tonight's festivities. There's bound to be a large plant or two you can hide behind."

I turn to look at her, my face a wild mixture of shock and amusement.

She winks at me, and I notice for the first time that her hair is beautifully braided into a ring around her head. Each piece is carefully woven together.

"I'll wear the dress if you can braid my hair like that," I say.

She beams at the compliment and begins working quickly on my hair. "It might take the majority of the day."

I nod, thankful to have her company until the banquet. "Any advice on how to avoid offers tonight?"

She snorts a laugh and brushes my hair tenderly. "May I speak freely?"

I nod my head quickly, sadness filling my chest that she had to ask that question at all.

"Most of the men here are looking for women to fall at their feet. The higher you hold your head, the less likely they are to approach you."

I smile. I knew I liked her for a reason.

"You're strong, miss, I sense that about you. Sometimes you just have to play their games long enough to get what you want."

She's right about that. This all seems like one big puzzle I have to place just the right way to make it out how I want to.

"Only you can decide your future, you just have to be strong enough to take control of it." Avery is wise far beyond her years. Her pale skin is smooth of any wrinkles, her wide eyes thoughtful and observant.

I smile at her, this time a real and genuine smile. She continues working on my hair until the sun begins to lower in the sky.

"Let's get you dressed. The faster you get to this banquet, the earlier you can leave."

I laugh, her words easing the tightness that's been building in my chest.

The dress falls perfectly against my body. The skirt ends just before it hits the ground, giving me room to move without tripping. I lift my arms up and twirl side to side, testing the movement. It sways, flowing easily, but not too much. It catches each ray of sun that touches it, casting reflecting lights against the walls of my chambers.

This dress is the *opposite* of avoiding attention.

Avery nods her head at me, smiling, a pleased look gleaming in her bright eyes. She reaches up and adjusts the fabric loop that hangs off my shoulders, the lack of sleeves making me feel uncertain.

"The banquet will begin soon, miss." She slips flat leather shoes onto my feet, the comfort of them releasing my nerves slightly.

I smile gratefully toward her, glad to be in something other than the usual painful heels I've been wearing for events.

"I can't attend with you, but I can at least walk with you there. I'll understand if you need to let out a scream or two." She winks at me, and my nervous laughter rises in my throat.

She gives my hand a quick squeeze as we walk side by side down the corridor. The closer we get to the ground floor, the more people begin to fill the hallways with us. An excited energy buzzes through the growing crowd. I cross my fingers, wishing for time to stretch, but we arrive quickly. For once, the walk feels shorter than usual.

The standard guards are stationed at the entrance to the gardens. I nod a hello to them—without a response—and hold my breath as the doors are pushed open. I feel an edge of excitement mix with the nerves, curious to see what the gardens look like beneath the starry night sky.

The moment the night air breezes over me, I feel my lungs expanding, finally able to breathe fully. I almost didn't notice the structure that had been built in the center of the gardens. My nerves blur the world around me into a smudge.

I blink several times, turning to the sound of laughter and whistling instruments. The stars shine brightly above, twinkling and dancing in the unusually clear night. Not a single cloud covers their glinting routine.

Brighter than the stars, and even the full, round moon, the light emitting from the structure is almost blinding. From here I can see the building is made entirely of glass, giving a clear view to the banquet that is well underway inside.

For a moment, I forget the panic rising in me about the impending engagement announcement tonight. The closer I get to the glass building, the more entranced I become. A wooden flute weaves a strange tune, the stars above seemingly swaying to it.

The garden theme is continued inside the translucent building. The entrance is a wide opening that lets the cool air inside, giving the feeling of being outside even among the close quarters of the space. Plants of all shapes and sizes line the floors, and hundreds of small lanterns hang from the ceiling, causing a flickering light to ricochet off onto the party below.

I stand in awe for a moment as I take in the happiness plastered onto the partygoers' faces. Guests dance to the winding song, string instruments slowly joining the melody.

"Lovely, isn't it?" Avery interrupts my reverie.

I smile because she's right. "I wish you could join me. You'd certainly make for a better dance partner."

She laughs at the idea, knowing we'd get an endless sea of odd looks if we danced together.

Much to my disappointment, I find someone waiting for me by the entrance of the building. Standing beside the guards, but not interacting with them in the slightest, is Sir Christopher.

He walks over, ready to take Avery's place at my side, his tight red curls fixed snuggly to his head. He smiles slowly, his eyes traveling across the planes of my dress. It's the kind of smile that makes me want to run back into my chambers and slam the door behind me. Or to take my shoe off and hurl it at his red curls.

"Your father sent me to accompany you tonight. I must say it's the highlight of my stay thus far."

Avery clears her throat beside me, reminding us she's still present. "Enjoy your evening, miss."

Sir Christopher's gaze swings to her, his eyes narrowing and nose wrinkling. I expect her to be embarrassed at his sneering, but instead she holds her head high and smiles a tight-lipped goodbye to me.

He holds his arm out and I reluctantly take it, knowing there isn't a good enough excuse to deny it. I fix my gaze on the party. Out of the corner of my eye, I can see he has no qualms about openly staring at my chest. I bite the inside of my cheek, biding my time until the moment I can extract myself from this boy without it getting back to my father.

"Accompanying you tonight isn't the only thing that's made this the peak of my time here," Sir Christopher intones.

I grind my teeth together to remain silent as the doors are opened for us.

"Would you like to know why I'm so pleased?"

I really don't.

"I know you said you had to think about my offer for marriage, but your father has already approved it. We'll be the first to be matched of this entire event; your father suggested this event to the king so it could be announced." He leans in closely as we walk, his voice low and causing the hairs on the back of my neck to stand on end.

I jerk my head away from him, not realizing how close he was to me. So near to me that our noses were almost touching.

"No." The word leaves my lips without a thought, coming out in a gasp.

I am *not* going to marry this boy. Someone who so easily did whatever my father suggested.

"I'm afraid it's already set in motion," Sir Christopher drawls. "I'll give you a few moments to soak in the happiness of what's to come."

My throat closes tightly; I'm left sipping on short breaths as I try to process what could be done to escape this. He doesn't fight me as I drop my arm away from his, but simply steps forward with a slimy smile on his face.

"Sir Christopher! Join in on our night's bet!" A group of boys calls him over and he walks away without another word. The boys laugh, passing around various items of value as they traded bets.

The further he places space between us, the more the world around me adjusts into clarity. Father wasted no time in finding me a match, giving me less time than I thought to try and find a way out of Runnswick. I've wasted too much time since arriving here.

A wave of panic crashes into me at the thought. Sir Christopher, walking with the group of boys who called him away earlier, throws a smirk back at me. Dread winds low in my gut, my food from earlier threatening to come back up.

"You look wonderful."

I whirl around, not able to place the voice, my fear coating my senses.

Adrian takes a step closer, his hand reaching to gently cradle my elbow. His thumb slowly traces over my skin, gradually bringing my mind back down to the earth.

"Thank you for this." I run my hand down the silky material of the dress. "It's more than I can ask for." My voice comes out wrong. Shaky and soft. I don't mention how it's *much* more than I wanted. But the reminder of it having been a present, that he had gone out of his way to send it to me, is so kind I can barely mention it.

"What's wrong?"

I look up into his soft brown eyes, concern welling within them as he awaits my answer. His face is smooth and so unlike the roughness that mars the men at the camp—no scars or frosty winter nights to dampen the luster of his skin.

"My father is here tonight to—" I take an unsteady breath, my arms shaking in his warm grasp.

"You can tell me, Lu. You can tell me anything. That's what we agreed to when we became friends, right?" He quietly leads me to an empty corner of the room.

I look back out at the crowd, worried they'll take too much interest in our closeness. But the guests are already intoxicated with enjoying the evening—drinking, eating, and dancing with one another. Once we are safely nestled away from everyone else, I take another steadying breath.

"My father is here to announce my engagement tonight."

Adrian's concern grows tenfold, his eyebrows drawing together. "Your *engagement*? To whom?" Even with his voice just above a whisper I can hear the frustration in it, and a part of me is grateful he knows how unhappy I must feel.

"Sir Christopher Lander."

Adrian's eyes narrow at the name. His shoulders stiffen as he runs his hand roughly through his hair. "He's just a baron—why would your father suggest him? There's plenty of others here that have more money and higher positions. More than that, there's quite a bit more that aren't as seedy as he is."

I shrug, knowing that my father likely has a specific plan in mind. "Once he says it in front of others, I won't be able to take it back." I clench my jaw, feeling stuck.

"We have to do something about this," Adrian says. "I won't let you marry him. The things I've heard…" This time it's his jaw clenching; I can practically hear his teeth grinding.

The only way out of this is to run away—not an option—or to convince others I'm already promised to another. Which I'm not. But if I were…

"What if I were already engaged?" I stand upright, an idea building. The words rush out of me, tumbling from my lips in excitement.

"But you aren't?"

I take a small step closer to him, offering a conspiratorial smile. "But if I *was*, then I couldn't be engaged to Sir Christopher."

He nods, understanding that part but not putting together the rest. Suddenly his nodding ceases, his eyes widening. I tap my fingers lightly against my dress, waiting for him to speak and tell me how absurd this is.

"If I were to be promised to someone else..." I trail off, uncertain.

"I'll help you." His voice is so quiet that I almost think I've heard him wrong. His dimples deepen from the depth of the smile that spreads across his face. The smile, eager and bright, brings me back to the port, to the market boy who became my friend.

"You will?"

He nods and pulls me into a tight embrace, his arms wrapping around me in a warm cocoon. "I would do anything you asked of me, Lu."

I smile into his chest, thankful he can't see the silly grin I'm now wearing. His arms tighten a fraction as he rests his chin on my head, the perfect height to set it on top.

A brief tug of hesitation raps against my chest. The sinking feeling that I want this for a different reason than he might leaves me confused. He wants to help me, he always has. But is it more than that for him? He's a *prince*. Meaning one day he would be king, and if this was followed through to the end, then I would be queen. I shiver, the thought scattering fear down my spine.

"I would be honored." His words warm my heart, momentarily soothing the turmoil coursing through me. It may take some convincing, but who could oppose him?

"Let's introduce you to my father."

He drops his arms and steps away from me, the absence of his comfort leaving me cold.

I walk alongside him as he sidesteps everyone trying to stop and speak with him. We don't have any time to waste as we race against my father's announcement. The king is seated across the room from us, leaning heavily against a large wooden chair. Duke Wyman stands to his right, pouring what looks to be wine into his cup. We squeeze through the crowd, and I hold my breath the entire way until we make it to him.

"Father," Adrian begins, "you said you'd like to meet Ramsey's daughter. Lady Amira, daughter of the royal merchant."

King Avalon's gaze roams around before he finally realizes Adrian is speaking to him.

"Your Majesty." I bow deeply as I hear the king draining the contents of his cup. I rise back up, looking to Adrian with uncertainty. He nods, smiling at me with a confidence I don't fully feel.

King Avalon briefly acknowledges me before turning unsteadily toward the duke, motioning for him to speak as he looks back out at the crowd with unfocused eyes.

"Good evening, Lady Amira. Prince Adrian." The duke bows to Adrian, his age more prominent with the youthfulness of the room. Though he's much shorter than Adrian, the platform he stands on allows him to tower over us.

"What a celebration tonight is turning into," the king slurs happily.

"Oh, yes," adds Duke Wyman, "I suppose congratulations are in order, Prince Adrian."

Adrian and I share a worried glance. How could he already know of our plan?

"Uncle, what—" Adrian attempts to ask.

"Ah, Sir Graylen!" Duke Wyman interrupts.

Graylen comes to my other side, nodding his head at Adrian and ignoring the duke. I take a small step toward Adrian, feeling crowded by his towering height, a move that does not go unnoticed by the Prince's Snake.

"What are you talking about, Wyman?" Adrian's voice is clipped as he speaks to him, sounding more like a prince than the boy from the market.

Graylen looks between the two, watching with building interest.

Duke Wyman preens. "On your engagement to the princess of Penyth, of course."

The breath knocks out of my chest. I feel Adrian startle beside me, leaning on my arm for support.

"Did your father forget to tell you?"

I suck in a quick breath, immediately coughing uncontrollably and drawing unwanted attention. I can feel the anger radiating from Adrian beside me. All I can do is stand there as my perfect plan dissolves into pieces before it even truly took form.

"What do you mean?" Adrian's voice is so loud it causes the king to take notice of us, almost surprised we're still standing in front of him. As if he doesn't remember our presence.

"You must be Ramsey's daughter! You look just like him." The king roars with laughter, his round belly jostling with the movement, our brief introduction already forgotten. "He told me you are engaged as well—cheers to whomever it is." He lifts his drink into the air before finishing what was left of it.

Did Father tell him who it was, and he forgot? Or did Father simply just tell him to announce my engagement?

"You're engaged as well, Lady Amira?" The duke studies me.

I shift on my feet, heat spreading across my cheeks as I stumble for something to say. "I, yes, but—" My words meld together as I look around, desperate to find an answer that I don't have.

"Well? Who are you engaged to?" The king is watching us too, his attention free now that his cup is empty.

"Um…"

The duke raises an eyebrow, waiting for me to answer him. Adrian clears his throat, trying to buy me a moment of time, but falling as short as I am.

Suddenly Graylen takes a step closer to my side, winding his arm casually around my waist. I almost jerk away from his touch, but his words stop me.

"She's to be my wife." Graylen's face is a mask of calm.

I almost laugh at the words, positive he isn't serious. I open my mouth to tell him I am *not* engaged to him, but again I'm stopped as he turns his piercing green eyes to face me and winks.

A mischievous smirk dances on his lips. His declaration reminds of me Evans, of how he used me to get closer to my father. The memory threatens to stop my heart in this very moment—a ploy to use me, freezing me to my spot. But wouldn't I be using him too?

I stiffly turn back to the duke, his eyes bouncing between us, looking every bit as skeptical as I feel. I at least know what Graylen is capable of, but whatever my father is planning with Sir Christopher is a mystery.

"*Two* engagements to celebrate tonight! Musicians!" The king stands on teetering feet, the duke quick to steady him. The musicians quickly cease their playing, allowing the king to speak.

Adrian looks sick.

"It's with great excitement that I announce two matches tonight! The success of this event already coming to fruition."

I turn to face the crowd and see my father stepping easily through as the guests make space for him. Sir Christopher earns several glares as he bumps into people and shoves them aside.

"I'd like to congratulate Lady Amira personally on being one of the first to meet her royally sanctioned match. May the two of you be blessed for years to come! The combining of these two houses is a wonderful start to strengthening our kingdom!"

Sir Christopher visibly beams at the king's words.

For once, the king speaks at length instead of his short and confused bursts of speeches. By the time he's finished, my father and Sir Christopher are an arm's length from us, readying themselves for what they think is their announcement. Sir Christopher takes a step forward, my father looking particularly pleased with the attention we're getting.

"Sir Graylen Garriden and Lady Amira Ramsey! A match I couldn't have made better myself!" The king laughs joyously as he plops heavily back down in the chair, his allotted clarity all used up for the night. He motions once more for the duke to continue his speech for him as a servant fills his cup.

My father's hands are folded calmly behind him, his face doing little to give away the storm brewing inside. The room begins to fill with whispers reflecting off the glass walls and crashing back into me. The only thing keeping me upright is Graylen's arm still securely wrapped around my waist, as much as that thought brings a chill down my spine.

"Father, forgive him for not finding you sooner. It all happened so fast. Graylen proposed just this morning."

Graylen remains unmovable beside me. I still don't understand why he's going along with this.

"But—" Sir Christopher's voice rises an octave, nearing a whine. His body twists to my father, silently pleading him to do something.

My father's nostrils flare briefly, his annoyance beginning to show on his face.

Graylen's face slips into a slow smile. "There's a first for everything, Christopher."

I nearly laugh at how Sir Christopher's face turns bright red. I look at my father, his eyes narrowed, mouth pinched tightly.

"Then I believe congratulations are in order." Father nods his head in our direction, remaining composed, as I knew he would with an audience.

I try to keep my face from revealing my excitement at his acceptance, not yet allowing myself to think about the implications.

I notice the entire room is watching our exchange, their scrutiny causing my stomach to clench. They're going to watch Graylen and me constantly. But watching my father force himself to smile and congratulate me is almost worth their scrutiny. I let myself forget for a moment what the consequences might be if Father finds out about this ruse. About all the ways I can't slip up going forward— that his spies would let him know in a heartbeat if Graylen and I looked like we were faking it. For now I'm just relieved. I'll have to mourn my alone time in the library later.

My gaze flickers to Adrian. He's watching me, a hint of resentment stirring within his eyes. He looks like the cold, stoic prince I couldn't recognize. I try to smile at him but find it difficult, uncomfortable with the thought of how much I wish it were him beside me instead.

Like it always does, my dream is turning into another nightmare.

TWENTY

LEUCANTHEMUM

Duke Wyman steps forward, clearing his throat and trying to gain the attention of the crowd once more. The rumors have already begun to circulate the room, the guests trying to piece together how Graylen and I came to this point.

I'm wondering the same thing.

"Now! For the second congratulations tonight. Prince Adrian?" The duke motions for Adrian to come stand beside him.

I watch in half horror, half shock as Adrian goes along with Duke Wyman's announcement. There's likely nothing he can do at this point even if he wanted to—his father is still king.

"While the festivities of the matching took place, we were honored to have several Penyth diplomats join us for a short period." He pauses, letting that sink in for a moment. No one from Penyth *ever* came to the castle.

"There's no need to be afraid! The diplomats came on peaceful terms. They were under strict instructions that no witchery or tricks would be committed while on Crea's soil. They were thoroughly searched, questioned, and researched."

People around me share nervous glances, uncertain about having Penyth sleeping in the same castle without anyone realizing it.

"On behalf of King Avalon, I'm pleased to announce that a decision was made to bring peace to our kingdom. In exchange for their commander, the one you all met at the celebration ball, they agreed to an alliance." Dramatically, he waits once more, letting people gasp and whisper loudly at the implication. Peace hasn't been obtained since the split of the empire so long ago. My father, my father's father, and their fathers before them hadn't seen the two kingdoms united as one. No one in our lifetime thought we'd ever see it either.

"For now, we've all agreed to a truce. Prince Adrian will marry Princess Leda of Penyth." Shock reverberates through the room, and my vision blurs. Graylen's steadying hand is suddenly my only lifeline as I stumble. The duke forges ahead, ignoring the murmurs sounding throughout. "Their union will solidify the peace treaty. We will not attack Penyth, and they will not attack us. Nor will they perform any volatile acts." Duke Wyman beams as the king's eyes drop closed, a light snore sounding from his throat.

The crowd is frozen for a moment, silence suspended in the air at the impossibility of an actual alliance with Penyth. The kingdom that has spent hundreds of years tormenting Crea, while we do nothing in turn.

How can we expect things to be solved by a simple marriage treaty? The hatred between the two kingdoms runs deeper than the dodders infesting the land. In my world, things don't just fall into place. Yet here we all are, waiting around. Hoping that peace falls into our laps instead of war. But sometimes, war is inevitable.

The quietness in the room erupts into loud clapping and hearty cheers. Soon everyone in attendance is laughing and dancing, spinning around the room and raising their cups in salutes and praises.

A single voice rings out over the crowd. "Peace to Crea! Long live the king and Prince Adrian!" Everyone quickly joins in the chant.

As the music resumes, my father approaches me, Graylen still at my side. With the news of Adrian's engagement, ours is already irrelevant.

"Amira, we need to speak." Father's voice is laced with a dull rage.

Graylen remains unmovable beside me and tilts his head. He stares at my father with more intensity than most people would dare. "Actually, we were just leaving. Maybe some other time."

My jaw threatens to unhinge as Graylen wraps a hand around my waist and walks with me through the room. He laughs softly to himself at the impatient noise that escapes my father. A smile slips onto my face when our back is turned to him.

"Thanks," I whisper. Graylen's laugh dissolves, and he nods without looking at me. My smile, too, disappears when I remember who Graylen is, and what he's done.

He is everything about this kingdom that I hate. He treats those that he considers less than him unworthy. He's arrogant and unable to be trusted. He sees someone that's an easy target and takes as he pleases. But I can't say that yet. Not when I need him. I just need to remember it's all a game to him. The court is his game board, and he holds all the cards.

How could I keep letting myself forget these things? His easy words and rare smiles don't negate the things he's done. *Pull it together*, I curse at myself.

"We'll begin spending time together tomorrow. I can escort you to eat in the great hall." Wonderful. "I'll deal with your father, go ahead before he reaches us."

I turn to see Father weaving his way through the crowd. Graylen walks with me as far as the entrance to the glass house, motioning for me to exit.

"Reichardt," I hear as the door closes behind me, Graylen's voice long and drawn out.

I hug myself tightly against the chill of the evening, quickening my steps to get further away before my father sees me. The moon still blazes brightly in the night sky, the stars strung up and glistening.

Even covered in darkness, the gardens are far more beautiful than anything else in the castle. I quickly gather my dress in my hands and delve deeper into the labyrinthine paths. The guards remain fixed and ever-present along the path, but make no attempt to stop me.

As I pass the shrubbery maze, I duck behind one of the spiraling trees, peeking around the side in time to see Father and Sir Christopher walking toward the castle. I smile, glad that they assumed I went inside. My father really doesn't know me at all.

I relax into the tree, leaning against it while my mind tries to unweave the tangled web of tonight's events. The leaves attached to the tree are dull and slightly withered. I pluck one of them off of its branch, running my thumb along the rough surface. It falls to pieces in my grasp.

"You shouldn't be so sad. You have the best seat in this whole place," I whisper quietly to it. I sit down beneath the skinny tree and pick up some of the dirt beneath it, watching as the soil slowly falls from my hand and back onto the ground.

"You're going to ruin that dress."

I jolt at the voice and jump to my feet. The voice came from the other side of the tree, so I cautiously stick my head around to see who spotted me. Her long white hair drifts across her face with the breeze.

Addie stands across from me, her head tilted far to the side as she watches me with concern. Her delicate brows are pulled together, and her arms are firmly crossed. For a moment I'm jealous of how carelessly beautiful she is, her smooth, dark skin glowing with an almost silver sheen in the moonlight.

"What are you doing away from the party?" I try to keep my question light, hoping she doesn't ask me the same in turn.

She waves her hand in the air like it's nothing. "It's boring."

I gape at her. How she thinks the events of tonight were *boring* seems impossible.

"Are you okay? Shouldn't you be at the party gushing about your soon-to-be husband?"

I cringe at the word. "It's a lot to take in."

She nods, considering my words. "It's certainly unexpected. Want me to stay for a bit?"

I smile at the question. Something about her is far more inviting than most of the guests here. "Maybe next time." I step fully around the tree, feeling silly to still be half hiding behind it. "I was heading in soon anyway."

Addie shrugs, unbothered. "We've got to stop meeting like this, you know?"

Despite how the evening has gone, I laugh. The last time we were out here, I was hiding from Edith. Coming closer to her makes me feel so short in comparison. Addie's taller than all the girls—and some of the men—here.

"Next time we're out here we should go on a proper walk together." Her eyes are sparkling with a genuine offer. Then she turns and leaves me to my hiding, walking toward the castle, casting an exaggerated salute to a nearby guard.

I twist around to sit beneath my tree a while longer, blowing out a long breath.

The spiraling tree has a strange gleam coming off it. I rub my tired eyes, taking this as a sign to go to bed. With my heart returned to its normal rhythm I can feel the weight of my eyelids attempting to pull shut. I need the solace of sleep to quiet my thoughts. I'm not ready to think about what a fake engagement with Graylen will be like.

"The gardens will be closing soon, miss. You need to go back inside or back to the party. We'll be locking up after this last song."

I jump at the guard's voice, almost forgetting their presence.

With a relinquishing sigh, I dust my dress off and go back into the castle. Each step brings a sense of dread.

TWENTY-ONE

ILEX

AVERY BRUSHES MY HAIR QUIETLY, humming a sweet melody that draws me in, allowing me to forget where I am for a moment and bask in its tune.

"What are you humming? It's beautiful."

The brush pauses halfway down my hair. I wait for her to answer, the brush resuming its attempt to untangle the knots.

"It's an old one." She doesn't elaborate or continue. Most of the tunes played in the castle are monophonic and boring. Besides the winding flute from last night, most of the stringed instruments play the same sound over and over.

"I could bet my life that I've heard it before." She sets the brush down and I turn to face her, ready to get dressed and get this meal over with.

"Let's get you ready for Graylen." She bustles over to my trunk and rifles through its contents. "Ah, this one will do nicely. What do you think?" She holds up a deep navy dress, the material stretchy and plain. Exactly what I would choose myself.

"Do you mind dressing yourself this once? I forgot something." She hands me the dress and slips out. I wouldn't mind dressing myself every day.

I take my time pulling off my comfortable night shift, finding that once I put the dress on it's almost as easy to move in as my cotton nightclothes. I adjust my hair behind my ears and wish I could throw it into a braid.

I sit down on the lounging seat as I wait for Avery to return. Unease creeps its way into my thoughts about the impending mealtime with Graylen. I have no choice but to interact with him. This engagement, as fake as it is, is the only thing keeping my father off my back for the time being.

Unable to keep still, I stand and walk around the room. I adjust my dress, re-brush my hair, and take my tonic. Thankfully, it's not long before Avery is hurrying into the room with a small pouch in hand.

"This is for you, miss." She hands me the pouch, a smile stretching widely across her face. I've never seen her this happy before.

I pour out the contents of the pouch into my hand. A hairpin rests in my palm, the silver glinting against the light. A lily—the kind that has small, drooping bells, and rests deep within hidden valleys.

"I can't possibly accept this." There's no telling what a piece like this would cost her. Possibly an entire season's worth of wages.

"Don't be silly. It's a gift. It's customary where I'm from to gift a newlywed. I didn't think you'd mind receiving it a little early."

Guilt eats away at me. How can I accept this knowing I'm not *actually* going to marry Graylen? I'll just have to give it back when we figure out how to get out of this.

"Thank you, Avery. I don't deserve such a lovely gift. Can you help me put it on?"

She practically glows at the question. I pull my hair to the side for her. With light and gentle fingers, she places it in my hair. It matches perfectly with my necklace.

A knock at the door sends Avery hustling to open it. "Enjoy your day, miss." She beams, casting a sidelong glance at the door.

"Thank you, Avery. I'll see you later?"

She inclines her head toward me and opens the door for the guest. My stomach sinks when she opens it fully. I debate running into the washroom before he sees me, but it's too late.

Sir Christopher stalks into the room, his eyes verging on murderous. I circle out of his path, edging toward the open door, ready to make my escape. When he turns to face me, his anger looks more laughable than intimidating, seeming more like a toddler that had their favorite toy stolen.

"You truly are incompetent, aren't you? You had one job. Stand there while your father makes the announcement."

"Excuse me?" I take a step toward him, my fingers itching for a blade.

"You stupid, selfish girl. Do you think your father—" His words die in his throat. I feel an arm wind around my waist.

"Please. Finish that sentence." Graylen's voice is venomous. Where Sir Christopher's angered expression looked harmless moments ago, Graylen's rage rolls off of him in threatening waves.

"Amira and I—"

"*Lady* Amira." The hand firmly splayed across my ribs pulls me closer. His thumb sweeps across my side in a circular—almost soothing—motion. It's almost as if he can sense the rising anger in me. When I rotate toward him, he locks eyes with me, his resolve unwavering. A muscle feathers in his jaw.

"Of course," Sir Christopher stammers out. "Lady Amira and I were just talking."

"Talking?" Graylen laughs bitterly. "She was likely a breath away from burying a knife between your ribs."

I'm still too angry with Sir Christopher to register what he says. But Sir Christopher does. His eyes dart between us.

"If I were you, I'd get out while you still can. Otherwise, she might change her mind." I almost laugh at the way Sir Christopher's eyes widen but stop myself when I remember whose arm is wrapped around me. "But don't worry. If she doesn't, I still know where you sleep."

That catches my attention, and it's enough to send Sir Christopher blubbering an apology.

Graylen ignores his attempt. Instead, he turns to me. "Ready to go eat?"

I nod, tossing a glare at Sir Christopher, and leave the room nearly buzzing. The look on his face is almost entirely worth it. The risk of this ruse getting back to Father would probably land me back in the camp. But the tension bunching in Graylen's shoulders told me he was as annoyed with Sir Christopher as I was. The further we get from my chambers—and Sir Christopher—the calmer he becomes.

Outside the heat of the moment, I realize I've gone from the hands of one tormentor to another. Graylen's hands weren't innocent either.

"I don't need you to rescue me," I snap.

"Are you sure about that?" He smirks.

I bristle, hating the idea that someone like him thinks he's some savior. "Why are you playing this up so much, anyway? No one was watching back there."

"It's fun."

"So you're risking treason because it's fun?" I huff out.

"I'd risk a lot of things for you," he murmurs.

The heat of his hand brushes against my back, drawing me closer to him. I immediately jerk out of his hold—or try to. His arm is firmly locked into place. But it's the kind of hold that has warmth pooling in my stomach, making me all the more uncomfortable by my body's reaction to his.

"Don't you want to talk about this?" I push, needing to know what's going on in his head.

"Later." He shrugs, keeping his arm in place as we draw closer to the great hall.

We walk silently down the corridor, descending the stairs to the second level. The corridor is mostly empty besides the guards. By the time we reach the great hall, it sounds as if everyone is already seated. Loud chattering and clinking spoons filter over to us, so different from the camp where everyone used moldy bread to slop up their thin gruel.

A guard opens the door for us, the clinking and chattering pausing. Every head in the room swivels to watch us enter. I clench my jaw. Graylen leads us over to the far end where several empty seats are grouped together, hopefully separate enough that we won't have to speak with anyone.

"We haven't had time to get our story straight," I whisper furiously through my teeth while keeping a smile plastered to my face. Graylen doesn't bother. People would likely be suspicious if he *was* smiling.

"There's nothing to get straight if we don't talk to anyone." He pulls a chair out for me to sit down. Several girls around us are openly staring as he helps me scoot into the table. Their wistful gazes trail up and down his body.

"Congratulations. How'd you get him to say yes?"

I fight rolling my eyes at Edith's sneering comment.

"Careful, Edith!" Addie sits down next to me. Edith's eyebrows pinch together as she looks down at herself, checking to see if anything is out of place. "Your jealousy is showing."

I swallow back laughter. Edith's face grows red as the girls around us giggle at Addie's remark. I knew I liked her.

"So, Amira, tell me *everything*."

Maybe I don't like her. She props her elbows onto the table, lacing her fingers together and setting her chin atop her hands. Her crystal blue eyes are wide and expectant. These were all the questions I was hoping to avoid wrapped up into one. I look to Graylen for him to answer and find him glaring at Addie. Her smile is sickly-sweet and unbothered.

"It's a long story," we both say at the same time.

She shrugs, her mind already moving on to the next thing. "Beautiful necklace." Her icy eyes jump to Graylen, likely assuming he gifted it to me.

He remains entirely unhelpful, fully silent. I smile, but don't offer more than that.

When I look out at the room I find Edith watching us with narrowed eyes, studying the way Graylen and I interact. Sir Christopher strolls in behind us, his spine stiff as he walks straight to Edith. He plops himself down beside her. It's the two worst people I could think of interacting with each other. Do they know it's a lie? Both of their gazes turn to us, a knowing smirk playing on Edith's face.

My thoughts are momentarily cut off by the hand reaching up to tuck a loose strand of hair back. Graylen's fingers slowly round the curve of my ear. With our closeness I can see golden specks sprinkled into his green eyes, their intensity blazing into me.

"Like that?" His voice rumbles softly, deliciously deep.

I swallow, looking away from him and clearing my throat. I hear an agitated noise rumble from Sir Christopher down the table, nearly impossible to miss with a matching sound coming from Edith beside him.

A chair screeches as it pushes across the stone floor. Everyone turns to the sound as a boy stands from his chair. I realize it's Milo, the boy I met during the speed sessions event. His hands tremble lightly at his sides.

"If I could have everyone's attention," he says with a shaking voice. "There's someone here that I've come to know. She's the kindest soul in the room, and I would be remiss if I didn't take this opportunity to wed her."

The girls in the room gasp, some of them shifting in their seats and staring hopefully at him.

He walks a couple chairs down and sticks his hand out, offering it to someone I can't see. A delicate hand slides into his. He helps her to her feet.

"Sarah, would you be my match?"

I scoot to the edge of my seat, watching in growing excitement as Sarah nods yes. The room erupts into cheers and clapping. I can't help but join in, genuinely pleased that the two of them found each other.

Sarah lunges forward and wraps her arms around Milo's waist, squeezing tightly. I smile when he returns the embrace with just as much enthusiasm, gathering her into his arms and spinning her around.

"Congratulations, Sarah and Milo!" someone shouts. The room echoes the sentiment, the couple quickly swarmed with excitement.

Wine is brought out, cups raised and emptied as people begin to celebrate. The lightness in the room thickly coats everyone inside.

Sarah turns to hug someone, our eyes meeting. She smiles at me with a face full of joy. At least I've done something right since being here. My introduction during the speed event went further than I thought it would.

For the first time, it makes me feel as if this event isn't such a bad thing. I couldn't think of two better people to have found each other in the midst of this forced matching. I feel Graylen's hand come to rest on the back of my chair, casually placed around me without really touching my back, and pulling me back to reality. My reality. That I'm not like Sarah.

As much as it pains me to admit, I can't help but wonder what it would be like to feel loved like that by someone. To have that kind of closeness and know without a doubt I had a place beside them. But I haven't ever really had a place to call mine. I've always been a token to gamble whenever it benefited the person playing me.

I plaster on a smile in an attempt to cover the pain stabbing at my chest, like I've always taught myself to do. Play the game, find a way out.

TWENTY-TWO

TRACHEOPHYTA

MY DOOR SWINGS OPEN AND I groggily swipe at my eyes, expecting to find Avery coming in. Instead, Graylen appears. I sit upright, alarmed. His hands casually rest in his pockets as if he's done nothing wrong.

"A knock is typically offered prior to bursting into someone's room." My face burns red with the state of my sleeping gown. The thin cotton does little to conceal my body.

"Afraid I'll catch you indecent, Amira?" He leans against the wall and stares at me like he's already bored with this conversation.

I cross my arms and pull the covers further up.

"Adrian told me to pass a message on to you," he continues, unbothered. "Seems like he's afraid you'll disappear, *darling*."

I roll my eyes, but knowing Adrian has been thinking about me sends a thrill through me. A small smile tugs at my lips and then quickly dissipates when I remember the treaty, remember he's engaged now. Like me.

Graylen tilts his head to the side as he studies me. "A royal engagement doesn't promise a marriage will actually take place."

"Why would that matter to me?" I snap, the words stumbling out of my mouth, each one tripping over the other.

Graylen makes a humming noise.

"So? The message?" I push, irritated with his games.

The right corner of his mouth slants into a smirk. "He would like to speak with you soon but he's not sure when, with the meetings lined up the next several days. I told him it was probably for the best if you two spoke."

My pulse quickens at the thought of seeing Adrian. We have a lot to discuss.

"I'll be waiting on the other side of the door. Unless you'd like for me to stay while you change?"

I glare at him with every ounce of *go away* energy as I can gather. The corners of his mouth twitch, unsmiling but coming close to breaking.

I wait for him to exit the room before flinging the blankets off. Without bothering to eat the pastries Avery left out for me, I throw on the nearest dress and swallow down my tonic. I pocket the leather pouch that holds my powder, giving it a good pat to make sure it's still there. I take a deep breath; things are going to be complicated here.

We walk silently to the fourth level where the library is located. The climb up the stairs is quiet until we pass two girls walking together.

Graylen casually brings his hand to the lower part of my back, keeping his gaze ahead while noticeably stepping closer to me. One of the girls audibly sighs at the gesture, while the other ignores us entirely. The moment they pass us I hurry my steps so that his hand falls away.

"You're the one who said we need to make it convincing."

I huff. He's right, but it doesn't change that it feels weird to me. I'm out of my element here.

Graylen walks into the library and over to a small, exposed staircase. I follow behind him, gathering the absurd amount of velvet composing my dress, and ascend the steps.

We walk on a narrow path; bookshelves line the left side, while the railing overlooking the library boxes me in on my right. My dress brushes against either side, bigger than the walkway.

"So," I attempt.

He turns his head and pins me to my spot with his glare, his green eyes ablaze. "Not yet." His gaze darts back to the entrance of the library.

Irritated, my face twists with frustration, but I remain quiet.

We walk to another set of stairs and ascend. I would stop and admire the library from this height, but curiosity over Graylen's explanation tugs me forward like a string stuck in my stomach, pulling me along behind him. An invisible force yanks me along.

He stops abruptly and turns to look at me, his face unreadable. He overlooks the library, his eyes searching. We're alone; no one ever comes here.

"This is the first time I've been here with someone simply wanting to *talk*." He smirks, though it doesn't reach his eyes.

I glare at him, uncompromising. My teeth clench together, my fingers balled into tight fists at my side. His gaze flicks down to where my knuckles are beginning to turn white, the corners of his mouth twitching upward.

I make the conscious decision to stay further than arm's length away from him. His reputation precedes him; unlike other boys I've known, I know there's real danger behind his promises. There's a specific way a well-trained soldier will carry themself. I can see the way he moves with a confident purpose. Each step is sure, and every gesture is intentional. A man his size is usually on the slower side, easy to diminish with speed, but I have a feeling that wouldn't work with him.

"I don't want to marry you, Amira."

I relax slightly, but the skepticism remains. I nod at him, silently telling him to continue.

"And *you* don't want to marry me. Seems like the perfect arrangement."

I laugh, half-crazed. He's only stating the obvious.

"Adrian and I have been friends for a long time. He tells me everything, including his little trips to the market. Where he met a girl unlike any he's met before, and all she talked about was how to escape her life and everyone in it. About how much he wanted to help you." He smirks.

I narrow my eyes at him, my head tilting back to look up at his towering height.

"He wouldn't stop talking about you for days. Still does."

"Adrian and I are friends; it's why he's helping me." I shake my head and turn to grip the railing. Even if a part of me wishes it to be something more. That's clearly out of the realm of possibilities now.

He laughs and crosses his arms. "You truly think that's the only reason he's helping you?"

No, but I'm not ready to admit that yet.

"I think he's the kind of person who would do everything in his power to help someone else, with nothing expected in return," I say firmly.

I believe that so strongly that I would bet my life on it. Adrian had already proven as much when he learned where I lived. Even though it didn't happen how I wanted it to, he still got me out of the camp. I can't help but feel indebted to him for that.

"And I'm not someone who would do that?" He leans forward.

"You know, I'm not always talking about you."

He lifts an eyebrow, latching onto my words without missing a breath. "That doesn't mean you aren't thinking about me."

Does he even realize how serious this is? I turn my face toward the entrance of the library, thinking through all the possibilities of how this could go wrong.

"You certainly aren't helping from the kindness of your heart. So why?" I push, knowing there's more to it.

"Our engagement doesn't mean anything. It's clear by your lack in talking to anyone here that you don't want to be married any more than I do." He shrugs. "All we need to do is spend enough time together to convince the court we're an honest match, and then we end it when the time is right."

I turn to look at him, the cold metal of the rails biting at my hands as I steady myself.

"And what if we're found out?" I ask, raising a brow, wondering how the snake will get us out of that one.

He slips his hands into his pockets and leans back against the bookshelf. "I won't let that happen." His eyes darken. The mood shifts in the air around us, his playful demeanor momentarily gone.

"Oh, so the snake is afraid of something after all? Because I'm pretty sure faking a royally sanctioned engagement is a treasonous act. At least my father is—"

His jaw tightens. "Your father won't be able to help you either if this gets out. A woman's honor being tainted will make her a pariah. The only way we can do this is if I reject you, and scorn you later to make it convincing that you were innocent all along. It wouldn't end well for either of us."

"What made you step in, then?" I scrutinize his movements, hoping he lets his curated mask slip for a moment. This puts both of us at risk, and he seems well aware of the consequences. So why?

"I have little to no desire to be married. I prefer to not be bound to someone. If I made a promise to be faithful, I wouldn't break it."

Graylen's eyes bore into mine. "But that's not a promise I'm looking to make right now."

That's at least something I can understand. What worth is a person if they don't keep true to their word?

"Besides, you were panicking. That much was easy enough for anyone to see. I didn't become the Prince's Snake without learning to read people. I saw my opening and took it." His indifference is back, laced into every word. The seriousness from moments ago is gone, and back is the selfish man I'm used to. But the two sides of him aren't adding up.

"And what opening would that be? How does this arrangement even benefit you?" I press.

I've spent enough time with my father to know there must be more to it. Nobody gives out favors without a goal in mind, not someone like Graylen anyway. Unless they're Adrian or Linnick. That's why I gave Adrian my furs, and brought Linnick here. They need protection.

Graylen is the kind of person I'm protecting them from.

I chew on the inside of my cheek, uncertainty gnawing at me.

"I'm sure you've heard by now that my interest doesn't typically align with a singular woman." He smirks. "I'm being pressured by many people at the court to find a match as well. How does it look to have the prince's advisor not participating in the royal invite to find a match?"

I roll my eyes. "Couldn't you actually get married and still do whatever it is you want behind closed doors?"

"I told you; I have no interest in being married. This relieves some pressure against me for the time being." He shrugs.

I let out a short breath, frustrated he still hasn't fully answered the question.

"I haven't even seen you interact with anyone."

"Not everything is as it seems." He waves his hand in the air dismissively.

"Are you sure you just aren't jealous?" I surprise myself with the question. But it's the only thing that makes sense: he knows Adrian cares for me. Rather than feel offended, I'm relieved to have an answer. I'm just a tool in his game.

"What would I have to be jealous of?" He kicks off the bookshelf, taking a single step toward me.

"Your best friend will have the entire kingdom at his fingertips one day. He'll get to do what he wants while you're stuck playing the game. But you're good at that, aren't you? Playing games."

"Nearly as good as you are at it. I'd love to know what your secret is so I can take note. You're the one who crafted this arrangement. I simply took the place of someone else." His eyes flashed with delight as he said it, a game he was all too eager to play.

I turn away from the blazing fire brewing behind his gaze. My fingers curl around the railing. The library is still empty, and from this view it's easy to see if anyone were to enter.

Graylen rests a hand on either side of me, caging me in. There's enough space between us that I can easily slide away from him. But I don't. My heart pounds in my chest, and my feet stay planted, unable to move.

He leans in close, his voice dropping to a whisper. "The idea is to convince the court that this is real, isn't it? We'll need to make it compelling." His chest brushes against my back, and I lean into the warmth. "I can handle it. Can you?"

His words clang around in my mind as he steps away. I shake my head. Was I really leaning into *Graylen*?

"We both have to be able to handle it now. We're in too deep to just walk away." My voice comes out shakier than I meant for it to.

The decadence of the castle comes to be more suffocating than freeing. The library becomes my favorite haunt to spend my days, full of resources I never even knew existed before coming here. It's the only place I've come to find comfort—within the yellowed scrolls and literature.

I hunch over various maps and books on territories near and far. I reread the same map until it's memorized, hoping I can find a place for Linnick and me to escape to one day.

Graylen ambles in, knowing where to find me. The guard at the entrance of the library noticeably takes a small step away as he brushes past. He notices too much for me to risk being so obvious with what I'm reading. I slowly slide a small script of poetry over my current read, not wanting to be asked why I'm studying maps and territories. Because then I would have to lie, and lying to Graylen Garriden is something I'd rather avoid.

By the time he reaches the oak table I'm seated at, I've effectively covered my territory literature, though his eyes linger where my hand is covering the edge sticking out beneath the poem.

"Oh look, if it isn't the prince's rat. I mean, snake. Or would you prefer rat? Both seem quite fitting, scurrying around in the dark and such." I cross my arms as he takes a seat across from me.

"Find anything particularly interesting in your reading today? Or are you just using it as a front, so you can scheme?" He leans back, fully at ease.

"You know, now that I think about it, I'm overdue for some scheming. Have any twisted games that you're playing on someone for your amusement lately?" I shoot back.

His mouth twitches as if he wants to smile, but he doesn't. "You'd be the first I'd tell," he says.

"You mean manipulate?" I ask.

His wink is nothing short of arrogance incarnate. "Wouldn't dream of it, Ramsey."

I shake my head and look down at the book on the table, ignoring him.

"You might enjoy bothering someone else for the day." I try to steer him in another direction, hopefully a direction *very* far away from the library. My interest itches to look over the maps.

"That's reserved for you." He smiles.

I sigh, knowing he isn't going to relinquish.

As much as I'd rather be alone, at least he keeps the few away who wander into the library. A young couple burst in through the entrance, their laughter disturbing the quiet.

The way they're huddling together and rushing makes it seem out of the realm of possibility that they're here to read. The man, almost in a run, pulls the woman along by the hand, her cheeks pink and flushed. But the moment they walk in and spot Graylen, they immediately turn and leave.

He doesn't glance up from what he's reading after their hasty exit. Or the next two hasty exits. I watch in amusement as their eyes widen and bounce between us, two of the most disliked people in the kingdom banding together. Anger used to churn my stomach when people made faces at me, but now I have to stop myself from laughing.

"Do you miss the camp?" Graylen asks abruptly.

I snort a laugh. No one misses the camp once they get out.

"Only the training part." I've grown weaker without it.

He eyes me, his ankle propped up and resting on his knee. I can see a plan forming in his mind. One corner of his mouth slants up.

"Then we go to the gardens to train each night. That's typically how I spend my evenings anyway. We'll need to be discreet about you being seen in your army leathers. Do you still have them?" he asks, his eyes crinkling at the corners with mischief.

Sneaking quietly through the castle alone with him isn't my idea of fun. Especially when the gardens are empty. Though my ability to fight would likely throw him off enough to allow me to have the upper hand, even if only for a moment. My eyes drop to his arms, the muscles easily defined even beneath the fabric of his sleeves. The possibility of being out there without any guards wins out.

"I'd sooner get rid of these ridiculous dresses than them." I sigh. "We should use this time to test each other on our likes and dislikes. In case it comes up around others."

He doesn't laugh. Just assesses me with a lingering smirk.

"How do you plan on getting in and out? They lock the doors at night."

This time he does laugh, a low and quiet rumble sounding from his chest. "I have a key," he says proudly.

Of course he does. Likely to sneak out and do horrible things on behalf of the crown. I don't trust him any more than I did before, but for the first time I feel like I can use him back. And something about that feels a little closer to freedom.

TWENTY-THREE

CYPRIPEDIUM

I HAVEN'T SEEN ADRIAN MORE than occasionally in passing. The only thing that's kept me occupied is the surprising distraction of Graylen knocking on my door each night.

"Think you can keep up tonight?" he calls out from the other side of my door.

I bristle at his question and choose to not answer him. When I pull open the door, I find his tall frame leaning against the corridor wall, face smirking. He has traded his linen tunic for black training leathers.

"I think this will be better than the sheet you've been tossing over yourself the last few times." He hands me a bundle of fabric.

I quickly throw on the thick velvet cape, one long enough to cover my clothing entirely. I fasten the velvet hood over my head and give him a tight smile, a tug pulling at my chest that he thought to bring this. We walk to the ground level, anticipation surging my steps forward. With the moon set high in the sky, I know the majority of the castle is asleep.

Once we arrive at the entrance to the gardens, he pulls out a long iron key. Perks of being the prince's advisor. He turns the key until it clicks, propping the door open for me to step through.

I pause at the opening of the gardens, breathing in the crisp night air. Small, loose strands of hair gently lift and tickle my face. My hair is in its old style, braided against my back, and I feel more like myself. I hear the sound of the door clicking again, locking us out of the castle for the time being. My heart gallops in my chest.

I walk forward and let the tips of my fingers graze over waist-high shrubs. The tightness that always accompanies my lungs eases the moment I touch them. I smile to myself, looking out at the trees not too far away. The crashing of the Andronicus sounds like a lullaby in the distance.

"Ready when you are."

Without glancing back at him I shrug off my cape, my old training leathers moving with me as I stretch out my arms.

Veiled under the blanket of the stars, no one would see us if they looked out their windows. There's something about being surrounded by the night that calms my nerves: no people to impress, no lies to keep straight.

Among the stars and trees, I can be whoever I want to be. The trees watch me without judgment. The creatures and critters rest gently with little to no interest in me. I keep my focus on the task ahead—eventually I'll have to leave the castle. I can't remain here forever, or marry Graylen.

I push myself until my calves and thighs are begging me to stop. Still, I don't give them the rest they're screaming for. I force myself to match his pace. His movements are quick, and his breathing steady. Gaining momentum with each swing of my arms, I move my legs as swiftly as my trembling body will allow, racing against my thoughts as I press through the burn until my only focus is on the ground beneath my feet, and the short gasps of my breath.

I don't stop until we've reached the cliffs, needing to feel the openness of the water laid out before me. Staring out at the darkness of the water, I can feel my mind ease from the exhaustion of my body. The vast expanse stretches further than any eye can see, giving me a sense of calm at the possibilities that lie beyond.

"You're much more relaxed out here than in there." He nods to the castle.

I remain silent. It's not something that needs a response. The trees that shroud my view of the castle give me the feeling of being somewhere else entirely.

"What do you enjoy doing?" he asks when I don't respond.

I haven't thought about it before. I've mostly focused on what I *could* enjoy doing if I left Runnswick.

"This," I say shortly.

He sits down in the patchy grass, his arms coming to rest over his bent knees as he looks out at the dark sea. "I can't very well say that if someone asks me. 'Sure, she enjoys sneaking out at night, dressed in leathers, running about when the doors are supposed to be locked.' I doubt that would be received well. Just make something up." He rolls his eyes.

I join him on the grass, keeping distance between us. "I enjoy reading," I relent. That's believable with the amount of time we've been in the library. It's also not a lie. I pick at the grass, a single blade at a time.

"So you're stunning *and* smart." His flattery slips out like it's second nature. He seems to be the kind of man to get what he wants, even if through trickery.

"You don't have to play the game out here," I say impatiently, tearing the blade of grass down the middle.

"Practice makes perfect." He shrugs.

In the distance clouds are gathering, and the sea crashing heavily against the rocks gives way to the brewing storm.

"You also enjoy walking the gardens during the day," he adds.

Why would he know that? I haven't seen him out there.

"You've been watching me." I turn to face him, holding his gaze.

He winks, not the least bit bothered that I accused him of it. "I watch everyone."

At this, I stand, ready to place more distance between us. "Creepy," I mumble, mostly to myself. But hoping he heard.

"How is it that your words are so sharp, when you manage to leave a trail of flowers in your wake?" he asks.

I haven't the faintest idea what that's supposed to mean. No one has ever accused me of leaving *flowers* behind me. Is it his way of flirting? If it is, then I don't understand how that's come to work in the past.

He notices me studying him and narrows his eyes. "Is there something you'd wish to say?"

I mutter an answer under my breath, and he motions for me to speak louder.

"I was simply wondering how you've become so…likable among the court."

A harsh laugh escapes him. He has the strangest effect on people. Either they're terrified and running in the opposite direction, or women are throwing themselves in front of him.

"You know why, Amira. You've heard the stories, I'm sure," he says, unbothered.

My cheeks redden. I can feel the tips of my ears heat up. "Of course, if everyone were smart, they would seek a friendship with you just to gain the ear of the prince. You must be strongly disliked for people not to try that ploy."

He smiles, even though I intended for my words to have the opposite effect. Nothing seems to bother this man.

"Not everyone here is as smart as you are, it seems." He wiggles his brows up and down.

That's not at all what I meant. He knows just what to say to get under my skin.

"Well, I don't trust you," I say plainly. There's no point in pretending otherwise.

He looks at me like I'm a puzzle he's trying to solve. We stand staring at each other, the silence stretching thickly between us. The image of him hurting that servant hasn't left the forefront of my mind.

"I would be disappointed in you if you did." A hint of a smile plays at his lips.

The wind carries a strong, icy breeze through the garden, picking up my already messy hair and whipping it around my face. Strands loosen from my braid and fly into my line of sight with each gust that smacks into me. The only thing worse than rainy days is the bite of frigid rain falling.

"Let's go before the rain begins." He stands up, brushing the grass from his trousers.

Well, this was a wonderful success. I hardly feel as if I know him any better than I did when we started the night. One wrong question from Edith could reveal how little I know about him.

Even with the coolness of the night, sweat still pours down my body, my shirt sticking to my back. I wipe my sleeve across my forehead, feeling a weight heavy in my chest.

"Adrian wants to visit you in the morning before the event."

That one sentence steals the breath from my lungs, my pulse racing.

"What event?" I ask.

He brushes past me without a response. But I'm too distracted by the idea of Adrian wanting to see me. I've missed my friend. And I was starting to wonder if he missed me.

In celebration of All Souls' Day, you are cordially invited to an afternoon of merriment and masquerade. Located in the great ball, you will find entertainment unlike any you've seen thus far where you may find yourself speaking to someone you had yet to notice. You are encouraged to eat, drink, and mingle with a potential match. Furthermore, a costume is required. Your entry upon arrival is dependent on your participation in the costume and mask. Once the sun reaches the horizon, the festivities will begin.

I glance out of my window, annoyed to find the sun already setting. I crumple the invitation and toss it onto the small table beside my bed. All Souls' Day. What a joke.

A soft knock raps against my door.

"May I?" a gentle voice says through the door.

The way Adrian asks for permission makes me smile. We haven't spoken since the night of our engagements.

"Of course." I sound more eager than I meant to.

He takes a step into the room, his richly embellished tunic reminding me of who he is. Golden lacework had been stitched into the thick fabric, winding up the center and lining the edges.

"How are you?" he asks hesitantly, his arms folded behind his back.

I shrug, not really sure how I feel.

"I'm sorry I haven't been to see you. With the news of the engagement, things have been…busier than usual." He unclasps his hands and scratches the back of his head, looking adorably shy.

"I suppose an engagement was always in your future if it suited the kingdom," I say to try and lighten the mood.

He snorts a short laugh and turns his head to look at me. His gaze reveals his struggle, and the dark circles accumulating beneath give away the many sleepless nights since I last saw him. My eyes trail the planes of his face, falling over the short, tousled hair and landing on the deep definition of his jawline.

"You mean an engagement that suits my father. I don't know if he plans for the marriage to go through, but somehow he thinks we're getting something from this arrangement." He sighs and shoves his hands into his pockets. "He's been so out of touch with directing the kingdom, and I'm surprised he was able to do this without me knowing."

I nod my head, remembering all the times I've heard about the king doing anything other than actually making decisions.

"I keep thinking through that night. How things could've gone differently. If I had just announced it sooner..." He takes a step toward me, his gaze sweeping my chambers.

He lets out a long, pent-up breath and runs his hand through his hair. I briefly wonder what it would feel like to do that to him. I shake the thought out of my head, my cheeks tinting pink.

"At least I'm not stuck with Sir Christopher." I shrug.

But Adrian doesn't seem that relieved. "I've never known Graylen to settle down. Hopefully others won't feel the same. His interest in women ends after just a single night." He sighs, worry evident on his face. "I just hope you don't get hurt before he can end it."

"If I don't hurt him first before this is all over with," I mumble, mostly to myself.

"You'll get used to him; just give it some time." He smiles, but it's forced.

"I still don't see how you two have become so close. He's endangering my sanity with each conversation." It's doubtful I'll *ever* get used to Graylen and his arrogance.

Adrian laughs, but I don't find it funny.

"And yet you've both escaped something, it seems," he says.

So it seems. While Adrian is left chained to Penyth instead.

"Maybe something will change before you have to marry the princess," I say softly.

He nods, his mouth slanting into a frown. "It's moments like these I wish I had a brother or sister to take my place. Sometimes it seems so unfair." His voice cracks, his emotions rising to the surface like a wave about to crash.

"The world is unfair, Adrian. Linnick losing his farm and being subjected to servitude here is unfair. The people that are starving because of the dodder infestation is unfair." A flurry of tension fills the room as I list the unfairness eating away at the kingdom.

"I know." He lowers his eyes to the floor.

"I'm sorry. Just because your problems are different doesn't make them any less painful." Sometimes, I feel as if I'm begging for someone to see the pain that I feel.

He takes another step closer. I stare at his mouth, his lips parting as we gravitate toward each other. When I look up at him, I find his gaze fixed steadily on my mouth in return. His face mirrors the longing welling up inside of me, the air in the room now shifting to a different form of tension.

A knock at the door causes us to jump apart. He scratches the back of his neck, looking anywhere but directly at me.

Avery shuffles into my chambers, her arms full with a fluff of fabric piled so high she can hardly see over it.

"Time to get ready. Oh—Your Highness." She bows quickly, the mountain of a dress teetering.

"I'll leave you to it. I hope to see you at the masquerade." Adrian gives me a lopsided smile and slips out. My chest does a flop at the sight of him leaving.

"Your costume, miss. They didn't give us long to prepare them, but I had a feeling this one would suit you. I made a few alterations." She lifts it in the air for me to see, the skirt dragging across the ground.

I gasp, my eyes widening in excitement. The dress is a shimmering teal and turquoise. The fabric on top is sheer and entirely see-through, falling lightly over a black skirt. I can't quite figure out the pattern laced into it.

"Here. It'll make sense once you're in it."

I quickly shrug off my clothes and step into it, eager to see what it's like on. The black sleeves run down to my wrists snuggly.

"Hold your arms out like this." Avery demonstrates, spreading her arms out at her side.

I open my arms, material coming with me. I twirl around, looking down at the dress. It's wings, like a butterfly.

"Avery! I love it."

She beams at me and rifles through a small box. "Your mask is plain, but that's because the band that rests in your hair is so intricate." The mask is simple and black. She ties it around my face, covering my eyes and nose. Then she holds up a small black headband. Wires poke out in all directions, with small wooden butterflies strung throughout, painted the same shade as my dress. She slides the band onto my head, the wires bouncing slightly when I take a step.

"You were right. It's perfect." I smile at her, thankful that she's here.

She helps me into a pair of pointed and long-nosed shoes that pinch my toes together at the ends.

Someone knocks on the door. I smile, surprised that Adrian's come back. Avery opens the door.

My smile slips.

"Hoping for someone else?" Graylen's voice is teasing. He looks entirely like his usual self, save for the plain black mask he's wearing.

"Aren't you supposed to be in a costume?" I cross my arms, my eyes narrowing on his lack of costume.

He shrugs. "Not my thing. It clearly suits you well, though."

He makes a show of dragging his gaze from the bottom of my dress all the way up to my face. I fight against the blush creeping across my cheeks, thankful for the mask.

"Let's get this over with," I huff out. He offers his arm, and we make our way to the party. I pluck a glass of wine off the first tray we pass.

The great hall has been transformed into a flashy gathering. Minstrels, puppeteers, dancers, and small theatre troupes performing dramas have been set up in varying places around the room.

A dark, haunting song is being sung by two women. Their harmony stretches out among the crowd. Dancers sway along, stationed throughout the room and putting on writhing performances in skimpy outfits.

All of the costumes add a hint of eeriness to the party. People walk around with strange face coverings—some shaped like animals, others big and extravagant. Someone beside me turns their head, almost poking me in the face with the long bird-like beak of their mask. I jump out of the way, feeling a shiver trickle through me.

Graylen and I walk side by side, ignoring the looks cast our way. Someone steps into our path, blocking us from going further. Her back is to us, showing off a long, feathered mass covering the entire top half of her body. The showy iridescent feathers encircle her head, stretching out into a fan around her.

The feathers brush against anyone in the vicinity, earning several glares from the people near her. She spins around, her hands on her hips.

"Edith, how fitting your costume is," Graylen drawls.

I attempt to stifle my laugh by taking a sip of wine, though I don't think I hide it well enough. Her eyes cut to me, the slightest curl of her lip giving away her anger.

"So, Graylen, I'm still reeling from your match with Lady Amira." Her tone is accusatory.

My heart begins to beat a little harder. My fingers involuntarily squeeze where my hand still rests in Graylen's arm.

"It surprised me as much as it did you. I was unable to resist her from the moment I saw her," he says and turns his attention to me. "She's captivating."

I clench my jaw to avoid it popping open at his words. I shouldn't be surprised at his ease with lies.

"If you say so." She glances me over once, her nose lifting slightly in the air as she examines my dress. "Shocking someone can feel that way about her. What's your secret?"

I bristle at her insult.

"She clearly possesses something you do not." Graylen beats me to whatever words were about to spew from my mouth. I look up at him in surprise as he meets my gaze. "I'm just thankful she chose me."

Edith makes a strangled noise in the back of her throat. Her left eye twitches slightly. "Enjoy the gathering." She brushes past us and bumps her shoulder into mine. I tighten my grasp on Graylen to stop myself from whirling around to face her.

"Easy," Graylen whispers down to me as if I'm a stomping horse preparing to trample someone. He leads me to a corner of the room where couples are dancing.

I begin to shake my head. I barely know any dances.

"Do you want people to believe us?" His question stops the refusal sitting on the tip of my tongue. He pulls me into the middle of a dance, getting in line with the other men. I nervously line up with the other women.

The minstrels pluck fretted stringed instruments, the tune light and hoppy. The women all spin and float over to their partner. I do the same, a step behind.

Graylen winks at me as if he knew I wouldn't know the dance. I try to watch the women around me. If anyone were to look twice at me, they would quickly notice I have no idea what I'm doing.

The other dancing partners hold their right hand up to mirror each other, each couple spinning in a circle. I look to Graylen, trying to follow along.

"May I?" a familiar voice asks. The song changes tune as a man steps up to us. His mask covers the entirety of his face. A hood is drawn over his head, a tassel tying together his flowing robe.

Graylen looks at me, an eyebrow raised. I realize he's waiting for me to respond. I nod and the song shifts into another.

"I'll admit I'm not very good at dancing," I deflect, not wanting to dance with someone else—someone I don't know. At least I know what to expect with Graylen.

The man laughs, his shoulders shaking slightly with the movement. "With a beauty like yours, I doubt it matters much," he answers slyly.

I fight back a grimace at the flattery.

"Breathtaking, isn't she?" I flush at Graylen's statement. "It's a wonder she's mine." There's an edge to his voice. He says it so convincingly, even I almost believe it's real. But it's not, I remind myself, my chest fluttering.

"May I steal her for a quick dance?" the man presses.

Again, Graylen turns to me, awaiting my decision. His eyes are unreadable but focused entirely on me. I need space from him before I do something I'll regret. Like forget who he is, and forget that I used to care about what that meant.

"I would love a dance." The words taste bitter in my mouth.

The familiar stranger smiles. Graylen's eyes dim a fraction.

The man whisks me away, his hand slightly lower than I would deem respectable against my back. I hear a throat clear behind me.

Judging by the way the man immediately raises his hand to a more appropriate position, it likely came from my brooding date.

Graylen disappears as we twirl away from him. Something in my stomach sinks at the thought.

"Tell me, have you enjoyed your time in the castle?" my new partner asks while I focus on not stepping on his toes.

I squint. His voice is familiar, but it's hard to tell who he is with his face fully covered. "How could one not?"

Years with my father have taught me how to appease men like this. I may not recognize him, but I instinctually raise my guard.

Before he can speak again, someone claps a hand on his shoulder. We stop dancing, but the couples surrounding us continue.

"I believe I was promised a dance, Lu."

I smile at Adrian's voice. His mask is encompassed with tiny strands of hay, resembling wiry hair. He's wearing a tan tunic with matching trousers, and a small tail has been tacked onto his back. Like a lion.

My dance partner turns, studying me. "Lu? I thought you were Lady Amira?" the man questions.

"It's a nickname, Uncle." Adrian waves him off.

I pause. That's why I recognized him. No wonder I felt something was off.

"Where did the name come from?" Duke Wyman tilts his head to the side.

"It's something my friend and I made up when we were younger. Just a little game we used to play when we were children." I shrug as Adrian steps between us.

He grabs my hand, pulling me into a dance, but my focus lingers on the duke. His hands clench tightly at his sides as he watches us.

"You look beautiful," Adrian says with a grin.

I can see the outline of his dimples as he smiles down at me, his eyes glinting with playfulness. No one has noticed it's him yet, otherwise all eyes would be on us. But everyone near us dances in their own world, lost to the sound of the melody.

"Interesting party." I turn my head away, watching people around us. We're standing in the center of the dance floor.

He huffs out a laugh. "You don't enjoy people not knowing who you are for a while?"

I shrug. Duke Wyman and Edith didn't have a problem figuring out who I was quickly.

"Well, I think it's quite nice," he says and takes a step closer, one of his hands on my waist, the other holding my arm.

I shiver at his closeness, wishing there wasn't any space between us. But people know who I am, and they know the lion I'm dancing with isn't Graylen. Instinctually I step back, but he holds me firmly to him.

"Someone might notice," I whisper quickly.

His eyes bore into mine, searching my face for something. He tilts his head down toward me, his lips parting.

A burst of laughter draws my attention, my head snapping away. A court jester bounces around in a circle through the dancers, a bell on each foot jingling noisily as he tells his joke. People point and laugh.

Adrian and I quickly step apart. We almost kissed. In front of the entire court. I shake my head, frustrated at myself. We could've been caught. I'm briefly terrified of what that could have meant, what the consequences would have been. And even more worried that if another moment had passed, I might've stopped caring long enough to let him kiss me anyway.

TWENTY-FOUR

TRIFOLIUM

I SLIP THROUGH THE DANCERS, weaving my way through. I hear Adrian call out after me, but he doesn't follow. His voice is immediately recognized, and a crowd gathers around him.

I walk around in search of something to distract myself from what almost happened. Maybe the drama being performed is less humiliating to the performer than the jester's act. It's hard to make it through the thick crowd; groups of people are bunched together, forcing me to squeeze through them.

I try my luck on the edges of the room, but end up getting stuck behind a group of girls talking. The wall's on one side of me, and a tray of food on the other. The only way to get past them would be to go straight through. I turn around to backtrack, but their conversion makes me pause.

"The Snake is a good place to start," a sneering feminine voice says.

"They say he's made his way through half of the women in Crea."

A burst of laughter sounds from the group. My heart drops in my chest.

"Gross," another voice adds.

"I haven't heard a single one of them complain," the first voice tosses back.

"I was one of the lucky winners." The girl sighs wistfully. "It was one hell of a night."

I curl my fingers into a fist. I shouldn't even care. But something has rooted my feet to the floor, unable to move.

"Maybe he'll be up for round two," another says with a laugh.

"Good luck trying that. He hasn't taken a single woman up on their offer since the night of the first ball," yet another says with a wistful sigh.

"Strange he wouldn't, with how many willing participants there are."

The girls pause while a servant refills their glasses of wine.

"Well, how else are we supposed to curry favor here? He was my ticket in." Another sigh.

Something snaps inside of me at the way they're talking about him like he isn't a real person. As if he's just a stepping stone to what they want. It's a feeling I'm painfully familiar with.

I spin around, my cheeks ablaze.

"He's engaged now, so perhaps that's reason enough you shouldn't try for *round two*." I don't even know why I said it. Or why my voice lowered in a warning. I shove away the irrational jealousy clawing at my stomach.

The girls go silent. At least two of them have the decency to look embarrassed.

I stiffly stalk away from them before I say something else. Or look too much into my reaction. Graylen had been a willing participant, and from the sound of it, the feeling was mutual. I can't blame them. Most women would find him attractive. He's tall, built entirely of muscle—his arms are ones that could wrap wholly around you and make you feel safe—and he has eyes like the plushest field, the kind you want to lie down in.

But the person I've come to know is so much more than that. And whether I trust him or not, nobody deserves to be used like a tool so others get closer to power. No wonder he's a loner, I realize. Just like me, everyone wants to go through him to get closer to who he knows. And just like me, they run when they realize they can't handle it.

I shake my head. The wine is strong tonight. Our engagement isn't real. He didn't *choose* me to be his wife. He saw an opportunity for something to benefit him and he took it, just as I did. So why is a smile tugging at my lips knowing he's rejected every advance since meeting me? And am I kidding myself that it's more than a coincidence?

When I make it to the stage, I find the actors in the middle of a scene. I force myself to focus on their play.

"We won't align ourselves with your evil! We will be our own kingdom, and one day we will rid the world of yours!" the actor wearing Crea's insignia shouts loudly to the other, an old wobbly woman, hunched over while holding onto a wooden stick.

"I hate this one."

I jump at the sound of Graylen's voice. His attention is set on the drama playing out before us. A shiver claws its way up my spine as his hand reaches up and brushes across the curve of my back.

People clap and cheer, chanting, "Long live Crea! Long live the king!"

I look at the audience gathered around us, everyone shouting and pointing at the actor portraying Penyth. Not very festive.

"The Valon Empire will be ours one day! We are the rightful rulers of our once sacred empire."

More cheers sound from the crowd. When I look to Graylen, I find his eyes hardened. He doesn't join in clapping like everyone else—not that I expected him to.

"Amira! Graylen! Power match of the season!"

I grin as Milo and Sarah walk over to us. Milo's voice is loud and sloppy, sounding like he's been enjoying the party very much. He holds his cup in the air to greet us, the wine tipping over the sides and splattering to the ground. I half expect Sarah to be upset, but she seems to be enjoying it just as much, her giggles following his goofy gestures.

"Another drama is about to start! Come join us!" Sarah says with a grin.

We walk past the singers, the music loud as it reverberates through the room.

Graylen walks stiffly at my side, not attempting small talk. A few of the sconces on the wall have been snuffed out, causing the room to be darker than when we first entered.

"This one is supposed to be really good. The actors traveled from Prince's End," Sarah whispers excitedly.

The drama is starting as we arrive. It's just two actors, a man and a woman. They move around each other silently. The woman mimes walking with her back turned, and the man jumps around behind her, trying to get her attention.

The actress sighs and turns, facing a different direction but not looking at the male actor. It's as if she doesn't see him at all. Everyone in the crowd shouts at her to turn around and look at him. His shoulders slump and he grabs his chest, heartbroken he can't get her to see him.

"Can't you see that I'm in love with you? Please, just notice me!" the man shouts. She continues moving about as if she didn't hear him. Another actor joins the drama. The woman looks to the newcomer.

The newcomer and the woman embrace, winding together and kissing. The man behind her falls to his knees, begging her to stop.

"He doesn't love you! He doesn't see you like I do," he calls out, heartbroken. But the woman ignores him, entwined with the other. Some in the audience clap, and some point to the man again. Everyone watching is hanging on to their every move.

The man with which the woman is wrapped around hands her a red rose.

This only angers the unseen man further while he watches the pair. "Her favorite flower is the orange star-shaped kind you can only get in Saltain! It reminds her of the sun. Do you even know her favorite thing to eat? It's a slice of fresh bread with honey drizzled over it."

The man she's focused on presents her with a small cake. Her nose scrunches slightly, but she accepts it.

"What about the look she's giving you now? It means she isn't pleased. If you knew her, you would know she prefers a walk in the orchards over a gift or dessert. How can you say you love her without truly seeing her?"

The girl hugs the man for all of his presents, though there aren't any she truly likes.

"What's with these dramas tonight?" Graylen mutters.

Surprisingly, I agree. I haven't found either one of them to be entertaining. Though Sarah looks entirely entranced.

"Let's go find something to eat," I whisper to him.

"Or drink." That too.

Several drinks later I feel bolder than I ought to. Graylen walks me back to my chambers, leaving the party still rolling on behind us. We finally stop in front of my door, sleep calling out to me.

This place is suffocating, I think to myself.

"Then why stay?" he asks, tilting his head to the side.

I twist to Graylen. Did I say that out loud?

"You wouldn't understand. It isn't that simple," I grit out. He does as he pleases through the castle. No one would dare question him if he walked right out of here.

"Try me." His tone is challenging.

"You do what you want, when you want. It's not like that for me." I throw my hands into the air.

He makes an amused snorting sound. "It is if you make it like that for yourself. I didn't magically become this way. Be free. Leave."

I grind my teeth together at the ease of his comment. "Don't you think I've tried?" The words rush out of me on accident, likely the wine's doing. I rip the mask off my face, feeling smothered.

"Not hard enough if you're still where you don't want to be." He shrugs.

I roll my eyes, tired and annoyed. "I know your type." I point my finger directly at his chest. "You slink around in the shadows, doing what you want because you're stronger than everyone else. I've been around that type my entire life." I don't realize I'm shouting until the words bounce around the empty corridor.

"Have you?" says Graylen. "So you must have me all figured out."

"I do," I say, though my voice goes small, uncertain.

His face lowers to the shell of my ear; it's an effort to not pull away just to spite him. "You don't know me as well as you think you do, Ramsey."

"How is it you use people so often? You should have a little more compassion considering they do it to you just as easily." My words come out slightly slurred, lessening the sting of them.

His jaw sets firmly. "I'm well aware of how people use me. As are you, I suspect." I swallow down the pinch of guilt in my throat. "That's what we're doing here, isn't it?"

He spins around and leaves me standing there, unable to get the last word in. I tear open my door and stomp into the chambers.

"Miss?" a soft voice cuts in.

I whirl around. "Avery! You scared me." My hand flies to my chest, trying to calm my racing heart.

"I'm sorry. I thought you might want help getting out of the costume. I can go if you'd rather."

"No! It's okay." I still feel heat prickle the tips of my ears. Still stewing over Graylen thinking I don't know him. I've *seen* with my own eyes what he's done to people. Not to mention the countless stories that circulate the kingdom about the things he's done. The people he's hurt.

"How was the party?"

I shrug.

"At least you had a good date."

Without meaning to I let out a disbelieving laugh.

"Was he not a good date tonight?" She asks, her brows draw together in confusion.

Actually, I found myself having fun with him. He didn't buy into the silly dramas everyone else seemed enthralled by. "He's a difficult man to understand. He acts one way here and another way there."

Avery hums to herself. "He's different with you. I know what most people say about Sir Graylen, but he isn't all bad." She removes my hairpins, causing my hair to cascade around my shoulders.

"What makes you say that?" I haven't heard a single person say anything remotely kind about Graylen.

"I was stationed here in the castle before the event. Graylen was always kind to me and the other servants. He knows all of our names, each and every one of us." She smiles, looking down at her hands. "There's been more than one occasion where he's slipped us extra wages."

My brows shoot up as I remember my first day in the castle and his treatment of the servant outside the window.

"I wouldn't think he's capable of that extent of kindness. He seems rather focused on himself." Much like my father.

"One might think that. But the more you give yourself the chance to get to know him, the more you'll understand." She walks over to my bed and fluffs the blankets out for me to climb under.

"Well, if that side of him exists, I haven't seen it." My voice comes out rougher than I mean for it to.

"May I ask you something, miss?" she asks hesitantly.

I twist around to look at her. I nod, urging her on.

"Why are you so angry with Graylen? Sure, he's a little rough around the edges, but you said yes to his proposal for a reason."

Right. A reason that has nothing to do with actually wanting to be with him, as one might suspect. I take a deep breath and look at her. "I saw him doing something when I first arrived. Something horrible to a servant."

She nods but doesn't seem surprised. "What did you see?" Her voice is gentle, making me feel safe to be honest with her.

"I don't even know where to begin. He was punching a servant, over and over. I haven't seen that servant since that day." My eyes lower to my feet.

"Oh. I see. Why didn't you say something sooner? We could've cleared this up ages ago," she says with a laugh.

My gaze flies up to hers. "You know? How are you okay with this?" Hundreds of questions fly through my mind.

She lets out a long sigh and walks over to the lounging seat, patting the cushion for me to join her.

"He was doing it to protect me. We servants depend on him to help keep us safe. No one cares what happens to us. No one except him."

My mind reels with this information. "What do you mean?" I ask. I've spent all this time hating Graylen for what he did to that servant. Was I wrong? I know what I saw.

"The servant you saw him hitting wasn't helpless, and he certainly wasn't innocent. Most of the staff knows to stay in line and not pick on the others, or they'll have Graylen to deal with. He watches over us. This particular servant was new. He didn't know anyone cared what happened to those of us that can't defend ourselves."

I hang onto her every word. Her voice trembles as she recalls the night.

"That servant needed to be stopped. He was harming one of the younger girls, and I ran to get help. Graylen came immediately. He saved the girl's life." She shakes her head. "The servant is still alive, though I'm sure he'll have quite the limp for the rest of his life. He cast him into the market that day and made sure he could never show his face here again. Graylen's done countless things like that for those of us most cast aside."

I rub a hand over my face, confused. He's been *protecting* the servants this entire time.

"Not all clouds bring rain, miss." Avery pats my hand and leaves me to sit with my guilt.

He was right—I don't know him at all.

TWENTY-FIVE

ALSTROEMERIA

AVERY TWISTS MY HAIR INTO a single braid down my back and secures it with pins. Her nimble fingers quickly weave my hair into the simple yet elegant style. She braids a small piece to frame each side of my face and pulls it around to the back. Somehow, she manages to meld that with the braid. It's so close to the way I'm most comfortable having it, but graceful enough to wear around the castle. I smile, feeling slightly more myself as opposed to having it in elaborate twists and curls.

She holds up a mossy green dress. "This one suits your eyes well, I think."

I smile brightly at her. Her thoughts always seem to flow on the same wavelength as mine. This one has far less fabric around the skirt than the others, its soft and stretchy material making it look more like there's room to breathe in it. I nod and she helps me into it. She applies a rose coloring to my lips and a light charcoal to my eyelids.

As nice as it should feel to be pampered each morning, I can't help but yearn for the simplicity of how my mornings used to be. I used to throw on my training leathers and go.

My smile slips as my old friend enters.

"Well, hello to you as well." The wrinkles around Linnick's eyes crinkle further as he smiles at my expression.

Avery bows quickly and slips out.

His breathing is heavier than the last time I saw him. "You look lovely, Lu. Different, but lovely. The castle life suits you, kid, even if you'd rather be fightin' in the mud with idiot soldiers." He winks at me, but I look back to the door one more time to see if anyone else is behind him.

"It's good to finally see you again," I say with a smile.

"Expecting someone else?" he asks, giving me a knowing look.

"Adrian said he was stopping by today." Disappointment settles into my chest.

"I passed *Prince* Adrian this morning. He wants you to know he's getting pulled into another meeting, but says he'll come see you soon." Linnick pats my shoulder. "He's a good friend to you. He sure is lucky to have met you."

I smile; he always knows how to bring one out of me.

"He's easy to talk to," I admit, my cheeks heating. Every secret I could possibly have is safe with Linnick.

"Graylen Garriden, though? I hope you know what you're doing," he warns, raising a brow.

"I know. We have this arrangement. We pretend to be engaged long enough for me to get my father off my back, and he can do as he pleases without women wanting a long-term commitment." It sounds silly saying it out loud, but all I need is for it to work.

Linnick scratches his chin, considering the idea. "It might be just crazy enough to work."

I hope he's right.

"I'm still so sorry that I get to sit here playing dress up, and you spend your days tirelessly working in the kitchen," I say guiltily.

His smile remains on his face, and he shakes his head at me. "Don't be sorry, child. The kitchen is my happy place. Before my farm was overrun, I'd bake pies when the market wasn't selling. Sometimes, I'd sell the pie the next day, and sometimes I'd keep it for the children in the village or the workers on the farm. My favorite was using the tall lemon tree by my bedroom window. You wouldn't believe how a lemon pie topped with raspberries would taste after working in the fields all day." He looks out the window, longingly dreaming of a simpler life. "I'd use lemon on every bite of food if I could."

I have to admit he looks far happier here than I could've predicted. While looking worn from the labor, he at least doesn't have the weight of the farm hanging over his head.

"Anyway, it didn't take them long to realize that I know my way around a kitchen. Honestly, it's easier down there. People respect me because of my skill, and no one asks each other about their backgrounds because no one cares." He gathers up a smile. "We have a job to do, and we all just do it."

I feel tears prick at my eyes, and I quickly blink them away. Not many people would find a bright side to the situation he's been thrust into.

"Linnick, I need you to know that you've given me hope that decent people still exist. I couldn't trust my father to give me that, but you freely love those around you." I pull him into a hug and he stills, surprised. "Thank you for always being my friend."

He lets go of me and pats my knee, giving it a little squeeze before standing up slowly. "All that bullshit your father talks about power is nothin' if you don't have someone to share it with. And that man is going to be miserably alone for the rest of his life. You got to have someone to have your back," he grunts.

I nod my head in agreement, and we sit in a comfortable silence.

"Care to join me around the palace for a while?" I ask, not ready for him to leave.

He smiles warmly at me, laughter dancing in his eyes. "I'd be happy to, Lady Amira."

He offers me his arm as we make our way to the only place we can sit mostly unbothered, hopefully far enough detached no one wanders in to see a servant in there.

We spend the rest of the afternoon in the library, rummaging through book after book. I show him what I've found most useful so far as possible places to go. I point out small and relatively unknown villages, while he tells me what he's heard about some of them through his time at the market.

The further from my father and the castle, the better, but I feel a small tug in the center of my stomach at the thought of not seeing Adrian again. I quickly push away the thought and focus on the story Linnick is telling about an old village where he used to sell fruit.

"There's this one town filled with different types of trees to trade for. I sold them a few extra crates of fruit in exchange for a couple of sapling lemon trees. They scooped them right up out of the earth and placed them in woven baskets. Took me a while to get the hang of growing them," he says with a smile, his eyes distant and lost in the memory. "Only one tree made it through the mistakes, and that's the one left in the remnants of my farm. Gave it all the love I could. I told it every day how nice and pretty it was. Guess the compliments paid off."

I smile at him, wishing I could see his home in its prime. "What town was it?"

He flips a few pages in the book and scrolls down the map with his finger until it rests on a dot northwest of us, nearer Penyth.

"Lyland. Small town and simple people making an honest living." He holds the book up for me to see the little town that nestles near the border, not quite at the edge.

Graylen comes into the library and eyes us curiously. I introduce Linnick, left without much of a choice. I discreetly cover the books on territories by placing a history ledger atop it, and Linnick does the same with the closest book to him as Graylen sits down at the table.

"So, you're the one that's been making the prince's pastries. I'll be honest, he's been too stressed to even notice food in front of him, let alone eat it." Graylen grins and says, "But I have no issue with taking that off his hands for him."

I roll my eyes. Of course he doesn't.

"They're delicious. Truly," he adds.

I blink in surprise that Graylen managed to compliment someone, still not used to this other side of him Avery told me about. Though maybe I haven't allowed myself to see it.

Linnick seems unfazed and thanks him with a small tilt of his head. "So, you're the one who spends every day with my Lady Amira. Are you as respectful to her as you are to me? Or do you treat her with the same *respect* as the others in the castle?" he inquires firmly, his voice resembling that of a protective father.

My head whips to Linnick, shocked at his brazen question.

But Graylen laughs. A real and deep laugh rumbles through his chest. "I like you more than anyone I've met at the castle thus far. Not including Lady Amira, of course."

I don't miss how he uses "Lady" when speaking in front of Linnick. Graylen gives me what he thinks to be a charming smile, but it comes across as more arrogant than flattering.

Linnick isn't impressed. He crosses his arms and stares unblinkingly at Graylen, who laughs, amused with the game Linnick is playing.

"You seem awfully protective of Amira to be just a servant," Graylen says with a nod.

This cracks Linnick's stoic expression.

"We've spent several seasons together in the market," I explain. "He's one of the only people on this planet I trust. Sometimes a servant can establish more trust than, perhaps, the future royal advisor could." I stare pointedly at Graylen, and he lifts an eyebrow as if to say *Fair enough.*

"Do the markings on your skin have any significance?" Linnick questions, eyeing him warily.

I keep my eyes positioned on Graylen's face, hoping for a reaction of any kind, eager to change the subject. His face reveals no hint of emotion, almost as if I've said nothing at all.

"Yes." He doesn't elaborate further, and the temptation to push him is just too hard to ignore.

"Are you going to keep it to yourself?" Linnick presses.

I study the markings that peek out beneath Graylen's sleeve and the collar of his shirt. It's an odd, swirling pattern that doesn't make any sense.

"Yes," Graylen says shortly.

I exhale as exaggeratedly as possible and roll my eyes, hoping he notices my antics. The castle can get so boring sometimes; the least he can do is get annoyed with me.

"Is it the story about how you became such an ass?" I bite out, but the words come out more playful than angry.

At this, he lets out a soft laugh. The quietest one I've ever heard. My lips turn up of their own accord in response to the sound. If it weren't for the emptiness of the room, I wouldn't have heard it at all.

"Something like that, Ramsey." Graylen smirks.

Linnick looks at me, exasperated. But Graylen seems more amused than annoyed.

Linnick and I spend the rest of the evening exploring more of the library and subtly flipping through books, hoping to form a plan on how we can leave. We need to find a safe place to escape to, and hopefully figure out the wage issue when we get there.

We search as much of the texts as we can with Graylen present. He doesn't speak to either of us the rest of the night and we don't speak to him. As the sun begins to set and the light dances around the library, I motion for us to leave. We tell Graylen good night and I let Linnick lead me out of the room, glad to get a break from an evening with my usual companion. Things feel different now that I know the truth behind what I saw on the day I arrived at the castle. I'm not sure where things stand anymore.

With the castle mostly empty and everyone eating, Linnick and I take our time going back to my room. He needs to return to the kitchen soon, and I'm not ready to be left alone just yet. Linnick is the only one I don't have to be Lady Amira around. He treats me as if I'm not the daughter of the royal merchant. I suppose the same could be said for Graylen.

"Is he truly being respectful? I've heard about what that boy does in his spare time with women," he whispers softly as we walk down the hall.

The conversation I overheard at the masquerade flashes in my mind, filling me with confusion. He hasn't been with anyone since we met. I don't know where to even begin explaining that part.

We turn the corner and stumble into a couple.

"Excuse us! We apologize," a familiar voice echoes at the same time I say, "We're sorry."

The beautiful blonde's eyes widen once the recognition takes hold. She gazes with her mouth open as her eyes bounce back and forth between us.

Opal.

TWENTY-SIX

ARBORVITAE

I GRIP LINNICK'S ARM TIGHTY as a mixture of shock and nausea hits me. Has Opal been in the castle this entire time? We both stare at each other, frozen in place, both of our eyes wide. No one speaks for a moment, then she rushes forward at the same time I do. We hold each other firmly for as long as we can. She's still the same Opal I remember, my childhood friend.

Her long blonde hair is pulled into a delicate knot at the nape of her neck. Her smile lights up her entire face as she hugs Linnick, even though she's only briefly met him. The only difference is the jewelry adorning her, and the army leathers replaced by a dress. I suppose the same could be said for me.

I hold her at arm's length, studying her beaming face. It's only then that I finally notice it's not just the three of us. Duke Wyman watches us with intrigue, his peppered hair styled so neatly it doesn't budge as he tilts his head to the side. Why is he with her?

"Why are you here? You look so different! How is your hair like that? You finally let someone do it!" Her words come out in a rush, her questions flowing one after another in bursts of excitement. Her hand reaches out to hold a strand of my hair between her fingers as she examines it.

I struggle to find the words. "Opal, how are you here? Where's your husband?" A sprout of guilt springs up that I haven't been asking around about her.

She loops an arm through the duke's and squeezes. "He's right here. I have so much to tell you." A faint blush creeps across her cheeks.

She's married...to *the duke?*

He had to know Opal and I were friends. I narrow my eyes, opening my mouth to speak, but he cuts me off.

"I'll let the two of you catch up. I apologize, I didn't realize the friendship." Duke Wyman clears his throat as he looks between the two of us. His words are softer than they've been when he's spoken with me, which only fuels my annoyance. He *knew*, of course he did.

Opal nods, keeping her eyes on me—too shocked to register what he said.

"My father thought to include me in this matching event." She makes a *tsk*ing noise when I pause, and I know what her reaction is going to be to the next part. "Remember the mystery boy I met at the market on my weekly runs?"

She nods, her eyes big, hanging onto my every word.

"Well, he turned out to be the prince. He's kind of my friend." The last word feels like ash in my mouth. Guilt eats away at me about my plan to leave. But now that she's here it has my mind in a tangled heap.

"*What?*" she practically squeals, her voice bouncing around the corridor.

Linnick and I both laugh, happiness warming my insides and spreading across my chest. She's just as I remember her.

"I'll tell you soon, I promise. I'm sorry I didn't find you sooner. I tried but…" I open my mouth to tell her how sorry I am, but she stops me before I can speak the words.

"I think we all know your father wouldn't have allowed you to visit her—even if you knew where she was." Linnick finally speaks, having given us a moment to catch up. He isn't wrong in his assumption.

Opal nods. "It would've been near impossible to find me. I sent you letters, which I assume your father never allowed you to receive," she says sadly.

I shake my head as her face scrunches in a grimace, but none of us are shocked. It'd be foolish to be surprised anymore by his cruelty.

"It was worth the try. I've missed you so much, Lu. I've needed my closest friend," she says, reaching out and squeezing my hand.

My heart stutters at my nickname. My oldest friend is standing directly in front of me. Tears shine in both of our eyes at the unexpectedness of the last few minutes.

"Is the duke good to you?" I ask.

She smiles brightly and nods her head, her face changing colors for a different reason entirely. Though my question is laced with suspicion, she doesn't notice. Does she not think it's odd he didn't make the connection between us?

"I know how strange it is to think I could be happy with someone his age, but he's so kind, it's difficult to explain. To have a husband, a real home, the land, and titles? It's more than I could ask for," she says wistfully.

Most of the castle believes I'll be right along with her as a new bride. With her married to Duke Wyman, can I tell her it's all just a ruse?

"There's so much to tell you. Where can we meet tomorrow?"

The duke's shoes click against the stone floor and we rush to make a plan.

"The library just after daybreak," I whisper quickly and she nods her head. Her blue eyes still glisten with unshed tears. As the duke gets closer, she gives me another quick hug, squeezing so tightly she steals my breath for a moment.

She turns to the duke and says, "I think I'll stay in tomorrow while you go out to the market."

Duke Wyman looks at her with concern evident in his eyes. The tenderness with which he brings his hand up to cup her cheek is surprising. His words are even more gentle than his touch.

"Of course, my darling. Whatever it is you need. I'll bring you back something special." He smiles at her and kisses her forehead briefly before nodding in our direction. I watch them as they walk away, my head still spinning in more directions than I can count.

"What do you make of the duke not telling either of you about you both being here?"

Linnick's question leaves me stumped. He doesn't press my thoughts as we walk back to my chambers, and by the time we arrive, I still don't have a response.

"I don't know, but I'm going to find out. I can't believe she's been here the whole time, Linnick. How could I possibly leave her here now?" I huff out a tense breath, close to banging my head into the door.

"Let's just hear what she's got to say tomorrow. I'll be in the kitchen, but fill me in when I get the chance to come back."

I hate that he has to go back to the servants' quarters, even if he does enjoy it. He deserves more.

He leaves me to my chambers, and I strip off my gown forcefully, pulling on my trousers and blouse. I undo any pins shoved into my hair and separate my hair into two braids. I glance into a mirror on my way out and catch sight of myself. With my braids tied at the end by a frayed ribbon and my regular clothing, I look more like my old self. I study my face; it looks fuller than when I was at the camp. No longer hollowed out.

Most days, I was lucky to eat one meal. The camp sludge wasn't very filling, and the likelihood of seeing Father was too high. Other than the times I could eat with Opal before our chores, I dreaded the thought of being within sight of him.

Now my muscles are growing stronger with the consistent meals, even with less training each day. Only managing to train once a day, I suspected I would lose the muscle I've spent so long building. But as I look into the mirror, I see how wrong I was.

My body is more toned than it's ever been. My arms are strong and firm. My hips and thighs are slightly fuller with the added muscle, making me feel powerful. A small part of me feels like smiling at this victory, but the other half is drowning in a sea of worry about Opal's life since I last saw her.

A knock at the door has me hustling to pull it open, ready for my mind to be filled with the earth beneath my feet, limbs burning with a long run.

"Ready?" Graylen says, leaning against the frame.

By this point we've fallen into a comfortable routine. He isn't the least bit surprised to find me in my training leathers. I jog back to my lounging seat and grab the velvet cape he gave me. When I meet his stare, his eyes are unreadable.

He's better than anyone I've met at concealing his thoughts, his mask always perfectly in place. I may know the truth about his reasons to protect the servants, but that doesn't mean he's stopped getting under my skin.

We weave silently through the dimly lit castle until we find ourselves at the entrance to the gardens. Our routine here has become my favorite part of the day. I never tire of the way the night air fills my lungs. Even Graylen is more likable out here, someone I can almost get to know.

He pulls out his key, looking to either side to ensure the corridor is clear. When he finds it empty, he unlocks the door. A smile edges the corners of my mouth.

We normally remain quiet at the start of the night, stretching our bodies wordlessly as we listen to the frogs sing and trees rustle. The stress that tugs at my chest begins to melt away, allowing me a moment of reprieve.

When it's just us and the night sky above, I feel as if I can think clearly. Graylen stays so far within his own mind I sometimes forget he's there. We begin our pace at a jog, silently agreeing that tonight is going to be a long one.

We pass the half-dead tree I hid beneath the night we got engaged, noticing how beautifully it's now growing. It must've needed the day or so of rain to give it a bit of life back. I smile, happy that its leaves are now brightly green and growing longer than before.

"Morning or nights?" Graylen asks.

I consider it a moment, his voice coming out steady while mine is still verging on breathless.

"Nights. As long as it includes getting out of the castle." And especially if that means getting into the gardens. I look at him out of the corner of my eye and ask, "You?"

"Mornings," he says without elaborating.

Not what I expected him to say.

"Next?" I ask.

He huffs out a laugh. "Would you rather travel on a ship, or ride a horse, sleeping beside a fire each night?"

He doesn't seem to mind I make him ask the questions. I pick up the pace and he matches it.

"I don't know, I haven't done either. Riding a horse, I guess. Easier to see more towns that way," I answer.

He makes a humming noise.

"What, you don't agree?" I ask, unsurprised we don't have the same answer. The trees blur past us. My words come out choppy from the near wheezing of my breath.

"A ship is easier and safer." How is his breath always so steady while he talks and runs?

"Doesn't sound like much room for an adventure, though," I say.

He shrugs and says, "So you like adventure? Does that mean if you could get the chance to explore Penyth, then you would?"

I trip over a small root peeking up from the ground and slow down a little. "Of course not."

My words come out too fast. He narrows his eyes, hearing the lie. Though I can't openly admit it, there's something alluring about exploring *everywhere*. Even Penyth.

"Would you explore it?" I press, curious if he would go to such a forbidden and dangerous place.

He's silent for a moment. The sound of our feet pounding into the dirt is the only thing filling my ears. We're finding our stride now. I've pushed through the breathless wall, my attention turned to him.

"Wouldn't dream of it. Winter or summer?" He moves on.

"Neither. Summer is too hot and suffocating. The winter is bitterly relentless. So...spring and autumn, I guess. You?" I ask.

"Winter." He shrugs. "Less people around."

I snort a laugh. "Of course. Would you rather be a bird or a bear?" I echo Opal's words from the night we sat by the fire at the camp together. I can see him glance at me out of the corner of my eye.

"Anything with wings will be my answer," he says.

I bite back a smile. "That's what I said!"

We laugh, finally finding at least one thing we can agree on.

"Instead of running the rest of the night, we could work through a fighting series?" he suggests. "Hand-to-hand is something every woman in this kingdom should familiarize themselves with."

"I'm good with running." I shake my head, remembering the last time I allowed a boy to train me. I move my legs faster, hoping he doesn't notice the frown tugging my mouth down.

He shrugs, not taking offense.

We run until we're both breathing heavily and gasping for air. The faster I try to run, the more he matches my pace. It's like a game of seeing who can run the farthest each evening, but it typically ends in a draw. Though I sometimes get the sneaking suspicion he just stops whenever I do.

We quietly stretch before going back inside. He raises his arms into the air, leaning from one side to the other. The movement causes the bottom of his shirt to lift up, revealing his toned stomach. I can't help but watch the muscles move as he leans into the stretch. I feel my cheeks flush. At least it's night out.

"Need something?" His voice is light and airy. Laughter rumbles in his chest as my eyes dart up to his.

"Nope. You don't have to walk me back to my chambers," I say, not for the first time.

Graylen simply shrugs and walks with me like he always does.

Either way, I'm eager to get to the basin of water to clean the sweat and insanity of the day off. My thoughts center on what Opal will say tomorrow, hoping I've worn my body out enough to sleep tonight.

After just a couple nights of coming back from training, Avery started leaving water for me to wash with. Though she made no comments about doing so, I know it's her. The water has usually lost most of its warmth by the time I return, but I'm just as grateful for it.

As we round the corner, I hear a laugh ring out from the entrance to my chamber. A laugh that sends a swarm of butterflies flitting about my stomach.

A man bows to Adrian and walks away from us. Adrian's eyes flicker with something closely resembling anger when he sees who I'm with.

"I'm sorry. I should've told you I was coming; I wasn't anticipating having free time tonight. I didn't expect you to be out of your room so late," he says as he takes in my disheveled appearance and a deep crease forms between his brows. He looks to Graylen, his mouth pressing into a line.

I fumble for an answer, wanting to ease whatever thoughts are running through his mind. "I find I sleep better when I exercise before bed, and it's the best time to spend with Graylen without being interrupted." I look between them, tacking on what should be an obvious explanation: "So we can be prepared if anyone questions us…"

My heart pounds, thoughts escaping me at the sight of Adrian here. It leaves me more thrilled than I care to admit.

"Of course. I just thought I'd come over to see you for a while." Adrian folds his arms behind his back, his voice growing hesitant.

"This must be my hint to leave," Graylen grits out, staring at Adrian. He must not like being told what to do; I can understand that.

"Thanks for the run, Graylen. See you tomorrow." I open my door, leaving Graylen behind as Adrian follows me into my chambers. My heart races as I fight a smile. Adrian wants to see me.

"If you two smiled more at each other, you might not have to spend so much time with him." He sits down on the lounging seat, relaxing into the plush cushions.

I walk over and take a seat beside him. I hope I don't smell.

"I won't be at the castle forever," I whisper so quietly that I'm not sure if he heard me, wondering if he can read between my words. I won't be staying in Runnswick forever either.

He lets out a long sigh and leans his head back, closing his eyes. "I know."

Unable to look into the depths of his brown eyes, I look down at my hands, at the grime coating my fingernails. A lifetime of scars covers them.

"And I hopefully won't be engaged to the princess of Penyth forever either." Strange for him to be in this position at all.

"Have you two had any correspondence?" I try to push down the little seed of jealousy filling my thoughts.

"Nothing. My father has been his usual self since announcing it. If my mother were here, things might be incredibly different." His voice drops to a whisper. "She was always able to get through to him in ways others couldn't."

I wonder if my mother had the same effect on my father.

"And now he's making decisions for you," I say briskly.

"My father is a good man. He's just naïve to the world around him. Around our kingdom. Not to mention he enjoys a pint of ale more than giving orders. We're lucky to have Wyman to help; otherwise, I'd be drowning more than I already am." He looks away and stares up at the ceiling. I have a feeling he doesn't talk about this very often, so I silently listen.

"He believes things will work themselves out and doesn't feel the need to initiate anything himself. Whether it's from him not knowing how or just laziness I don't know. He truly is a great father, but we all know that he's a terrible king. Someone has to rule this kingdom, and it isn't him." The weight of the pressure he's been under is heavy in his voice.

I've never had a decent father, let alone one that's a king. I lean my head against the seat and stare up at the ceiling too, unsure of how to respond. After we sit in silence for a while, I start to think he's fallen asleep. As I part my lips to speak, I feel the warmth of his fingers lace through mine. I freeze. Fear and excitement stir inside of me. The temptation to rip my hand out of his is hard to fight against, but for some reason I don't move. It's been a long time since I've allowed someone to touch me in this way. It's kind of nice.

He curls his fingers around mine, and I mirror his motion. "I'll try to come see you more—" his voice is a soft whisper, "even if I'm being selfish for it."

I fall asleep with my hand attached to his, my thoughts unusually quiet.

Twenty-Seven

COREOPSIS

IT'S EASY TO FORGET HOW comforting it is to have someone to talk to. With Linnick and Adrian both busy, I've done nothing but interact with people who are here for the matching and keep the charade with Graylen up.

But now, with Opal peppering me with questions, I find myself remembering the days I was able to spend hours with her just talking.

"So, wait. The prince held your *hand*! In your room...*alone*?" she squeals.

I sigh dramatically at the one thing Opal chooses to focus on. But it ends as a laugh, unable to stop myself with how much I've missed her.

"He's engaged, Opal," I whisper through gritted teeth. "But we do spend time together when he's free."

She jumps up and down while squealing loudly, her voice bouncing off the stacks of books that surround us.

"*Shhh.*" I look around to make sure no one else is in the library. "He says he'll be back to see me, but he hasn't yet. I see Graylen on a daily basis, far more than I see Adrian."

With the confusion swirling on her face, I choose this moment to tell her, though she likely has already heard.

"I spend more time with Graylen because I'm engaged to him," I say with a grimace.

Opal's mouth pops open, unable to speak for a moment as she processes. "*You,* Amira Ramsey, are *engaged?* To the prince's advisor!" She shrieks the last part, saying it with such astonishment it doesn't sound like a question.

"It's a long story but the short answer is yes," I admit.

After a moment of throwing her hands into the air, making several strange noises, and finally turning back to me, I can see the hundreds of questions brewing behind her eyes.

"How did this even happen? I've only met him a handful of times but he's certainly...different from most of the suitors here." She giggles, covering her mouth.

I nod, realizing I can't tell her yet that what Graylen and I have is a temporary arrangement. The duke has to believe it's real or the whole thing could unravel.

The last thing I want for Opal is to have her keep a lie from her new husband, whom she somehow seems to be happy with. I can't steal that happiness from her, even if it means hiding the truth from the person I care most about in this kingdom.

"I'm not like most of the other women here either." I shrug.

She nods, accepting this answer, and pushes ahead. "Then why were you with the prince last night? Does your father know? Oh, I would love to see his face when he finds out. What is Graylen like?" She laughs so loudly I can't help but join in.

"Honestly, Opal? He makes me feel *insane.* He somehow manages to crawl beneath my skin every time I'm near him. Everything I say, he says the opposite. I say up, he says down. I say no, he says yes. It's infuriating!" My eyes widen, afraid I said too much.

"Oh. You really do love him." Her mouth stretches into a wide grin. Did she not just hear me?

"Did you really not know? Everyone at the castle knows by now." Then I realize I haven't seen her at any of the castle events, even if the duke was present. She looks down at her delicate hands, twisting a gold band around her ring finger.

"No, I don't spend much time at the castle. We have the most beautiful estate not far from here. Oh, you have to come! It's so lovely it makes it difficult to leave." She sighs dreamily. "Especially when the duke is on business while he's here."

I study her as she fixes her gaze on her ring, which now holds her attention.

"What about you? How does it feel to be the duchess of Runnswick?" I wiggle my eyebrows up and down, causing her to laugh. Redness spreads across her cheeks at the formal title.

"It's quite strange as well. The day my father stuck me on the horse and had me ride straight to the chapel, I thought my life was over. I wanted to be a wife but not like that. I spent the first week of our marriage in tears. I'm not proud of how weak and horrible I probably seemed to him." She swipes away a rogue tear slipping down her cheek.

She always had a romantic notion of marrying for love, and at first it looked as if she would never get the chance.

"But how could I not be upset? I was ripped from my life. Even if we were miserable in the camp, the unknown was scarier than the nightmare I was used to living each day," she says softly.

"Of course you were upset—everything happening so fast," I reassure her. She has to know that she's allowed to have these emotions, even if we were taught to repress them in the camp.

"I was shocked when I began falling in love with him. From the moment I met him, he was nothing but perfect. We went on our honeymoon at one of his estates and slowly I began to warm to his presence. Now he lets me do as I please around our Runnswick estate, and if I'm bored, he has a carriage drawn to accompany me to our Grantford or Saltain estate. He has one in almost every town!" She sighs wistfully with one of her hands propping her head up.

From where we are—huddled on the second floor of the library, sitting with our backs resting against the shelves—I feel as if we can speak freely. "I'm so happy for you, Opal." Even if it's a little weird that she's married to the duke. I smile at her, and we clasp hands, still unable to believe our luck at being here together.

She nods her head and says, "Who would've thought that the Lu I know is now a friend of Prince Adrian and engaged to his advisor."

We laugh in disbelief. Our lives have turned out so differently from where we were not so long ago.

"Lu?" a voice says.

Both of our heads jerk up, startled. My panic eases: it's Adrian standing on the first floor.

"Your Highness!" Opal quickly stands as he makes his way to our level. Her eyes dart to me, shooting me a look just before he gets to us. He stops, his hands resting casually behind his back.

"Adrian, this is Opal. One of the three friends I was telling you about back at the port," I say, shifting awkwardly.

Adrian nods to her, a smile lighting up his face. "You mean one of the *four*? Good to see you again." He directs the first question to me, then turns to her, offering his hand in greeting.

My eyes bounce between the two of them, confused. His blond hair has been trimmed shorter since the last time I saw him, and I can't help but wonder again what it would feel like to run my hands through it.

"We met briefly at the wedding," Adrian says with a smile. "I wish I would've known the girl that was stolen away to be married was your friend; it would've gotten rid of a lot of those tears."

Opal blushes furiously, likely remembering the day.

"Duchess Wyman, I hope this means you'll be joining us more at the castle," he adds hopefully.

She groans and puts her head in her hands. "Please just call me Opal. I don't think I'll ever get used to that." She speaks through her hands, and we both start laughing.

"Well, you're certainly the first of the three to have a fancy title," I tease her.

I know for a fact she loves the big decorum, and she deserves it. I notice Adrian watching me carefully, and he smiles when I look at him. Something about his smile doesn't reach his eyes this time.

"Four," Adrian leans down and whispers. I look at him, not understanding.

"Four?" I repeat, my brows drawing together.

He smiles at me and looks down at the cold floor. Now, I'm second-guessing if that's what he actually said.

"You again said you have three friends, but you have four." He nudges me in the side.

Opal looks like her smile is about to crack her face in half, and I have to stop myself from doing the same.

"I suppose you're right. So, now there's the one who got married off, an old man, a dog with no name…and the prince. My collection of friends makes quite the group."

This time, the gleam in his eye matches his smile, the dimples fully present and his golden-brown eyes sparkling with amusement.

We sit on the floor, Opal and I sharing stories about our childhood. Adrian absorbs every word and laughs at every tale we tell of two little girls surrounded by soldiers.

"One time, we found two discarded swords and tried to practice fighting with them. We were only eight at the time, and our fathers were both *furious*. They said girls have no place handling a sword, so they made us clean the stables for a month." Opal laughs as she narrates, but the story brings unwanted memories. That was one of the lighter punishments my father gave to me.

I bring my knees to my chest and listen to her continue the tale.

"Lu was so angry after having to clean the stalls. She decided that we should learn how to fight properly, so the two of us snuck out back to the creek every night to practice. We would watch the soldiers and try to mirror the movements when we were alone."

Cleaning the stables wasn't my motivation; the way my father effortlessly fought other soldiers was. I wanted to be better than him.

"Eventually, we got stuck once we learned what we could from watching," she says with a wicked grin. "I told one of the twins if he didn't teach us in the sparring ring then I would rat him out for sneaking off to the market to see a girl."

At this, I bite back a smile. Mica was always easy to blackmail. He got himself in trouble more times than both of us could count.

"And your fathers were just fine with that?" Adrian asks.

Opal and I share a look, her mouth lifting up at one corner, a mischievous glint in her eye.

"We told them if they ever wanted to make money off us marrying someone, they would have to let us train out in the open," I say with a grin and look at Opal, the memory swirling in my mind. "Otherwise, we would intentionally scare away every potential suitor and they would be stuck with us forever."

We didn't want to be stuck with them either, but we knew it was a risk they couldn't take.

"Prince Adrian?" a guard shouts into the silent library.

Adrian lets out a small groan, his brown eyes rolling at the interruption.

"You're needed in the throne room for the council meeting," the soldier continues, evidently used to Adrian hiding away.

"Duty calls." Adrian nods his goodbye to Opal, but his eyes linger on me. He's watching me in a way he hasn't before, like he's trying to figure me out. My eyes track his movements as he walks away, unable to stop myself.

Surprisingly, Graylen doesn't wander into the library the rest of the afternoon, which is fine by me. It gives Opal time to fill me in on the feud between my father and her husband.

"In the last offsite council meeting, your father accused Wyman of collecting extra taxes from a village, where he has one of his houses." She looks down at her hands. "Of course, it isn't true, but the one time the king decided to be there, he was inclined to listen to your father. He threatened to strip Wyman of his title and take his land away."

I gape at her, though not completely surprised. Father is good at convincing others, but it's still a bit much that the king would oust his own brother.

"Maybe the king was too far gone that night," I suggest. "I've heard he doesn't make many decisions anyway. He likely forgot with the ale clouding his thoughts shortly after."

She nods, unconvinced. "The duke was mad with your father. He never mentioned you were at the castle, but I supposed he's been fairly busy with smoothing things over since that council meeting. He's nothing but gentle with me, but when it comes to your father and the king…"

I nod my head, knowing my father is capable of driving people to do things they wouldn't normally do. Maybe that's why the duke always acts strange around me. He wouldn't be the first person to treat me differently.

"I know," I say softly.

Quiet tension forms in the air, and we decide to stop talking about my father. He's always hungered for power, and we both know he'll do anything to get more of it.

"Does this mean you're going to stay?" Opal whispers.

When I first came to the castle, my mind constantly raced with how to escape, and when. But sitting here with Opal today, the thought hasn't crossed my mind once. I can feel my plan of leaving easing to the back of my mind until she mentions it. My life really could be different now that I have Opal and Linnick here. But the thought of being trapped within these walls makes my stomach turn.

I reach over and squeeze her hand. "I really don't know."

She squeezes my hand back, and we sit there until our bellies growl with hunger. She walks with me back to my room and pulls me into a tight hug.

"Maybe after your wedding, we can really spend more time together. Like an entire weekend in another village. You would love it," she says brightly, trying to lighten the mood.

But it wouldn't be my life. It would be hers, and it would only be temporary. Her arms squeeze me tightly. Guilt gnaws at my chest.

"Are you staying here in the castle?" I ask.

She nods. "Only for a night or two. Our estate is so near it's just a short walk to it. The duke said I'll be more comfortable there. Maybe you, Linnick, and I can all spend some time together soon?"

I smile. It sounds too good to be true. But it does bother me slightly that she refers to her own husband as "the duke."

"What do you say we meet before sunset in the gardens?" I offer.

She nods, giving me one last hug. I find it difficult to let her go. My two closest friends are both here with me now. I hardly have my father to deal with, Linnick isn't fighting to survive without his farm. For the first time in my life, I feel like I should be able to relax.

So why is it I don't feel that way?

TWENTY-EIGHT

LISIANTHUS

I PULL THE DOOR OPEN just as Graylen is raising his hand to knock on it, his dark hair falling into his face as a hint of surprise flickers in his eyes. Almost as soon as it's there, it disappears.

"Am I that predictable?" he asks with a chuckle.

I find myself wanting to smile but don't want to give him the satisfaction. Instead, I shrug and breeze past him, eager to get through mealtime to meet with Opal and Linnick. Hopefully Avery was able to get my note to Linnick about where and when to meet.

Our shoes make light pattering sounds against the stone floor. I keep my gaze focused on the dark corridor ahead, needing to squint to see fully. "You'd think they would put larger sconces through here. Or at least more in between them to light the way better."

Graylen turns to me, lifting a brow. "Maybe. But then the light would wake all those friendly spiders in the cracks of the walls."

I involuntarily shiver at the thought and say, "That's one way to look at it."

I take a step further away from the wall beside me, in turn moving closer to Graylen. Even in the poorly lit walkway, I can see him as he winks at me.

"Careful. Don't fall in love with me, Ramsey," he says with a smirk.

My back straightens as I bristle at him calling me that. "We at least need some pretense of liking each other," I snap without really meaning to. I clear my throat.

We both remain silent after that. It isn't until we get to the great hall that I finally speak.

"You don't need to walk me back to my chambers after we eat," I say quickly—before we have to pretend again. The room sounds full of people already.

"Have a date planned?" His voice is casual but his jaw flexes.

I slip my arm into the crook of his elbow. People hardly look our way as we enter. We're hardly considered gossip now.

"In fact, I do." I don't bother to tell him the *date* is really just meeting with my two closest friends.

He says nothing as we find our usual place with several empty chairs. We sit side by side, our knees almost touching.

"I'm far better company," he whispers into my ear.

My pulse quickens as he reaches forward and twists a piece of hair between his fingers. People are watching now. I blink several times and remember the part I'm supposed to be playing.

I turn to look at him, holding his gaze. His finger still twirls a single lock of hair. I reach up and brush the hair from his eyes. The darkness matches his ever-present black tunic.

"Do you only own one shirt?" I whisper through a fake smile, our seats positioned with enough space no one can hear me.

"Why? Do you want to go to my room and see them?" He says this a little too loud. The girl sitting closest to us gasps, and immediately turns her head to the person next to her. The comment quickly makes its rounds through the room. I continue smiling but narrow my eyes at him. He shrugs, playing the game.

I make to move my hand away from his hair, but he catches it, slowly bringing my hand to his mouth and placing a light kiss on the inside of my palm. I force myself to not snatch my hand from his lips. Luckily, I'm wearing a shoe with a point on it today, which easily finds its way to his shin as I dig it in. He grimaces, dropping my hand. But the faintest outline of a smile plays at his lips.

"How far do you want to run tonight?" he asks.

I huff. "I already told you, I'll be busy."

"Suit yourself. Adrian said he wanted to see you in the morning, by the way. Early," he says and leans away from me, turning to his food. A muscle in his jaw feathers as he clenches it tight.

"Thanks," I bite out.

Why does it feel so tense?

We eat quietly; all the while my stomach does an unusual flip over and over. I press my lips into a thin line, trying to interpret what it means. But not having to interact with anyone around us, he doesn't try any more unsolicited touches. He hardly looks my way. The moment I finish the last drop of soup, I stand from my seat.

"Good evening," I call out after him, but his back is already turned to me. He doesn't return the goodbye as I breeze out of the hall.

It doesn't take long for my friends to show at the entrance to the gardens. Opal's smile is as happily relaxed as Linnick's. I clasp my hands together, eager to squeeze away the feeling of Graylen's mouth on the inside of my palm.

I motion for them to walk with me. I'm itching to get as far away as I can from the castle before the sun sets and we have to go back inside. I nod to the guards, not expecting any sort of response.

"Enjoy dinner with Graylen?" Linnick's eyes are light, dancing with amusement.

"What?" says Opal, clearly disappointed to be out of the loop. "Did something happen?"

I can't stop the blush that creeps across my cheeks. "You heard already?" I say weakly. Word sure does spread fast.

"Almost the moment it happened. One maid came to the kitchen for a tray refill and told the whole kitchen, who told another, who told another. It didn't take long for your swoon-worthy breakfast to touch every corner of the castle," Linnick says.

At this, Opal's shoulders fall. I can tell she's frustrated to be so behind, especially after having missed the engagement too. If she would've just come to one event, we could've been together this entire time. Or if her *husband* would've said something.

"That boy sure does know how to play up—"

I cut him off, forcing a laugh. "I told him not to be so affectionate in public, but I guess he can't help it."

"Right," says Opal dejectedly. "Well, I'm so happy for the two of you."

Linnick turns to me, one of his grayed brows lifting in accusation. I shake my head and he remains quiet. I'm not ready to involve Opal in this tangled lie yet.

"It's good to see you two together." Linnick smiles at the two of us, his short stature forcing both of us to look down slightly. He still walks with his head high, his wrinkled eyes filled with life.

"I wouldn't want to be anywhere else." And in this moment, I mean it.

Our path is dim but enough of the sun is still out that we have time to spend. We walk through the maze, laughing and talking about our market days. The guards positioned along the path remain perfectly still, as if unaware of our presence.

"They're kind of eerie, don't you think? Just standing there like statues. Do they ever leave?" Opal says and shivers.

I almost tell Opal they do at night but keep it to myself.

"Maybe both of you can come to our Runnswick estate. I'm sure the duke could pull some strings to get you out of the kitchens for a day. We could sit in the dayroom or sit by our small pond. Really anything we wanted to do I could arrange for us." Her face beams brightly.

We walk until we reach the back half of the gardens, a part Graylen and I only come to on our longer runs. This area has small trees scattered about and is far enough away from the cliffs that I can hardly make out the sound of crashing waves.

The oak tree we stop in front of is the largest in the entire garden. Even with it being so distant from the entrance and the maze-shaped hedges, it can still be seen from the steps of the castle. The top of it sticks oddly above the rest of the shorter tree line.

"Up for a game?" Linnick says with a wink.

I smile, knowing Linnick is just trying to distract me from what lies within the castle. Opal claps her hands together and sits beneath the large oak. We both join her, the last of the tension leaving my shoulders as I rest against the cool bark. A buzzing energy hums through each spot where the trunk connects with my back.

"See that empty space on the ground right there?" He points to a small open area just past us.

Opal's eyes widen, waiting to play pretend together like we did when we were children.

"It's the perfect spot for a special seed to be planted from a..." He trails off and I pick up quickly.

"From a lemon tree," I finish.

He laughs half-heartedly, knowing he would've picked the same kind. He pauses for a moment, and I can see the longing in his eyes for what he's been forced to leave behind.

"It's no ordinary lemon seed, though…" Opal jumps in, sensing the sadness and wanting him to forget about it for a moment. "Whoever plants the seed will feel the benefit of the healing tree."

I stare at the empty space in the dirt and feel my thoughts drift to it. "I have to spend each day walking out to this spot to water the seed," I gently carry on. "Each time it's watered it has to be with happy thoughts or it'll spoil the fruit."

Linnick rests his head against the tree, closing his eyes as he listens to us continue the story. Opal does the same, the tree large enough for all of us to lean against.

"Right. And you have to talk to the tree, *especially* as a sapling. You have to spend time beside it, telling it about your day and how you wish it could join you instead of being stuck in one place," Linnick says with a gleam in his eye. "Sapling trees can be so fickle, you know?"

Opal and I giggle, picturing ourselves talking to a tree like it were a person. I know Linnick has done just that.

"Through the years it grows tall, bearing dozens of lemons. Any time I need a wound healed I can come to this tree and squeeze the lemon onto it. The juice will burn and sting, but it'll sew my wound up in the blink of an eye."

Linnick smiles at where I pick up the story.

"It doesn't heal just flesh wounds, though. If consumed, the citrusy juice will heal anything from within." He points to his chest before continuing. "It'll mend a broken heart, cleanse the hate toward another, and calm a worried mind."

I sigh and pick up a handful of dirt beside me, letting it run through my fingers.

"I wish a healing tree was more than just a game of pretend." Opal speaks the words we're all thinking. Though part of me feels whole the moment my feet step onto the earth, mending my anxious thoughts when I connect with it. With no thick walls blocking my view of the world around me, I can relax into my own mind.

It makes me imagine what it would be like if our kingdom could be healed in that way. If we could all be washed of our hate and pain. Would the three of us even be forced to be here right now?

"We'll find a time to do this again soon, right?" Her voice is low and uncertain.

But our kingdom doesn't work that way. The question lingers, unanswered.

TWENTY-NINE

NARCISSUS

THE MORNING IS CLEAR AND cold. Not a single cloud can be seen in the sky, allowing the sun to attempt to warm the world below. The brisk air seeps in through the windows of my chambers. I absentmindedly rub my hands over my arms to ease the chill.

"Hello? Earth to Lu?" Adrian smiles, his dimples deeply on display. His boyish grin is what my eyes drift to as he laughs. His lips morph into a lopsided smile. "I can't wait to see the look on everyone's faces when you win today."

I tilt my head forcefully away from him and his lips, focusing on the marketgoers through my window.

"Win what?" I ask, narrowing my eyes.

He shrugs, a mischievous glint in his eyes.

I groan. "Another event today?"

His laugh is like a lullaby in my ears. "That is why you're all here, isn't it?"

My smile falls at the reminder. "I should go down then before they begin." I move to step past him, and he does the same, blocking my path. I step to the other side just as he follows suit, causing him to laugh uncomfortably. He finally steps fully out of the way and sweeps his arm out.

"After you," he says softly and gestures to the door. "I'll give it a moment before I leave too."

Right. Don't want anyone getting the wrong idea. I yank the door open harder than necessary and come face to face with Graylen's raised arm about to knock. His dark eyebrows flick up, displaying more emotion than usual.

"I came to escort you. Since we're engaged." His words hold an edge to them, aimed at Adrian. I don't know why he's surprised; he's the one who told me Adrian wanted to see me.

"I know I told you I wouldn't stay so late, but we lost track of time." Adrian shrugs apologetically before turning to me. "I'll try my best to come see you tomorrow morning again."

"You should be more careful. Everyone is leaving their chambers on the floor below to head to the games," Graylen grits out.

Be more careful? There aren't any other guest chambers on this level. The likelihood of running into someone else is fairly low.

Graylen offers his arm to me, which I reluctantly take. I cast one last smile over my shoulder at Adrian. He waves goodbye to me, and I leave him standing in my room alone.

We're both silent on our walk to the gardens. Though we join the cheerfully chattering crowd, we don't speak. We all pour out of the castle where extra guards and an announcer are waiting.

"Pair up! One woman to one man!"

A burst of energy erupts from the gathering crowd. The sun beams down on us, though it does little to ease the frigidness in the air. Various games and objects have been set up in the gardens, transforming them into some sort of competition.

Unsurprisingly, my partner is Graylen. We silently watch the flurry of women trying to find someone to pair up with. Sarah and

Milo are a given, their pair forming as quickly as ours. Everyone begins matching up, even Sir Christopher, who—surprisingly, but somehow also making complete sense—pairs up with Edith. Both of them stand with their crossed arms, glaring at me.

We have to beat them.

"Does everyone have a partner?" The announcer smiles, pleased with the silence. "Wonderful! We have an exciting day planned for you all. There will be a series of games lined up for you to play. Your partner and you are a team, playing against the others!"

Excited whispers are shared among partners at the promise of a prize.

"What do we win?" a man from the crowd shouts.

"This is not that sort of competition. The idea is to get to know your partner in the process. You're here to find a match above all else."

Grumbles ensue with the lack of a prize.

"Welcome to our first ever garden games! If you beat the opposing team, you will receive a token. Whoever has the most tokens at the end of the first round will advance to the next; anyone without tokens will be eliminated."

A group of spectators filters out into the gardens. My breath is stolen away when I see who's among them as they're led to the edge of the games area. Father is pointedly *not* looking in my direction, his gaze set on Sir Christopher instead.

I haven't seen him since the night of the engagement. A tremble surges through my body. I squeeze my hands into fists, trying to steady them. I feel a warm hand slip into mine, forcing the tension to slowly ebb away.

"Don't allow him to see the effect he has on you."

I turn my attention to Graylen. He nods with an arrogant smirk over my shoulder—in the direction of my father. His mask firmly in place.

Graylen leans forward until his mouth is close to my ear. "I'm a sore loser, Ramsey. So I don't intend to lose today."

Lose? Right. The game.

"Try to not look like you hate me. Remember we're supposed to like each other?" His voice rumbles deeply.

It's impossible to forget when he keeps reminding me. I look down to where Graylen's hand covers mine, trying to ignore the skip in my heart.

Beside Father is Duke Wyman and Opal. She looks especially radiant in a light blue frock, but her face is pinched and tight. The remaining spectators are other lords and ladies I don't recognize. Adrian comes around the group, planting himself in front of them. When our eyes meet, he nods, a small tilt to his head. His eyes narrow to where Graylen's hand is connected with mine.

"Try and focus," Graylen whispers into my ear.

"I wish I was on someone else's team just so I could beat you."

He laughs softly and pulls away from me. "I don't think you'd come out victorious, sweetheart."

I balk at the name and contemplate making a gagging noise.

"Sweetheart? Who knew a woman could get Graylen Garriden to use those words," a tall, curvy, dark-haired girl says to him. "It certainly isn't the word you used with me."

I try to ignore the sour feeling that rises in my stomach. I take a step closer to Graylen.

"Amira isn't just any woman, Florence. Have you seen how beautiful she is? It's difficult to focus on much else when she's around."

The girl rolls her eyes and walks away, her hips swishing back and forth, turning more than a few heads.

My cheeks burn at Graylen's compliment, though I know it was for the benefit of keeping our deceit alive.

"Pick any station!" the announcer calls. "When the bell is rung, you may begin!"

Graylen gestures for me to choose the first game. I take a deep breath and walk over to where a wooden table has been set up.

A servant stands nearby to preside over the game. "As a team, you are to strategize where to move the piece," she explains. "The winner will receive their first token of the day."

I haven't a clue what I'm looking at. Small pieces have been whittled into various objects. A small castle-like one, the head of a horse, one with a small cross, and many more with odd, rounded tops.

The other couple has their heads bent together, strategizing. They don't look nearly as confused as I am.

"Any ideas on what our first move should be?" Graylen inquires.

I shake my head, not wanting to admit I don't actually know what game this is.

Graylen's eyes search mine for a moment before he finally says, "I'll take this one. Adrian and I have spent from sunup to sundown playing chess. Better pull your weight on the next one though, Ramsey."

My face twists at the name. How difficult is it for him to just say my name like a normal person? But there's no use in complaining, not when I would have to admit I don't know how to play. There's not a lot of time for games at the training camp.

People around us fill the gardens with noise: those winning cheer and shout, while groans sound from those not doing as well. It's hard to focus on the board laid out in front of us. They swiftly move pieces about, so fast I can't figure out how it works. Some move side to side, while others are only moved diagonally.

Graylen's expression remains focused through each move, his eyes hopping around from piece to piece. The couple across from us glance nervously at each other, whispering before making their next move.

Graylen lets out a soft laugh. "Checkmate."

The boy on the other team jumps up, examining the play closely. The servant, quicker to catch on, hands us our first token.

But the boy looks furious. "You cheated somehow, Snake."

The girl grabs her partner's arm to quiet him. I stiffen, but Graylen seems entirely unaffected.

"Rematch!" the boy shouts at the servant.

"I apologize, we were told no rematches." The servant keeps her voice quiet, her eyes trained on the table.

"Then forget we played our first one," the boy snarls and takes a step toward the trembling servant. Her lower lip wavers, and she shrinks back from him.

Graylen takes a step forward before I can. "Throwing a tantrum isn't a good look on you, Henry. Tell me, how is Fourteenth House doing without their highest-paying customer visiting them every day?"

The boy pales, while the girl at his side drops his arm like it's made of fire. Her face twists into a scowl, and she stalks away from the table.

I stifle a laugh. Fourteenth House is the same madam's house that James frequented. Everyone knows that lords will occasionally spend time there, but no one outright says it. Except Graylen, apparently.

"I won't forget this," the boy spits at the servant.

"Yes. You will." Graylen's voice is cold and clipped.

The boy turns to face him and, to his credit, attempts to hold his gaze. But something in Graylen's eyes must make him lose his boldness because he takes a step back.

"Fine." The boy spins around and trudges away from us. His partner is very pointedly walking in the opposite direction.

"Ready for another?" Graylen asks casually.

I blink a few times. His face is now entirely blank, as if nothing had happened. When I don't say anything, he laughs.

"What? I'm competitive."

"What did the competition have to do with protecting that servant?" My brows pinch together.

He smiles without answering. The kind of smile that has my stomach fluttering. I peel my tongue off the roof of my suddenly dried-out mouth and lick my lips, trying to wet them. Graylen's eyes flick down to the movement, taking notice. I press my mouth into a thin line and quickly look away.

"Are we going to talk or win another game? Of course, if you don't think you can win any of the games, tell me now so I can find a new partner."

I narrow my eyes at him. "Let's find another one then."

I look around the gardens, my peaceful sanctuary infested with people who trample over low-hanging branches without a care in the world.

"Perhaps one you'll be helpful in?" he suggests.

I punch him teasingly. He feigns a wince and cradles the wounded arm.

"I just didn't know the rules of that one," I bite out, my cheeks heating. "You got lucky."

He smirks at me. "I could get luckier."

I roll my eyes, no longer offended by his hollow words. "You seem to talk a lot more than you act."

He doesn't miss a beat. "Would you rather I act on it then?"

He winks at me. Heat crawls across my chest and cheeks.

A loud squeal draws attention from the crowd. Sir Christopher is down on one knee, holding Edith's hand. She's vigorously nodding her head up and down.

"I accept!" she shouts, sending birds flying from their branches to escape the horrible noise. I wish I could follow them.

"A match made in heaven," I mumble. Graylen must have heard judging by the small laugh he breathes out.

"They'll eat each other alive," he whispers to me.

He's right. I look forward to the day that happens. I smile, clapping along with everyone else. Edith wraps her arms tightly around Sir Christopher's neck. But his gaze is on me, pure hatred in his eyes as he watches me. Perhaps expecting some sort of reaction?

"But then again, isn't it more fun that way?" Graylen adds.

Again, that wink.

"Let's go to our next one," he says and walks alongside me to the nearest game. This one is two long, lined areas side by side. A handful of wooden figures are stationed at the end.

"One player from each team will take a turn rolling this ball toward the pins in their lane. The team that takes the least amount of tries to knock them down wins," the instructor explains.

Sounds easy enough.

We position ourselves at the start of our lane, the other team laughing and not looking particularly invested. I smile when I realize I know one of them. I step up to roll first, shaking out my hands at my sides. Addie moves at the same time I do, waving when she sees me.

"Amira! Please put me out of my misery and win so I don't have to do this any longer." She leans in close to me, lowering her voice. "I'm going to try and convince my partner to sneak off into the orchids with me." She winks, her ivory hair long and flowing around her waist.

I take my first roll, knocking over at least half the pins, while Addie only gets one. Graylen trades places with me as her partner does the same. They each get two pins, leaving only three left on our side and a handful more on Addie's.

"I know you can do it." Graylen hands the ball to me, his hand catching my wrist. He smiles down at me, his thumb tracing circles over my skin.

Addie stifles a laugh at his encouragement. Maybe she can see through him more than the others, most of who are staring dreamily at our exchange.

I glance over to the spectators' area, finding more sets of eyes on us. Adrian is watching with a firmly set jaw, mirroring my father's expression. Opal is smiling, clutching her hands to her heart. I turn my back to them and roll the ball with so much force it sends the rest of our pins—and two of Addie's—scattering.

"Well done!" Addie claps, much to her partner's dismay.

The servant hands us another token.

We continue to another game. Graylen shoots arrows at a distant target, striking a perfect bullseye with each turn, securing us a token faster than any of the other games yet.

A bell is rung, and everyone finishes their game. We have three tokens. Several teams immediately join the spectators, having no winnings to advance them to the next level. Less than half the people that started remain.

"Four tokens already, my dear. We're certain to be the winners today," Sir Christopher says louder than necessary as he passes us.

One more token than us. I march over to the closest station and sit down at the card table. I hold a small hand of four cards, studying what to play.

"This one." Graylen points to one with hearts on it.

I glance at the other team, scrutinizing their hand. "Are you sure?" I whisper furiously. He couldn't possibly know what to play yet.

"Just play it."

I huff, but do as he says. I lay the card down and wait for our opponents to do the same. They lay down one with diamonds. I tap my foot against the grass as the servant flips over the card at the top of the deck. Hearts. Graylen was right.

"Hearts win." I smile widely, taking the token from the servant and thanking him.

By the time the next bell rings, there are only a couple of teams left, Sir Christopher and Edith among them. The entire castle is now watching us, cheering different teams on and passing bets on whom they think will win. We've reached the only game we haven't played. This one is a small ball several paces away.

"You have two tries to get your ball closest to the one over there," the presiding servant explains. "Whoever is the closest wins."

I let the other girl go before me, holding my breath as her ball lands so close it's almost touching the targeted ball.

Graylen goes next, getting his ball a hand's length away. Then the other team comes nearly as close when they throw.

The onlookers clap and chant the opposing team's name, which only spurs on my drive to win. I take a deep breath, trying to filter out the noisy clamor around me. I close my eyes, feeling the breeze brush against my cheek.

I swing my arm back and release the ball. The crowd goes silent as it flies over the grass, time stretching thin. The faintest sound of my ball tapping the targeted one is all that's heard for a moment. Then, the spectators erupt into cheers. I turn around and throw my arms around Graylen's neck.

"We did it!" I shout, a rush of adrenaline surging through me.

He smiles at me, tightening his arms around my waist and twirling me around in a circle.

"You did it," he corrects, his voice surprisingly soft.

I laugh, several whoops coming from the guests. He sets me down, a smile playing on his mouth. He picks up my hand and gently kisses the back of it. His lips press against my flesh, searing into it.

"This should settle any doubt for the time being." He tips his head toward my father, who is most definitely watching our exchange.

We hand our tokens over to the announcer, and all I can think about is Graylen's comment.

You did it.

"Great game, Amira! I was rooting for you two." Addie breezes past us with an easy smile. She winks at me, dragging her partner behind her and through the crowd.

"We have a tie it seems! Sir Christopher and Lady Edith." Cheers burst from the crowd. "And Sir Graylen and Lady Amira."

"A tiebreaker!" someone says, followed by agreeing shouts.

"We have one last game in store to determine the winner. Prince Adrian, will you assist with this one?" The announcer waves Adrian over to us, and his eyes are fixed on Graylen as he approaches.

The crowd cheers, eating up the spectacle before them. A servant brings over a long rope with two white cloths tied to it, a wide, empty space in the middle between the two knots. Another rope is laid across the ground, creating a barrier between the two teams.

"Each team, if you would grab an end of the rope. The game is simple: Prince Adrian will stand in the middle and watch the cloths. Whichever side allows their cloth to cross over the middle line loses," the announcer says.

Graylen is much larger than Sir Christopher. Judging from the redness rising on Sir Christopher's face, he knows it. Graylen stands at the end of the rope, while I stand closer to the middle. Lady Edith's face is set into a determined glare.

"Begin!" the announcer shouts.

Adrian remains neutral, not cheering for one side or the other. We begin pulling, having an obvious advantage when the rope starts to move in our direction almost immediately. Sir Christopher and

Edith both dig their heels into the ground, pulling up dirt along with them as they slide.

Graylen and I have trained together in the gardens night after night. Doing something that requires physical strength is a comfort we both relish. Sir Christopher leans forward and whispers in Edith's ear, and a smile forms on her face. Just as I turn around to tell Graylen they're up to something, I feel the rope slacken in my grip.

The momentum sends me flying backward onto the ground. From where I was half-turned toward Graylen, my face slams against the dirt. Graylen, who is much quicker on his feet, was able to remain upright.

"We...have winners!" The announcer walks over to hand us our token, but Graylen bends down to help me. I rub at my face, my cheek throbbing.

"Are you okay?" Graylen's voice sounds genuinely worried, though I suppose it's a good opportunity to put on a show. He brushes his fingers across my face, lightly dusting the dirt from it. When I nod to him, he relaxes, though his eyes harden as his gaze shoots to Sir Christopher and Edith. Tension bunches at his shoulders, and I can feel the anger like a static charge between us.

"Amira, are you hurt?" Adrian squats down on my other side, offering his hand as well. I look between their hands, stilled by indecision before ultimately ignoring them both and pushing myself up to my feet. I spin to face the other team, glaring at them.

"I apologize, Lady Amira. A complete accident." Sir Christopher walks over to me, offering his hand as an apology. When he's close enough not to be heard, he mutters, "Or you could go back to where you belong. Covered in dirt suits you better." His voice is low and brittle.

"Excuse me?" Adrian steps between us, forcing Sir Christopher back a step.

His eyes widen when he realizes he was overheard. "Your Highness, I—"

Adrian cuts him off. "You're dismissed. You have your match. The two of you should begin your lives together *away* from the castle. I suspect you'll be out of the castle within a matter of days."

Sir Christopher bows deeply, still stammering his apologies.

"Let's get you inside," Adrian says to me, then begins to walk ahead and snaps, "Graylen, walk with us."

I stand there, shocked. Sir Christopher makes to walk past us, but is stopped. Graylen reaches for him and grips his shoulder, his forearm tense. Sir Christopher flinches, a grimace on his face. Graylen leans close to him, his words too quiet to be heard from here. Sir Christopher's eyes widen, the blood draining from his face at whatever Graylen is telling him.

"Understood?" Graylen says loud enough for those around us to hear.

Sir Christopher nods once, quickly scurrying away the second Graylen removes his hand.

Graylen turns back to me. His eyes swim with an emotion I'm unable to read. He simply offers me his arm and walks alongside me back into the castle.

Out of the corner of my eye, I see Opal get up, but Duke Wyman places a hand around her waist, keeping her at his side. She smiles and waves, mouthing, *Sorry.* I wave back, trying to ignore my father's presence. He shakes his head and turns his back to me.

We pass the guards at the entrance as Graylen and I follow Adrian into a room down the corridor. It's just a small space with a few chairs, likely a sitting room—so unused I've never noticed it on all my walks down this hall.

"I've got her." Adrian steps forward, dismissing Graylen.

I move to slip my hand out of his arm, but Graylen hesitates, his arm tightening. His gaze lingers on me.

"Do you promise that you're okay?" he asks and his eyes catch mine, leaving me unable to look away.

"I promise." I give him a small smile.

"I'm sure you've had worse hits." He grins. "I'd pay a year's worth of wages to see you give it back to him in return."

I laugh. He knows me better than I thought. A soldier once stuck his foot out when my arms were filled with laundry. Clothes went scattering about, and blood poured from my nose until the sun set.

Another time I convinced a new recruit to mock combat, but I was too untrained to be doing that. He had me pinned to the ground with a deep slash down the side of my arm.

Then there was that time I tried to escape, and I was caught. The deep scar across my abdomen never fully healed from that night.

"I bet you my year's wages that he would cry," I joke.

Graylen laughs and gives me a sad smile. "He without a doubt would cry."

I grin, feeling better. He turns around and leaves us in the room alone. Once Graylen disappears, Adrian turns to me, his brows drawn together as he studies me.

"You two have gotten on better terms, it seems," he says tightly.

"We mostly argue. Only occasionally do we get along." I shrug.

"I can't believe Sir Christopher did that. He looked ridiculous with his nose upturned, thinking he's better than everyone else." Adrian's anger is double my own.

In fact, I feel like laughing. The whole day seems strange, and this was minor in comparison to my entire childhood. Even so, the high of winning soars above the other teams' games. Not a single piece of me is surprised that Sir Christopher and Edith did what they did.

"You didn't have to send him away like that."

He whirls around, his eyebrows drawn together in disbelief. "Of course I did. He's a rat that scurries around infesting the kingdom. And he hurt you."

If Adrian only knew how many times I'd been pushed down at the camp. This game was literal child's play.

Still, his concern leaves butterflies in my stomach, my throbbing cheek forgotten as he steps closer to me.

"They shouldn't have had that game in the mix. It won't happen again." He laces his hands with mine, squeezing them tightly.

"I'm fine, I promise," I say quickly. My breathing catches in my throat as he closes any remaining distance between us.

"I can't bear the thought of something happening to you," he grits out through clenched teeth.

My pulse quickens. "It won't," I say. Though I'm not sure that's entirely true.

"Don't leave the castle, Lu." He grips my shoulders tightly. "I want you to stay here."

I pause, not knowing what to say.

I thought love was out of the realm of possibilities for me, but Adrian makes me feel as if it's within reach. He's still the goofy boy I met at the market, the very one that helped me to get out of the camp and away from my father. There's a safety with him that I haven't felt before. He's the first person that has wanted to protect me, and has the means to actually do it.

He sent away Sir Christopher with one command. For me.

"Why?" I ask, breathless. A part of me hopes he gives me a reason not to go.

"Because I want you. You're all I think about. From the moment the sun rises, to the moment it sinks below the horizon," he says, his eyes wide.

I struggle to believe what I'm hearing. When he brings his hands to either side of my face, I melt into him, not considering what tomorrow will bring or what this will change between us.

"You're engaged." I shake my head. I don't mention I am too. This feels far more real and possible.

"I'm working on that." He lets go of me and pinches the bridge of his nose. "There are forces among the kingdom of Penyth I can't begin to explain. They're evil to their very core. I've been told stories of the crimes they're capable of since the day I was born. I can't marry someone tied to that."

My heart constricts, tearing in half for the duty he's bound to, his pain evident in his eyes.

"I think about you too," I whisper softly.

His eyes widen and then he's leaning down, his mouth meeting mine.

Unable to think a rational thought, I don't stop him when he kisses me—not even when his warm lips are moving against mine and we're both breathless. His hands trail down to my waist, gripping me tightly and deepening our kiss.

My heart pounds in my chest, so loud I wonder if he can hear it. I reach up and run my hand through his messy hair. It feels as soft as I thought it would. He is everywhere, all at once. Invading my space and thoughts.

Steps echoing in the hallway pull my attention back to the present, and I break away from him. We stare at each other, our chests heaving in unison. His face breaks into a wide smile, his dimples indenting his cheeks.

"I don't think I could ever get enough of that." His words ensure my smile is as big as his. I couldn't agree more. "I promise I'll find you soon."

"I'd like that." I bite down on my lip. "A lot."

I float back to my room, smiling and humming to myself. The moment with Adrian was entirely unexpected.

As I settle into my room, preparing for bed, I can't help but think about how surprisingly well the day went. For some reason, winning the games with Graylen is the last thing on my mind.

THIRTY

ADIANTUM

A YAWN FORCES ITS WAY out of me, followed by a wide grin that hasn't left my face since yesterday. I touch the tips of my fingers to my lips, the weight of the kiss still lingering.

Avery silently watched me this morning as I hummed to myself, grinning wordlessly. I don't regret being up so late, but I would've thought sleeping until midday would've eased my tiredness. But it didn't, not even a little. I trudge my way to the library, my feet heavy and dragging.

"She honestly thinks she can keep a guy like him—"

I round the corner and the voice immediately cuts off. The two girls talking look up at me from where they're lounging beneath a window. They hardly wait for me to pass before their whispers resume. I fluff out the dress I'm wearing, needing to do something with my hands. Let them talk.

The library is as quiet as usual this time of day. I look around, expecting to see Graylen seated at his usual table in the center of the room. I find myself smiling at getting the room to myself for a bit. Though it feels unusually long since I've seen him.

My smile fades. I forgot about training last night. He must've tried to come by when I was with Adrian. I rub my palms against my arms, trying to brush away the guilt. Is he not here because he's upset? The thought makes my chest ache in an uncomfortable way.

I amble over to the map section and rifle through it until I find several new territories I haven't looked at yet. I pause, the feel of Adrian's lips against mine resurfacing in my mind. I shake my head and continue to pull more books from the shelves.

As I'm stacking them into my arms, I notice Graylen walking out of a room beside me. He's here. My stomach drops at the sight of him. He isn't avoiding me.

Graylen stops when he sees me, his eyes widening a fraction. He seems to take a moment before decisively slipping out of the room, a slender book in his hand. Then he winks, holding the door ajar for me, and strides out of the library with his finger to his lips.

I stand there with my mouth agape, like a fish trying to catch their breath. A door has been carved straight out of the wall, one I've never noticed before in all my days spent here. My books teeter in my hands and I quickly place them on the table beside me before they end up scattered across the floor. I *know* I haven't seen that door before. With the amount of time I've spent hiding away in here, I've explored every corner.

My curiosity instantly drives my feet into the room, closing the heavy door behind me before I can think better of it. Delight and surprise cause my breath to stall in my throat. I can feel my smile stretching so wide across my face my cheeks begin to ache. I blink, my body fully alert and awake now.

The room is small, no bigger than the few tables and chairs placed inside. Candles line shelves that sit at shoulder height, causing the room to twinkle and dance with shadows. Even in the dimness of the room, I can make out the old bookshelves that are stuffed together against the walls. A cold draft leaks in, bumps pebbling my arms.

Crammed into the tiny room are old, worn shelves filled with odd-looking books. Their spines are embellished with strange markings of gold paint that shimmer against the candlelight. I laugh, amazement tumbling from my lips.

I could spend a full day in here and no one would ever find me. The cobwebs over the chairs and shelves suggest no one has stepped a foot in here in ages. In fact, the books don't look like any I've seen in the library so far.

Why would Graylen leave this for me to explore? I bite the inside of my cheek, suspicion keeping me from examining the books closer. None of the names of the books are ones that I recognize, but something feels familiar about them, drawing me in.

One of the leather books is peeking out, so I gently slide it off the shelf. Even if it weren't slightly askew, I would've grabbed it anyway. It's calling out to me, a whispering chatter that I can't ignore.

I sit down at the small, rickety table and set the tome softly on the scarred wood surface. I immediately cough as dust flies into my face. I wave my hand around until it settles, and carefully wipe the cover of the book. A fresh candle has been lit in the center of the table, casting enough light to let me see the inscription across the front. Likely Graylen's doing.

I run my fingers across the leather case, pausing at the title— *The Healers: Creatures of the Wood*. I gently open the book to the beginning and hear the leather crackle with the movement. The smell is old and musty from the age of the pages.

The hair on my arms rises as I read the first line:

Creatures of the Wood are revered and protected. Their magic is entwined with nature itself, and—

I snap the book shut. Is Graylen *trying* to get me in trouble? I leap out of the chair, causing it to fall back onto the ground with a loud smack, more dust blowing up in its wake.

I rush over to the shelf and pull out another book, this one reading *A Diary of Shadows and Dreams, written from the perspective of a Nocturna Fae.* I shove it back into place, my heart thudding heavily.

I yank another out of its resting place, this one golden and shimmery. *An Aegis Fae Training Guide.* I let out a frustrated breath, squeezing it back onto the shelf.

If anyone found me here reading books banned from the kingdom, I could be cast out of the castle, likely worse than that. Adrian's great-great-great grandfather outlawed hundreds of books that promoted any sort of ill word about Crea. That included anything that suggested there was anything more powerful than the king. Magic certainly fell into that category.

The sound of my heart pounding in my ears is the only thing I can hear as I ensure all of the books are just as I found them. I peer out of the door, making sure no one else can see me leaving. I hurry out, an exhilarated smile tugging at my lips despite the slightly panicked rhythm of my heart.

I turn back to the room and blink. It's gone. I spin around, looking side to side. The library is just as I've always seen it. Shelves line the walls as they always do, no new door in sight.

Graylen is most certainly playing some kind of trick on me.

Maybe Linnick would know something about the books. He's traveled to more towns than anyone I trust enough to ask. Opal certainly hasn't been to many places other than the estates of her husband. I burst through the library doors, looking around wildly. One of the guards jumps and takes his helmet off.

"Lady Amira?" A hint of concern laces his voice, but I hardly take notice as I gather my dress in my hands and rush through the hallway.

"Are you able to lead me to the kitchens?" I call out over my shoulder as he follows closely behind.

"That isn't a place for a lady."

I continue ahead, stopping to ask anyone who will listen to give me directions. The guard still follows behind me, reluctant.

"Can you tell me how to reach the kitchens?"

A young girl with a pink velvety dress stares at me like I've lost my mind. "No? Why would you want to go there? Just ring for a servant to bring you something."

I huff in frustration at her response. I quickly make my way through the long hallways, taking flights of small staircases down until I've reached the bottom floor.

"Please, can you point me in the direction of the kitchen?"

A slender maid with a linen bonnet raises her finger and aims it a few doors down. Just as she does, the loud banging of pots and pans echoes down the hall.

"Thank you," I say in a hurry as I all but run to the kitchen door, yanking it open.

"Miss, you really should return back upstairs," the guard calls out.

I ignore him and search the room for Linnick. Metal pots of various sizes hang from a large bar that stretches across the entirety of the ceiling. An area has been carved out of one of the walls, housing a sizeable cauldron sitting atop a fire. The smell of carrots and boiling stew wafts over me.

"Miss? Do you need something?" A cook steps forward, a long ladle in hand.

"I'm looking for Linnick," I wheeze, my breath coming out in pants.

The cook's eyes grow wide. "Linnick? He's probably in the kitchen a few corridors down. Take a right out of this one, walk past the stairwell, take a left, and then another left and you'll be there. You'll smell the bread baking the closer you get. Can't miss it."

I smile appreciatively and spin around.

I don't care about the many looks I get, their disapproval indicating that a lady isn't supposed to be down here. I don't feel like waiting days upon days to find Linnick and ask about the books. And the further I go, the more I'm set on edge, my heart pounding faster. The guard still insists we turn back, but I'm so worked up at this point I'm nearly sprinting.

I take a right, swiftly pass the stairwell, take a left, and finally the aroma of baking bread fills my nose. I breathe in deeply, the scent like a beacon leading me home. I take the final left and find the door wide open, servants bustling about and quickly stepping around each other.

I walk across the threshold as a servant tosses powdered dough into the air. I watch in amazement as it spins around and lands back in their hands perfectly. Another servant is rolling a wooden pin across a lump of dough and flattening it out, their arms shaking with the pressure.

"Can someone tell me where Linnick is?" I shout, my panic growing.

Someone pinching the edges of a pie looks up at me, confusion on her young face.

"He hasn't been in here today," a servant that looks like her mother grunts. "He was supposed to, though. Left me with ten pies to bake alone." She slams a freshly baked pie against the table, not looking in my direction.

"What do you mean he hasn't shown today?" I demand. Linnick hasn't missed a single market day in all the years I've known him. Come rain, shine, or sickness, he never missed a day.

"I mean he skipped. Probably to sleep, or see his fancy friend that brought him here." After she realizes what she said, she looks up, her face reddening as she looks at me.

"Well, he doesn't sleep in, and he definitely wasn't with his *fancy* friend. So where is he?" I bite out.

The child takes a step closer to her mother. The woman shrugs, unapologetic.

"Someone here has to know where he is." The volume of my voice increases, causing the bustling room to pause and look at me. Everyone shakes their head and resumes their duties.

"Where are the servants' quarters?"

The servant I've been speaking with looks ready to bolt out of the room. "You really shouldn't be down here, miss. It isn't a place for a lady."

A baker steps forward, nodding his head in agreement.

"He sleeps in the room next to mine," another man says. "I'll pass the message along you're looking for him."

I'm not convinced, nor does this make me feel any better.

"Was he in his room this morning?" I question him.

The man's forehead creases as he thinks about it. His mouth turns into a deep frown. "Can't say that I paid much attention to it. His door was closed and that's about all I could tell you. Though he's usually awake before the rest of us, getting an early start on the day."

Unease burns through my core like poison had been poured into my body. Even the guard stops insisting, clearly curious as well. I clench my teeth together in an attempt to focus my mind against my pounding pulse. I can't shake the feeling of a painful ache swirling in my stomach.

"Come with me, I'll show you."

THIRTY-ONE

LYCORIS

"HIS CHAMBERS ARE JUST A bit further," the servant leading us says. He's close to my height but still has to hunch forward to avoid hitting the low ceiling. The passageway feels crammed even for me; a thump and a grumble sounds from the castle guard every few steps as he struggles to squeeze through.

I rub my hands over my arms, trying to warm them up, a cold draft sweeping through the passageway. The majority of the castle is already poorly lit, but this passageway is even darker in comparison.

We pass several doors left ajar, one room fully open to anyone passing by. There's a woolen cot on the ground and a worn trunk beside it. With no windows to let light in, it makes it almost impossible to see. Other than those two items, there still wouldn't be enough room for more than one person to stand in the center of it.

Linnick never mentioned how it was down here, yet he seemed just as content as ever.

An icy drop of water drips onto my forehead, rolling down the side of my face, followed by another drop. I look up to the cracked, mold-infested ceiling as more water leaks from above. The entire hallway smells worse than the camp stables. I don't know how they stand to be down here with the stench of it. I cough into my hand, trying to avoid gagging.

"This is his," the servant says and steps to the side for me to knock, his foot tapping impatiently.

"We can manage from here." I thank him and, without needing more encouragement, he slips past us hurriedly to resume his baking.

I knock twice and wait. Nothing. I rap my knuckles a little harder against the thin wooden door. I'm met with silence and the sound of water dripping onto the stone floor.

"Linnick? It's Amira. Can I come in?" I put my ear to the door. The continued silence probably means he isn't here. I sigh, not sure where to look next.

"Maybe he went somewhere and left a note inside," I say, more to myself than to the guard.

I slowly push the door open and have to wait for my eyes to adjust to the darkness of the room. His quarters look identical to the others we passed from what little I can make out through the blackness. It's just as crammed and smells much like the rest of the passageway. I take a step deeper in search of some sort of clue as to where he's gone. The guard has no choice but to wait outside since there's nowhere for him to stand in here.

"You can go back up, you know," I say over my shoulder.

The guard makes an impatient noise. "I'll wait for when you're ready to return to the main level."

It makes no difference to me.

I squint into the darkness, feeling across the top of the trunk to see if Linnick left a note, but find it empty. I knew it was a long shot anyway. I open it and feel around, hoping he doesn't mind me rifling through his things.

Only a single spare pair of linen trousers and a tunic rest inside. I push them around just to make sure I haven't missed anything.

A sigh escapes me, sounding louder in the tight room. "Where did you go?" I mumble to myself.

I turn toward the bed as my eyes finally adjust. A breath of relief whooshes out of me as I see Linnick sleeping on his cot. Squatting down to the makeshift bed, I gently shake his shoulders to wake him.

"Linnick. You have to wake up, you missed your shift. Plus, I need your help." I peer over my shoulder at the guard. The darkness enveloping him makes his lurking presence look more like a shadow than a corporeal body.

When Linnick doesn't stir, I wiggle his shoulders with more force.

"Okay, it's time to wake up. Linnick?" This time I speak louder as I shake him, my hands becoming clammy from where they grip his slender shoulders. "Linnick, wake up."

The sound of the guard's boots scuff as he squeezes as far into the room as he can.

"Shit. Linnick. Wake up!" I yank the thin blanket off him.

A light flickers to life behind me, illuminating the tiny room. I twist around to see the guard holding one of the sconces in his hand. He leans closer so I can see better.

Nothing could've prepared me for what the light reveals. My eyes fall to a dark, sticky substance covering the blanket. My gaze remains fixed on it, not wanting to look at my sleeping friend.

My eyes travel across the puddle. My mind races to catch up with what my eyes are seeing, flitting from one possibility to another like a hummingbird racing from flower to flower, only to find each one empty.

Linnick's body lies lifeless in his bed.

"You have to do something!" I scream at the guard behind me. He stands as immovable as the stone beneath us. The flame stutters as dancing shadows leap across a deep wound in the center of Linnick's chest, the blood already half-dried.

I've tended to wounds of soldiers at the camp before, but never any this bad. Is he still alive? My hands fly to cover the gaping wound, trying to push the blood back in. *Think, Lu, think.*

"Linnick, please wake up," I beg. "I can't do this without you."

He said he wouldn't let me do this alone. Cold, sticky blood coats my hands. The wound lies directly above his heart, his chest quiet and still. My hands fumble to find a pulse on his neck, but I'm met with more stillness.

Pain explodes in my chest. Darkness clouds my vision and threatens to wholly consume me as I stare at him, unmoving. My gaze snaps to his face that is no longer his usual vibrant color, his eyes staring into mine but no longer seeing. Tears blur my vision and I furiously swipe them away.

"We need to go find who did this! They might still be down here." My throat constricts at the words, my voice breaking.

"Lady Amira, I need you to step away from the body now. You're going back to your chambers." The guard's words float through the air and disperse into a vapor, not coming close to reaching me.

"Lady Amira. Stand up, *now.*" I feel a hand clasp down on my shoulder, enough to peel my eyes away from my friend's body.

"I need to get you to safety; I know he was your servant, but we're leaving." The hand still attached to my shoulder begins to tug.

I bring my hand up and close it around the wrist, trying to push it off. "He wasn't my *servant!* He was my *friend,* and he didn't deserve this."

My pulse drums in my ears, the voice behind me sounding as if it were underwater. I push until the hand falls away. Who would do this to him? Why?

Arms wrap around my waist and wrench me away from the cot. I beat my hands against the arms and try to elbow my way out. They remain tightly fastened around me, a piercing scream reaching my clogged ears. I realize the scream belongs to me. I'm pulled away and left with the image of Linnick's open eyes and bloodstained body seared into the backs of my eyelids.

"Wait! At least let me look for the knife that did it."

The guard pauses and I slowly feel his arms release me, my mind momentarily clearing. There aren't many places it could be. I fall to my knees and run my hands frantically across the hard floor. The guard brings the flame back so I can see.

"Lady Amira."

Something in his voice sends a chill down my spine. When I look at him still hunched in the threshold, I find his eyes on Linnick again. My head snaps in the direction of where he lies, hope filling me.

He reaches down and tries to grab a knife clutched in Linnick's hand. I rush forward, batting him away so I can do it myself. Linnick's hands are so stiff I have to pry each finger away from the blade, flinching at each pop or crack of his bones. The hilt of the blade is covered in fine jewels, sparkling ruby red through the sheen of crimson blood coating it.

"He didn't do this himself," I breathe. "You know that, right?"

The guard's eyes are narrowed on the knife, not giving away what he thinks.

"He would never do this." I stand and feel my body sway to the side. I brace myself against the wall with my free hand.

The edges of my vision begin to fade. I feel my body become weightless as it's lifted off the ground and tossed over the guard's shoulder, the blade clanging to the ground before I can study it further. I claw at the arms, desperate to get to Linnick. I *will* find justice for him. A feral noise tears out of me as I'm dragged away from his body.

"I'll need to inform the other guards. You have to go back to your room now."

His voice rings hollowly in my mind as I try to fight my way out of his grasp. My attempts weaken the further we get from Linnick, and the heavier my pain gets.

I don't even remember making it to my chambers. By the time I realize I'm in my bed, I let sleep take the hurt away. Anger and grief consume me as I drift into nothingness.

I am made of glass. I shatter and splinter into a thousand tiny pieces. A sob escapes my gasping lips as my breath catches in my throat and the air in my lungs freezes. I collapse onto the hard floor of my chambers as the image of Linnick's cold body floods my mind.

"You're all right. You're going to be okay." Avery's gentle voice does little to soothe the pain. She hesitates for a moment before wrapping her arms around me, rocking me side to side.

We sit there for what feels like an endless amount of time. I can't be certain how long. We sit in silence before she finally peels me off the ground and helps me into bed.

"He was a lovely person, miss. Everyone in the kitchens enjoyed being around him." She pulls back the covers and waits for me to slip into them, tucking the sheets up to my shoulders. I feel her dainty hand fall over mine, her strength pouring into me, urging me to not fall apart entirely.

"I can stay here tonight if it helps. Or if you need time to grieve, I'll be here at first light with a tray of pastries and steaming tea," she says softly.

I nod, having no idea what I want right now. "I'll manage." My voice cracks, unconvincing.

"Just send word if you change your mind." Her warm smile helps to push back the wave of emotions stirring just beneath the surface.

Just when I think my tears have dried, I hear the door open and shut softly. Avery stands and quietly slips out of the room as the weight of my bed shifts with another sitting in her place.

Adrian pulls me to him and refuses to let go. The grief is too much. I cannot accept this. I didn't bring Linnick here just to die alone. I turn slowly in Adrian's arms and look at him as I speak with more strength than I thought I possessed.

"You said we'd be safe." My voice lacks any real anger, instead just sounding broken. "And now he's dead."

He holds my gaze and bends down to rest his forehead against mine. "I am so sorry, Amira."

The anger momentarily subsides. He leans back and loosens his arms to reach down and grab my hands.

"When word reached me that a baker was found dead, I couldn't believe it. Then I heard that it was the one that accompanied the merchant's daughter, and I had to come find you." His voice is pleading. "Please tell me what I can do for you—let me help."

I shake my head and pull away, but his hands remain firmly grasping mine. "I need out of the castle for a night, without a guard."

His jaw hardens at the request. "It's not safe for you to go out alone—"

I can feel the tears threatening to spill over, the floodgates close to opening. "I *need* this Adrian, please. This is what you can do for me." My voice comes out smaller than I mean for it to. A single tear sneaks out of the corner of my eye, followed by one after another.

"I'll need a few days to arrange it," he says tightly.

Or a few days to try and convince me to change my mind.

Fear shines through his golden eyes, begging me to stay. We both know I might not come back.

"I know the loss of his farm was great, almost too much for anyone to bear." He looks almost *sorry* as he says the one thing that threatens to tear me apart. Like he believes Linnick may have done it to himself.

My nostrils flare. "He didn't do it."

Adrian nods, looking unconvinced. Pity fills his brown eyes.

I'll find out who did this and make them pay. Even if it's my father. He's meticulous, but only if he's doing it himself. Who's to say he didn't hire someone, and they did a poor job of it? Leaving Linnick's body without covering their tracks? Was Linnick just a loose end my father didn't care to have around? Question after question fills my head.

But something feels off. Having Linnick in the kitchens was in my father's best interest, where the most illicit gossip spreads like wildfire. Something about the way he died doesn't feel like something my father would do, and yet who else could possibly be to blame? I can't stop the sinking suspicion that in some way, it has to do with me.

My entire body trembles, and Adrian smooths a hand over my hair, murmuring he's here for me. But I don't need someone to hold me. I need someone to believe me. I wait for him to leave, needing to be alone with my thoughts. I don't sleep.

I lie awake, running through any and all possibilities.

THIRTY-TWO

ALLIUM

EVERY DAY HAS BEEN THE same since I lost Linnick. I wake up, get out of bed, take my tonic, and get back in bed until it's time to run in the gardens. I dismissed Avery for the rest of the week. I told Opal and Graylen that I need space. I told Adrian that I need time to process things. I'm still telling myself that I can do this.

A piece of paper slides beneath the door to my chambers, where I haven't left other than to run each night with Graylen to try and chase away the sadness. We haven't said a word to each other yet. I walk over to the note and feel my chest constrict at the words:

It's arranged for you to leave tonight, on one condition. I hope you can understand. Here's the other thing you asked for.

- Adrian

My eyebrows draw together as I reread the note. The sun slinking down means I don't have time to consider what he means.

I pocket the little seeds he gave me and toss the note onto the floor. I twirl the pendant of my necklace against its chain, my fingers trembling.

I take a long, deep breath to steady my shaking hands. As I walk to my door, I feel like my mind is detached from the rest of my body.

"Amira."

I jump at the sound of the voice to my right, not having seen him lurking in the shadow outside of my room.

"Not now, Graylen," I try to say firmly, but it sounds more tired than anything.

He'll manage if I miss one night of training. I brush past him, trying to hold my head higher. He quickly catches up with me, matching my hurried strides.

"Yes, now." He steps in front of me, cutting me off. "I'm your ticket out tonight."

My feet slam to a halt.

"Adrian couldn't just let you leave the castle. He sent me to protect you. Though I'm fairly certain you can handle yourself." He looks at me, one brow raised, waiting for me to snap back at him. I don't. There's no point.

I sigh and say, "Just stay out of the way. It won't take long."

I can feel his questioning gaze at how easily I relented.

"I'm sorry, Amira. About your friend." He apologizes, but I don't want him to. It doesn't change what happened.

I clench my teeth together, ignoring the stabbing pain in my chest. We come to the ground level and Graylen stops walking.

"We need to leave out of the gardens," he says.

I squeeze my fists tightly and nod, then flex my hands and impatiently drum my fingers against my thighs as he unlocks the doors.

We walk past the tall, spiraling trees and toward the far end to which we usually don't bother going. The ground is soft and muddy from the days of rain that followed Linnick's death.

Thunder rumbles through the night sky, and the stars are covered by another storm rolling in. We walk deeper through the garden, pushing our way through thick trees and tall bushes. There isn't a flower in sight with the current conditions in Crea, not even a small flash of hope to lean on as I walk through the brush—nothing more than scattered dodder weeds choking any plant that tries to rise from the ground.

"Almost through," he mutters.

I follow behind, beginning to doubt Graylen knows where he's going. A branch swings around and smacks me against the cheek, sticks and leaves getting tangled in my hair in the process. We continue to shove aside the thick coverage.

Just as I'm about to ask if he really is just lost now, he disappears out of the brush, leaving me to get thwacked with at least three more branches. I take a deep breath and push through to the other side.

My breath loosens when I realize I'm staring at the back half of the market. Graylen brings a finger to his mouth, signaling for me to be quiet. He points up to the wall above us, soldiers laughing and drinking ale together.

We flatten our bodies against the cold wall, noiselessly side-stepping until we get close enough to an empty cart to duck behind. The guards stationed on top of the wall laugh again, unaware of us leaving. My heart pounds at the freedom of being out of the castle for the first time in almost a full season.

"You're welcome." His voice is light, almost teasing. The freedom vanishes at the reminder that I'm not truly alone. My lip wobbles, fresh tears welling. "Hey, I'm sorry. It isn't easy to lose those we love. I'll follow your lead."

I avoid his intense stare, sometimes feeling as if he can see directly into my thoughts.

The sky begins pouring, mimicking the flow of tears now leaking from my eyes. If Graylen notices, he doesn't say so. We walk until the cold seeps through my bones and the rain soaks through my clothing.

Linnick's farm is easy enough to find. I don't bother wiping the tears away, their presence concealed by the rain falling from the clouds above. The traveling trails are quiet tonight with the weather keeping people in their homes.

Linnick told me once that his farm was so close to the castle he could hear the sounds of parties at night, back when the castle was bustling with guests and hosting lavish parties. Just down the south trail, a right at the double-twisted oak tree, the last farm on the left.

The sound of the rain falling to the earth mutes our footsteps. Graylen's so quiet behind me, I have to check that he's still there. His long hair is plastered to his head, the rain dripping off the ends. As much as I wanted to be alone to do this, I can't help but be slightly thankful someone's here.

The first farm we pass has half-dead vegetables filling large barrels, the deadly vines covering them in the darkness.

"Dodders must've just taken that one over," I remark.

In the short amount of time it takes to walk to Linnick's farm, the rain slows. His farm is just as I expect it to be. His house isn't anything overly nice, but it's in far better condition than most of the other farms. It's made of strong, amber-colored wood. When well-kept I can see this being a safe place for anyone to live.

But now thick dodder vines stretch out over the front door, which currently hangs off-kilter from its hinges. They strangle the front of the house, weaving out like veins across the majority of it. The steeply pitched roof, which likely used to be pointy, now sags down.

I walk to the back of the house. Graylen waits at the front, giving me space. The remnants of Linnick's farm almost pull the earth from beneath my feet. His field is twice as large as the others we passed on the way, the soil dry and covered so heavily with dodder vines it would take days upon days to clear just one small section.

The vines twist together and dive back into the ground, sprouting up and tangling together with new ones, making it nearly impossible for any farmer to clear the land once it's fully infested. Once you pull the vines up, new ones replace it the next day.

I squeeze my eyes shut, guilt seared onto my heart at having brought Linnick to the castle. Even seeing his limited options, it doesn't make it easier that I was the one who asked him to come along. He deserved a life so much better than he had been given at the castle. He shouldn't have been stuck feeding the same people who allowed this to happen. This was his home, his heart. I drift back to the front of the house, unable to look at the ruined field any longer.

My knees sink deeply onto the soft, muddied earth. I avoid letting my eyes wander. I can't bring myself to look at Linnick's favorite tree yet. If it's infested with dodders I might fully fall apart. I let the tears fall once more, accompanied only by my memories and the rain. The creatures of the night are all hiding away from the storm as it closes in around Runnswick. I crawl forward on my knees and dig.

I pull the earth apart with my hands, creating a carved-out pocket deep within the ground. My hair is now caked to my face, damp from sweat and rain. I drop the lemon seeds into the soil and cover it as my tears mix with the wet dirt. I fashion a makeshift grave in memory of the kindest soul I've ever met. He was more of a father to me than my own claimed to be.

"I promise I'll get us out of here. We'll go to the town you talked about, and I'll plant a dozen more lemon trees. We'll have lemon on every bite of chicken, lamb, and cow. A day won't pass without the memory of you flickering within my mind." My voice breaks as I cover the last of the seeds with soil.

Lying down on top of the freshly planted seeds, I cry until the sky decides we have watered the earth enough for one night. Graylen doesn't make to comfort me, and I'm thankful that this moment is mine.

I finally turn to where Linnick's lemon tree is rooted in place. A hysterical laugh escapes me. I rise to my feet and run over to it, pressing my palm firmly to the perfectly intact bark and resting my forehead against it. It's as if the dodder vines stopped growing once they reached the house, not a single piece of soil upturned with the curse of the deadly plant.

The tree is short, but the leaves are a vibrant green, full of life. The fruit isn't in season yet, so no lemons grow, but they soon will. I smile for the first time in a week, feeling closer to Linnick.

I reach up and pull my necklace out, twirling the pendant around, feeling calmer with its weight against my chest. The rain has fully ceased now, replaced with the glow of moonlight. I turn back to Graylen, my hazy mind clearing with the strength of saying goodbye.

"Let's stay out a little longer." His voice is gentle, and in this moment, I'm more grateful for Graylen than I ever thought I could be. The small reprieve has lifted so much weight off of me. I've never been this close to being alone without a guard.

I sit down beneath the tree, pulling my knees tightly to my chest and hugging them. Graylen slowly walks over and sits beside me. I stare longingly out at the road. The center splits down the middle: one path leads back to the castle, and the other leads to another town I've never been to.

"I've never been out this far without a guard." I don't mean to say it out loud, my mind still jumbled.

"You can leave if you want. I won't try to stop you," he says softly. I turn to him, surprised, then look back to the empty path.

"What? You didn't think I'd notice, when I watch you train every night to run away? When I look at you, all I can see is someone who's begging to be free." He gestures to the road. "So go."

I blink, too stunned to speak. An overwhelming sense of comfort fills me that I could go right now. It's never been an option for me.

"You wouldn't say anything?" My voice cracks on the last word.

"No. Being chained to something by choice is entirely different than it being out of your control."

My brows pull together and I ask, "What do you mean?"

"If I walk into the cage with the key to get out in my pocket, what would I have to be afraid of? But if someone shoves me in, slams the door closed behind me, and throws the only key away? Then I'm screaming and fighting until I can get out." Each of his words holds a bite of anger.

"Has that happened to you?" I ask in a whisper.

He's quiet for a long time. I assume he's not going to answer, but he surprises me when he does. "I chose my cage. But right now, I can't find a way out of it. Hell, I *made* the cage I'm in. I can't help but wonder what my life would be like if I hadn't."

I angle my face to look at him. His eyebrows are drawn together in thought.

"You aren't what I thought you would be," I say in a tentative voice. "Why do you let people think the worst of you?"

He shrugs, letting out a long breath. "It's easier that way."

Sitting this close to me, his presence is overwhelming. He smells like the fresh scent of rain about to fall. But he's not a pleasant drizzle: he's a downpour coming down so hard you can't see more than a few steps in front of you. He's the unpredictable storm that rolls in on the clearest day. And somehow, I don't mind the thought of getting caught in his storm.

When I look back to him, he's pushing his sleeves over his elbows. My eyes catch on the fascinating symbols covering his skin, surprised by how different they look in the moonlight. For a moment, I swear I can see an image in them. I blink, wiping the moisture out of my eyes, but the image remains: the senseless swirls connect, spelling out a word.

I shake my head as he moves his arm, my mind fuzzy with the commotion of the night. My eyes snap back to the road. I can't just leave, can I? I clench my hand around my pendant and run my thumb across the back. The ridges in it feel different too.

I suddenly turn to him, for some reason feeling he knows why. Because everything feels different when it comes to Graylen. Something I can't put my finger on. Like the odd room full of books on magic.

"Graylen, the other day, in the library—"

Loud drums interrupt me. The noise travels through the woods, followed by horns.

The deep, steady rhythm of the instrument freezes my insides, the sound carrying through the air and bringing farmers onto their porches. The drums are only marched through the town on one occasion.

"The mourning drums," I whisper. I cast a fleeting look at the path that leads away from the castle, my opportunity swallowed up by each thump pulsing through the trees.

"Adrian needs us," I say, almost to convince myself, my feet moving swiftly toward the castle. I hear Graylen's feet sound behind me, catching up easily. He doesn't question me, matching my pace stride for stride. There's no time to look back, to mourn my friend Linnick and the chance at freedom left behind me.

The drums can only mean one thing. The king is dead.

THIRTY-THREE

CHRYSANTHEMUM

AVERY HAS PUFFY EYES AND tear-stained cheeks as she slips into the room. I feel a tremble tear through my body at her distress. I see my training boots sticking out beneath the bed and scoot them further under with my heel, having hardly made it back before first light.

We both remain quiet while she helps me bathe and dress. While she's preparing my bath, I grab my tonic pouch off the table beside my bed. I methodically grab the amount I know is needed and stir it in with my tea.

I wrap my hands around the warm cup and slowly sip until it's empty, the tightness in my chest quickly easing.

After I bathe, she holds up a simple, black frock for me to wear. "This one is for today, but there's more to come. It's customary for the entire castle to wear black until the next king is crowned. Even if it's alone in your room, you still need a black dress. It's bad luck for the old king to pass into his next life without his kingdom mourning him."

"How did it happen?"

She looks at me, alarmed and too stunned to speak for a moment. "You haven't heard, miss?" she asks. "The king was found dead in the middle of the night. The prince will be crowned shortly after the funeral."

I chew on the edge of a nail and stare out the window. With my window facing the market, I have a small view of the one place I ache to go to right now. The docks sit tauntingly in the distance, freedom so temptingly close.

"Tell me how it happened." I clench my teeth tightly and look over my shoulder to where Avery is seated.

"He was found lying by his door, believed to be natural," she says solemnly.

I begin my pacing, thinking through the events. It feels wrong. King Avalon isn't old enough to die like that.

"Who found him?" I hold my breath, hoping it wasn't Adrian that had to see him like that.

"He was found by the prince. I just can't believe what that boy is going through." The dried tears on her face are replaced with fresh ones.

"And he just died?" I ask.

She sniffles, blowing her nose gently into a cloth. "It's hard to believe the word passed among the servants, but they say he had been dead for some time."

Was it really a natural death?

"How was he there so long without someone finding him? Doesn't someone come to clean his room or bring him food?" None of it makes sense.

"The king usually drinks ale or has female companionship in his room during the day; long ago, he said he was not to be bothered unless he himself decided he required something."

A fatal mistake on his part, then. If he'd had a heart attack with guards closer by, he could've been saved.

"It was kept quiet for as long as possible," Avery adds.

Nothing stays quiet in the castle for long. Adrian's face presses into my memory, and my heart breaks for him. He may be used to running the kingdom, but he still had his father to rely on.

"I really must be getting back to the servants' quarters, miss. They want us all there to begin preparations for Prince Adrian's coronation." She gives me a brief hug that surprises me before opening the door to leave. The words sound strange coming from her mouth.

When she opens the door, she startles with surprise. A guard is stationed at the entrance.

"Who are you?" I step forward.

"Prince Adrian ordered me to stand guard for your protection. He was very clear that I am to keep people from entering who aren't your routine visitors, but you are free to exit if need be." The guard turns back to the hallway, sword and shield in hand.

"The castle is going to have more guards about until the prince is safely crowned. The kingdom needs this transition to happen smoothly," Avery says with a hint of irritation in her voice.

I nod, understanding. "How are there enough guards to stand at everyone's room? Shouldn't you all be focusing on who did it?" I ask.

The guard and Avery share a look, and a small smile appears on Avery's face.

"It was a natural death. I don't think anyone else has guards to protect them, miss. I presume he only sent an extra one for you." She smiles.

"Oh." A blush spreads across my face and I hope Avery doesn't investigate too much.

"I'll be back soon." She smiles goodbye and I close myself back in my room.

I lean heavily against the door and slide down to the ground. I need to see Adrian. I yank the door back open and walk to his room—easy to spot with the amount of guards stationed outside the door.

"I need to see Prince Adrian," I demand.

The guards step in front of the door, blocking me out. "No one is allowed in, miss."

I grunt, frustrated.

"Tell him it's Amira. He'll let me in."

"He said no visitors under any circumstances." The guards don't budge.

I consider shouting for Adrian but think better of it. My own grief is fresh enough to remind me that sometimes being alone is necessary.

"Can you just tell him I was here?" I relent.

The guards nod, satisfied I'm done trying.

I twist my necklace around, feeling as if I imagined the entire conversation with Graylen last night. He was almost…nice. Maybe in my grief I hallucinated the whole conversation. The only way to know is to find Graylen, and to try and see what version of him I get today. Maybe he knows something about the king. I roam the corridors of the castle, trying to find him.

I start by walking through the library. There are now double the number of guards stationed. The feeling of more eyes on me, trapping me in, makes me question why I didn't leave when I had the chance.

Inside the library I find no door to the banned book room in sight. No Graylen either. I walk to the gardens, making my rounds but finding it mostly empty.

"Time to come back in, Lady Amira," a guard calls. "The gardens are closing for the evening."

The cool, wintry twilight shoves the sunlight away, the day ending too soon.

My stomach rumbles loudly, reminding me I should at least force down a bite or two. The walk to the great hall is short. I pass fewer people than normal, but the few I do are dressed in as much black as I am.

I search the eating area for Graylen, my shoulders slumping when I find he isn't among the faces. A sea of black fabric and hushed whispers accompanies the room tonight, the usual clamor, bursts of laughter, and bright colors all dulled in the mourning period.

"Amira! Come join us for a while," one of the girls says.

I try to find an excuse. It's not that I don't want to. I just don't have it in me to be social right now. At least with Graylen, I choose to sit in silence or talk. But I smile when I see Sarah wearing one of the dresses I had sent to her room. It fits her perfectly, such a deep navy that it can pass as black.

"Sorry," I say, "I'm looking for Graylen."

The girls nod, understanding.

"It's so sad what happened to the king," Sarah says quietly. The others nod in agreement "I get it. I had to find Milo right away this morning. His smile brings me so much comfort."

Her genuine look of concern is endearing. Though that's not why I'm looking for Graylen.

"I told my parents I wouldn't accept a proposal unless I could feel myself falling in love. They can't just cart me off to be matched and expect me to spend the rest of my life with someone I hardly know," a girl I don't remember seeing before says, her eyes glossy with unshed tears.

I join their sympathetic nodding, endeared. She isn't wrong.

"Have any of you seen him here?" I ask, and they all shake their heads. I sit down with them, smiling through quick bites of food. Everyone is speaking in low voices, just above a whisper—honoring the dead that are no longer around to care.

I make my way around my room, lighting the sconces before the sun sinks below the horizon. There's just something about the flame eating up the end of a sulfur stick, the small spark that ignites and begins to swallow it whole. Unless snuffed out, it'll devour itself entirely, burning brightly until the light slowly dims.

I hear thunder slap across the sky and bounce between the growing clouds. The moment I light the last flame, rain begins to pour.

The heavy drops of water smack against my windows. I wrap my arms around myself, suddenly cold. I open my door to find the same guard still stationed there. Despite the circumstances, I fight back the sudden urge to laugh. I likely could defend myself better than he could. I doubt he's even seen real combat. The castle guards are all passed through the hands of my father at the royal training camp, his political sway like a gilded collar around their necks.

I sigh and shut the door, sitting down heavily in my lounging seat. The past day feels like it's lasted a full winter's season.

The sound of a door clicking open cuts through the room. I look to my door, finding it still closed.

"Lu."

I jump to my feet and spin around toward the wall beside my windows. Adrian is standing there. His golden hair is a mussed mess flying in all directions. Even when I thought he was a beggar in the streets, I never saw him in a state like this.

I take a tentative step forward. "Adrian?" The setting sun casts an orange glow throughout the chamber.

"Lu." His voice breaks as he whispers my name. He clears his throat and speaks louder. "There's a passageway that connects our rooms. I've wanted to use it before, but with everything going on…"

My heart loses a piece of itself, floating to his feet. I take a step closer to him.

He meets me in the middle and grabs my hand, lacing his fingers through mine as he pulls me to him. We stare at each other for a moment. His jaw is tense, and his eyes are red and swollen. I try to calm my breathing to stop it from being so loud, but all I can hear are my short and heavy breaths filling the space. He looks down at my mouth briefly before flicking his eyes back up to meet mine.

"Adrian, I'm so sorry. I can't imagine... I'm sorry."

He studies me, his eyes bouncing between mine. After a moment he releases a heavy breath. He rakes his hand through his hair and squeezes the back of his neck, then leans forward and looks at me with so much heartache that I have to look away. I don't deal with pain; I run from it.

"It's not your fault." His voice is strained and rough from crying.

I reach forward and comfort him in the only way I know how. I brush his hair from his forehead and run my fingers down the side of his face. I cup his jaw and brush away the single tear that falls.

More tears fill his eyes, threatening to spill over. I remove my hand from his cheek but he doesn't try to stop me. He swallows thickly and looks away from me.

"If there's anything at all that I can do, please tell me," I whisper. "I know how much this hurts." The sting of losing Linnick is almost too fresh to talk about still.

His brown eyes search mine, desperate to hold onto something other than the pain he's feeling. "Okay." He gathers me into a tight embrace again. When he starts to pull away, I wrap my arms around him as tightly as I can, hoping I'm pouring a sliver of strength into him. He buries his head into my shoulder.

I feel my resolve begin to break when his silent tears start to freely fall.

We stay like this for a long while, both of us exhausted and unsure about what tomorrow will hold.

"I'll be there at your coronation," I murmur. "If you feel like you can't do it, just look for me and I'll be there."

He nods his head into my shoulder before bringing his face up to mine. "I don't deserve you, Lu. Graylen is one of the only friends I've ever had, and I don't even fully trust him. He's too good at his job sometimes." The corner of his mouth turns up slightly. "But you, Lu. I trust you. I don't know if it's because I could be myself with you when we were in the market, but I can't stop myself from thinking about you. Even after I lied to you, you still forgave me. Not because I'm the prince, but because you wanted to."

My pulse quickens as he brushes a stray hair from my face and tucks it behind my ear, causing all of my thoughts to disappear. He takes a step closer to me, so close now that nothing separates us.

He trails his hand from the top of my shoulder down the length of my arm to my fingertips. He laces his fingers with mine and studies the scars on my hands, his thumb tracing each scar as his brows furrow deeply. I watch him, unable to move or breathe.

He leans down until his forehead is resting against mine. He closes his eyes, squeezing them tightly shut, trying to block out the world, but mine are wide open.

"I'll be king soon. Who I marry may change, but if you don't want this…" His hands begin to shake, and I can't take the pain he's in.

For a brief moment, time is suspended between us. The world is frozen, but we're still spinning around the sun. His hands cup my face and his golden eyes stare into mine. They're so much brighter with the tears coating them, his gaze drifting down to my mouth.

We stand there, our foreheads bent together and pain mingling together. There's nothing I can do to bring him comfort from this pain. I know it too well to think otherwise.

"What am I going to do if you leave?" he asks.

My heart splinters. I don't know if I can leave anymore. I blink, unable to process or form any semblance of a thought.

"Be a king."

THIRTY-FOUR

Salix

I RUB MY TEMPLES, THE tender spot aching with frustration. The blankets are suffocating, and the moonlight is streaming so brightly through the tall windows I can't fall asleep again. I fling the covers off my body and walk over to the window.

I draw my knees close to my chest, wrapping my arms snugly around them. My body leans heavily against the side, the coldness of the stone biting into my back.

From where my window is positioned, I can make out the edges of the market in the darkness. Its usually bustling square is empty and desolate with the night well underway. With nothing better to do, I close my eyes and settle for playing a game of pretend.

I dash quickly through the night-shrouded market and hope I'm heading in the direction of the port. My feet hasten their steps, and my breathing increases tenfold. I look down at the piece of paper in my hand and hope the poorly written timestamp is correct for when the ship is setting sail.

I squeeze my fist tightly around my travel sack and start to sweat profusely, even with the night's frigid temperature. Just as I begin to give up hope, I see the top of the mast in the distance. I let out an audible sigh and continue toward the ship.

Spending time near the castle was nice for a few days, but nothing compares to the seas of the Andronicus. It's unrelenting with its sheer power and dominating presence. I make it onto the ship just in time, and the moment I step on the crew begins to reel in the boarding plank.

I find a spot easily on the mostly empty ship, sitting at the front just before the foremast, where I'm less likely to be seen. I may have needed to get on this ship from dry land, but I won't be exiting it that way. I rest my head against the wooden floorboard and listen to the world around me.

The stars above me shine so bright I have to wrap my arm over my eyes to lessen the light. The sailors that are still awake are singing loudly amongst themselves. With every passing hour I can hear their songs threading together in strings of confusing words. The ale they're drinking has something to do with that. I try to focus on the crashing of the waves as the ship plows through. The ship so large, and the sea so calm, I can only feel a slight sway with the movement of being on water.

The wood creaks and groans in protest against the slow speed it trudges at, the crew not noticing the lack of wind will likely lengthen the journey considerably. Without there being many other passengers due to the lateness of the night, I look over the deck anyways to make sure there are no prying eyes pointed in my direction.

Once the moon is securely positioned high in the night sky, I begin removing my dress. The majority of the crew are half drunk or gathered near the captain's wheel.

I check behind me once more just as I begin to feel the call back home. A few more paces and we'll be there. The ship drags forward through the water, and I step toward the edge.

I hear a shout behind me as someone urges me to not get too close to the railing. I hear footsteps grow in number along with the voices yelling at me. Leaving all of my things behind, I jump into the darkness of the Andronicus. The cool water cocoons me.

The shouts above me fade as I sink further into the depths of the sea. My body adjusts to the change, and I feel my breathing filter the water in the place of air. I wasn't planning on being seen, but from the looks of it, the ship is continuing along just fine.

My legs disappear beneath me, turning into one singular fin. My hair finally loses its heaviness and floats around my head as it moves with the water. I smile at the weightlessness of my body without gravity dragging me down.

Fish swim past, paying me no mind. I swim closer to the floor of the ocean, not wanting to be seen by anyone else who might be out this time of night. I find a place among the coral that's glowing with luminescent fish, their soft light emitting shades of pink and purple across the reef.

Finally, home, I lay down and stretch out among the fish. I stare up toward the surface of the sea and smile to myself, the moon so bright it shines all the way to where I'm laying. A sea turtle glides into my view, followed by several freshly born hatchlings, its massive shell and webbed feet just an outline with the light cast from above.

I watch them for as long as I can, until they're just specks in the distance. The world down here is so much quieter. I can get anywhere I want just by swimming there. Going from place to place is so much harder in the human world.

Between needing money and a man to get me from one place to another, I think I need a break from going to the surface for a while. Plus, I haven't quite figured out how to use a horse yet. If only the humans knew how to share and not be so selfish, then—

My face slams into a hard surface. I peel myself off of the cold, stone floor and rub my throbbing cheek. I look around, blinking, confused with being suddenly awoken. I stand to go back to the massive bed, where I lay my head down and slip back into my dream world.

My eyes peel open at the sound of Avery entering my room with a fresh gown and food, feeling as if I had just fallen back asleep. To my surprise, the sun has already passed its highest point in the sky. Somehow I feel as if I didn't get a moment of rest.

She sets the meal atop a small table and hands me a heavy black dress. "This is for the funeral tonight," she says softly.

I run my fingers down the silky material. It's unlike any dress I've been given since arriving. Most of the garments have been sewn with cotton and linen, but this dress is made almost entirely of smooth silk. The sleeves are full-length, like all the others, but this one is loose, given the lightness of the fabric. The dress hugs my waist snugly and falls straight to the floor.

"Can I get more dresses like this?" I ask.

Avery smiles at me and nods. She adjusts the fabric around my neck and straightens the tie wrapped around my waist.

"Another dress will be delivered to your room before the morning of the coronation. It'll take me a few more days to make, but it'll be ready in time," she promises.

I gape at her. "You're the one that's made all of these dresses for me?"

She nods as embarrassment flushes her cheeks, motioning for me to sit down so she can do my hair. "Most of them yes, save for the few when you first arrived." She ducks her head slightly and trains her eyes on her fidgeting feet.

"Why did you never tell me? They're lovely. All of them. Thank you so much, Avery, truly."

She twists my hair into a knot on top of my head and places several pins throughout with delicate stones on their ends. "You deserve much more than the life you're living," she quietly says.

Quickly speaking before I can thank her, she adds, "I apologize for speaking so plainly, Lady Amira."

I shake my head, twisting around to look at her. "Please don't apologize. You're always welcome to do so around me."

I reach for her, pulling her into a quick hug and she squeezes me back before letting go. I straighten my skirts, fiddling with the buttery-smooth fabric. I shift, uncomfortable with how she seems to see straight through me. My necklace rests on the wooden table beside my bed. I have a feeling I'm going to need its calming pressure against my chest today.

"Avery, will you help me?"

Even with the somberness of the funeral looming over the castle, she's practically glowing. "Of course." She takes the necklace from me, smiling down at it.

A knock raps at the door. Avery hurries to open it.

Graylen's funeral attire is no different from his daily clothing. "Ready?"

"I was just about to put her necklace on. I'll wait outside." She holds her hand out, offering the necklace to him instead.

Without a moment of hesitation, he walks over and takes it from her, coming to stand in front of me. I toss an exasperated glance to Avery, but her smile is too big to disappoint her.

I reluctantly turn so he can put the necklace on. His arm slips around me so he can adjust and clasp it. His fingers brush the nape of my neck, sending a streak of lightning down my back. I lean into his touch. My shoulders ease the tension I hadn't realized crept into them.

"It's the king's funeral. I doubt anyone will be paying attention to us tonight. There isn't a need for us to attend together, if you'd rather—" My words get caught in my throat as his hand gently rests against my shoulders, lingering longer than necessary. The weight of it calming me.

"Better to be safe. Your father is attending," he murmurs against my ear.

I've drifted so far back I'm nearly leaning into his chest. I step forward, forcing his hand to drop back to his side. Adrian needs me right now. The mention of my father painfully reminds me of why he's coming. Adrian's lost so much in such a short amount of time. He's lost his father, but he's also lost any semblance of freedom he may have had. His entire world is shifting, thrust into being in control of the entire kingdom. Far sooner than he expected, and without any warning.

The thought of having to stomach being around my father is almost too much to bear. I cross my arms, not ready to see him yet.

"I wish he wasn't. I'd rather not be subjected to his disappointment today," I mutter.

"Only if you allow his words to have an effect on you." He offers me his arm and gently pulls me tighter into his side.

I take a deep breath. I can do this.

He leads me out of my chambers, where we're met with Avery's bright eyes. "You two will join behind the prince's coach with the rest of the nobility on the funeral march."

She'll be with the servants. I smile at her, my chest constricting at leaving her behind.

Our steps echo through the emptiness of the corridor. The sun is already gone for the evening and the chill chases its absence. A cool breeze begins to seep through the cracks in the windows.

We join the second-floor guests leaving their rooms, all dressed in black like us. Silence seems to be the theme of the evening, the others staying just as quiet. The passageway leading to the castle entrance is just as dark and smelly as last time. Instead of just two guards at the castle doors, there are nearly twenty.

Pain shoots through my chest at the memory of the last time I was here—when Linnick was by my side, and we didn't know what our time here would hold.

So much has changed since then. Back then the most I hoped for was a short reprieve from the camp. But now I know for certain I'll never go back to my old life.

A soldier speaks out into the passageway, repeating himself every few breaths. "Seek your respective families to walk with during the processional. You all are to walk behind the prince's coach until the march has concluded. Only the king's family will be allowed into the abbey for the burial."

The tunnel breaks open into the market, and my lungs fill with a full breath at the sight of it. I begin to unwind my arm from Graylen's, but he tightens his hold. I turn to him, my eyebrows raised.

"We're supposed to go to our families," I say, confused.

"I have none. I believe that implies I can walk with you." Graylen shrugs, but a surge of sadness shoots through my chest.

"Sir Graylen, a word?" A castle sentry leads Graylen toward the edge of the crowd. I try to read the words coming from their mouths, but people keep stepping into my line of sight.

"Amira?"

I spin around to the familiar voice. A grin overtakes my face; I can't help it. It's been so long since I've seen an old friend.

Mica's tone is light. Without his twin attached to his side, he lets his guard drop a fraction. The trademark Lyle-blue eyes stare back at me, open and curious.

I can't stop myself from throwing my arms around him and pulling him into a crushing embrace. He stiffens beneath me, not used to me displaying any sort of affection. Honestly, I'm not either. But being in the castle has even made me miss the twins.

Mica finally relaxes and wraps his arms hesitantly around me.

"Is Emeril here too?" I crane my neck to look through the crowd for Opal's youngest brother. My heart warms just at the thought of seeing the little guy.

"He stayed at the camp with Ember," Mica says. Now it makes sense why his twin is nowhere in sight. Usually, if you see one then you're soon to see the other. "Neither was too pleased to have to stay."

"Why make them?" I ask.

"We couldn't very well leave the camp empty after Penyth's attack earlier this season. A unit stayed behind to keep watch," he explains.

The Penyth soldier I fought flashes into my mind. I shiver, remembering the look of agony in his eyes.

"I'm glad you're here. Opal will be excited to see you." I smile. Then my gaze shoots to his, wondering how much he's known and for how long. "Did you know she was here?"

"Beryl was able to get it out of our father when the king died." He leans in closer, dropping his voice to a whisper. "We're painfully aware of who he married her to."

An uneasy silence sits thickly between us. It seems I'm not the only one who is unsettled by the duke. Mica brings a clenched fist to his mouth and clears his throat.

"How are things here?" His eyes hold a question I can't decipher.

"Different than I thought they would be," I admit. Like faking an engagement with the prince's advisor, who has a knack for making people disappear. Though I'm not so sure I believe those rumors anymore.

Mica smiles and pokes a finger at my hair, pulling my attention back to him. There's a mocking fear in his eyes that something might bite him if he gets too close.

"Different isn't a bad thing. Though I've always wondered if women hide things in this pile of hair." He reaches out for my hair and I slap his hand away. We both laugh, lifting the heaviness of the last few days off of my chest for moment.

"Tread lightly, Mica," I warn.

"Well, I'm certainly surprised with how well the castle life suits you." His eyes move down the length of my black dress.

"I'm not surprised. Everything suits her," a deep voice rumbles.

Mica's eyes widen at the grumbly shadow that appears behind me. He takes a step toward me, almost in a protective gesture, and his gaze hardens, but the moment Mica reaches out for me, Graylen snakes an arm around my waist. Mica's eyes nearly bulge out of his head, taking notice of the movement. And that I don't step away.

"Graylen, this is Mica Lyle, Opal's brother."

Mica gives Graylen a short nod. The way they're glaring at each other makes me feel like they've met before, but I plow ahead anyway.

"Mica, this is Graylen, he's—"

"Soon to be her husband," Graylen says with arrogance. A spike of irritation pokes at me.

Mica's head snaps to me, waiting for confirmation. I guess his father didn't tell them everything. I shrug, trying to brush it off, though the tips of my ears burning red are likely giving away my rising anger.

"Mica! We need to find Father before the ceremony begins." Beryl's booming voice cuts through the crowd. He shoves his way over to us. If he's surprised to see me, he doesn't show it; he gives me a curt nod, though his gaze lingers on Graylen.

"Beryl." Graylen's voice is dripping with venom, and his arm tightens around my waist slightly. "How's the camp these days?"

Beryl narrows his eyes in response. He jerks his head toward the front of the crowd, motioning for Mica to follow him. Mica hesitates, his eyes sweeping over me one last time before he finally gives me a half-hearted smile. The kindness slips from his face when he looks to Graylen. I can practically feel the molten anger seeping off Graylen, though I'm not sure why.

Once the brothers disappear through the crowd, I turn to Graylen. The motion forces his hand to fall from my waist, the spot cold in its absence.

"Do you have to be rude to everyone you meet?" I hiss through my teeth, trying to keep myself quiet and not draw attention to us.

"Does that question still apply if I've already met them?" he says with a smirk.

I narrow my eyes at him. "Beryl, I understand. But Mica is nice."

"Never trust a Lyle," he mutters.

Except Opal, I think. Although I guess she isn't technically a Lyle anymore.

"You don't trust anyone," I mutter at him.

He takes a step closer to me. "I trust you." His words deepen into a primal growl.

I take a wide step back, bumping into someone. His gaze snaps to something behind my shoulder. Or rather *someone.*

"Heard about your servant. Next time pick one who isn't so weak-minded." Father's voice causes every nerve in my body to buzz with anger.

"He didn't—" I start, but he waves me off.

I open my mouth to fight with him, ready to prove him wrong, but then I stop. Father thinks Linnick did it to himself, and he only gloats when he's certain. He doesn't know he was murdered.

"I suspect the wedding will be happening soon. No use in waiting." My father's voice drips with disappointment. A tone I'm all too familiar with.

The sound causes my nostrils to flare, anger heating my cheeks. I feel Graylen shift his body, an almost unrecognizable motion to place himself just slightly between the two of us. His words float into my mind; I'm in control of how I let my father affect me.

So, I look to Graylen to avoid looking at my father. His eyes darken, pure hatred rolling off him in waves as he fixes his unrelenting glare on my father. I expect him to have something to say back, a sly remark or comment. But he remains silently positioned at my side.

"It can't come soon enough," I say with a fake smile.

Father narrows his eyes at me, likely sifting through each word to catch me in my lie.

"Petals, for the king's carriage." A soldier drops a handful of crumpled petals into my palm, the small pieces wilted and withering. There's no telling how much it cost to bring the amount of flowers required to hand people petals. Even the townspeople gathering are given small handfuls.

"The king is dead, long live the king!" a single rider dressed in black calls out. He gallops on his horse past us, creating a path down the center of the market. He plays a solitary horn, weaving a solemn tune. The sound of hooves thundering against the ground accompanies the melody. The crowd parts to make way for the forty horsemen following the leading rider.

They all wear the same black cape with a hood positioned on top of their heads, their faces obscured from sight. Each one of them carries a long torch with a blazing flame, the light from the mass brightening the market enough to see the crowd that has formed to watch the king's coffin for the processional.

After the horsemen pass, the coach carrying the king's coffin is pulled through. The carriage housing the king's body is long and wide, the top of it adorned in red roses. It rests in a horse-drawn carriage pulled by six large steeds.

The carriage passes us, and the nobles begin tossing their petals. So many float in the air, it looks like the first snowfall. I squeeze the petals into my fists, in awe of the spectacle. It makes its way through the parted sea of nobles and townspeople.

Each person the carriage passes yells out, "Peace be!" The standard sign of respect to wish the king well into the afterlife. But as Adrian surfaces behind the carriage, the crowd gathered begins to quiet. The townspeople all wear tired expressions, the night not dark enough to mask their exhaustion.

"Long live King Adrian!" someone shouts, followed by one, then three, and finally the entire gathering chanting in unison, apart from the nobles, who share looks with each other, trying to decide whether to join in or not. He's not *King* Adrian yet. Not until his coronation

"They're not tossing the petals ahead of the carriage," someone gasps beside me. From what we can see, the flowers that are supposed to be tossed toward the carriage as a sign of respect don't fall, the nobles' petals already cleared from the air.

Instead, now that Adrian is going through the parted sea of people, the tiny white petals rain down over him. Several people around me shift uncomfortably with the display of the townspeople, so obvious with being tired of King Avalon that they don't do what tradition demands when burying a king.

"They have to show their respects to the king," someone behind me grits out.

But they don't understand the townspeople like I do. They haven't seen them joining the army just to send every wage they earn back to their starving family. Nor have they seen them begging on the streets for a single scrap of food. The people want change, and all their hope is being placed on Adrian's shoulders.

With Adrian's back to me, I'm unable to see his expression. He's surrounded by several guards on their horses, and at least fifty walking on foot behind him. People cheer, saving their petals for when Adrian passes. I drop my hand to my side, letting the petals slowly drift down to the ground.

We're led to walk behind the soldiers surrounding Adrian, but the townspeople grow restless with each finely made dress that swishes past them. A few of them hold their hands out, begging for a coin to be tossed their way.

With all the time I've been stuck in the castle, I didn't see it get this bad. There's always been hunger—but never like this. We walk behind the processional, my father just ahead with his head held high in the air. The begging turns into louder pleas. With the soldiers ahead, and Adrian so far away, they begin to break out of their place lining the path.

"Please, a single coin!" a woman near me yells, her arms holding her newly born child, who's screaming loudly. "My baby is starving!" Her yell turns into wailing.

I pull away from Graylen, my feet gravitating toward her to help. Before I can reach her someone else hands her a coin. I spot Sarah's saddened expression, her eyes wide at the brewing storm around us. People gather around her when they notice her handing a coin out. She's quickly surrounded and cut off from where I can see her.

But the crowd grows angrier. A man beside the begging mother plucks the coin from her hand, saying, "I have a sick child at home!" I gasp as another person shoves through the crowd to take the coin for themselves.

In a flurry of motion, the people gathered break into pushing and yelling. The parted sea crashes together, dissolving the path of the funeral march. My pulse races at feeling closed in as I'm separated from Graylen and my father. A fight on one side of me, and the nobles on the other.

It's impossible to see where to go. The nobles begin to push their way back to the castle, trying to escape the fighting. Soldiers plunge into the mass of people, yelling for everyone to settle down. The horsemen leading the processional are already on the path to the abbey, taking the light with them, leaving us with a sliver of moon to see by.

For a moment, I'm boxed in between people, the crowd pressing into me and leaving me in a breathless panic. Someone beside me gets struck in the face, falling to the ground. A woman's screams pierces through the noise, followed by another.

I look wildly around, trying to find someone I know or an escape route. I feel an arm wrap around my waist, dragging me away from the angered crowd. I kick against them until I spot the familiar swirls of ink.

"This way." Graylen grabs my hand and pulls me through.

"Wait!" I slam to halt. "We can't just leave. Sarah might need our help."

"She's not my priority. You are," he shouts over the yelling.

I yank my hand out of his. I turn my head, absorbing the scale of the riot with some distance.

"I'll go back for her, first—"

I cut him off. "There's no time. She's young—one of the smallest here." I spin around, squeezing through the tumultuous crowd to find her.

More soldiers have gathered to break everyone apart. "Nobles, back inside! Everyone, return to your homes!" Guards attempt to shout over the crowd, but their voices are swallowed up by the screams of panic.

I'm elbowed in the back, causing me to stumble forward. I see Sarah's small frame hunched in on herself, tears streaming down her face.

"Sarah! Over here." I push through people until I reach her. "Come with me, Graylen can get us back." I turn around and find him hovering close to me. He looks out at the empty path, a familiar sense of longing in his eyes. A look I know better than anyone.

"Graylen. We can't see above everyone. You have to get us back."

Graylen nods once and takes my hand again. I grab Sarah with my other hand and pull her along with us.

It's a disaster trying to get back inside with the nobles all pushing their way back in. Adrian's stiff shoulders on top of his horse are all I can think about as we're herded back in like cattle. I hope he was far enough away he didn't hear the crowd turn into a mob. He deserves to lay his father to rest in peace. Because from the looks of tonight, there'll be no peace going forward.

THIRTY-FIVE

AQUILEGIA

"*CLOSE YOUR EYES, SWEETIE, DON'T look.*" *Her voice calms my nerves, but I can't stop the tears from streaming down my face. She told me to be strong, but I don't know how to do that.*

"*Quick, you need to hide.*" *The swirling hazel of her eyes is a mixture of green, brown, and worry. They mirror my own and I've always liked that about her.* "*Lulu, please, you need to let go of me for a moment.*"

I furrow my brows in confusion. "*Why aren't you coming with me?*" *I place my tiny hand in hers and try my hardest to tug her with me to the hiding place below the floorboards.*

She pulls me into a fierce hug and murmurs her love for me against my hair. "*I can't fit in there. It's just big enough for a brave girl your size. Hide here until me or your sister come for you.*" *She opens the latch and I crawl into the carved-out space.*

"*Close your eyes, my love. Play pretend until we come back for you.*"

I nod my head and sit down, curling my knees to my chest. I look up at her from where she's now hovering over me. She keeps looking behind her as loud clashing noises grow closer.

"I'll pretend I'm boarding a ship to a land where everyone has wings. Then when I get there, we can both get wings and fly around all day."

She smiles just as a crash clangs through the room, causing us both to jump. She takes one final look down at me and mouths, I love you.

She's not crying like I am. She's brave and going to get us out of this scary day. She quickly places the boards back over my head, sealing me beneath.

I shut my eyes as I hear shouts ring through my ears. "Be strong like she says," I command myself. I don't like it when Momma is disappointed with me.

I jolt awake at the sound of my door opening. My heart has been beating so hard lately that I'm afraid it's close to giving out on me. Avery is carrying a pale yellow gown in her arms that's covered in gold beading.

"Avery? Why do you look so worried?" I ask. She's rushing around my chambers, moving things about. It makes me wonder if things got more out of hand last night after we were locked back inside.

"There's much to do today," she puffs, breathless and distracted. "With the unrest following the funeral march, the coronation's been pushed ahead. The kingdom needs stability right now, and it's being said crowning Prince Adrian sooner will solve that."

I freeze on the edge of the bed. "The coronation is happening *today?*"

It wasn't supposed to be this soon. Adrian was supposed to have time to mourn.

"I'm afraid so, miss." She motions for me to follow her into the washroom, quickly scrubbing me down and combing out my hair. She quietly helps me finish washing, her brows furrowed in thought.

"Avery, this is stunning. I feel like this is my coronation with how beautiful it is. Thank you. I love it."

She looks me over and checks the dress to make sure everything is in place.

The entire bodice is covered in gold beading. The neckline dips into a deep V and hangs loosely at my shoulders. Beading also covers the long sleeves in the pattern of vines wrapping around my arms, climbing their way up to my shoulders. The waistline meets the bodice's beadings and trails down the sides of the dress, creating an illusion of golden vines encasing it.

"Open up!"

I smile at Opal's voice on the other side of the door, feeling less on edge as she bursts in.

"Are you okay? That was insane last night!" she half-shouts as I open the door.

I laugh as she hugs me. She pulls back and holds me at arm's length, studying me.

"Wow. You look beautiful," she says with a smile.

"It wasn't the night anyone expected. Thank you, so do you."

Her hair falls in waves down her back like spun gold. The dress she's wearing matches the rosy tint to her cheeks.

"Up for a game before we go to the coronation?" She walks over to my lounging seat and plops herself down.

"Before *we* go to the coronation? Are you not attending with the duke?" I ask, and she waves her hand in the air.

"He's in meetings helping the prince get ready." She shrugs.

I nod, my thoughts elsewhere.

"I'm sorry I didn't come see you after Linnick." Her face grows serious. "It's just been so busy... I know you two were close."

I swallow down the building emotion. It would've been nice to have her around.

"Let's play pretend," I say, mostly to distract myself from thinking about Linnick. "You know the formation of stars that make a small bucket? When the stars fill the sky, I go there to borrow that bucket. I fill it up with as many stars as I can gather, and then when the sun rises, I store them in a big glass container so I can look at them all day. They show me any memory I ask them to replay."

She's recovered enough to give me a small smile. "And while you're filling up your bucket and working hard as usual, I'm wearing my best star-hopping boots and bouncing from star to star. Then I hop all the way to the moon, where I collect moon dust to sprinkle over myself."

I let out a half-hearted laugh. "What does the moon dust do?"

She's silent for a moment, lost in thought. "It transports me anywhere I want to go. I just have to close my eyes and think of anywhere in the kingdom and *bam*, I'm there."

I long to be transported anywhere but Runnswick.

"You better get going, miss. The great hall will be filling up quickly." Avery shoos us out the door.

Opal and I loop our arms together, her excited chatter not really reaching me. The closer we get to the great hall, the more people cram into the corridors. We walk shoulder to shoulder, though there's plenty of space around us. The only people present are the guests that have been at the castle to be matched, along with their families and other well-known lords and ladies. The gathering is likely smaller due to the outbreak among the townspeople at the funeral.

Even with the crowd smaller than it would be if the doors were open to everyone, I still find it near impossible to see a few feet in front of me.

The guards at the entrance to the room are stopping people and ticking them off a list before we're allowed to enter. Their presence is heavier than usual.

"Wow," Opal whispers, admiring the décor.

Even with the rush of pushing the coronation forward, the décor still manages to be overwhelmingly beautiful. Deep violet cloths are strung across the ceiling. Tall iron stands line the perimeter, with candles burning brightly on top. All of the guards present are dressed in freshly washed garments, the bright red making it easy to see them even through the thick crowd.

I see the throne that Adrian will be seated on positioned at the far side from where we're standing. It's elevated enough to where the entire room can see him from any vantage point. A priest stands at the foot of the throne with Graylen on the other side.

He is dressed in all black—his usual attire, but a surprising choice for today. The majority of those in attendance are wearing bright colors in honor of the new king, no longer needing to wear all black with the promise of a new leader.

Graylen's green eyes find mine and a slow smile spreads across his face.

Someone steps in front of us, cutting my view off before I can roll my eyes at him. But I feel my lips tugging into a smile too.

Trumpets sound throughout the room, and the crowd falls into a thick silence.

Adrian walks toward the throne with his head held high, a look of determination on his face. His eyes are red, and I wonder if he has been crying. He walks directly to the priest, the crowd silencing as a buzz of energy surges in wait of the ceremony to begin. Everyone holds their breath as the exchange of words is made.

"Do you swear to serve your kingdom, on this day, and each day forward, until your dying breath?" The priest's voice booms throughout the room.

Adrian kneels. The priest holds his arms out, hovering with the crown above his head. The structure of the crown resembles two vines woven together.

"I, Adrian Stewart, shall serve and protect my kingdom, on this day, and each day forward, until my dying breath," Adrian vows and the priest lowers the crown onto his head.

"Long live King Adrian!"

The shout echoes through the room, followed by silence. The moment is still as tension follows the voice. One by one, more voices follow and soon the entire room is chorusing, "Long live the king!"

Adrian stands and turns to face the crowd. The radiant splendor of his voice sweeps through the room as he commands it with confidence: "May the kingdom of Crea reign supreme."

The crowd cheers. He stands patiently, waiting for them to quiet back down.

"As your king, I want my kingdom to know that I will put you before all else." More cheers sound through the room. "My first act is assuring you of the prosperity and safety that will follow my succession. That can only be obtained if the current link between our kingdom and Penyth is removed. We cannot bind ourselves to the horrors creeping through that kingdom, lest we fall prey to it."

My gasp is covered by the excitement coming from the crowd.

"I will not marry the princess of Penyth. We will find a way to rid ourselves of their infestation."

The crowd erupts into cheers. Somehow Adrian's eyes find mine and my resolve begins to crumble. The air around me thins, and I find it difficult to breathe. He's *not* going to marry the princess of Penyth. Did he really just do this for the kingdom?

"Lu, are you okay?" Opal's look is filled with concern, and I nod.

Leaning heavily against her, I fan myself. "It's just hot in here," I whisper and hope I look convincing.

The celebration around us grows and beats along with the drumming in my chest.

"King Adrian!" someone shouts from the crowd several times until he gets his attention. Adrian turns around, a smile stretched across his face as someone approaches his throne. Several guards shift closer.

"That's close enough to the king," one of them says, his hand resting on his sword.

The man straightens, staring daggers at Adrian. The crowd takes notice, collectively holding a breath as the man speaks.

"Lord Samson. Is something the matter?" Adrian's voice is strong, but his brows flick up in surprise.

"Do you plan to uphold the decree your father, and his father before him, set against Penyth? Will you outlaw our attempt to save you?" Lord Samson demands.

No one says a word. Not a single sound to be heard. The way he used the word "*our*," like he's aligned with them, doesn't go unnoticed by anyone in the room. The guards take a step closer to him.

"*All* of the current decrees will remain in place," Duke Wyman calls out. I bristle at him speaking before Adrian. He's all too eager to answer for him.

The lord doesn't acknowledge Duke Wyman's statement; his attention remains fixed on Adrian.

Adrian clears his throat. "As Duke Wyman said, these laws will remain in place. We don't need saving from Penyth." He spits out "*Penyth*" like it tastes sour on his tongue.

The soldiers draw their swords when the lord takes a step closer.

"Why are you keeping this banned?" Lord Samson asks. "You *need* us." His voice is near begging.

"Us?" Adrian says at the same time Duke Wyman spits out, "Not another word."

"You'll all die in a few short seasons." Lord Samson spins around, facing the crowd. A few people scream at the man's declaration.

"You openly admit to your allegiance with Penyth?" Adrian demands. "You and your house have spent years serving the crown. You would so blatantly choose to align yourself with the kingdom that promises death?"

We all hang onto the question, a shock rippling through the room as Lord Samson nods his head.

"Guards!"

Duke Wyman's voice is muffled by a burst of fire. The crowd pulls back, pushing toward the doors. But I can't tear my eyes away, transfixed by the waves of fire rolling off the man's outstretched palms.

Heat prickles against my neck, a sensation I can't ignore. Someone's watching me. My eyes meet bright green, the intense gaze like two precious emeralds gleaming in an abandoned cave. Chaos ensues as guards move in a flurry of movement. At the same moment, Graylen takes a step toward me, his focus set on me, his eyes swirling with concern.

He's cut off from my line of sight. The guards quickly overwhelm Lord Samson, the flame dying out as a sword pierces his flesh.

"Everyone, stay calm! Please exit into one of the celebration rooms while we sweep the area."

The duke is the only one speaking. Adrian's face is pale as he watches the man die. His gaze swings over to meet mine. His guards surround him, but he's frantically talking to them and pointing to me.

Two of them immediately turn in my direction. They swiftly move through the crowd. "King Adrian sent us to stand with you until the room is secured."

I peer around them and find Adrian still watching me as the crowd filters quickly out through the doors. That's what he's worried about right now? Even in the midst of panic, his thoughts still find their way back to me. The whole interaction causes my mind to spin in a thousand directions, barely able to stomach Opal's inquisitive stare.

"Amira."

The sweat collecting against my forehead freezes at the voice. Shards of ice splinter through my veins.

I turn around, my back stiff as my father stands with his arms folded neatly behind his back. His expression is tight and his gaze narrows on Opal, waiting for her to excuse herself. Finally, he says, "I believe you are to be with your husband while this ordeal is dealt with."

Opal hesitates, but the small smile I give her has her bobbing down in a quick bow and walking away.

"He sent guards to protect you?" Father says with a sly grin. I can see the wheels turning in his brain. "This is your chance."

"My chance to…" My voice trails off. The image of the lord's hands on fire burns in my mind still, but my father plows forward, unbothered.

"To marry Adrian. Sir Christopher was a fine choice, but Adrian? Our new king? I didn't think it could be something you could obtain before. But he sent guards to protect *you*—and only you." I stiffen at his words. "This is your chance to be queen."

He wants me to marry Adrian. The thought nearly sends me to the ground.

"Do what you need to make this happen. He can easily fix this *thing* between you and his advisor."

My words stall in my throat, unable to claw their way out.

He shoves a leather pouch into my hand. "Here's a new supply of your medicine. It'll last you through winter while you're preparing to become queen."

I shove the pouch into my pocket, attempting to fight the wave of nausea rolling through me at his words.

Little does Father know I'm already preparing for the same thing, a part of me yearning to be at Adrian's side.

THIRTY-SIX

TAGETES

THE REST OF THE EVENING is filled with room after room of different celebrations. People seem to forget what happened during the coronation, the wine flowing freely and drowning their worries.

Who was that man with the fire erupting from his palms? I can't help but feel frustration with the duke speaking over Adrian. He never spoke over King Avalon. He at least let him attempt to speak, and even then, would only address the room once the king allowed him to. Something feels off with the way he easily ran over Adrian. As if he thinks he's the one in power instead.

I walk around with Opal, glad to have her by my side and away from the duke. There's something not right with him.

The room we walk into has dancers streaming from the ceiling in long, lavender skeins of fabric. Their limbs are like extensions of the flowing fabric, writhing and fluid. Opal stares with her mouth wide open as the girls twirl and spin through the air.

The room is only lit by a couple of flickering flames, causing shadows to soar across the walls. Opal watches them in wonder, but

I can't focus on the spectacle. My heart is pounding too loudly in my chest, all of my focus devoted to calming my breathing. Thankfully, Opal is too distracted to notice.

I can feel the walls around my heart being rebuilt brick by brick, each stone slab firmly put back into place where he previously tore it down. He's the king now. There's nothing he can promise me. Surely, he wouldn't put the entire kingdom at risk for me.

I pull Opal away from the dancers as we make our way to the next room, where twenty musicians play various instruments. More than two hundred candles surround them while they play their haunting melody.

Their music is slow. A woman is in the center, singing an unfamiliar song in a foreign tongue. A girl beside us is singing along.

Opal pokes the girl and asks, "What is she singing about?"

The girl bends her head close to ours so she doesn't disturb those around us. "She's singing about the promise of a new king," she says in wonder. "It's a story about a boy being made into a man. Not because he's a king, but because of the woman he goes to when the crown is too heavy. It's her love that makes him a man worthy of leading the kingdom."

I feel a silent tear spill down my cheek. I angle my head away from Opal so she doesn't see, the dimly lit area hiding my emotions well. I don't bother wiping it away as more tears follow in its wake.

The singing woman's voice haunts me, dragging up all of the pain I've felt over losing Linnick and bringing it to the surface. The string instruments build, and I can feel the tears gather by the bucketful.

I clear my throat and say, "Let's go see another room."

Opal is so entranced by the singer that she doesn't even look my way as I pull her away from the melody and candlelight. We make our way from room to room, eating and drinking until we both can hardly stand.

"Oh! I have to go congratulate them on behalf of the duke. I'll find you later," she promises and gives me a kiss on the cheek.

My eyes follow in the direction she's headed, unable to stop my face from twisting as she wraps her arms around Edith and smiles at Sir Christopher. The wine does little to conceal my thoughts.

I wander around the party, hopping from room to room without any true direction. The rooms all feel hot and sticky. People around me blur, their pearly teeth bared as they laugh, their bodies bumping into mine as they dance.

There's a small room that sits at the end of the corridor. The door is closed, but it sounds empty. I press my ear to it, listening. Nothing.

I check around to see if anyone's watching and sneak into the room. It's quiet and dark, not a soul occupying it. I shut the door behind me. Just a moment to breathe and I'll return. I place a hand on my stomach, trying to relax myself.

The sound of voices and a small screech draws my attention to the far side of the room. I step forward as quietly as I can manage. The scream now sounds stifled. It's coming from the back corner, though I didn't think any more rooms were in this hall.

I see a flicker of light shine through a crack in the wall. I bring my eye to it as more muffled cries echo through.

The man that attempted to attack Adrian is still alive. He's in a small room, hardly large enough for the four men positioned around him. He's seated in a wooden chair with his hands bound behind him. A cloth has been tied around his mouth to gag him. His body is bloodied and pale.

"Reveal to us something of use," Duke Wyman demands.

My hand flies to my mouth to cover my sharp intake of breath.

Duke Wyman is crowded over Lord Samson. A swirling pool of darkness winds its way around his body. The man's head lulls to the side as he struggles to remain conscious.

The duke is doing something that is strictly forbidden in the kingdom, manipulating the shadows that writhe around him. He lifts a single hand and sends the shadows barreling into the lord, whose body convulses and slumps over. Lifeless.

The shadow sucked the life from within Lord Samson without a trace. If he weren't already wounded, it would've looked nearly like a natural death.

Much like the king's.

I stumble backward, not believing my eyes. The duke *himself* just announced the same laws would be upheld under Adrian's reign. I gather my skirt and leave the room behind, a sickening feeling clawing its way up my throat.

I make quick work of finding the room closest to me and drink another cup of wine, trying to wash away the bitter taste of the darkness shrouding the duke. It felt so…*wrong*. It's treason for him to be using anything of the sort.

My body sways. I put my hand on the wall to steady myself, a panicked giggle bubbling to the surface. I slap my hand over my mouth to stop more from tumbling past my lips. The wall I'm attempting to steady myself on suddenly moves, and I turn to place my other hand on it, unable to hold myself up.

The moment I put my hands on the strange moving wall, my nose is pressed into black fabric. Odd for a wall to be covered in black fabric tonight. The wall suddenly speaks, and I jump back, almost falling over myself.

"Amira, how about I help you back to your chambers?" It's not a wall. It's Graylen.

I roll my eyes and let out a loud, annoyed sigh. "Nice try, Graylen, but you aren't going to my bed."

He smiles with a lazy curve of his lips, and I have to blink a few times to make sure I didn't imagine it. Do his lips always look like that?

"Ramsey, you would know if I were trying to take you to your bed."

I narrow my eyes at him. "You know I don't like it when you call me that."

He laughs despite the glare I'm attempting to give him. "That's why I say it." He points to my lower lip. "I like it when you do that."

"Calling me that only reminds me of my father, and all that comes along with that." Which typically results in my insides twisting together. Why did I just admit that to him?

Something in his face changes—a look of understanding.

"I know what you are." Is my voice slurring? The wine is giving me courage.

He lifts an eyebrow, amused. "Please tell me what I did so I can apologize immediately." He wraps a hand around my waist and leads me away from the table of wine. I snatch another cup off before he can stop me.

I throw back the bitter drink and feel it rush to my head, giving me more confidence. "You pretend to be engaged to me just so you can sneak into a different woman's bed when you please. But you don't really want that, do you?"

The amusement in his eyes quickly fades and he looks around to see if anyone overheard me. He pulls me through the crowd and takes the cup from my hand, tossing it on the floor without bothering to see it break into a thousand pieces. His jaw is set like an unmovable block of stone. He says nothing as we pass guest after guest, each so drunk with the celebration that they don't notice him dragging me down the hall.

"The men in the castle are so *strange*," I mumble. "At least you aren't that bad. Like the duke. You should've seen the shadows he was using—"

Graylen pulls me tightly against him, looking around. My head spins in a circle at watching his head move so quickly.

"Amira, you can't say that out loud. Do not let anyone hear you say those things." He catches me when I stumble.

"Let go of me."

The moment I say it, he complies. But when he releases me, my feet aren't sure how to properly work anymore, resulting in me almost falling on my face. He grabs me once more, stopping me from breaking my nose on the stone floor.

"Can I continue to hold onto you until we reach your room?" he asks in the tone one would use with a child.

I let out an audible breath of annoyance, but don't protest. The journey seems to move in slow motion, the walls around me spinning.

"Fine. But this is the last time," I relent, mainly because I don't think I can get there on my own.

He looks down at me. His head looks more like three as my vision sways.

"Because this is ending soon," I clarify. "With Adrian becoming king, this little game gets to be over. I don't need you anymore." My confidence stutters as I stumble again. I feel my body being lifted off the floor.

Strong arms encase me, cradling me gently. Too tired to hear what he says, I drift off. The last thing I remember is being set down on my soft bed and my covers being pulled up to my chin. Sleep calls out to me, and I accept it greedily. The events of the night fade from my mind, almost like a dream.

Thirty-Seven

DATURA

THE NIGHT OF THE CORONATION fades from memory. Filled with restlessness, I spend my days training with Graylen, and Adrian's too busy to see me. The fact that he's no longer engaged is still heavy on my mind.

I pace the length of my chambers, my leathers allowing me room to run a rut into the ground with my constant movement. I slipped into my leathers far earlier than necessary, eager to get to training in the garden tonight to distract myself. My fingers trace the stitching of my leather pouch, now full after the new supply Father gave me.

I reach up to release my hair, intending to remove my lily hairpin, but pause at the sound of the hidden door clicking open.

"Can I come in?" Adrian's voice calls out from behind the door.

I rush over to where the door is partially cracked and yank it open. Adrian and I stare at each other. It feels different. There's always been something between us, blocking us. An invisible barrier shoved between our minds.

When he steps fully into the glowing dusk-filled chambers, I freeze. My eyes widen, and a small gasp rushes from my lips. His face is worn and shadowed. His usually glowing presence is dulled. He's lost weight in the few days since the coronation.

For a breath, I'm too stunned to speak. He takes a hesitant step toward me. When I don't back away, he takes another, one step at a time until he reaches me. He stands in front of me as a wave of familiarity washes over my body.

I throw my arms around his neck, squeezing tightly.

"Amira…" He hesitates before finally wrapping his arms around my waist in a loose hold.

"The coronation—" A flash of Graylen carrying me back to my chambers makes me grimace slightly.

Adrian releases me and rakes a hand through his hair, already looking every bit of a king with the weight of the kingdom on his shoulders.

"I meant what I said." He slips his hand into mine and leads me over to sit on the edge of the bed. He looks down at our fingers laced together, squeezing tighter. "I won't marry the princess. Not when there's someone else."

My palm turns clammy in his grasp.

"I know you've always wanted to leave Runnswick, but I don't think that's a feasible long-term solution." His fingers curl tighter around mine, holding our hands in his lap.

"And what do you suppose *is*?" I ask.

A soft tremble rakes through his hand, trailing up to his shoulder pressed lightly into mine. "Amira, I want you to be my queen. To rule by my side. You could never be safer than at the side of a king. Your father could never order you to do something ever again. Eventually, I might be able to let you go out with a company of guards so you can explore. Like you've always wanted. But this way, you're truly safe." He steps closer to me, his eyes wide with fear. "I couldn't bear it if something were to happen to you."

My throat closes tightly as I press my lips into a thin line. The offer he's handing me leaves me reeling. Rather than feeling an overwhelming sense of happiness, I just feel…overwhelmed.

"Amira?" His voice cracks.

I slip my hand out of his, needing the space. The walls are closing in on me. I stand from the bed, frustrated when he follows behind. He reaches forward to cup my cheeks in his hands, which are now cold as ice. His eyes are wide and wild.

"There are things you don't understand, dangerous things. I just want to keep you safe," he says quickly.

I bite the inside of my cheek at the desperation laced within his tone. The words land oddly within me, clanging warning bells within my mind.

"What dangerous things?" I ask, needing him to give me more of an explanation. I can't just blindly follow him.

He shakes his head, running his hand through his hair and gripping it at the ends. "I can't, you wouldn't—"

"Friends tell each other things," I spit out, throwing his words back to him—the same thing he said to me when we were just two people hiding away from the world. But we can't hide any longer.

"Will you stay if I tell you the truth?" he asks. "If you understand the weight of what could happen to you out in the kingdom?"

A kernel of fire rushes through me, the smallest burst of anger causing my eyes to narrow on him.

He takes a deep breath and walks over to the window, staring longingly outside. "I made a mistake. To protect you." He turns his back to me, fully facing the window. His shoulders drop forward, the heaviness of guilt evident in his posture.

"What did you do?" My words come out breathless, quiet.

"My father's death wasn't an accident. Not entirely," he says as he turns around to look at me, his face twisted in pain. I still. He takes another long, drawn-out breath, the moment stretching out into an eternity. "I killed him. And now I can't take it back."

I numbly lower myself onto the bed again, not trusting my legs to hold me up any longer. Adrian doesn't move toward me. He remains beneath the window, his jaw clenching and unclenching. Did he say what I think he did? Maybe I heard him wrong.

"You couldn't have. It was a natural death."

He's shaking his head before I can finish, his movements jerky and his breathing uneven. "Certain poisons can mask their involvement, making it look like a natural death," he says softly.

My eyes widen. I stand and take a step back. For the first time, I feel cold in his presence.

"This is coming out all wrong. I'm just going to say it, okay?" He holds his hands up, showing me his palms.

I nod once, torn between not wanting to hear another word and *needing* to know the full story.

"He called me to his room the night it happened. He wanted to talk through my engagement to Princess Leda. He hadn't brought it up since the night it was announced, but out of nowhere he tells me it's to happen soon. Much sooner than I was ready to let you go." He ducks his head down sheepishly, gathering his thoughts before continuing.

"After he told me it was going to be planned quickly, he began pacing his floor and mumbling wildly to himself. Sometimes when he drinks, he says things that don't make sense. He says he sees things that aren't truly there. I usually ignore it, but he was coherent enough to tell me about a servant he let die."

My lower lip trembles. He pauses to look at me, his brows pinched in concern.

"He told me he needed information about the servant's master. A guard was to question him thoroughly, but he took it too far. My father watched as his guard killed Linnick. He promised it was something he just took too far, like everything else in his life. Him sitting idly by while the kingdom falls apart piece by piece. I was so incredibly angry with him. He kept rambling on about me focusing on making this wedding happen."

I grip the hem of my shirt tightly in my hands, trying to steady the shake plaguing them.

"Tell me this isn't true," I manage to get out. Hurting someone to further your *own* agenda is something my father would do. Not Adrian.

"I thought he was drunk. He wasn't making any sense at first. He said he was the king and his word was final." Adrian takes a step toward me.

I wrap my arms tightly around myself to stop him from reaching out to me. His mouth continues to move, but no sound reaches my ears. What did I just ask him a moment ago?

"What?" I croak. I blink rapidly, trying to clear the blurriness of my vision. My pulse pounds in my ears, thumping loudly.

"My father yelled at me to leave. Explosive anger is fairly common if he hasn't had enough to drink. I didn't even think. Poison is something all royals keep on hand. I poured it into his pint of nightly wine and left it at his door like his servants do. Besides, he's been poisoning his mind and body by wasting away from his alcohol, right?"

Nothing about this seems right, but I don't know how to tell him that. My lips are clamped shut, rendering me unable to respond.

"As I was walking away, I heard his door open. I listened as he gulped it down. I was so angry, Lu. You have to understand. I regretted it the moment I heard his body hit the floor." His voice is frantic. I stumble back another step, needing space from him. His voice sounds less like he regrets it, and more like he's desperate for me to understand.

"You killed him?" It isn't something I thought he was capable of. Even hearing him say it, I can't bring myself to believe it.

"You don't understand. I didn't have time to think. He let Linnick die, Lu!" I cringe at my nickname, but he forges on. "He was forcing my hand with Penyth. There was only one way to escape that engagement. My mind was only on protecting you. Under my father's rule the kingdom wouldn't have lasted much longer."

Searing hot anger bursts across my vision. "How could you do this?"

A mixture of my anger swirls together with the hurt etched across his face. His father has neglected the kingdom for years, and he's only noticed now that it affects him. My anger grows quicker than the sun is setting, casting darkness into the room. The absence of light veils one side of his face in shadows.

"Lu, I know you're upset. I understand why. You don't have to forgive me now, but the quicker we get married the safer you'll be."

My chest is rising and falling with such force I'm afraid I'll pass out. "I need to think."

Adrian takes a step toward me.

"Alone," I say. "Please leave."

I nod to the door for Adrian to go. He holds my gaze, so many emotions swirling behind his eyes.

I reach out to comfort him, maybe to soothe my own trembling mind too. I don't know. But when I reach for him, I see a strange glint flash in his eyes—tears not of sorrow, but of frustration—angry that I don't agree with him. My vision fades into a blur, the room tilting to the side.

I feel Adrian's hand wrap around my arm, holding me steady. I snap back to my chambers. As if awaking from a nightmare, I look down at my body and remember I'm still here, his fingers wrapped so firmly around my arm it hurts. Can this be the same boy I met in the market? The same person who knows what it's like to feel trapped in a life you don't truly want?

"Adrian, you're hurting me." My eyes shift into focus.

His face nears mine, his golden-brown eyes now deeply haunting. The vibrant life I'm used to seeing dance behind them is dimmed. Instead of releasing me, the pressure of his grip tightens to the point I know it'll leave a bruise. He doesn't even seem aware he's doing it.

"There's nothing stopping us from being together now. Don't you understand? It isn't as if you and Graylen planned to go through with the engagement. Don't go. Marry me. We can have it planned quickly, Lu." Without realizing it, he's echoing the words his father said to him, the very words that set him off to murder his own father. He jerks me closer to him, pulling me flush against his body. Something I once thought I wanted.

This is what my father wants. To secure our family name with the Stewart line, a family that is tangled within the shadows of the castle. I can't bring myself to stay surrounded by the darkness within these walls any longer.

I look at Adrian's desperate eyes, no longer seeing the thoughtful boy from the market within the depth of his gaze. I've lost the person I thought I knew.

"Only my friends call me Lu." I yank my arm out of his grip, his untrained movements too slow to stop me.

He rushes toward me in a panic, his arms outstretched and his face reddening. I bring my knee to the center of his stomach with all the strength I possess. He stumbles back, bending forward and coughing.

"Wait!" he chokes out, kneeling on the floor. The feeling of him roughly pulling my arm is enough to send me flying out of the room, leaving him.

THIRTY-EIGHT

Cuscuta

I'M RUNNING AS FAST AS my feet will take me. I barrel through the corridor, my breath coming out in gasps. With the sun not yet fully set, I know what awaits me at the entrance to the gardens. I just have to get past the guard there, then I can figure out what's next. There's something inside of me screaming to keep going.

I stumble down to the second floor, flying past people who turn to look at me in alarm. A few of them run back into their rooms, assuming I'm running from something. Anything is better than this. I can't go back to the camp, and I refuse to stay here. I furiously wipe at my eyes, willing the tears to not fall.

The first floor is mostly empty, other than the guard looking at me with confusion as I round the corner. I won't have long before Adrian catches up with me. The guard knows who I am by now. He sees me running at him full speed and doesn't register my intent until I'm about to shove past him.

"Lady Amira? Do you need help?" He takes a quick step in front of the door to the gardens, blocking my exit.

"Just need a stroll," I breathe frantically.

"Sorry, we'll be locking up soon. Everyone left out is being called back in. Maybe tomorrow night."

I don't have until tomorrow night.

His sword is sheathed, but he positions his hand to rest on the hilt. I slam my elbow into his nose, causing him to yell out, but he recovers quickly.

The guard grabs my shoulders and slams me into the wall, the wind momentarily knocked from me. On pure adrenaline and anger, I smash my forehead against his. He releases me, stunned. I wince at the throbbing pain splintering through my head but try to ignore it.

I take the opportunity to burst through the gate, the stragglers outside jumping at the commotion. I look around, trying to find the best way out of this. My forehead begins to bead with sweat as the panic worms its way into me. *Think.*

"Amira?"

I whirl around, coming face to face with Sarah's stricken expression.

"Sarah, can you do something for me?" I rush to ask.

"Are you okay? What can I do?" Her small eyebrows draw together.

"I need a distraction." I cross my fingers, hoping it's enough.

Her eyes bounce between me and the guards coming closer. She nods and falls to the ground.

"Someone help her! Quick!" Milo yells, rushing over to us. He doesn't even look my way as he surveys her on the ground. "Guards!" he shouts.

The soldiers closest to us rush over, bending down to assess her. It's just enough of an opening to go. I silently thank her and sprint through the gardens, the fully set sun on my side. I make it halfway through the garden before I hear someone shouting again.

"Stop!" a guard yells from behind me. His booming voice gains the attention of anyone that's not helping Sarah. I'm almost to the spot Graylen showed me, but not close enough to make it without them catching up.

I unsheathe the small blade I brought with me, wishing I had two of them. Six guards face me, their chests heaving from running with all of their armor. I twirl my blade in my hand once, readying myself.

The guard from the entrance comes at me first. His movements are slow and driven by rage. I can't take them all, but I can at least go down fighting. He rushes toward me. I bend down low to swipe my blade across his thigh and gain the upper hand to breathe, when a back presses against mine. I spin around, bringing my blade up to the guard.

"What are you doing?" Graylen says, his chest heaving in his sweat-slicked black tunic, dark hair falling in his eyes.

I'm too stunned to speak. I raise my blade, prepared to fight him. For once, I'm not confident I can win this one.

"If you're leaving, we should probably go now." He nods his head to the brush lining the exit of the gardens.

We?

A loud groan draws my attention, and I notice the other five guards lying on the ground. My eyes widen, horror rolling through me.

"They aren't dead, just passed out," Graylen mutters. "I don't know what you're doing but if you're trying to leave, I'll help. You won't get out alone."

Too stunned to question it, I run past him, squeezing through the brush and hearing him follow behind.

"I need to know where the duke's manor is." I just hope Opal is there.

Graylen grunts. "You don't want to go there."

The sound of guards shouting fills the space behind us.

"Please, show me how to get there," I say, nearly begging.

Graylen hesitates. The rustle of bushes being pushed aside and boots stomping against the ground must be all he needs to agree. We stay crouched low to the ground and make a run for it.

With the sun gone for the evening, the night sky is on our side. Clouds cover the light of the moon and stars, giving us a blanket of darkness to slip between. The night is so dark it's difficult to see more than a few steps in front of us.

"Find them!"

The shout rings out from the top of the wall. Our nights of running together send us swiftly through the empty market with ease. The soldiers at the wall shoot flaming arrows at piles of hay on the ground, a stone barrier encircling the brush. Flame engulfs it and lights the way for the soldiers to see. But we're too far out for it to do the soldiers any good.

We don't break our stride, our legs moving in unison without signs of slowing down. I don't look back at the castle as we sprint through the woods, the sounds of yelling soldiers fading behind us. I slow my pace slightly, the only thing surrounding us now a blur of trees.

"How'd you find me in the gardens?" My voice comes out surprisingly steady. Even with our bodies straining to reach the duke's manor, I feel a weight lifting off me with every step away from the castle.

"Adrian found me before running to the guards. He sent me to find you." He pauses long enough for us to jump over a fallen tree. "It wasn't difficult to figure out you would go to the gardens. It was the first place I looked."

I mull over his words. "So, you're going to take me back." I tense, my eyes searching for an escape.

"Of course not." Graylen abruptly stops and pulls me into a crouching position behind a tree. I relax at the sincerity in his voice. He juts his chin toward the entrance of a large manor, its white columns peeking out through the bushes ahead. "I'll wait for you."

I stand, but he grabs my wrist, stopping me.

"If you want to leave, you shouldn't waste time on goodbyes. Leave her a letter and get out while you can."

I'm grateful for his help, but he doesn't need to understand my reasoning. "Is the duke a good man?" I ask.

His eyes darken. A shadow crosses over his face as he releases my wrist.

I'm not going to say goodbye. I'm going to convince her to come with me.

"We won't have long," I hear him say behind me as I creep up to the manor. The grounds are quiet and still.

My gaze travels up the front of the massive white stone estate. Ivy trails up the sides of it, curling around the door decoratively. The heavy oak door takes up enough space for several people to walk through at once. I swallow and walk up to it.

I knock on the door several times, bouncing lightly on my feet. My pulse races as I wait for the door to open. I tap my knuckles against it again, this time louder. Finally, it creaks open.

"Lady Amira?"

I freeze at the duke studying me on the other side. I thought he stayed at the castle most nights.

"May I help you with something?" His eyes narrow as he takes in my disheveled appearance. He peers around my shoulder and into the empty woods behind me.

"I just wanted to speak with Opal." I force my voice to come out steady. A slimy feeling rolls down my spine at his gaze on me. Remembering the life he drained from the man bound in the chair,

I almost want to take a step away from him. But I don't. I push my shoulders back and hold his dark gaze.

"I'm afraid she's asleep. You should get back to the castle." He makes to shut the door, but freezes.

"Is someone at the door?" Opal's voice floats over to us, light and curious.

Duke Wyman's face tightens the closer her footsteps get. "A friend came to see you, dear. I'll give you two a moment." He gives her a peck on the top of her head, his eyes glaring at me.

"Amira! What are you doing here? Is everything okay?" She grabs my hands in hers, worry etched across her face.

I wait until the duke disappears into the manor before I squeeze her hands lightly and pull her onto the front steps outside. "Opal, I'm leaving Runnswick. For good. And I want you to come with me."

Her delicate eyebrows draw together, processing what I'm telling her. "Why would you want to leave? Wyman told me King Adrian was going to ask you something extremely special." She winks at me.

My stomach drops at her excitement. "I know. He already asked me. I don't want to marry—you know that, Opal."

She pulls her hands out of mine, looking confused. "Why not? He's the *king*. Don't you know what that would make you? I'm sure the thing with Graylen can be dissolved quickly."

I let out a frustrated breath. "It's a lot to explain right now, but he isn't who I thought he was. I don't want to be queen." The thought of his hand squeezing my arm to the point of pain skitters into my mind. I take a deep breath, hoping she doesn't walk inside and slam the door in my face. "I want you to come with me." My voice comes out as a whisper.

She takes a step back. "What? No." Her face is drained fully of its color. I reach out to her, but she jerks away from my touch. Tears brim her eyes.

"I think the duke is on the verge of doing something horrible," I whisper. "He *knew* we were friends, and yet he didn't tell us we were both here the entire time. He speaks for Adrian, acting as if he's king. There's something not right about how he constantly allowed his brother to be the drunken king for years. What do you make of that?" I keep my voice as low as I can, hoping he can't hear us.

Before she can speak, the distant sounds of horses' hooves pound against the ground. I twist toward the woods, seeing a faint glow of torches.

"I know this is a lot to process, believe me, I understand. But we need to leave, now."

She blinks rapidly, unmoving. Voices yelling in the distance begin to sound closer with each moment that ticks by.

"I can't," she whispers softly, definitively.

I take a step toward her. I try to keep my voice even and soft, careful to not scare her. "We'll figure it out, Opal, we always do."

"No, *you* always do. I'm not like you. I'm not brave or eager to explore the world anymore. My world is here now."

A lump forms in my throat, closing my airway off. "What are you saying? You can't stay here."

She shakes her head and wraps her arms around herself. "I'm sorry. I'm a wife now. I can't just leave the duke and my home. I know you don't understand our relationship, and that's okay. He's just misunderstood." A single tear slides down her cheek, dripping off her nose and onto her dress. "Be safe. I'll miss you, but this is my choice."

I fight back my own tears at her words. It was my decision to leave Crea; it must be hers too. The door opens behind us, revealing a sneering Duke Wyman.

"I didn't realize you hadn't notified anyone of your leaving. I took the liberty of sending a rider to the castle so you wouldn't have to walk back in the dark alone." He steps beside Opal, placing an arm firmly around her waist. A shadow coils around his wrist.

"Opal—"

She stops me abruptly. "Goodbye."

A smile creeps across Duke Wyman's face at her words. He gives her another peck on the forehead and steers her back inside.

"The duke said she was here!" comes a shout.

I dart away from the entrance of the manor, quickly hiding behind the nearest tree. Sir Christopher leads the charge, their heads on a swivel as they search for me. My heart pounds in my chest. The duke *told* them where I was. My fingers curl into a fist, ready to fight.

"I told everyone she was up to something! Find her so she can pay for the heartbreak she's caused our king!" Sir Christopher's tight red curls spring out around his head in a frizzled mess. He raises his sword high in the air.

I silently unsheathe my blade.

"She's not to be harmed—king's orders are for her to be returned safely," a soldier barks out at him. I make myself as small as I can behind the tree as they circle the area, searching the grounds. "You're here on a volunteer basis only. No fighting."

I stifle the urge to laugh at the soldier chastising Sir Christopher. The laughter dies before it reaches my lips when they circle closer to me.

Adrian sent them to chase me down. Hurt hits me in the center of my chest that he would go so far as to drag me back to the castle.

I slowly rise, trying to get a better view of my escape route. A hand grabs me by the elbow and jerks me back behind the tree. The smell of rain about to fall washes over me, leaving my hand to relax from the grip I have on my blade.

"Are you trying to get caught? Stay down," Graylen hisses, annoyed. "I told you we didn't have long."

I narrow my eyes at him. "The duke sent a rider to alert them where I was."

He rolls his eyes. "Are you surprised?"

I bite back a response as the sound of horses treads near us. I hold my breath, waiting for them to pass. My stomach clenches when one of them passes just a few paces away, though the night and trees give us enough coverage the rider doesn't see us.

"Search the other side!"

We stay crouched low to the ground, our backs pressed against the trunk. The shouts of their search fade to the other side of the manor. I release a short breath, unable to fully let it out.

"We need to wait until they're farther away," Graylen states as if that wasn't obvious enough.

We sit in silence, our ears straining for the sounds of the soldiers. I look down at his arms, flexing where his hand is gripping his sword. His sleeves are shorter than usual, allowing me to fully admire his ink markings. The word I saw swirls across his arm.

"So, why Lunaria?" I whisper to him.

His green eyes sear into mine, flickers of surprise running across his features. Even in the darkness, his eyes are ablaze.

"Why did you say that?" He makes another face, leaning toward me and causing me to press myself further into the tree to create space between us.

"Lunaria? It's marked onto your arm?" I point to the word engraved into his skin. Though it's written in a curved and spiraling lettering, I'm surprised it took so long for me to notice it.

He lets out a long breath. His eyes drop to my necklace. Acting as if he's been stabbed, he falls back heavily against the tree.

I instinctively reach for the pendant, feeling the grooves. They're different again, like at Linnick's farm. I peek down at it. The word *Lunaria* is hazily formed on the back of it. My eyebrows draw together as I try to make sense of it.

"Graylen. Why does my necklace say the same word that's marked onto your body?"

Emotions I didn't know he was capable of flash across his face, one after another—from surprise, to joy, and landing on confusion. His guarded gaze now wild, he stares at me as if I've grown a second head.

"Why do you have that?" he whispers, the sound of the soldiers now completely out of hearing range.

"My mother gave it to me."

He scratches at his stubbled jaw roughly, struggling to speak for a moment. "I can't believe it's been you this entire time." His laugh is quiet, his face so close to mine that his breath tickles my cheek.

I squint at him, not understanding.

"You look so different grown up," he says.

"What do you mean?" I ask, my heart racing.

He shakes his head. His gaze bounces around us, fully alert to our surroundings. His shoulders bunch with tension, though the woods are silent.

"Your real name is Lunaria Manor. Not Amira Ramsey. I've been looking for that necklace for a very long time, because I was told it would lead to you. Though your mother enchanted it a little too well."

The words sink deep into my soul as I process the name. When I don't speak, Graylen does again, his voice soft and gentle:

"Evelina Manor is your mother, and your sister is Leda Manor. Your mother is the queen of Penyth, and I've been sent here to take you home."

THIRTY-NINE

LEONTOPODIUM

"*WHAT?*" I BURST OUT, A little too loudly.

Graylen's hand flies over my mouth to quiet me. His mouth is moving, but I barely hear him. The queen of Penyth's daughter. *Me.* And a sister who happens to have been previously engaged to Adrian.

The sounds of soldiers circulating the area grow increasingly louder, causing me to snap back to what's happening around me.

"My mother is the queen? She's still alive?" My voice breaks on the last word.

A deep crease forms between Graylen's brows. "She's very much alive. She's spent your entire life trying to find a way to bring you home. I was sent here to find you on her order, along with a few specially selected subjects. I've spent years in different towns trying to find you, though it hasn't been easy." He shakes his head, his eyes bright. "Your father didn't have a single earning to his name when he stole you away. I wasted so much time looking for a poor farmer with a daughter your age."

I can't figure out which thing to unravel first. My *mother* being alive, or that she's the queen of Penyth. Or that Graylen has been a spy living in the castle this entire time. There are too many things winding together, creating a tangled mess in my brain.

"Your father changed his name and wormed his way into King Avalon's inner circle. He made himself who he is through trickery and lies. We still don't fully understand how he was able to steal you away that day in the forest." He pauses to let me soak it all in. His words trigger a memory of the golden forest. The slender, faceless man, always jolting me awake. The nightmare always ended before I saw whom the face belonged to.

The soldiers rounding the other end of the manor shout, "Keep looking!"

"What if you left Crea entirely?" Graylen asks.

My pulse accelerates at his question. It only takes a single breath to consider it. There's nothing left for me here. This might be my only chance to leave and get the answers I've so desperately wanted.

"Show me the way out."

Graylen nods, his face fiercely focused. He stands up and closes his eyes.

"What are you—"

My question sticks in my throat as the soldiers still, as if frozen in time and unable to move. The wind picks up around us, and a gentle breeze works its way through the trees.

Graylen's posture is relaxed, his hands folded into his pockets. His eyes open, a small smile tugging at one corner of his mouth. He looks down at me, offering a hand.

"Let's go. I have a few friends we need to meet up with before we leave."

I stumble as he tugs me along, watching the frozen soldiers. "What did you do?"

He pulls me ahead faster, remaining silent. "By now, my friends have gotten the message to meet me. We need to go before they wake back up." He nods in the direction of the soldiers. Their eyes are open, but they remain unmoving.

We quicken our pace through the woods, the clouds now clearing enough for the moon to stream through the trees. My mind reels with shock.

We run deeper into the woods, so far it seems impossible he knows where he's going. Are we lost within the forest? The question tugs the corners of my mouth up. I've never felt this close to freedom. He keeps a hand firmly clasped around mine, as if he's afraid I'll slip through his grasp.

I almost stop when the thought hits me. *Is Graylen even human?* Whispers about the *unnatural* and *inhuman* ways of Penyth float into my mind. What he did to those soldiers wasn't just a human using banned spells, like the old woman who tried to sell me the illegal rhyme. This was something more. Something stronger.

"How were you able to do that?" I demand, desperate for answers.

"Do what?" When I stall, he says firmly, "Don't slow down."

"You aren't human, are you?" I breathe out.

He looks over at me, his green eyes bright. "I think you know what I am. But we don't have time—we need to hurry."

"You couldn't have done that sooner?" I mutter.

He rumbles a deep laugh. "You would've had a lot of questions I couldn't answer."

I still have a lot of questions I want answered. "Are they…"

He slows his pace, forcing me to do the same. "Dead? No. But they'll have a headache when they become fully aware."

I nod, understanding. We halt in front of two fallen trees crossed over each other, forming an X.

"What'd we miss?"

I whirl around, coming face to face with Avery and a familiar icy white flash of hair behind her.

"Avery? *Addie?*" I say in disbelief.

"Everything, as usual. Are you two ever on time?" Graylen drawls.

I don't think I've ever seen them interact more than once or twice. Now I'm truly lost.

"We left the moment your message reached us. Not too difficult to do when half the castle guards are out looking for her." Addie rolls her eyes.

I shake my head, stepping back. "You're all from Penyth?"

I survey each of them. Addie has a sheepish grin on her face, Avery looks slightly guilty, and Graylen's face is unreadable.

"So, you know now?" Addie smiles, clasping her hands together in front of her.

"See, I told you we would find her soon! I had a feeling. And you were starting to doubt it!" Avery smacks Graylen's arm, and he rolls his eyes at her—the way a friend would.

"All you said is, 'I have a feeling she's near.' That isn't much to go off," Graylen mutters.

I step forward, bringing their attention to me. Are they *all* not human? "I'm sorry, can someone tell me what's going on?"

Everyone seems to know more about me than I do.

"It's nice to finally meet you, Lunaria. I'm Avery, and this is Addie, as you well know. Both born to the land of Penyth, and loyal to its queen. We accompanied this overly joyful brute here to aid in finding you."

"What else do I not know?" I ask. Addie and Avery share a look. "How many of you are there?"

"Just us three! That's all." Addie offers a small smile.

"I'll ask you one last time," Graylen says suddenly, more serious than the other two. "We want to give you the option to return with us. It's your choice."

Avery and Addie shoot Graylen a displeased look at his offer. He watches me intently, waiting for me to decide.

I've never been given the choice before. I came to the castle on my father's orders. I was told to stay on Adrian's orders.

My voice comes out stronger than it has all night. "I want to go with you."

Graylen smiles, a full and breathtaking smile that catches me off guard. Addie and Avery visibly release a breath at my decision.

"How long will the ship take?"

They all share a look again. It's not even in the realm of possibilities to consider going through the mountains. No one that went in has ever made it out.

"We aren't taking a ship," Graylen says as he searches the forest.

I frown. "Then how would we get there?"

Addie loops her arm through mine and squeezes, her tall, slender frame light against me, as Avery positions herself on my other side. The way they carry themselves makes me feel like they're soldiers trying to keep me safe.

"That." Addie points to my necklace.

"How does my necklace help?" I ask, confused.

"It works like a map. It'll lead us to where we need to go." She explains it as if this makes perfect sense. Instead, it leaves me feeling uneasy.

"And where exactly could it lead us, if we aren't taking a ship?"

Addie shrugs. "It's better if we show you."

In the distance, a voice carries through the forest, calling out for me. "Amira! Please, come back!"

Adrian. I stiffen, my jaw clenching.

"Time to go. They'll be close soon," Addie urges.

More voices ring out, yelling my name. Addie squeezes my arm before letting go; I didn't realize I was shaking.

"Okay. What do I do?" I stare at the three of them standing shoulder to shoulder, the shock of them knowing each other still not subsiding.

"Your necklace, what does it say?" Avery asks quickly.

I lift it up, moving it around until the moonlight shines onto it enough for me to read it.

"It says *Lunaria* again. My entire life it's never been legible. Why would it appear now?" I study it harder, more words appearing on the back.

"It reveals itself when the owner feels safe," Graylen explains gently "You must've felt safe enough for it to reveal itself partially earlier. It's an enchantment so that a random person can't just pick it up and use it. Your mother designed it specifically for you. What else does it say?"

I choke back the tears welling behind my eyes. I don't mention I saw it appear that day on Linnick's farm after he died, but I know I felt safer there than I ever did at the castle or the camp.

The voices grow, getting closer. There's far more than just a handful of guards this time. Graylen's focus stays set far out into the woods behind us.

"You have to say it out loud," Avery says. "Once you do, the enchantment will begin and take us to where we need to go."

I focus on Avery's calming voice, trying to steady my trembling fingers. Graylen tenses as he slowly pulls out his sword.

"*Of my own free will, I return home.*" My feet move of their own accord, one foot in front of the other. I grind my teeth together, trying to make my legs stop. But my own body isn't listening to me. My feet continue their path forward despite my protests, moved by some unforeseeable force.

"Um, you guys?" I stutter out.

Graylen's head turns with every snap of a branch around us. "It's taking us to where we need to go. Don't fight it," he says, keeping his voice low.

We go as quickly as the enchantment will allow us, not quite placing enough distance between us and the vast number of soldiers on horses. We half-jog through the woods, the pull intensifying with every step, drawing me along faster. Darkness and trees surround us, obstructing the space between us and the charge Adrian is leading.

The woods around us turn into a familiar path. One I've only taken once before.

"The portal we need to find moves," says Addie, seeing my puzzled expression. "Magic is funny like that. We had no way of knowing where to even begin looking without the necklace. Where it was a hundred years ago is likely not where it is now."

My heart pounds when I realize where we are. Graylen realizes it too because he catches up to walk alongside me. I feel the ghost of a caress graze my shoulder, though when I look at him, he's looking forward.

Linnick's farm morphs into view through the darkness of night. My breath hitches as I feel the draw of the necklace weaning. Out of nowhere, my feet stop, causing Graylen to bump into me, and the girls to bump into him. The force of them all running into my back sends me lurching to the ground. We pile on top of each other, and I let out a groan. Someone's elbow jabs my side, and Addie lets out a laugh.

"Ouch?"

They all scramble off me, muttering their apologies.

"This is where it is?" Graylen's voice is as hesitant as I feel.

"And why does being at Linnick's farm help us?"

No one answers me as Graylen walks over to the front of the crumbling farmhouse.

"Magic seeks a safe outlet." Avery walks carefully around the farm, investigating. "The enchantment must've felt drawn to being here." Then she points. "Specifically, that tree. See how the dodder vines don't reach it? The portal must've transferred here before they began to take over. He must've nurtured and cared for this one deeply."

It's Linnick's lemon tree. It looks just as content as the last time we were here. A little sprout pokes out of the ground just beside it where I planted the seeds all those nights ago.

"You're sure?"

Addie feeling the need to ask fills me with unease.

"Positive. Graylen, you're up." Avery's voice is steady.

Graylen quickly steps up to the lemon tree, turning around to me. "There's only one of these left in Crea. It'll take us directly to Penyth. The four of us each have a part to play in getting it to open. It started with you getting us here. Once we go through it can never be used again, closing the last portal between the lands."

I nod, mostly confused but grateful for some explanation. Even if it makes no sense.

Then comes a shout. "There! Stop!"

Graylen lets out a frustrated grunt. They've found us.

FORTY

CONVALLARIA

GRAYLEN QUICKLY TURNS BACK TO the tree, bringing his sword to his hand and slicing it open. He smacks his hand against the trunk, pressing it deeply against the bark. His blood seeps in instead of rolling down.

"Graylen, hurry." Addie bounces on her toes as the horses tear through the woods and close the distance quickly.

"I believe I know you better than you would've guessed."

My breath catches as my father's voice causes us all to freeze.

I spin around, needing to see him to believe it. He's standing on the rotted porch of Linnick's old farmhouse, a smug smile stretching across his angular face.

Graylen, Addie, and Avery immediately come to stand by my side. Near enough that I don't feel afraid.

"Of course, I'm not surprised you're running away from your responsibility. I've always known you wouldn't be able to handle being in a position of power." His words don't infiltrate my chest like they normally would.

I've never been able to face him alone.

But I'm not alone anymore.

"Goodbye, Father. Enjoy adding to the darkness of Crea," I say without an ounce of remorse in my voice.

His eyebrows pinch together in confusion. "I will not allow you to leave." He takes a step toward us, his eyes ablaze with anger.

I square my shoulders. "It's not your decision to make."

Avery takes a step closer to my father the moment he moves off the porch. She lifts her hands into the air, and the sound of earth moving fills the space between us. I watch as dodder vines burst from the ground and wind around Father's legs, holding him in place.

He stumbles, catching himself on the ground. "Amira! Do *not* leave." His voice has lost its composure. He pulls at the vines, attempting to get them off, but they stay securely wrapped around his legs.

The sound of hooves pounding into the dirt grows nearer. We all turn to the noise, watching as the group gets closer.

Avery hurries to the lemon tree, winding her hands in an odd motion through the air. I open my mouth to tell them to hurry, but I'm silenced by the sound of splintering bark.

The tree splits open down the middle, a crack wide enough for us to squeeze through sideways.

"Come on, everyone in." Graylen steps into the tree first, followed by Avery. Addie gives me a little nudge, and I go next. I squeeze in through the opening, the inside somehow big enough for us to all stand in it. "Close it up, Avery."

In the darkness, the sound of splintering bark fills my ears once more, closing the last bit of bark and encasing us in darkness within the tree.

"Where did they go?" Adrian's voice bellows from outside. Horses' hooves stomp from just beyond our hideout. My heart pounds at his closeness, fearful.

"They're in the tree! Your snake is loyal to Penyth!"

Father's declaration sends Adrian into a panic. The sound of nails scratching against wood vibrates throughout the tree. Almost as if someone is trying to rip it apart with their bare hands.

"Amira, are you in there? I'm going to get you out! Just hold on."

The clawing turns into a steady hacking.

"Someone help me! My sword can only go so fast on its own!" Adrian shouts, but his voice sounds like he's a world away. "I swear, Graylen, if you hurt her—" He chokes out the last part, his voice thick with emotion.

"I think you've hurt her enough, Adrian." I can't see Graylen within the darkness, but my head whips toward the sound of his voice.

"Amira, *please* say something so I know you're okay. I promise, I'm going to get you back!"

A flame flickers to life in the center of the tree, resting in Graylen's palm without burning him. The light brightens the entire inside of the hollowed-out trunk, and a gasp escapes my lips at what's inside with us.

Sunken into the inside of the tree is an old, long mirror, buried deep into the bark itself and covered thickly in dodder vines—as if it's been here for a century, though Linnick planted this tree when he was in his middle age.

Adrian's voice sounds like he's across the field, his words receding to the back of my mind.

"We need to leave." Graylen transfers the flame to a thick stick. He hands it over to me, the end of it staying lit without the fire engulfing the wood. Still, it's not the strangest thing to happen to me tonight. "Let it burn, Lunaria."

I take the stick from him and hold it up to the mirror. The dodders are eaten away by the fire, the bark somehow untouched by the flames. They disintegrate, leaving nothing behind but a burnt pile of ash at my feet.

"My turn," Addie says quietly. She reaches forward, skimming her fingertips down the mirror. A water-like ripple rolls through the surface once the last of the dodders are swept away. The three of them turn to me.

I reach forward and touch the hazy surface of the old mirror, another ripple flowing through like a pebble striking a pond from where my finger grazes it. More than a hundred boots stomping against the field around us rumble through the tree.

"It's time to leave," Graylen says. I turn back to the eyes watching my every move. "We won't have long before the enchantment wears off and the portal closes. The necklace has to go through last in order for it to close fully. Avery, are you good with leading us through?"

She nods and wraps me in a brief hug. "I'll see you on the other side." She gives us all a big smile and steps through, disappearing entirely. I gasp as I watch her vanish in front of us.

"After you, princess."

My eyes narrow at Graylen. "I'm not—"

Addie cuts me off. "Can you two shut it long enough for us to leave this place? Maybe before we get caught?"

I toss a scathing glare at Graylen and step aside for Addie. Without hesitation she steps through the mirror. And then, she's gone too. Leaving Graylen and me alone. He sticks out his hand to take the necklace. I hesitate, then hand it over to him.

"Here goes nothing," I mutter to myself. In the reflection of the mirror, I can see a flicker of concern cross Graylen's face. I turn around to see him better, only to find him wearing his smooth mask of indifference. Maybe I imagined it in the murkiness of the mirror.

"Perhaps some time before the sun rises?" he suggests.

I roll my eyes at him. I can make out faint yelling through the old mirror, urging me to hurry. A shimmering wave shudders down it.

I take a deep breath and reach my hand out in front of me, fascinated at how it glides through the mirror as if it weren't a solid surface at all. I wiggle my fingers, making sure they're still intact even though half my arm has disappeared.

Without thinking, I step fully through. For a moment, it feels like I'm submerged beneath the sea, pressure building behind my ears and eyes as I struggle to take a breath. The world around me becomes nothing more than a silent blur.

I'm plunged into darkness, my body heavy and slow. I force one foot in front of the other, struggling to push ahead as if I'm trudging through thick mud.

All at once the world speeds back up. A blinding light leaves me unable to see while my eyes adjust. I take a gasping breath and squeeze my eyes shut to try and ease the dizziness. I test out the movement in my limbs and find they're all moving as they should. I open my eyes to find a field of lilies. Their tiny, stringed bell shape fills the valley before me. They stretch farther than I can see, with no end in sight.

A memory stirs from years ago of lying in a field just like this one. Impossible. Flowers don't grow like this in Crea. With all the rain, mud, and dodder weeds, they can't manage to grow in abundance like this.

But then my mind pieces itself back together. I take a deep breath when I remember where I am.

Penyth is unlike anything I've seen before. I reach down and pinch my thigh, wincing at the pain. Nope. Still awake.

I take a hesitant step into the field, a castle peeking up in the distance, one that's more than twice the size of Crea's. The open air is so fresh that I can feel it stir something deep within my chest. There's a whispering call filling my veins, and my body sings in answer.

I twist around, finding Graylen, Avery, and Addie all watching my reaction. Smiles spread across their faces. Graylen takes a step closer to me, smiling wider than anyone else.

"Welcome home, Lunaria."

Acknowledgments

It feels surreal to be finished with my very first book. When I began writing Lunaria's journey, I never expected it to be something I would share with others. But I'm certainly glad I did! While putting myself out there is one of the scariest things I've done, the regret of letting that fear rule my life would have been worse.

I wouldn't be here without placing my trust in God. He's been my lifeline when my fears were louder than my passion. Before this, I have never truly felt like I fit in anywhere. But becoming a part of the indie author/reading community makes me feel like I will always have a place to call home. I will never forget the growth I experienced while writing my first book.

To all of my readers, thank you for reading my first novel. While I hope you join Lunaria for her next adventure in Book Two, I'm thankful you have come this far. For the you that I've known my entire life, have yet to meet, or am just getting to know—bonus points: you're even reading the section that most people will skim over. I hope you enjoyed this book almost as much as I enjoy snuggling up with my dog.

I can't have a dedication section without saying thank you to my beta readers: Justin, Sebastian, Clare, Keira, and Kasen. You read a typo-ridden, somewhat thought-jumbled, first full draft of my manuscript. With the majority of you having already authored your own books, your feedback was invaluable during such a fragile time in my writing phase.

To my ARC readers, THANK YOU! I was blown away by the amount of support for people who signed up to be a part of my ARC team. You all gave me the courage to keep going to put my debut book into the world (even if at times it was more than a little terrifying).

A special dedication is made to the people who were a part of making this book possible. I am so lucky to have such an incredible group of people in my corner to cheer me on.

To my husband for watching me write for countless hours and nights (and making me all the quesadillas!). When I'm with you, I know I'm in my safe place. You have consistently been my sounding board, my shoulder to cry on, and a smile on a tough day. I am so thankful to have you on my side as my best friend and my teammate.

To my amazing designer, Rena, for making this book come to life inside and out and giving me something to be proud of. You are mind-blowingly talented in all that you create.

Lastly, I owe so much of this to my editor, Sophie. For picking me up and dusting me off when I felt down. Thank you for your hard work on this and for taking a chance on me. You were one of the first to believe in me and read this book. You handled my book with so much care and love, and I wouldn't be here without your guidance and support.

I will forever be indebted to you all.

To anyone reading this that has ever felt less than, unimportant, or like they don't belong: You're not alone. You've got this.

Printed in the USA
CPSIA information can be obtained
at www.ICGtesting.com
LVHW040603070524
779484LV00004B/350